PRAISE FOR JUDI FENNELL AND HER NOVELS:

"The opening . . . is one of the best hooks I've read. I don't know who could set it down after the first few pages . . . an excellent choice."
—Joey W. Hill. national bestselling author

"One of the most exciting and fun reads I have ever encountered." —*Fresh Fiction*

"Phenomenally written novel . . . One of the best stories I have read this year, and I highly recommend it to anyone who loves a happy ending!" —*Sizzling Hot Books*

"Will keep the reader enraptured."
—*Publishers Weekly* (starred review)

"I had a smile on my face and a sigh of contentment . . . lighthearted but full of emotion. The story stirred in me feelings of falling in love all over again. It was just downright enjoyable to read!" —*That's What I'm Talking About*

"A light and breezy read for all . . . [will] amuse the reader to the very last page. Well done, Judi Fennell!"
—*Night Owl Reviews*

"Rip-roaring fun from the very first page . . . This book is one for the keeper shelf." —Kate Douglas, bestselling author

"A tale that shimmers, shines, sparkles, and sizzles."
—*Long and Short Reviews*

"Full of vivid imagination." —*Seriously Reviewed*

"Sizzling sexual tension, plenty of humor, and a soupçon of suspense." —*Booklist*

What a *Woman* Wants

JUDI FENNELL

BERKLEY SENSATION, NEW YORK

THE BERKLEY PUBLISHING GROUP
Published by the Penguin Group
Penguin Group (USA) LLC
375 Hudson Street, New York, New York 10014

USA • Canada • UK • Ireland • Australia • New Zealand • India • South Africa • China

penguin.com

A Penguin Random House Company

WHAT A WOMAN WANTS

A Berkley Sensation Book / published by arrangement with the author

Berkley Sensation Books are published by The Berkley Publishing Group.
BERKLEY SENSATION® is a registered trademark of Penguin Group (USA) LLC.
The "B" design is a trademark of Penguin Group (USA) LLC.

For information, address: The Berkley Publishing Group,
a division of Penguin Group (USA) LLC,
375 Hudson Street, New York, New York 10014.

ISBN: 978-0-425-26829-2

PUBLISHING HISTORY
Berkley Sensation mass-market edition / March 2014

PRINTED IN THE UNITED STATES OF AMERICA

10 9 8 7 6 5 4 3 2 1

Cover illustration by Daniel O'Leary.
Cover design by Judith Lagerman.
Interior text design by Kristin del Rosario.

It's said that it takes a village. Here's to my village:

Mom, Dad, Jill, Chris, Joe,
Janice, Lisa R., Michelle, Jenny, Sheila,
Marci, Lisa T., Joanne,
Pat, Dale, Lisa F., Jamie, Beth,
Steph, Jenny, Lori, Dakota, April, Tracey, Ann, Daria,
Roberta, Leis,
and, as always, T, S, A.

Love and huge, huge thanks to all of you.

Guys' Night . . . Plus One

❧

SEAN Patrick Manley stared at the straight flush, nine high, in his hand. He really hated that he was going to win this game. Oh, he didn't mind taking his brothers to the cleaners, but taking his hardworking sister's money wasn't anything to gloat about. Still . . . she *had* asked . . .

"All in." He kept his poker face steady and slid the balance of his chips to the center of the table.

Bryan and Liam raised their eyebrows, but Sean didn't say a word. Mary-Alice Catherine had wanted to play "like one of the boys" and this was how they played: cutthroat. No slack because she was a poker novice—or their younger sister.

Bryan glanced at his cards, flicking the edges as usual. Distracting habit, which was obviously why Bryan had affected it. "I'm in." He stacked his remaining chips alongside Sean's pile.

Sean hid his smile. He didn't mind taking Bryan's money.

Liam leaned back in his chair and tapped the back of his cards with his index finger, unreadable as ever. "Mary-Alice, are you sure—"

"Don't, Liam," Mac said, bristling as usual at the use of her given name. "Play the hand as you normally would."

Liam tapped his cards. "Fine." His stack joined the pile.

Sean eyed it, then his brother. He could never tell with Liam.

Mac chewed on her bottom lip and fidgeted in her chair. Sean almost felt bad for her. Almost. But she'd bugged them enough to get in on their game. They'd tried to tell her that she couldn't afford the stakes, but she wouldn't listen. So, to shut her up once and for all, they'd let her in, figuring that once she lost the figurative shirt off her back, she'd stop bothering them. There were some things sisters just weren't supposed to be a part of.

"Okay, so how do I raise you guys if I don't have enough chips?"

"Mac, just put the rest of yours in. Don't go upping the ante. You can't afford to lose any more." Sean smiled at her.

He was surprised when she tossed him a look of pure anger. Who knew she had it in her? She'd always cajoled them into doing her will as a child. The fact that she'd been treated like a princess all her life by them, her knights chivalric, probably had something to do with it, so this behavior was out of character for her.

"Just answer the question. What rules do you guys have for that?"

Bryan ruffled his cards again. "We throw something big in. Like Sean's place for a week or my Maserati or Liam's island getaway. Since you don't have anything comparable, just call."

Mac looked at her hand again, now nibbling on the opposite corner of her mouth. She swept a strand of hair behind her ear. "I'm raising all of you."

Sean started to protest, but Bryan raised his hand. "What's the wager, Mac?"

Mac placed her cards facedown on the green felt in front of her. "If I lose, winner gets four weeks of housekeeping for free."

"And if you win?" Liam asked.

Mac folded her hands over her cards. "If I win, you each owe me four weeks' work, free of charge, for Manley Maids."

"What? Are you crazy? I'm not going to be someone's

maid for four *hours*, let alone four weeks." Bryan rammed back in his chair as if someone had electrified the poker table.

"Oh, well, if you don't think you can beat me . . ." She looked at Liam.

Liam studied her through narrowed eyes. "Four weeks, huh?" He tapped his cards. "I'll call. With the Kiawah place for the same time period."

Sean studied Liam. A bluff? Nah. The rent for the vacation home wouldn't break his brother, but Liam wouldn't risk servitude. He had to have a winning hand. If it was better than his straight flush, Sean would only be out the cash and the hotel stay, not be in danger of putting on an apron. "Me, too. A week at the resort when it's up and running." *If* it got up and running, but he wasn't planning on losing. Not with this hand. And not the resort, either.

Bryan looked at the three of them as if they'd lost their minds. "So, one of us is going to end up with two vacations, maid service, and the use of a Maserati for four weeks?"

"Unless I win," Mac said, drumming her nails on the felt. Typical newbie response. She was too anxious.

"You calling?" Sean nudged Bryan with his elbow.

"Hell yeah." Bryan threw a full house onto the table. "Come to Papa." He reached for the pile of chips.

"Hold on, Bry." Liam flicked his hand to the table. Four threes stared back at them. "Sorry about that, Mac." Liam stood.

Sean wasn't surprised about not getting an apology from Liam. The brothers each had had their turns winning. The money was immaterial; they enjoyed outplaying each other and getting together once a month. But Mac . . .

Still, he had to set Liam straight. "Good hand, Lee, but not good enough." Sean flourished the straight flush.

"Shit." Liam sat back down.

"Son of a bitch." Bryan always insisted on having the last word.

Only Mac didn't react. But at least there'd be no question of her joining them again.

Sean started stacking the chips, planning when he could take off long enough for the vacation he'd just won from his brother. Sooner rather than later, since there wasn't much he could do on the Martinson project until the whole inheritance mess was finalized.

Silence descended on the table as he stacked the chips. Over three grand. Not bad.

His brothers were trying not to look at Mac. Sean, too, but he did catch the flicker of her lips. Probably trying not to cry. Yeah, a grand was a big deal to Mac, especially when she was pouring everything she had into her cleaning business. Maybe he'd slip it to her when Liam and Bry weren't looking.

"Sorry, Mac, but that's how the game's played."

"Yeah, Mac. We warned you," Bryan added.

"I know." She cleared her throat. "It's just . . ."

"What, Mac?" Liam leaned an elbow on the table.

"It's just that . . . doesn't a jack beat a nine?"

"Jack?" Liam's face turned green.

Sean's stomach turned to ice. "Jack?"

Bryan's mouth opened, but, for once, he was speechless.

"Yes. Jack." Mac fanned her cards onto the table. Five hearts, in ascending order.

Jack high.

"I believe, dear brothers, you all need to be fitted for Manley Maids uniforms."

Chapter One

✦❧

THE doors to Hell—aka her familial estate—were wide and welcoming.

Well, there was a first time for everything.

Livvy Carolla jerked her duffel out of the back of the Baja and slung it over her shoulder, flouncing the bottom of her peasant skirt around her, which sent the peacock that was meandering around the well-manicured lawn of her grandmother's estate scurrying to safety.

Who had peacocks roaming their lawn in suburban Philadelphia as if they were maharajahs or something?

Her paternal blueblood relatives, that's who.

Home sweet freakin' home. Wouldn't *Daddy dear* pitch a hissy if he knew she was here?

There was some satisfaction in entering the old man's lair. Especially now that it was hers.

Who would've believed it? That her reputation-protecting, society-conscious, paternal grandmother would outlive her reprobate of a son and leave it all—*all*—to the granddaughter she'd barely acknowledged.

Mr. Scanlon, the estate's attorney, had assured her that all she had to do was fulfill the stipulations in the will over the next two weeks, and the house and the accompanying funds would be hers to command.

Ah, the irony. Her grandmother, from what her mother had told her in a rare lucid—make that *sober*—moment before Livvy had been taken away, had threatened to disown her own twenty-year-old son who'd dared impregnate a barely-high-school-graduate from the wrong side of town with zero money to her name and less than zero prospects other than trapping the local rich boy in the oldest way possible.

So Merriweather Martinson had swooped in and finagled a way (translation: bought Mom off) into gaining custody of Livvy, who, at the tender age of five, had wanted nothing more than a loving family with food on the table, since Mom wasn't capable of the latter and Dad had been . . . well, *absent* was a kind description. Then there was the car accident that had taken him from her life for good.

So Livvy had found herself shipped off to boarding schools without so much as an acknowledgment of their blood ties or a kind word from her new guardian. Hell, the woman had never even cracked a smile, and Livvy's letters begging for some kind of a connection, a visit, a trip home, *something*, went unanswered.

Except for that one time when she was seven. That was it. The old lady had allowed her one visit, and then Livvy had never wanted to return.

Yet here she was. All by virtue of that very same grandmother who'd wanted nothing to do with her. Too bad Mom wasn't alive to see it, but then, the twenty-four-year-old single parent hadn't done much in the way of keeping in touch after selling her child, er, signing over custody, so perhaps *Mom* wouldn't really care that Livvy was back at the scene of the crime.

Ah, but it was water under the proverbial bridge. She'd survived, managed to keep herself employed, and lived her life on her terms. If not for a stipulation in Merriweather's will, she wouldn't even be here.

But here she was, so best to get on with it.

Taking one last bite of her apple, she gazed up at the monstrosity. That was how she'd always thought of this place. The

Martinsons, her father's family, were ancient English nobles who'd immigrated back in the eighteen hundreds, apparently bringing half their English manor with them, complete with mullioned Tudor windows and carved oak doors the size of elephants. Stone lions guarded the drive, and the gargoyles on the roofline blended into the backdrop of gathering clouds. Ominous. Foreboding. She'd been overwhelmed on so many levels during that one visit, and her feelings hadn't changed. The place was ostentatious. Overdone. Obscene.

And now it was hers.

Livvy tossed the apple core into the flower bed—good compost—and grabbed Orwell's travel cage from the back seat, being careful the cover didn't allow any glimpse of the scenery. The African Grey went nuts when he was caged outside, so what the loudmouth didn't know wouldn't hurt her ears.

She hiked up the white marble steps to the front door, her boots leaving scuffmarks. Oh well. Something for the butler to do.

"Hello?" She pushed open the door to an empty hallway. Strange, twenty years ago the butler—Rupert? Jeeves?—had guarded the door like a mother bear. Clearly, things had slipped since her grandmother's death.

Grandmother. The word felt odd. Livvy closed the doors, realizing she'd never really thought of the old woman as her grandmother. But, technically, as the bearer of the worm who'd knocked up her mother then took off at the first sign of pregnancy, that was who Merriweather Knightsbridge Martinson was.

"Anyone home?" Livvy peered around the massive foyer, vividly remembering the burgundy and cream striped walls crammed with gilt-framed, musty paintings of portly ancestors trussed up like Easter eggs. It'd probably been centuries since anything had changed here. These people were so hung up on their heritage that she could feel the heavy mantle of Martinson ancestry forming a chokehold around her throat.

Not that she'd have anything to do with it. They hadn't wanted her as a child; she sure as hell didn't want them as an adult.

"Hello? Rupert? Jeeves?" *What was his name?* She stepped farther into the silent entranceway.

"No Rupert or Jeeves here."

She jumped as a guy walked out of the doorway on the left. Tall, dark, and yummy, with the body of an Olympic athlete and the face of one of their gods, he had wavy black hair that swept the top of his collar and set off a pair of eyes so blue they might have been fake—except there was nothing fake about this guy. From the set of shoulders that appeared to have been created solely for the purpose of wrapping strong arms around a woman, to washboard abs that had her mouth watering, to legs with muscles that strained the seams of his pants, this guy was all man.

"What can I do for you?"

There was probably a lot he could do for her. And to her, and with her . . .

"Who are you?" She tugged the front of her blouse closed over her camisole, but it was kind of hard to do one-handed.

"Who are *you*?" he shot back, hefting a . . . *vacuum*? in his hands.

"I asked you first." What was he doing with a vacuum?

"You . . . *what*?"

"Uh, I mean . . ." She tossed her curls and raised her chin, trying to make herself appear taller. Not that she was ashamed of her height—or lack thereof—but it helped when she was feeling out of her element. And she definitely was, because being in this place, with a hot guy holding a vacuum cleaner, was so foreign she wouldn't be surprised if she had fallen down Alice's rabbit hole. "I, um, asked you a question."

"And?" He set the canister down, then leaned on the wand attachment.

"And I'd like an answer."

"And I'd like to be hanging out on a tropical beach, but we don't always get what we want now, do we?"

"You know, you're pretty cheeky for the pool boy."

"In case it's escaped your notice, *this*," he rattled the wand, "is not a skimming net. It's a vacuum cleaner."

"So that makes you, what? The maid?"

He glanced away. Score one for her.

"Look, who are you and what do you want? I don't have time to stand here all day." His jaw was doing some furious ticking.

"Why? Got some shelves to dust?"

Red crept up his neck from where his mint green polo shirt opened in a V, revealing some nice curly black chest hair just to the left of the insignia . . .

Manley Maids.

Oh, man. He *was* the maid. This was just perfect!

"Look, miss. Is there something you need?"

Uh . . . yeah. She bit her lip trying to swallow a smile. Her grandmother obviously had had one hell of a sense of humor. Maybe it wasn't such a good thing she'd never gotten to know the old battle-axe. "Okay. Sorry. It's just that I'm Livvy Carolla and I was looking for the guy who runs this mausoleum."

"*You're* Livvy Carolla? *Olivia* Carolla?"

She hated that name. Olive, Oliver Twist, Olivia Fig Newton-John . . . The nicknames hadn't been fun. Boarding school "chums" were simply better-dressed playground bullies.

"I prefer Livvy. And, yes, that's me. Why?"

Pool Boy—*Maid Man*—groaned.

"Hey, really, it's not cause for a meltdown. The name's Livvy and I need to see Jeeves. Rupert. Whatever."

"It figures," muttered Pool Boy, er, Maid Man.

She wished he *was* the pool boy—much better uniform. "I'd like to get settled, so if you could point me in his direction, I'd much appreciate it."

She set Orwell's cage on the floor to readjust the strap of her duffel. A few feathers and seed husks puffed out from beneath the cover to scatter on the floor.

"Hey, I just cleaned that," Pool Boy said.

"You're kidding."

"No, I'm not." An eyebrow went north. "And it was a pain to do, so if you wouldn't mind cleaning that up, I'd appreciate that."

He looked so indignant. "Okay, *Mr. Belvedere*, I'll make you a deal. I'll clean up the mess if you tell Rupert I'm here."

"Sorry, lady, right now it's just me, and, well, me."

"You."

"Me."

She raised her eyebrows. She'd been working on raising just one, but so far that trick had eluded her. "So, you're running the place then?"

"Princess, running this place is nothing compared to what I do in real life."

"Oh? So this is some fantasy you're acting out? Not quite the maid's outfit that typically goes along with that sort of thing, but whatever floats your boat. Just don't call me *Princess.*"

"Sorry." Pool Boy scratched his chin. "Okay, so here's the deal. The will pensioned off every single employee. Right down to the ten-year-old newspaper delivery boy. No one's here but me. And now you. And as I understand it, you're now in possession of this, what'd you call it? Mausoleum?"

She nodded, her amusement tempered. Everyone was gone? Was this some challenge the old battle-axe was issuing from the grave? Something to make Livvy prove she was worthy of the Martinson name?

Or to prove she *wasn't*?

Well, she wasn't about to jump to that woman's tune, especially not in death. In fact, Livvy was glad everyone was gone. That way she wouldn't have to fire them when she sold the place, which she would do as soon as she found out what stupid stipulations her grandmother had come up with to force her to live here for two weeks.

Okay, so maybe she was still jumping a little bit to the woman's tune. But not for much longer. Soon she'd be home free with millions to do with as she wanted. And she wanted to do so much good with them. Unlike her *illustrious* so-called family.

"So." Livvy hiked the duffel onto her shoulder and knelt to scoop the feathers into her hand. "This changes things. I was hoping the butler could show me the ropes, but I guess that's not happening." She repositioned the duffel as she stood.

"The only ropes I've seen are tying back some curtains in the living room, though I think there's a real bellpull in the chapel tower," said Hot Guy With A Vacuum.

"Yeah. It rings obnoxiously early, too." Oh how she remembered waking to it one Sunday morning. She still couldn't believe there was an actual chapel on the other side of the property. That seemed more than a little overboard even for *her* family.

Pool Boy smiled. "Actually, it's been quiet since I got here. No one to ring it."

She shared the smile. "A plus to the situation. Very good. Well, in that case, why don't I get my stuff upstairs"—she hefted the duffel and cage—"then I'll come back down and we can chat."

"Sure. Fine. I'll be in the . . ." He flicked his hand toward the far corner. "Whatever that room is, finishing up."

"Okay. See you then."

"Fine." He turned around.

"Uh, hey?"

"Yeah?" He looked back over his shoulder. Man, the way those pants hugged his butt . . .

"Your name? I didn't catch it."

"That's 'cause I didn't toss it."

"Funny. So what is it?"

"Um . . . Sean."

"Well, Um Sean, I'll see you in a bit."

SEAN felt her eyes on him all the way through the door. Her gorgeous amber eyes. On a five-foot-nothing body of screaming sex appeal with more curves than a racetrack, lips ripe for kissing, a face that'd put Helen of Troy to shame, and all the attitude to back it up.

How was he supposed to kick her out of this place when his first instinct was to drag her over to the closest piece of furniture, rip those gypsy clothes off that delectable body, and devour her for hours on end? Grab those auburn curls that tumbled down her back like an invitation and wrap them around his fist, arching her neck so he could—

Sonofabitch. The private eye he'd hired to investigate the will's stipulations hadn't mentioned that the granddaughter was a babe.

He also hadn't mentioned that she'd be moving in, or that they'd be the sole inhabitants of Casa Martinson. He'd thought living in was a good idea when Mac had gone over the job's specs, but now . . .

Sean set the vacuum down and headed to the curio cabinet. With the way he reacted to her, he'd better find out what those stipulations were and soon. Failure was not an option. This property was going to make his name in the resort industry and validate everything he'd been working for. He was banking on it, to the tune of millions of dollars in revenue.

His Heritage Corporation bought historic buildings, most in disrepair, and brought them back to their former standard and beauty as bed & breakfasts. So far, it'd been a win-win situation. Localities loved saving their old buildings, and he loved the bottom line.

But his dream had always been to be bigger. He wanted luxury resorts. He wanted to be *the* destination in this part of the state, with an eye toward growing into other areas. To be as successful in his career as his siblings were in theirs.

The Martinson property was his chance to start expanding the company. The next tier of his dream. And as long as there was a chance to make it happen, he wasn't about to call it quits.

So when Merriweather had thrown the wrench in, jeopardizing his name, his bank account, and his brothers' money, his back was to the wall. He *had* to buy this place at the below-market-value price she'd promised or he'd lose everything. He really didn't need her change of heart or his sense of misplaced lust screwing this up.

Screwing was a bad word choice.

Sean replaced the porcelain statues in the glass-fronted case, careful not to ding them against each other. There were some prize pieces here. What in God's name had possessed the woman to leave this place to a granddaughter she'd never acknowledged? According to the detective, Mrs. Martinson hadn't sent even a birthday card to her only living descendant. No contact even when her son, Olivia's father, had died. Talk about cold. He hadn't had a doubt that his plan would pan out as she'd promised.

Yet there was obviously no figuring what was in someone's mind at the end of her life. And the old woman was thorough, dammit. His lawyer had tried to find some way to break the bequest, but no dice. It was airtight. Olivia Bombshell Carolla held all the cards.

The poker reference was ironically appropriate.

He'd thought Mac's win was a homerun when he'd seen

the Martinson name on her client list. He'd jumped at it; if Lady Luck had given him the means to secure the place for himself, he wasn't one to question her.

Until now.

Because with millions at stake, a babe for a boss, and just under three weeks to kick her out of her home, instead of being lord of the manor, he was the freaking *maid*.

Chapter Two

WINDING through the indoor maze of corridors that made up the second floor, Livvy paused to glance out one of the arched windows. Yep, the outdoor maze was still there. She'd gotten lost in the hedgerow monstrosity during that one visit all those years ago. The thing still creeped her out, just like the rest of this place. She couldn't believe she was descended from these people. If not for Mom's fling with the local rich boy on summer break, she wouldn't be.

That maze had to go. Along with the free-range peacocks. Peacocks were notoriously nasty and she did have her babies to consider.

But Pool Boy? She'd keep him around awhile. There was definitely something to be said for eye candy.

She placed her bag and Orwell's cage in the first room she found after climbing the curved staircase, the Blue Room, or some other bland misnomer, she was sure. Pale-blue-to-the-point-of-being-white curtains against cream walls, cranberry carpet and gilded French provincial furniture so ornate it was a testament to Pool Boy's cleaning expertise that dust bunnies hadn't set up colonies in the curlicues.

She removed the cover from the cage, bracing herself for

the parrot's rendition of "*Just a Gigolo*," his favorite wake-up song. She gave him some water and herself a quick once-over in the Roman bath of a bathroom to remove travel *ick* from her face, buttoned her blouse, then headed out to take a look at The Inheritance.

At the top of the stairs, she took one step down and stopped. She looked at the banister, glanced around, and smiled. No one would know and, for all intents and purposes, this *was* her house, right?

Right.

In the dimming rays of daylight streaming into the foyer through a massive oval window, Livvy hiked her skirt between her thighs and slung one leg over the banister. She unbuttoned her blouse so she could get a good grip on the banister, looked behind her, then shoved off.

The rush tickled her tummy like her hair did her cheeks as she sailed down backwards. She'd wanted to do this every day of the ten she'd stayed here during that long-ago visit, but with a butler whose face could've outwrinkled a raisin and a house-keeper whose disposition made a lemon seem sweet, there'd been only one opportunity. And Dragonlady had caught her.

Livvy reached the bottom without incident, banister surf-ing being one good skill she'd learned in boarding school. *Dragonlady.* Funny, she'd forgotten that nickname for the woman.

At the bottom, she landed on one foot and started to swing the other over the banister, but her skirt tangled in her combat boot. She grabbed hold of the closest spindle, twisting it as she tried to prevent herself from falling, while simultaneously attempting to unlatch the fabric from the rivet before one or both ripped.

Apparently her banister surfing skills were a bit rusty. Thankfully, though, no one was around to witness them.

The door to the *whatever* room opened and out stepped Um Sean.

Figured.

"You didn't really slide down, did you?" His laughter did not detract from his hot-guy saunter across the marble floor.

"Sure I did. What kind of kid wouldn't want to do that? I finally got the chance."

He bent down to unhook the hem of her skirt while she did a mad scramble to make sure all pertinent parts were covered.

Sapphire eyes met hers through the spindles, his glance resting briefly on the turned one. "What *would* Grandmama say?" He stood up with a *tsk-tsk* and set the baluster to rights.

"Well, what *Grandmama* doesn't know won't hurt her, now will it?" Shrugging, Livvy yanked the strap of her camisole back into place and crossed the edges of her blouse over her stomach.

"So, Um Sean." She tried a dignified march down the last step to the black-veined white marble floor, wishing she was wearing something more glamorous than combat boots. "What exactly are your duties around here? Have you been running this place for Merriweather for long?"

Sean slid his hands into the side pockets of the cotton work pants. "Long? No. Running the place, well, that'd depend on your definition of running it." He swept his hand toward the far corridor. "You want something to eat? I was just going to get lunch."

"Works for me. Lead on, MacDuff." She swept out her hand for him to precede her.

"Princess, it's Irish, not Scots."

Black-haired, blue-eyed, sexy, skin-shivering Irish.

They passed an old suit of armor her grandmother's former housekeeper, Mrs. Tidwell, had told her was haunted. Someone had probably rigged the thing to move its arm with fishing line or something to scare the old sourpuss. Livvy remembered being terrified of the housekeeper as a child. Merriweather certainly had had a lot of old cronies around her back then. Old cronies and no children.

That one visit had been enough. Funny that she was now the sole beneficiary. She hadn't expected it, though she'd be the first to admit Merriweather owed it to her.

Oh, sure, the self-appointed matriarch had picked up the boarding school bills, but Livvy wasn't talking about what, to her grandmother, had been a mere pittance. No, the woman owed her for Mom's untimely, sauce-induced demise, brought on by the free time the kiss-off money had afforded her after

Merriweather's attorneys had swooped in to take custody of Livvy.

Livvy shoved that nightmare back into the farthest closet of her mind. The worst part had been that she'd known what was going on—even at the tender age of five when they'd packed her off. If only Merriweather had given her a semblance of love. Hell, pity would've been something, but the silent indifference had gnawed at her all those years. Why wasn't she good enough to be called a Martinson? What sin had she committed? Why take the anger at her parents out on her, an innocent victim from all parties involved?

There'd been no answers, and after a while Livvy had stopped asking the questions. Stopped writing letters. Stopped hoping to belong. Instead, she'd found the determination in her soul to make a different life for herself. And once all the *I*s were dotted and *T*s crossed, she'd have the money to invest in proper facilities and equipment to make her organic bakery products and to give herself the life she'd always wanted, Martinsons be damned.

The archway into the banquet hall, aka the dining room, took longer to traverse than the entire farmhouse where she lived.

"Memories?" A deep voice behind her yanked her from her thoughts.

The toe of one of her boots caught the heel of the other. *Memories.* "I guess you could call them that."

The arched door leading to the kitchen was ajar. *Tsk-tsk,* indeed. Jeeves/Rupert had never allowed the door to be unlatched. Why, the kitchen was where *the help* did all the nasty work. He'd always made sure to secure that door whenever she'd skipped in for a treat.

Or maybe he'd been under orders to keep her contained. Who knew, but with the family's wish to keep the heir's *little indiscretion* from becoming tabloid fodder, it certainly was feasible.

Livvy pushed the door open the rest of the way.

Oh, hell. The kitchen had been updated.

She stepped onto the polished oak floor that was a couple hundred years old and covered now by what must be a dozen coats of polyurethane. Wax didn't give off that shine. Wax also wouldn't protect the floor from the thousands of pounds of stainless steel appliances now ringing the walls. Sub-Zero, Wolf, Bosch, Viking . . . The high-end products gleamed at her. Granite countertops, speckled black, with double ogee edges. A baking-level prep counter with a wagon wheel of copper pots hanging overhead. Mini fridges and ice maker. Sinks of all sizes, and two six-burner commercial-grade ranges.

The original room-sized fireplace still graced the back wall, and through the window on the back door she saw the herb garden was still thriving.

With all this new equipment and the best of the old kitchen, she could have the perfect place to make her breads and pies. It'd be heavenly to have this much workspace, and with the herb garden so well established, she'd have her own organically grown ingredients to be able to—

Livvy stopped mid-stride. She had to halt this train of thought before it left the station. The only thing she'd *be able to* do was sell the place. Period. She didn't need a *thing* from her grandmother and the family that had all but disowned her the moment she'd been conceived, except the money the sale of their pride and joy would bring.

SEAN tried not to bump into her when she stopped, but his momentum carried him forward. He caught her as she stumbled. "Olivia? What's wrong?"

Not a damn thing, his hormones answered. She smelled of lavender soap and apples and something way too feminine for his state of mind.

"Huh?" She swung around to look at him, a wine-colored curl catching on the tip of her nose, and Sean found himself drawn to her eyes.

Confused, vulnerable, a little lost . . . Then there was a sexy quirk to a kissable mouth that was entirely too close for his comfort—

Back away from the enemy, Manley.

His brain was on board with that, but the rest of him was staging a mutiny. Back away? Right.

"Sean?" Her voice was soft as she licked her lips, her slim hand gripping his arm.

If his name were whispered like that in the middle of the night, he'd have no defense.

"Did you want something?" She peered up into his eyes.

Oh, he wanted all right.

"Uh, lunch. You want lunch?" Damn these flimsy pants— his body's reaction wasn't easy to hide. Mac really needed to change the uniform. Jeans would be better.

Or that suit of armor.

He headed to the counter, hoping the granite would cool him down. But then he looked back at her, her hair fanning out as she spun around to follow him, her curls tumbling over one shoulder to drape across the prominent curve of her breast, and Sean found himself battling the granite for the title of Hardest Thing In The Kitchen.

He strode to the Sub-Zero fridge, turned his back to Olivia, and hoped an arctic blast would take care of the problem— but, of course, *the problem* followed him over.

"Is food shopping on your list of duties?" She peered around him.

The half-empty jar of ketchup, two eggs, and a hot dog mocked him. "I was planning to get to it," he spat out. "No one sent a list of your likes and dislikes, Olivia, so I figured I'd wait for you to get here. I think there are a few frozen dinners in the freezer."

"The name's Livvy. Unless you want to go back to being Pool Boy." *Livvy* opened the upright freezer beside the fridge. "A chicken pot pie?" She picked up the package. Perfectly arched eyebrows headed skyward as she looked at him. "This is what you're subsisting on? Forty grams of fat, sodium tripolyphosphate, monosodium glutamate, liquid and partially hydrogenated soybean oil, mono and diglycerides, sodium benzoate . . . Do you want me to continue reading about the clogging of your arteries?"

"What are you, some kind of a health nut?"

"I find that term extremely offensive, you know." She crossed her arms, making her curves all the more prominent. "Just because I've decided not to fill my body full of chemicals doesn't mean I'm nuts. People who eat additives, preservatives, and whatever other poisons big-time corporations put into their food"—she punctuated the last word with air quotes—"are the crazy ones."

"So what do you eat? Lettuce and tofu?"

"No. I eat normally. And so do my customers. All natural products with no hormones, no preservatives, no pesticides, just food as nature intended. Organic."

Customers. Ah, yes. Princess Olivia Bombshell Carolla—*Livvy*—was a wannabe farmer. Sean had had a good laugh over that. A co-op living, organic baker-slash-farmer had inherited the Martinson fortune; a fortune made of and invested in any number of companies that'd have her running for the hills when she read their portfolio.

He pulled a carton off the shelf. "You're welcome to the eggs."

"Styrofoam? Why not just toss mercury into the ground while you're at it?" She spun around, giving him a quick glimpse of sexy leg beneath the skirt. "Do you have any idea—oh! They're here!"

Sean shook his head at the change of subject. It was like trying to follow a hummingbird as it darted from flower to flower. "Who's here?"

"My babies!" She skipped over to the back door, flinging it open with no thought to the chink the brass handle would put in the countertop behind it.

Sean never moved so fast in his life. Mrs. Martinson had spent a small fortune—no, make that a *large* fortune—updating this kitchen. It was one room he wasn't going to have to touch when he took over. As long as he could keep Livvy from destroying it until he got her out of here.

But . . . *babies*? She had *kids*?

Sean shook his head. That detective had a lot to answer for. Nowhere had the guy made mention of children. Christ. How the hell was he supposed to throw a woman with kids out of their ancestral home?

Millions of dollars, Manley.

Oh yeah. That's how.

Chapter Three

꧁꧂

ALMOST tripping on a brick that had unwedged itself in the winding pathway, Livvy reached the truck just as the driver climbed from the cab.

"Where do you want them, ma'am?" He handed her a clipboard.

Livvy ran down the list, making sure her neighbor Kerry hadn't forgotten anyone. She signed the delivery slip and glanced at the ominously cloudy sky. "There's a barn just down this lane. I'll ride with you and we can unload there." The barn had been the first thing to pop into her mind when Mr. Scanlon had called her out of the blue with the news of her grandmother's passing and The Inheritance. How well she remembered escaping the gloomy *Wuthering Heights*-ness of the house all those years ago for the sweet-smelling barn with all those horses and cats.

She hopped into the cab and smoothed her skirt over her legs. The driver had made good time. She hadn't expected him for another hour or she would have changed into jeans already.

She shrugged. If the "kids" ruined her skirt, she was finally in a position to afford a new one.

The barn, backlit by a gray sky, was just as she remembered, down to the hibiscus in the flower beds beside both doors. *Who landscapes a barn?*

The same people who had free-range peacocks.

Those free-range peacocks darted out from the back of the building and ran across the lawn.

Cedar shingles topped the stone building that, with the same arched mullioned windows as the house and dove gray shutters, could pass for a homey cottage. Her babies were going to get the star treatment.

The driver backed the truck up to the barn doors, then went around to the tailgate and pulled out the ramp. Livvy followed, remembering the last time she'd been here. The stalls, all ten of them, had been filled with hay, and the windows along the back let in lots of fresh air and sunshine. The Martinsons had dabbled in horse breeding, though those assets had been sold off before Merriweather had gotten ill. Pity. Livvy wouldn't have minded horses, but since she wasn't keeping the place, it was a moot point.

"Ya got leashes or anything, ma'am?" the driver asked.

She shook her head, smiling. "Just let them out. They'll mind me."

They'd heard her voice. The doors swung open to a chorus of grunts and brays and bleats as the mini farmyard version of Noah's ark emptied into the yard. Kerry was sending the dogs later. They tended to nip the sheep's heels when excited, and the trip here would most definitely excite them.

The ram and his ewes rumbled down the ramp, followed by their babies. Her own next generation. How she loved their soft wool coats that would eventually end up matted and dingy like their parents'. She hated that part, but their dingy wool kept them in hay.

She picked up Buttercup and rubbed the lamb's cheek against her own. Three days between the trip to the law offices and their arrival here seemed like a lifetime to be apart from her little family. Buttercup bleated and stiffened her legs. Mama Daisy gently butted Livvy's thigh. "Okay, Dais, here you go. I just missed you guys."

The goats kicked out of the truck next, followed by the

alpacas. Rhett spat at her, which was not unexpected. He usually spat at her. Scarlett followed right behind him. The *hembra* had become more subservient since Livvy had caught them "in the moment." Hopefully there'd be baby alpacas this time next year, though with The Inheritance, the price their fleece would bring was no longer the big issue it had been.

The gaggle of geese and ducks waddled out behind to form their ritual circle around her for their feed. She had to shuffle through to the truck to grab one of the feed bags, but pretty quickly everyone was munching away happily, the squawks giving way to contented pecking. Well, okay, Calypso might have just taken a bite out of Calliope's wing, but that wasn't anything new.

Once the birds settled down, Livvy climbed into the back of the truck. Sure enough, there sat Reggie on his blanket in the crate, his black snout rooting around in the folds. She wondered how many dog biscuits Kerry had hidden there to keep him content for the ride.

"Come on, Reggie. Let's get everyone settled." The pot-bellied pig snorted at his name, then clambered to his feet, his harness jingling with the bells she'd hung there. Reggie thought he was a cat. And he'd actually learned the stealth of a feline, but, sadly, lacked the grace. The bells warned her before he pounced—on her, on the furniture, the lily pads in the pond back home . . .

She grabbed a pair of chicken pens, lifting the clucking birds out of the truck, and clicked her tongue to herd the menagerie into their new home before the storms that were predicted for today—and the gray sky attested to—hit.

The driver, a larger feed bag tossed over one shoulder, opened the barn door, and he and Livvy came to an abrupt halt.

Someone had filled the barn not with hay, but boxes. Stacks and stacks of cardboard boxes. Floor-to-ceiling, taped and labeled as if it were a warehouse. Wooden crates containing blanketed and shrink-wrapped lumps that looked like furniture filled every stall, and the aisle along the front was cluttered with lawn furniture. Mice would be hard-pressed to find a nesting spot, never mind the menagerie she'd brought.

"Uh, ma'am? Are there pens around here somewhere for whatever used to be in that barn? I have to get going. More deliveries to make."

Pens. Of course. Around back were open-air pens. She'd have to find some tarps to construct a temporary shelter—or grab the bedspread from the Blue Room—but the pens would have to do in a pinch.

While the driver unloaded the rest of the feed bags onto a stack of benches just inside the barn door, she herded the animals around to the back. Pens wouldn't be the Ritz, but then they hadn't exactly been living like kings at the other place.

Except it didn't look like they'd be living *anywhere* because there *were* no pens.

Her kids were going to have to go back home. Livvy closed her eyes and tried to come up with someone she could ask to take care of them for her while she was stuck at this place. But the list was the same as the one she'd come up with before arranging to bring them here: no one. Kerry helped some, but he and Sherwood had their own farm to run. Same with Sheila and Marci and Jenny. Richard had scooped up all the college kids for his vacation before she'd had the chance. Life was busy for their co-op community, and caring for her animals would only burden everyone else.

Watching the driver and his truck head back down the lane, Livvy plunked her butt on the manicured lawn, made springy by what she was sure was a zillion dollars' worth of chemicals so that the darn thing looked like a golf course, crossed her legs beneath her, and rested her chin in her palm.

Green for acres. Artistically placed, white-shingled gazebos. An ornamental pond with gurgling waterfall. Pergolas covered in wisteria above wrought iron café sets. Topiaries in the shape of mythical creatures. All this land and not a useful thing to be found. All for show.

Why was she not surprised?

Reggie came over and snuffled in her ear, his usual greeting when they were at home on the sofa. She scratched him under his chin. Reggie closed his eyes, hunkered down, and stretched out his neck, grunting with pleasure.

The sheep started rooting around the grass, followed by the goats and the alpacas. Livvy jumped back to her feet, dislodging Reggie's chin from her knee. She did not want the animals ingesting whatever poison had been spread on the lawn. She herded them back toward the front of the barn, trying to figure out her next move.

Maybe they could sleep in the chapel. After all, there was precedent. Two-thousand-plus years of precedent, so it wasn't as if God had anything against sharing a place to sleep with a bunch of barnyard animals.

Then a black cloud edged over the top of the barn with a rumble of thunder. They wouldn't make it to the chapel before the storm hit.

She had no other choice. Only one place left to go.

SEAN climbed off the ladder. No way was he taking those drapes down. They looked harder to put back up than an entire pallet of rafters on a hip roof.

He reached the bottom of the fourteen-foot ladder, then eased it down onto its side, careful to miss the loveseat he'd moved before setting it up. The magnificent dimensions of the room would allow for great entertaining opportunities once the renovations were complete. This space, with its French door access to the slate patio, would make the perfect reception room for an intimate wedding. The landscape designer he'd had look over the place had suggested moving one of the gazebos from the croquet lawn close to the patio so the ceremonies could be accommodated in the event of rain.

Sean retrieved the rolling cart and angled the ladder onto it. Even with his pickup truck just outside, he didn't want to heft the awkward thing even a few feet and risk dropping the ladder or damaging any of the millwork. Now that he'd finished up with the ground floor rooms on this side of the house, he'd get this ladder back to his truck, then move upstairs where the ceilings were a little lower. With another whole half of a mansion to clean, he was going to need the entire month to finish this place.

He maneuvered the cart and ladder to the patio doors, thankful for the rain holding off—and for the twenty-foot-wide terrace. The slate out there needed some touch-up, but he knew just the guy for it. Provided, of course, he ended up with this place.

Jesus. How the hell was he going to get her out of here? The poor, discarded bastard child with a chip on her shoulder had just walked through the door of the family bastion, reclaiming it for herself. She wasn't going to leave for just any reason. And he had to be careful he didn't get himself fired before the rest of his time was up.

He had to become her new best friend. Charm her, befriend her, become her buddy. Play Working-Man to her Wronged-Heir. Us-Against-The-Family. Make them kindred spirits. Cajole her into thinking he had her best interests at heart. None of which would be a problem. The problem would be when he found out what those damned stipulations were and had to beat her at them.

The idea hadn't sounded bad about an hour ago. He wasn't into losing his brothers' money, but he hadn't met her then. Now she was a living, breathing woman. With kids.

Damn it all. Who would've thought Merriweather Martinson had a heart buried somewhere beneath the layers of starched collars and fur stoles?

Sean unlocked the French doors and wheeled the ladder through. Maybe once he ran Livvy off and got this place up and profitable, he'd give her a monthly stipend. She'd have money to fix up that ramshackle farm she called home, and he'd feel less guilty for sending her and her kids away. A win-win for everyone.

The eruption of barnyard sounds should have warned him it wasn't going to be that easy.

Chapter Four

❧

SEAN spun around at the commotion, shocked to see an unruly crowd of birds and farm animals headed his way. With one boot-shod gypsy running alongside them.

He stood there, disbelieving—and appreciating—until something hit him in the shin. Sonofabitch!

Sean tore his gaze from the stampede to see a gray-horned head backing up for another shot at his leg. A goat?

Feeling like an inept matador, Sean sidestepped the annoyance, managing to keep from tripping over the large white duck on his right, but getting a shoulder clipped by a llama.

A llama.

A llama that was running into—

"No!" Sean twisted around and ran back into the room he'd just spent the better part of the last day and a half cleaning, only to find two goats on the white loveseat, another chewing the edge of the rug, and the stupid llama literally preening in front of the glass cabinet.

And was that what he thought it was in front of the sideboard? Oh, God, it was. At least the duck had dropped that little "gift" on the marble, not the carpet—not that the goats would care.

"Oh, no!" Livvy's distress call was weaker than the one he wanted to utter.

The furniture was going to have to be re-upholstered, and if that llama scratched its ridiculous neck on that cabinet one more time, it'd knock it over. And forget about the goats. The rug was a write-off in all of fifteen seconds.

He turned around just in time to see the rest of Noah's ark waddle through the doors. Including a pig.

A pig. Who the hell had a pig?

Well that was a no-brainer. Obviously it was the woman around whom the hounds—okay, *goats*—of Hell were congregating.

"Rhett, stop that!" Livvy yelled, swatting at the llama. *Rhett.* It figured. "Dodger, get off that settee right this minute!" The goat looked up from the fringed pillow it was denuding with a flicker of its eyelashes, then went right back to munching. "Calliope! No! Outside! *Outside!*"

Yeah, Calliope the goose wasn't paying attention. Or didn't care.

Not that it mattered anymore. The rug was toast.

Livvy ran onto the rug, shooing and kicking, her skirt flouncing all over the place.

The animals just dodged her and found something else to ruin.

Sean looked from the chaos to the ladder on the patio, and quickly came up with a plan.

He ran outside, bypassing the ram that tried to nail him in the nuts, then dragged two wrought iron settees across the porch and butted the sides against the house. Then he maneuvered the ladder cart up against them and stuffed the cushions into the escape holes, creating a makeshift corral. All he had to do was get the Pied Piper to lead them out.

"Livvy! This way," he yelled over the chorus of squeaks, honks, and brays.

Livvy flipped a swath of curls out of her face when she peeked over the back of the llama she was pushing and relief shone in her smile. "Good idea."

One by one, she shooed, hustled, or carried the animals through the French doors. Sean then closed them and barricaded them with his body to keep the hellions from running back in.

It took a good ten minutes, and more of the Aubusson rug than could ever be repaired, but all of the creatures were soon ensconced in the improvised pen.

Livvy leaned against the door next to him, her curves heaving way too much for his liking.

Well, no, that wasn't exactly true. He definitely liked. But he definitely didn't *need* to be liking.

"Thanks," she said, trying to catch her breath. "I don't know what came over them. They're normally fine in the house."

"You *let* them in your house?"

"Well, not as a general rule. But when my barn was leaking during a hurricane, I didn't really have a choice. Other than the necessary, um, calls of nature, they behaved quite well."

"Yeah, well, looks like they forgot their manners today. And what gives with the menagerie?"

"They're my pets."

"They're barnyard animals, not pets."

"Why can't barnyard animals be pets?"

"You want me to agree that having a pig is like having a dog?"

"Actually, Reggie's more like a cat than a dog."

Sean gritted his teeth. "Same difference."

"Not a cat lover, I see."

"I'm more of a dog person."

"Good. The dogs will be here soon."

More insanity? "Lucky me."

"Look, Pool Boy." She poked him in his side and it hurt, dammit. "It's my house and they're my animals. Live with it."

"Did you see what they did to that room? Is that how you want to live? Your ancestors didn't build a barn out there for nothing, you know."

"Leave my ancestors out of this. I don't care what they did, or what they want. It's my place now and if I want the goats to have a playground in the reception room, it's no business of yours."

"You can't honestly say that you're going to allow those animals to destroy all that antique furniture."

"Why do you care?"

"I care because . . ." Uh, yeah, good question. What was his answer going to be? "Because it's my job to take care of this place. I just finished cleaning that room, you know. Now it's a disaster."

She closed her eyes, shaking her head. When she opened them, Sean saw a hint of laughter sparkling in those amber eyes. "Sean, Sean, Sean. You really need to lighten up. It's just *stuff*. They've been cooped up in a truck for hours. If the barn were empty, they could've unwound out there, but someone stuck a load of boxes and furniture in there. I didn't have any other place for them to go without them eating all the grass."

"And tell me again why heirloom rugs are better for their digestion than grass? I thought grass was organic?"

"It would be if it wasn't soaked in enough chemicals to make the lawn golf course–worthy."

Exactly. That lawn was gorgeous. It wouldn't take much to turn it into an ideal fairway.

"So what are you going to do with them now?"

She twisted those pretty heart-shaped lips to one side and Sean wondered what they'd feel like against his. What they'd taste like—

Yeah, yeah, mind off the pretty and heart-shaped thing. And he could forget about kissing her. She was the enemy.

As was the pig that was trying to nuzzle between the two of them, the jingle bells on his collar sounding like a drunken Santa.

"I have to empty the barn before I can put them there. Any chance barn cleaning is in your job description?" She nudged him with her shoulder and looked up at him from under her lashes.

Not fair. That look had probably been created by Aphrodite to make men's knees and wills weaken. And Livvy had it down pat. Dammit.

Looked like he'd just added more work to his day because there was no way was he opting for an indoor barnyard in his soon-to-be Hideaway Hills Resort.

But then the skies opened up, unleashing sheets of rain worthy of Noah and *his* menagerie.

"Oh no!" Livvy flew off the door, rounded the animals up, then glared at him. "Well?"

"Well what?" He hadn't moved. Nor did he intend to.

"Aren't you going to help me?"

"Help you what?"

"Get them inside."

"Inside? I thought we just decided to empty out the barn."

"But they're getting wet."

"They're animals. They're used to it."

"No they're not. And I don't want them to get sick. Come on." She nudged the pig out of the way and yanked on the door.

Sean grabbed it before it moved more than two inches from the frame. "You're not letting them back in."

Spiked, sooty lashes framed spitting gold eyes. "Yes I am."

"No you're not. They're animals. Barnyard animals."

"Who don't have a barn. Now quit arguing and move!"

For a tiny thing she sure could pack a wallop. Her hip clipped him at mid-thigh and he actually had to sidestep to stay upright.

That was the break she needed. Just that quick, she grabbed hold of both door handles and flung them open. Animals stampeded inside.

Shit. You'd think they'd never seen rain before.

He could no longer say the same for the Aubusson. The only saving grace was that it'd already been ruined—as the furniture was now being. Oh, hell.

Thunder rattled the panes of the French doors.

"I better close those," Livvy, the den mother, said, pushing off one of the wingback chairs.

"Why bother?" Sean slicked his drenched hair off his forehead with one hand and grabbed her arm with the other. "The floor's already soaked. Besides, you wanted a barn. Now you've got one." With the décor of Versailles.

She had a finger already pointing his way, but, mid-turn, the words got stuck in her mouth. She looked at him, then at herself, then at all the animals, and promptly started laughing.

Which got him laughing.

But with her bedraggled skirt plastered against her legs

and the wet, gauzy, practically transparent fabric doing the same to her body, laughter died in Sean's throat.

It was replaced by something much heavier. Expectant. He couldn't look away.

She looked delectable. Rain tracked along her collarbone, a few drops pooling in the hollow before they slipped down her chest beneath the thin fabric of her camisole. Sean traced that line with his eyes, his breath growing shallower with every freckle he counted.

Livvy's laughter slid away and Sean met her gaze.

The vulnerability he'd seen before had been replaced by something . . . more.

He *wanted* more.

He didn't understand why; she wasn't his usual type. But it didn't matter. When Livvy looked at him like she was, *looking* like she did, it didn't matter. He wanted her.

He took a step toward her. A slight one, but her lashes flickered and her lips, slicked with rainwater, formed a small *O*. He wanted to lick it off.

So he did.

Somehow she was in his arms, their bodies touching, their breath mingling, her curls skimming his chest at the V of his shirt, and his tongue slid out to taste her lips. Just a whisper of a touch, but there was no hesitancy on her part. Her breath caught just enough for the small opening he needed and he deepened the kiss.

Thunder crashed through the room—or maybe that was the blood rushing through his veins as his body turned to fire. He wrapped his arms over her shoulders, pressing the impossibly small curve of her waist against him, her breasts—her wet, tight breasts—crushed against his chest, and he couldn't help but groan as her hips moved against him.

God, she turned him on and he didn't care if she knew it. Because really . . . how could she not?

He slid one hand into the tangle of curls he wanted to see spread all over the bed pillows upstairs, and held her head at just the right angle. His tongue swept in, meeting the thrust of hers, her lips nipping at his, her nipples pressing against his chest, sending riotous signals to every nerve ending in his body.

She was tiny, almost fragile, but, God, could she kiss. The fierce scrape of her nails on his back beneath his shirt, the way she leaned against him, holding nothing back . . .

The low moan in the back of her throat . . . It undid him.

He ran his hand lower, cupping her ass, pulling her into position. He'd love to wrap her legs around him, but that'd mean letting go of the sensuous fall of damp hair caressing his skin and that just wasn't an option at the moment. He could picture it draped over him as she straddled him, her breasts, heavy in his palms, swaying with their rhythm.

God, the image . . . He deepened the kiss, his tongue doing what his cock wanted to. He was so hard he ached . . .

He slid his lips to her cheek, tasting the hint of her arousal beneath the rain, tilting her head back, feeling her breath harsh against his ear. He dipped into the hollow below her jaw, her pulse pounding against his lips as he slid them up to her lobe, catching it between his teeth, tugging, and her head fell back. Moist, creamy skin his for the taking, a brush of his lips, the swirl of his tongue—

Hell, he was in a lot of trouble. This wasn't part of his plan. He was supposed to be devising a scheme to get her out of here, not kissing her senseless.

Yet he couldn't seem to stop. Kissing her might not be the smartest *business* decision he'd ever made, but by God, he thought it might be the best *life* decision he'd ever made.

And then the damn pig butted him in the ass.

Chapter Five

❧❧❧

SEAN jerked his head to look into those eyes he'd wanted to drown in moments ago—and wanted to go under again.

But, good God, this was a really bad idea.

"If your pig thinks he's a cat, why is he acting like a guard dog?" He needed to put some sense into the moment and if guard pigs were it, then he was definitely in a lot of trouble.

But it did the trick; Livvy's eyes danced with laughter. "Reggie's a little, um, jealous of anyone who gets more attention than he does. It could be Calliope, it could be Rhett. He doesn't have anything against you specifically."

Oh, yes, Reggie did. The pig's *snout* was against him. In a very inopportune spot. One toss of the animal's head and Sean would be singing soprano for a while. "Care to call him off?"

Livvy chuckled again and took a step back. Sean felt the loss immediately. But he also felt Reggie ease away. The thing glared at him as it did so.

Sean nodded at the animal. "Effective."

Livvy shrugged—and it did way too many good things to the thin shirt still plastered to her chest. If Reggie hadn't grunted a warning, Sean would have closed the gap between them again.

That, however, wouldn't be smart. He had to stay far, far away from Livvy Carolla.

But then she tossed her curls over her shoulder, the curve of her neck reminding him he hadn't gotten to taste that part of her yet.

"Why'd you do that?"

Because it'd been a better idea than getting her upstairs and out of those clothes. "You mean kiss you?"

She nibbled on her index finger and Sean wanted to groan. The tip of her tongue, a hint of pink, that sweet tart taste of apples . . .

"Uh, yeah. That."

"A guy needs a reason to want to kiss a sexy woman?"

She snorted. "Oh, puh-leaze. I look like a drowning poodle." She brushed her hands in front of her skirt and looked down . . .

And saw what he saw.

Those amber eyes shot back to his.

He tried to hide his smile. "I don't think so."

"Yeah, well . . ." She drew her hair forward and hunched her shoulders, crossing her arms for more protection. *His* protection, if she only knew. "Do you make a habit of kissing rain-drenched women? Must make you quite the popular guy. I'm surprised no one's rearranged your pretty-boy face yet."

"You weren't exactly fighting me off."

"You weren't exactly giving me the chance."

"Nice try, Princess, but your sigh and that tongue sliding into my mouth were pure come-on. Don't go putting all of this on me. I would've stopped any time you put up a fuss." And if he believed that, he'd have no doubts that he was going to end up with this place.

"I could fire you, you know."

"Yes. You could. But then who'd show you around? Give you the keys? Clean out your barn?" Sean used bravado to cover up the very real fear she *would* fire him. What had he been thinking? Breaking the contract with Manley Maids was the last thing he wanted her to do.

"Look, I'm sorry." He blew out a breath and raked his hands through his hair. "It won't happen again. I guess I just misinterpreted the interest." Right. That might not have been the reason her nipples had been saluting him at first, but she'd been as into the moment as he had.

But the project was what was important: getting her to fail. He'd do whatever it took to stay here.

Including keeping away from one hot Livvy Carolla.

MISINTERPRETED the interest. Oh, he hadn't misinterpreted anything, but Livvy wasn't about to admit it. What on earth had she been thinking, kissing him like that? The man was a perfect stranger.

"Perfect" being the operative word.

She certainly couldn't disagree with him. She hadn't put up a fuss because kissing him had seemed the right thing to do.

Right thing to do—sheesh. Now she was thinking like her mother.

Of course, if Mom hadn't thought kissing *the worm* was the right thing to do, Livvy wouldn't be standing here, staring at the most gorgeous guy she'd ever met.

"Fine. Apology accepted. Let's just not have a repeat, okay?" Thunder rumbled the panes of glass again as the rain picked up. Another flash of lightning made Rhett snort in the corner. Daisy started snorting and the goats jumped over each other, trying for higher ground. Reggie did what he always did during a storm—scrambled between her legs, coughing as if he had something stuck in his snout.

And then she heard the screechy rendition of "Yellow Submarine" echoing through the foyer: Orwell at his most frightened.

"Watch these guys," she told Sean as she herded Reggie toward him by the bell collar. "I'll be right back."

"Watch them?" Sean took the harness for a second, then dropped it as if it were on fire. "What do you mean, *watch them*?"

"Let Reggie stand next to you and don't let the others start nipping each other. Especially the alpacas. I need their fleece in good shape." If Sean had felt any attraction to her before that moment, it had to be gone now; he was looking at her as though she had a few screws loose. But it couldn't be helped. Orwell would only get louder and work himself into a state, and it'd take him days to calm down. A psycho parrot was not good company.

She bolted through the doorway, wincing as Orwell started in on the chorus.

Taking the steps two at a time, Livvy flew up them and into her room, swooping up the parrot's cage and high-tailing it into the closet. The moment darkness enveloped him, Orwell calmed down. Traveling and being alone in a storm: his two worst nightmares.

Livvy reined in her breathing and searched for the latch to the birdcage. He'd be fine once he was on her shoulder.

Sure enough, he hopped onto her hand, then scrambled up her arm, making her wish she'd worn long sleeves. He leaned over and, with a loud smacking sound, gave her the non-biting version of a parrot's kiss.

"Good boy, Orwell," he said.

"Good boy, Orwell." Livvy stroked his head, then opened the closet door.

To find Sean standing in the doorway to her room.

"What are you doing here?" she asked.

"What was that?" Sean asked at the same moment as another crash of thunder drowned their words.

Orwell stuck his head beneath her hair.

"Sean, what are you doing here? Didn't you hear me? You have to watch the alpacas."

"Alpaca watching is not part of my job description. And your damn pig almost broke my kneecap at that last bolt of lightning." He took a step into the room and looked at her shoulder. "A bird? You ran up here for a bird?"

She huffed and shook her head, then skirted around him. "Yes, I ran up here for a bird. Didn't you hear him screeching?" She headed toward the stairs. Rhett could get very temperamental, and Daisy could be overly protective of her lambs. Livvy couldn't afford to have their wool damaged.

She stopped on the second stair from the bottom. Actually, she *could* afford to have their wool damaged. Imagine that.

Then she shook her head. It didn't matter what she could afford; she didn't need neurotic animals. She'd worked hard to give them a sense of security after the instability of their lives before she'd rescued them.

She took the last two steps as Sean caught up with her. He followed her back inside the room to find—

Oh, joy. Rhett and Scarlett had found a new way to ignore the storm.

Right in the middle of the rug.

Chapter Six

OH hell. The animals were *doing it* in the middle of the room. On the half-eaten rug.

Sean started laughing. Insanity. Crazy, absurd insanity. Here he was in a room furnished with priceless antiques, planning to convert it into a reception room for no-expenses-spared weddings, and there was alpaca copulation going on. And one of the sexiest women he'd seen in a long time—whom he'd just kissed at great risk to his job and his company's future—was standing there in almost see-through wet clothing with a parrot on her shoulder.

A singing parrot. Whose off-key rendition of "I'm in the Mood for Love" was hysterically appropriate.

"Shh! Orwell! Bad boy! Bad boy!" Livvy tried to clamp the parrot's beak shut. "Ow!"

Yeah, she wasn't successful.

But Rhett, ol' boy, sure was. With a back-shivering grunt, the alpaca removed himself from his lady, then took to preening around the room as if he'd just performed the greatest service in the world.

Sean glanced at Livvy, whose nipples were *still* outlined beneath her shirt. He wasn't about to begrudge Rhett one second of crowing. Lord knew, *he'd* do the same thing if it wouldn't get him fired—making love to her *and* crowing about it, that was.

Sean shook his head. *Mind back on the job.* Not *the woman.* Even if she *was* the job.

And then the doorbell sounded.

"I'll get it," he said, leaping over a baby goat, almost taking one to the nuts as the kid jumped at the same time.

He left Livvy in the asylum and sprinted to the door, opening it as a flash of lightning outlined the man standing there like Lurch.

"Can I help you?"

Sharp eyes drilled him beneath an overhanging brow, rain dripping off an umbrella onto Sean's shoes. "I'm here to see Miss Olivia Carolla."

"She's a bit busy at the moment. I'm assuming you want to wait?"

"Thank you. I'm Benjamin Scanlon, her attorney. Or, rather, the estate's attorney."

Sean worked hard at keeping the grin off his face and the calculation out of his eyes. The attorney. The guy he'd been trying to talk to ever since Mrs. Martinson's death. The one who held the keys to this kingdom. And who was about to hand them over to Livvy—though not if Sean could help it.

"No problem at all. You can wait in here." He directed the lawyer to the Victorian-era study. "Want some coffee or something? A beer?"

"I'd love a beer, but in this mess"—the lawyer nodded as another crash of thunder reverberated overhead, complete with a bunch of snorts and whinnies from the room down the hall—"I'd better not since I'm driving. Coffee it'll have to be."

It was just the excuse Sean needed to make sure Livvy was doing okay on her own with the zoo. And that they'd keep her occupied long enough for him to get some info from her lawyer.

Ignoring his guilty conscience, Sean pulled the door to the study closed, ran down the hall to the living room, tiptoed past when Livvy's back was turned, went out through the French doors at the back of the hall, and slipped over to the ones from the living room to the patio, praying one curious lamb would find the opening he'd made with the door.

IVVY whirled around as Rhett tried to bite Orwell and Orwell tried to bite him back. These two never got along, and the storm's electricity only made them antsier.

Kind of what the electricity she had with Sean did to her.

Livvy snorted. She'd made out with the maid. Wouldn't the girls at school be surprised? And even more so once they'd gotten a look at said "maid." Good-looking and he could kiss. He'd probably had so much practice at the second because of the first that she really shouldn't be surprised.

Rhett hocked a big noisy one at Orwell, but the bird managed to dodge it, leaving her cheek the perfect target, erasing the memory of Sean's kiss faster than anything else could. Ugh.

"Knock it off, Rhett." She tried to shove the brute sideways, but he'd wedged himself next to the curio cabinet and wouldn't budge.

Total analogy for her life and the family she'd come from.

But things would change once this place was hers. She'd be able to do whatever she wanted with it. Sell it, donate it, or even tear it down, and no one could tell her otherwise. She'd finally be able to put the past behind her and pay them back for the disinterested hell they'd put her through. Mom, too.

And speaking of hell . . . The geese had settled onto the sideboard and were nipping at the kids as they tried to jump up with them. Randy, appropriately named, almost made it, but he slipped off and landed on top of Buttercup, who took off with a loud bleat and made a beeline for the opening in the French doors—

How in the world did *that* happen? She could have sworn she'd shut them.

And then it didn't matter how it happened because Buttercup slipped out into the storm.

Livvy took off after the scared little lamb. Daisy had the same idea. They met with a crash against each other and the doorframe, with Livvy's leg taking the worst of it. Or rather, her butt did as she landed with a spine-jarring thud, cold wet marble not being the optimal surface to land on.

Out Daisy went.

This only encouraged the rest of the ewe's triplets to follow. And then the kids followed suit, which, naturally, had their mother after them in yet another parade.

Livvy scrambled to her feet, shoved Digger aside, and launched herself through the door onto Daisy's back just before the sheep could ram into the wrought iron sofa and set everyone free.

Cursing the rain, her grandmother, Daisy, Buttercup, and most especially Randy for starting it all, Livvy managed to round them all up after fifteen minutes that felt more like fifteen years.

Where the hell was that sexy maid guy that had come with this place? It'd been much easier when she'd had him there to help her.

Finally, with hair so wet there wasn't a spring of curl left in it, her shirt doing double duty as a sponge, and the skirt more a hindrance than anything else, Livvy managed to corral all of the animals back inside where they went back to happily munching the rug. That reminded her; she needed to get them their feed from the barn where the driver had left it.

At least it was dry. Too bad she couldn't say the same for anything else in this room. Well, except for Orwell. Who was singing a Beatles' medley at the top of his tiny little bird lungs fifteen feet up in the air on the corbel holding up the curtains.

Now how was she supposed to get him down from there?

"ARE you sure she's not available yet?" The lawyer set the tiny little china cup—the only serving glasses Sean could find—onto the mahogany desk.

Sean had, luckily, found an old jar of instant coffee in one of the cabinets, and prayed he wouldn't accidentally kill the guy with rot before he got the answers he wanted.

"She'll be along in a little bit. Some, ah, husbandry issues."

"Husbandly? You're married?"

It *couldn't* be that easy, could it?

"Oh, not yet." Technically, it wasn't a lie. Scanlon hadn't specified *who* Sean was married to, and, he *had* been thinking about the equivalent of husbandly rights in that living room a half hour ago.

Yeah, yeah, semantics, but he needed this property—almost to the point of compromising his principles.

No. There was no "almost" about it. Principles had been compromised the minute he'd put on this uniform knowing that he was going to have a fight on his hands because of the will. But he needed this property. *Needed* it. The rest of his company, hell, his future, was dependent on this deal, thereby putting his principles out of the picture. But it'd be a hell of a lot easier if he didn't like her so much.

"So, um . . ." Sean set his own coffee cup down, hiked up the front of his pants, and sat in a chair beside yet another ornate fireplace. This house had ten, each a different style and each one with the original marble or stone surrounds. He'd done his research, and the description of each was already part of his brochure mock-up. Yeah, he was that far along in his plans. Had been for a while before Merriweather had tossed in her wrench. "What did you need to talk to Livvy about?"

Scanlon pasted an I-wasn't-born-yesterday-son smile on his face. "I'm afraid I can only discuss that with her. You understand."

Unfortunately, he did. So much for that tactic.

"Right. So . . . how long did you know Mrs. Martinson?"

The lawyer sat back and his lips relaxed into a shadow of a smile. "My firm has been representing the Martinson interests for generations."

"Bet you guys know where all the skeletons are, huh?"

Scanlon's eyes narrowed. "I'm not at liberty to discuss Martinson family matters."

"Of course. I just meant, Livvy's probably one in a long list that the Martinson money has hidden. It probably really got to Mrs. Martinson that her granddaughter was the only person she had to leave it all to."

Yes, he was fishing, since he already knew Livvy hadn't been Merriweather's only option, but what could the *housekeeper* know, right? And if he read the lawyer correctly, the guy had been either infatuated with, or in awe of, the *grande dame*. Either could have him defending her. And hopefully giving something up.

"Mrs. Martinson did not have to leave it to Ms. Carolla. She could do whatever she wanted with the estate. It was hers. Family has always been important to Mrs. Martinson, and that is why she chose to do what she did."

But with stipulations.

"Kind of a gamble, though, isn't it? I mean, her giving all that money and this place to the granddaughter she's barely spoken to? How did she know Livvy wouldn't blow it on parties or fortune hunters?" Sean pretended to take a sip of the coffee. "Could be Mrs. Martinson was, you know." He tapped his temple. "Old age and all."

The lawyer, no spring chicken himself, took the appropriate offense. "Merriweather Martinson was of sound mind and body when she wrote her will. I, personally, can attest to that. She knew exactly what she was doing. She wanted to give her granddaughter a chance to get to know her history. That's why the will was set up—" Scanlon set down his coffee cup. "Well." He cleared his throat. "That's why I'm here. I'm not at liberty to say any more."

The family history was the key.

"What if Livvy doesn't want to accept it?"

Scanlon's cup rattled in the saucer. "Not accept it? I highly doubt that will happen. Who wouldn't accept such a generous bequest?"

"True. This place has to be worth a fortune." It was. Sean knew exactly how much, down to the last nickel.

The lawyer eyed Sean's outfit. "I can see where that would be your first thought, but money isn't everything."

Said by a guy in a thousand-dollar suit and gold cuff links. Old money if ever Sean saw it. That "managed the Martinson affairs for generations" sealed the deal. The guy didn't know what it was like to be *this close* to making his mark. Didn't know what it was like to have everything hinge on one deal. Not like Sean did. And that was just the monetary aspect of it. Never mind that his sense of self-worth was tied up in pulling this off. That he'd be the least successful Manley sibling if he couldn't.

Sean didn't go there. All his life he'd had to work harder than his brothers. He was used to it. But this . . . This was out of his control unless he could figure out the stipulations and beat Livvy at them.

He didn't understand it. Mrs. Martinson had been on board with his plans for the last three years, always taking a look at the plans and suggesting other changes. She'd liked the idea of keeping the historic beauty of the place—as well as the continuing legacy of the family name. She'd even signed paperwork to that effect, but his attorney said legal maneuverings with her new will could make the battle tricky. And costly. So costly, he'd never be able to do what he wanted with the property *if* he eventually prevailed.

It'd been a calculated risk, but calculated risk was all part of his business.

All he had to do was convince Livvy to give it up.

Chapter Seven

LIVVY looked like a drowned rat when she opened the door to the study. "Hey, I was wondering if you could get that ladder— Oh. I'm sorry. I didn't realize you had company."

She turned around to leave, dripping enough water on the burgundy carpet that Sean was going to have to Shop-Vac it out of the padding or risk mold launching a colony in the fibers. If he had to replace any more carpets in this place, his profit margins were going to disappear.

And then Scanlon stood up. "Ms. Carolla?"

Livvy spun back around. "Mr. Scanlon?" She took two steps into the room. On the rug. Drenching it.

Lightning flashed outside and Sean sighed as he stood. Besides worrying about the possibility of mold, he'd also gotten an indelible picture etched into his mind—*again*—of the lithe body beneath the clingy clothes.

He shoved his hands into the front pockets of his pants to create some extra space so his body's immediate reaction wasn't obvious to everyone. He needed a cold shower.

Thunder rumbled overhead.

Or he could go outside. Same difference.

"What are you doing here, Mr. Scanlon?" Livvy ran a hand

through her hair, bringing the curls to life like tiny cork-screws.

Sean almost groaned. The words "screw" and "Livvy" should not be in the same sentence in his world. Ever.

"Hello, Ms. Carolla." The damn lawyer oozed more charm than a Swiss finishing school. "I was just telling your . . ." The lawyer looked over the glasses that were perched on the end of his nose and Sean felt as if he were getting a dressing down from the headmaster. "Your housekeeper, here, that we have some important documents to discuss."

Livvy snorted at the *housekeeper* term and put her hands behind her back, doing a sort of slow Texas two-step as she approached them, her lips twitching.

"Oh I'm sure my *housekeeper*," she winked at him, "was just about to come get me. Weren't you Se—"

"Of course I was." He didn't need her telling the lawyer his name, not if Mrs. Martinson had mentioned him. The guy would know who he was and the whole plan could blow up in his face. "So, can I get you something, Livvy? Coffee or—"

"A frozen dinner?" Her lips twitched again.

Sean's lips did the same thing. "I was going to suggest a hot dog."

"Ah." She nodded and leaned toward him. "I'm sure Mr. Scanlon appreciates better fare than hot dogs and frozen dinners. Isn't that right, Mr. Scanlon?"

The lawyer was looking between them as if they were speaking some foreign language. Sean could see why. No one could follow that chat unless they'd been there from the beginning of their relationship.

Whoa. Hang on. They didn't *have* a relationship. They *couldn't* have a relationship.

"*Bad boy!*"

Sean might have put that screech down to his moral sub-conscious if not for the bird that flew into the room and landed on Livvy's shoulder.

"*Bad boy, Orwell*," the parrot said again.

Livvy reached up to stroke the bird's feathers, and Sean could swear there was an expectant silence in the room as Orwell articulated what Sean, at least, imagined that touch felt like with an "*Ahhh*."

He shook his head. Don't. Get. Involved.

Right.

"*Bad boy, Orwell*," the bird said once more with feeling.

Mr. Scanlon stared at the bird for a moment before shoving his glasses farther onto his nose, then lifted a briefcase onto the desk. "Why don't we sit, Ms. Carolla?"

"Um, sure. Just a minute." She slid her fist beneath the parrot's talons and raised the bird so they were beak-to-nose. "What did you do, Orwell?"

"Do?" Both Sean and Scanlon said at the same time.

She glanced at them, then looked back at the bird. "Why were you a bad boy, Orwell?"

Orwell clucked in the back of his throat and the sound skittered up Sean's spine.

"*Timmmmmmmmmmberrrrrrrrrrr!*" the parrot screeched, tossing his head back as he sung it to the coffered ceiling.

Sean met Livvy's gaze. "Timber?"

She closed her eyes. "I don't like the sound of that."

Sean didn't, either.

"Well, perhaps your *housekeeper*"—the old guy just *loved* calling him that—"could check it out while you and I get down to business, Ms. Carolla?"

She looked at Sean. "If you wouldn't mind, Se—?"

"No, not at all." Sean cut her off yet again and took the bird. Mind? Yes, he minded. He wasn't a glorified pet sitter.

But he also had no legitimate reason to stay. So, with the two of them looking at him very pointedly, he took the damn bird and went back to work, trying to come up with some way to find out what they were talking about.

And then he did find a way. Looked like his principles were about to be compromised again.

S O, Mr. Scanlon, what are you doing here?" Livvy reluctantly took the seat across from the attorney, reminded too much of the last time she'd been here and *Grandmama* had given her the "this is what is expected of you" speech on her first day. That had set *quite* the tone for the rest of the visit. "I thought I signed all the papers I needed to in your office."

"You did. I'm just acting in accordance with your grand-mother's wishes."

Ah ha. *Wishes.* The oblique term for legal servitude had a nice ring to it. Too bad it still stuck in her craw. "Okay. So what are they? Do I have to not step out of the magic Martinson bubble beyond the front gates for the rest of my mortal life or something? Sacrifice my firstborn on the altar of Martinson to then become worthy? Lay prostrate in the hall of ancestral paintings until I atone for the sin of being born a bastard? What does dear *Grandmother* have planned now?"

The lawyer sat back, looking a little put out. Not that she could blame him, since she'd laid it on pretty thick, but come on already. An inheritance was an inheritance. What gave her grandmother the right to pull puppet strings from the grave?

And who'd know if she *didn't* follow the letter of the law? Mr. Scanlon? She'd just pay him off. Rich people did that all the time. You could get away with anything for the right amount of money. The girls in her dormitory at school had proved it time and again.

"Actually, Ms. Carolla, I do believe there is mention made of the gallery, but Mrs. Martinson left specific instructions."

"I'll bet she did," Livvy muttered.

"Sorry?"

Livvy shook her head. It wasn't the old guy's fault that her grandmother had had a God complex. She just hoped he was getting paid well. "Okay, fine. Whatever. Just lay it on me so I can get to it."

Mr. Scanlon arched his eyebrows, which, with the way they moved halfway up his receding hairline, made him look like Mr. Potato Head of the interchangeable facial parts.

She coughed into her fist to cover the giggle. He really did look like Mr. Potato Head.

"I can't just *give* them to you, Ms. Carolla. Mrs. Martinson left specific instructions, and the first is that I record the precise time when I give you the first document."

"*First* document?" Livvy leaned forward, her hands clasped in her lap. "There are more?"

Exactly how long did she have to jump to Merriweather's tune? The house was losing more of its appeal every moment.

And when a crash sounded in the next room, the appeal only lessened.

Although it did tick up a notch when she heard a muffled male curse that she was pretty sure was Sean's—she'd worked very hard to make sure Orwell's vocabulary was PG-rated at worst.

Mr. Scanlon unlocked the brass latches of his briefcase with a very loud and authoritative *click*. On purpose, she was sure. He'd hung around Merriweather too long.

Of course, given the fact that she sat up straight, crossed her ankles, and clasped her hands in her lap showed just what conditioning could do. Boarding school had been great—if that's what she could call it—at conditioning.

Except, hey, she was in her own house and didn't have to do what anyone told her.

Livvy lounged back in the chair, crossed one leg over the other, and put a little swing action into it, enjoying the fact that she didn't have to toe anyone's line anymore.

Mr. Scanlon handed her the first document. "If you'll read that, please." Then he wrote something down in the journal he also removed from the briefcase.

Livvy gnawed on the inside of her cheek and lifted the paper. It was her grandmother's handwriting. Livvy had seen the imperial scrawl often enough on the checks the headmistress made sure she saw. All part of that gratitude thing everyone thought she ought to feel.

She flicked the paper and the first word jumped out at her. *Olivia.*

Well, that covered it in a nutshell. No messy emotions like, "My Dear Granddaughter," or "Darling Olivia." As if that'd ever happen.

Livvy cleared her throat.

Olivia.

My attorney has all the pertinent documents making what I'm about to explain legal and binding, but I'm sure you can't be bothered by all the legalese, so I'll get to the point.

The Martinson name has been revered for centuries. Not just anyone should claim it, and those who do should know its history. Since studying history was not one of your strong suits at the Academy, I have created a series of clues for you to follow. The first will lead you to the next, and so on, until you reach the last.

You have two weeks to the minute from now to find the clues and present the last to my attorney's firm, whereupon you shall claim your inheritance, or the estate will be sold in accordance with terms I've specified to Mr. Scanlon.

I am aware, Olivia, of your hatred for this family. Of your desire to remove yourself from it, so I expect your first instinct to be to throw this away. But consider what turning your back on this home and our vast fortune means. Are you willing to give it all up? Willing to deny all the good your bleeding heart could do with it? The choice is yours.

The clock is ticking.

Don't fail me, Olivia.

Don't fail me. No signature because one wasn't necessary. Just the directive. Had Merriweather Knightsbridge Martinson ever *asked* for a thing in her life? Livvy doubted it.

She set the paper on the desk. Typical battle-axe self-centeredness. Livvy hadn't really expected anything else.

She would so love to tell the old woman to shove it, but that's exactly what Merriweather had expected. The woman had never had anything good to say to or about her. She was Larry's Indiscretion. Larry's Mistake. Larry's Unfortunate Accident. All in capital letters.

Well now she was Larry's Heir. Or, more specifically, Merriweather's Heir. Wasn't the irony delicious?

She wasn't about to blow this. Not when Merriweather had hit her at her weak spot. The money would enable her to do what she wanted: grow her business and help out the co-op. Take care of her animals and never have to worry about paying the rent again. She'd even be able to afford to donate to causes she felt worthwhile. It was her ticket to making her life everything she wanted it to be. "Okay, Mr. Scanlon. How do I do this?"

The lawyer removed his glasses and folded them carefully, then tucked them into the breast pocket of his jacket. "When I give you this paper, the clock will start."

Livvy contained herself. Such drama. "Okay then. Let's have it. Let the games begin."

Chapter Eight

✌︎❦︎✌︎

SEAN really hated poker. If not for that stupid game, he wouldn't be in this predicament.

The damn bird was worse than the goats, sheep, pig, and that pain-in-the-ass alpaca all put together.

Sean almost lost a finger trying to get the parrot to shut up, and the feathers the damn thing was molting all over the place were merely the tip of the iceberg.

Parrots needed diapers. Big time.

Actually, he realized as he surveyed the ruined Aubusson when he returned Orwell to the room, *all* of the animals needed diapers. Thank God the floor was marble; the mess would clean up easy, but he'd be the one doing it unless he could appeal to Livvy's sense of fair play.

If she was anything like her grandmother, Sean wasn't holding out much hope.

Dammit. He didn't need this nightmare. At this point, the room was a write-off anyway, and if he didn't find out what was happening in the study, he could write the rest off, too.

Checking to make sure the French doors to the outside were closed, Sean tossed Orwell into the air, where the bird swooped onto one of the curtain rods—that would no doubt

soon be covered in bird droppings—then he left the menagerie alone and closed the doors to the foyer.

He walked to the study door, listening at the opening he'd
deliberately left.

"So, what? Do I have to swear to name my firstborn after
the old battle-axe, I mean, my grandmother, or something?"
Livvy shook a piece of paper, then switched on the desk lamp.

"'This is the first clue for the first item you must find,'"
she read. "Great. A scavenger hunt. Wasn't she a little old for
games?" Livvy lifted the paper closer. "'You'll forgive an old
woman an indulgence in rhyme. It seems the game calls for
that and I find, at the end of my life, I like humoring my
whims.'" Livvy snorted. "*Now* she wants to get a sense of
humor. Her timing sucks."

"Please read on," Scanlon said with a sniff.

Sean liked the fact that he and Livvy were on the same
side in their opinion of Merriweather—the old battle-axe.
Yeah, he could see how the name fit.

He could also see Livvy's butt wiggle slightly in the chair.
Sean rolled his eyes. *Mind back on the problem, Manley.*

One of Livvy's combat boots rocked erratically. She tossed
her hair back. "Okay, then. So, clue number one."

Livvy's back went a little straighter, her chin dipped, and
her voice lowered an octave. She might have even put a slight
British accent to the words, which Sean also got. Merriweather
Martinson did seem like the upper-crust old paragon of British aristocracy. An image, he was sure, she'd purposely
cultivated.

> *The pages are old, hundreds of years,*
> *To when its benefactor instilled many fears,*
> *In clergy and nobles, and even the peasants,*
> *Though a loyal few did earn some presents:*
> *Like the first Martinson, who hadn't fled*
> *When a queen's mother lost her head.*

Livvy set both feet on the floor and placed the paper on
Scanlon's desk—her desk, actually. She tapped the letter.
"What's that supposed to mean? Where's the clue in there?"

Riddles. Sean cursed under his breath. He'd never had a

problem with numbers, but letters had always been a challenge for him. Dyslexia had tormented him through school, and though he'd come up with coping strategies, things like homonyms and homophones—and *riddles*—had made his life hell. It figured that his future would come down to riddles.

"So what is this supposed to mean? I have to find some old documents?"

The lawyer cleared his throat. "The only clarification I can make is that should you elect to pass on this opportunity or fail to complete it, you will be entitled to a small stipend from the estate. Beyond that, Mrs. Martinson's directions were clear."

"Yeah, yeah, I know. Follow the yellow brick road and I end up in Oz. Scarecrow included. Question is, does *Grandmama* see herself as Glinda or the Wicked Witch of the West?"

Sean knew which one he'd pick right now. Dammit. That old woman was playing both of them.

"Maybe it's a book." Livvy stood up and kicked the Louis XIV chair with the heel of that ridiculous boot.

Sean cringed. He hoped to God she hadn't put a dent in that chair or she'd just devalued it by several hundred dollars.

And then she stood just as more lightning flashed through the front window, streaming through her skirt, reminding him exactly what those legs had looked like draped over the banister, all smooth, creamy skin.

His damn pants were constricting him again. Sean bit back a curse. When was the last time he'd gotten laid? That had to be the explanation for this because frizzy-headed munchkins, with an attitude—and potential fortune—bigger than his, were not his cup of tea.

Tea. Oh, hell. He'd left the kettle on when he'd boiled the water for the coffee.

Great. Burning the place down would only make his problems worse.

Chapter Nine

'LL look forward to seeing you in two weeks, Ms. Carolla."

Sooner, if Livvy had her way.

"Drive carefully, Mr. Scanlon." She closed the massive front door. Two weeks and this would all be over. For better or worse, she'd be finished.

Why did she have the nasty suspicion that it'd be worse?

Sean materialized from behind one of the giant columns near the living room. She hadn't decided where he fell on the good-to-bad scale.

"Meeting go okay?" he asked, one eyebrow higher than the other. Oh, sure. *He* could do the eyebrow trick. Was there anything not perfect on this guy?

With the way those pants hugged his thighs (and butt, she reminded herself; let us not forget how they hugged his butt), the way the shirt rippled over the contours of that six pack . . . He was in the Better column.

No. Worse.

No. Better.

Ah, hell. He could be the Sexiest Man Alive according to whatever magazine was running the poll that week, but it didn't change anything. She was here to earn this inheritance so she could sell it and pocket the change, and he wasn't going to be very happy with her for doing him out of a job.

How about just doing him?

Now there was a thought. She already knew the guy was a world-class kisser, she'd bet he'd be a world-class lov—

"Hello? Livvy?"

A big, tanned hand waved in front of her face, cutting off that delicious image. Which was probably just as well because she could feel a blush starting and she didn't want to have to go explaining *that*. "Oh. What? Is Orwell all right?"

Sean winced. "Well, he's certainly a healthy eater. All your animals are."

Of course they were; that's what the organic food was all about.

"Did things go okay?" He motioned to the paper she'd dragged off her grandmother's desk as if it were a loan being called due.

And, yes, she did realize how appropriate that analogy was.

"Do you know if there's an old book around here anywhere? Something really ancient about a queen losing her head? Marie Antoinette, maybe." She couldn't name that many queens who had famously lost their heads.

"French Revolution?" Sean rubbed his jaw. "There's a library in the west wing if you want to check that out."

"That's right. I'd forgotten about the library. Good idea." She should have remembered. It was one of the off-limits-to-a-seven-year-old-with-sticky-fingers rooms. In the years since her one and only command performance with Merriweather, she'd never figured out if Rupert had meant sticky, as in the peanut butter she'd loved at the time, or, well, something else. Good thing that, at seven, she hadn't known that other meaning. "I'll just get out of these clothes"—she almost asked if he wanted to help—"and head there."

"Want me to come with you?" he asked as they headed for the front staircase. "I could help you look."

"Not liking my animals, are you?"

"It's not the animals I object to. It's their eating and sanitary habits."

"At least you're honest."

"Uh, yeah." He looked away and rubbed the back of his neck. "Sorry, but not everyone's an animal person."

"True. My grandmother, for one." Livvy took the first step. "She did have horses in the barn for a while, but I'm sure *dear Grandmama* would have a conniption if she knew goats were jumping all over her furniture. Could be why it doesn't bother me in the least."

"I take it you didn't like your grandmother."

She stopped mid-step and looked at Sean. "I didn't *know* my grandmother. She never gave me that chance. I did, however, know *of* her. Her reputation was revered at my school. Could be because she'd donated a few of the wings, but the woman herself? I don't know if anyone ever *knew* my grandmother. She was one tough cookie."

"When you have the kind of responsibility she had, you have to be."

Livvy shrugged. "In business, yes. But with your only grandchild?" She shrugged again. That hurt was so old it was forgotten, the wounds scabbed over and covered in new flesh. The tough, calloused kind. "Look, I'm soaked. If you do want to help, I'll meet you in the library, 'kay?"

Sean wrung the bottom of his shirt. "Yeah, I could use a change, too. See you in a few."

LIVVY yanked the handles on the library's mammoth oak doors that she hadn't been allowed to touch twenty years ago. Getting caught with peanut-buttery hands on the brass handles had been a memorable event—so was the hour she'd spent cleaning them afterwards under the stern eye of Mrs. Tidwell.

"So why are we looking up a book about a beheaded queen?" Sean reached over her and helped her open the door, his biceps flexing. Livvy caught a whiff of *man* as she passed him. Funny, she'd often thought of sweaty guys with an *ick* factor, but the faint hint of perspiration that lingered on him beneath the smell of the rain was definitely not *ick*.

And she shouldn't be noticing. She had a *job* to do, not a *housekeeper* to do. "In a full shocker to me, it turns out my grandmother has a sense of humor. And likes poems. Go figure. Anyhow, she said that I have to find something specific in this book or I don't get the castle."

"I thought the castle, er, the house, wasn't important to you." Sean ran a finger along the brass plates on the edge of a shelf above her head.

"That's one way of putting it." She checked the date on the one in front of her: 1100. She was pretty sure Marie Antoinette was after that date. "No, it's not the house itself. I mean, this place is too big for one person."

Sean rolled a wheeled library ladder along the rod that circled the room for that purpose. "You're not going to be single forever. This is a great house for kids. That suit of armor in the foyer could keep them entertained for hours."

Or freak them out.

"Kids are a long way off for me. If ever."

"You don't want kids?"

She was used to the disbelief; it was most people's reaction when this subject came up, but since she hadn't had the best parental role models, why perpetuate the angst? Not to mention, she probably wouldn't be very good at it, since she had zero idea of what constituted "normal," thanks to the way she *wasn't* raised. "Not every woman is programmed with the procreation gene, you know." She grabbed the book closest to her. William of Orange. *Bleh*. History had never been a strong point. She put it back.

"No offense meant." He stepped on a rung, then slid a book halfway off the shelf. "I can see why you'd want to unload this place in that case."

"That's the plan. Highest bidder gets the Martinson legacy and *Grandmama* rolls in her grave for eternity."

He tapped the book back in place. "Ouch. Harsh."

Okay, so maybe he had a point. She was, after all, a grown woman; her grandmother's disinterest shouldn't hurt her anymore. She had friends, her own four-legged family, a business. And now she'd have enough money to keep that family and business in the manner she wanted. All thanks to the woman who hadn't cared if she'd lived or died all those years. It made no sense to Livvy why Merriweather had left her anything, and especially this house.

Sean climbed up three more rungs of the ladder, giving

her a nice view. She laughed at herself. Still jonesing for the maid.

"Did you find something?"

"Not yet." He traced his finger down a book's spine, his lips silently mouthing the words. It was a cute mannerism and completely unexpected.

He climbed back down, rolled the ladder to the right and climbed back up.

She was going to have to find out who designed those pants because they did awesome things to a man's butt—though that might just be because Sean had a great butt.

"Livvy?"

She shook off the hormonal bath and looked up. Beyond his butt.

"Here." He held a book down to her. "Try this one."

"This isn't about Marie Antoinette."

"I know. It's a copy of Henry VIII's Great Bible, whose queen was—"

"Beheaded," she answered with him.

"Anne Boleyn."

"Queen Elizabeth I's mother." It fit. She opened the cover.

There, folded neatly, were two pieces of paper. The first one was yet another note from dear ol' *Grandmama*.

Well done, Olivia. You are holding the Martinson family bible. Henry VIII gave it to the first Martinson to make something of himself. We trace our lineage from him.

Actually their lineage could be traced from *that* Martinson's father, and his father before him, et cetera, but obviously, to Merriweather, unless there was a title after one's name, they didn't matter.

Which left Livvy where?

"What is it?" Sean asked.

Livvy held up the letter and unfolded the bottom part. "Another poem."

A family's honor to defend
A reputation to mend.

This inheritance I'll not be handing
Unless you identify the reward left standing.

To mend? Her reputation was just fine, thankyouvery-much. No matter what Merriweather thought, her illegitimacy didn't define her. She was an honest businesswoman. Hard-working. Delivered good customer service and a delicious product. Adhered to the standards she'd set for herself. She certainly had nothing to apologize for and did *not* have a bad reputation.

Ol' Larry the Worm, on the other hand, had more to atone for, but since he was dead, there wasn't much she could do about his reputation. Her grandmother couldn't honestly expect her to restore it, so this annoying riddle made no sense.

She unfolded the other piece of paper. Great. Latin. A lot of *-us* and *–um*, a bunch of *V*s . . . all of which didn't matter a hill of beans, since she knew Latin as well as she knew British history.

They hadn't exactly been her favorite subjects. Cooking and animal science, on the other hand, as well as the recycling and organic portions of her science classes, they'd been her thing.

"What's that?" Sean peered over her shoulder.

Livvy handed the notes to him. "Beats me. Another bad poem from Merriweather and a drawing of Henry VIII with a bunch of Latin. A love letter, maybe?"

Sean whistled. "One of your ancestors got a love letter from Henry VIII? And lived to tell the tale? That's amazing in and of itself. How's your Latin?"

"About as good as Orwell's singing."

"That good, huh?"

She rolled her eyes. "So now *Grandmama* wants me to learn Latin." Conniving, controlling, vindictive old woman.

"Or you can find out what kind of document it is and get it translated."

"And you know a sixteenth-century documents specialist, do you?"

"No. But the internet might."

Right. The internet. How could she have forgotten?

Mainly because she didn't have a computer. Discretionary funds weren't available for that purchase, nor for a cell phone with that capability.

She was going to have to chat with Mr. Scanlon about getting an advance against her inheritance. Although, the way Dragonlady was going about this scavenger hunt, Livvy wouldn't put it past her to nix any advances until this place was hers, free and clear. "They don't happen to have a computer around here, do they?"

Sean shook his head. "No computer that I've found. Other than the upgrades in the kitchen, this place is still firmly stuck in the last century. No remote controls for the televisions, no computer, and forget about Low-E windows."

She'd bet there had been a computer here. Merriweather wouldn't not have had one, if only to keep up on world markets. The woman had been old but shrewd, and Livvy would bet she'd had it pulled from the house just to make Livvy's search more difficult. "What about a public library?"

Sean thought for a minute, then nodded. "About a half hour from here." He checked the clock on the mantel above another monstrous fireplace. "But I think it closes before then. You don't have enough time."

She put the document back in the bible and placed the whole thing on top of another old tome on a stand in the corner.

Not enough time. She had a feeling that was going to be her mantra as *Grandmama's* little game played out.

T was all Sean could do not to run out of that library and into his bedroom in the servants' quarters. Mrs. Martinson might not have a computer around here, but he did. Ostensibly, he'd brought it to help with the running of his company, but since he'd sold almost everything, running his company consisted of making this work out to his advantage.

But he didn't need a computer to tell him what that document was. He'd seen enough letters patent when he'd done his research on this place, papers from the Crown gifting the title and lands over to the bearer, in this case, the very first

Martinson—the uppercase, italicized Martinson—to hold a title and the making of the dynasty.

If he could figure out how that document related to the next clue, it might be the *unmaking* of the dynasty, because he'd be one step ahead of Livvy and could get to that last clue before her. If he kept that up, he'd prevent her from fulfilling the will's stipulations.

Granted, it wasn't the most honest method, but all was fair when it came to business. Especially when he'd banked everything he had on this venture. He'd done the research, contracted the preliminary planning, and planned a tournament-sized fairway on the surrounding properties. Plus, he wasn't about to let his brothers down. This property would make his reputation. His company. His future.

Or break it.

Chapter Ten

❧

STILL planning on tripolyphosphates for dinner?" Livvy entered the kitchen an hour later, nice and dry from her shower—both from the rain and the one in her Roman bath—in a new outfit with Orwell perched on her shoulder. He'd buried his head beneath her hair and was snoring softly into her neck. Stress always tired him out.

"Actually, I was going for scrambled eggs with hot dogs. Want some?" Sean held up the pan of food that, by rights, shouldn't be as appetizing as it was, but that apple from earlier hadn't lasted very long.

"Is there ketchup?"

"You like bloody eggs?" He smiled, and when he did, *whoa, baby.* His eyes sparkled like sunshine, deep creases bracketed his mouth in a set of sexy dimples, and his lips formed the most perfect smile she'd ever seen.

Then there were the most perfect *lips* she'd ever seen—and kissed.

Well, technically, he'd kissed her, but she wasn't going to blame that on a technicality 'cause, *day-um,* she wouldn't mind getting technical all over again.

"Livvy?"

She shook her head. "What?"

"Are you okay? I asked if you liked bloody eggs and you zoned out on me."

She wouldn't mind doing a lot of things on him, but zoning out wasn't one of them. "Um, sorry. Hungry." She stroked Orwell's head, making sure he was still asleep. "Bloody eggs would be great," she whispered. The parrot didn't actually understand what she was saying—at least, that's what all the experts said—but she wasn't taking any chances that he'd take issue with her meal. She did try not to eat eggs or meat in front of the animals.

Sean served her half a plateful while she grabbed the ketchup from the refrigerator—the one healthy thing in it. And then she read the label. Okay, not quite up on the healthy scale; too much high-fructose corn syrup. That was why she made her own. Still, a little wouldn't hurt. But, boy, she couldn't wait to get to a grocery store and get some real food. Then Sean would see what he was missing.

"So you're heading to the library tomorrow?" Sean set a bowl of canned peaches in syrup and two disposable water bottles on the table, then headed back for his plate.

Livvy just shook her head at the plastic that would end up in a landfill and the processed sugars that would end up in him. "Yeah. First thing. Then I thought I'd head over to the grocery store. Are there any foods I should avoid?"

Sean straddled the chair at the end of the table and set his plate catty-corner to hers. "No. I eat just about anything."

Sadly, she saw that to be true. She picked up the rolled napkin he handed her and withdrew the fork from inside it. "So, do you live around here?" She took a bite. Not bad, actually. Although her arteries were probably going to start protesting any minute.

"You could say that." Sean shoveled it in as if he hadn't eaten in days.

By the looks of the empty fridge, that might be a good guess.

"What does that mean?" She declined the bowl of sugar that was supposed to pass for fruit.

"I have a room in the servants' quarters."

And just like that, Livvy was thrust into the past again.

The servants' quarters her grandmother had actually called them. *In front of* the servants. Livvy had been mortified on their behalf, though Jeeves had seemed to take it in stride. Mrs. Tildwell's left eyebrow, however, had twitched.

Livvy speared a hunk of eggs so fiercely that if they weren't already "bloody" from the ketchup, they would have been from her viciousness. "Sean, I think you should move."

Sean's fork clattered onto his plate. "What?"

Livvy set down her own fork. "I think you should move."

"Look, Livvy, I know I complained about the animals, but, you're right. Why shouldn't you keep them in the living room? It is, after all, your house. I promise not to say another word about them."

"What are you talking about? What do my animals have to do with where you sleep? The only place I'm planning to move them to after the living room is the barn. I'm certainly not going to toss you out just because you have your own opinion."

A muscle in Sean's cheek ticked. "Then why are you?"

"Why am I what?"

"Kicking me out?"

"What? Where did you get that idea? I'm not kicking you out."

"But you said you wanted me to move."

The light bulb went on in her brain. "Ah . . . You thought I meant to move off the estate. I didn't. I meant that you should move out of the," she gulped, "servants' quarters. There are a hundred bedrooms upstairs. One of them has to be better than where you are now."

SEAN hid a huge sigh. For a minute there, he'd thought she'd figured him out. But she'd been taking a shower when he'd snuck back into the library and grabbed a few pictures of that Latin-filled paper to decipher later.

"I don't mind where I sleep, Livvy. The room's fine." And far enough from hers that she wouldn't find his laptop.

"I don't care if the room's *fine*." She finger-quoted it. "You need to move into this part of the house. I insist."

It would look suspicious if he kept fighting her, but Sean couldn't say he was exactly overjoyed. He still had a company to run, smaller though it was. Still had calls to make, plans to follow through with. Being within earshot could put a wrench in his plans.

Although . . . by being closer to her, he'd be able to intercept or overhear any clues she came across.

"Okay. I'll move. It's your house after all."

"Not for long."

She took the words right out of his head.

"Ah, right. But why not stay? That'd keep your grandmother turning for eternity." Not that he wanted to encourage her, but he needed every bit of ammo he could get, and if there was a chink in her armor, Sean needed to know about it.

Livvy scooped a forkful of eggs into her mouth, the time it took her to chew and swallow ramping up his tension, though that could also have something to do with the way her tongue slicked over her bottom lip, catching the tiniest bit of egg there.

What had he been thinking when he'd kissed her earlier? Talk about a bone-headed move—on so many levels that his bank account was cringing.

His libido, on the other hand, was pleading for a repeat.

"True, but this place is a monstrosity. And obscene. It ought to be a museum or a university or something. It'll do more good for people that way than as a private residence. It should have been done years ago. What was my grandmother thinking, living here in this resource-hog all by herself?"

She'd been thinking that she had a legacy to pass on, but Sean wasn't about to share that since it ran counterproductive to his plans. But he understood Merriweather's reasoning. What was the use of building something with your life if there was no one to leave it to? He sure as hell wasn't building an empire to see it torn apart after his death. And Merriweather knew it. That's why she'd given him first dibs. He even planned to name the formal living room after her. The Merriweather Martinson Salon. After he'd had it fumigated now, thanks to the animals. The old woman definitely wouldn't appreciate alpaca sperm as a floor wax in her signature room.

"So do you have any offers yet?" Sean went for nonchalant, covering the urgency in his voice with the hot dog he stuffed into his mouth.

Livvy shook her head. "First I have to earn it, then I'll put it up for sale."

"Earn it?"

Her sigh was more expressive than words could ever be, and if Sean hadn't known the true situation, he would have been able to figure it out from that alone.

She explained about the stipulations, guilt shriveling his spine a little at the unsuspecting truthfulness in her answer.

"So, since it looks like I'm going to be exploring the house, I guess you're going to come in handy," Livvy said, finishing off her food.

Sean almost choked on his. "Handy?"

"Sure. You've probably been in every nook and cranny in this place. Who better to help me find what Merriweather has hidden than you? You *will* help me, right? I'll make sure Mr. Scanlon pays you extra."

Hopefully, she'd put the sick smile on his face down to the preservatives in the food. What could he say but yes? A guy in his supposed position would be all about the extra cash.

"Sure." He wiped his mouth with the napkin after he coughed out the hot dog that was blocking his airway.

"Great." She sat back and threaded her fingers through her hair, the resulting fan around her shoulders not helping the events in his pants any. The woman was going to kill him. Either with frustrated passion or frustrated dreams. "So you want to come?"

. . . So not responding to that.

Sean covered his mouth again with the napkin. "I, um, was planning to start working on the barn."

"Oh. Right. I guess that should be first on your list." She gathered her plate and utensils and took them to the sink. The *clink* when they hit the granite woke the parrot, who decided to imitate David Lee Roth.

Sean arched an eyebrow. "'*Just a Gigolo*?'"

The blush on Livvy's cheeks was too cute for words. Just like her. Which was becoming a huge problem.

"Orwell, like most of my animals, was a rescue. He'd lived

in a fraternity house for years until one of the pledges realized that nachos and cheese weren't exactly the best diet. The story goes that he was 'stolen' during Hell Week. Poor thing lived Hell *Years* until that kid did the right thing. I've almost cured him of the foul language, but the song has stuck."

"*Orwell wants a chip*," the bird said in the middle of the melody in a totally different voice.

Livvy smoothed a finger over the bird's gray crown. "Okay, Orwell, I'll get you dinner."

"Chips?" She complained about what *he* was putting in his body? He'd like to know in what jungle chips were native fare for birds.

She shook her head and some of her curls swept over her breast—not that Sean was noticing or anything. "The song stuck and so did his dinner vocabulary. I've got the perfect diet for him upstairs in his cage. I guess I'll head up. Don't forget to pick out a new bedroom for yourself."

"I'll do that." Right before he got to work on that document.

Chapter Eleven

"SURE you don't want to come with me?" Livvy asked as she tugged the giant front door open the next morning in another gypsy skirt that brushed the tops of her combat boots.

At least today she wore a baggy sweater instead of a camisole. He couldn't have stood another day of her body-hugging wear and maintained his sanity.

"I thought you wanted your animals in the barn tonight?" He sure as hell did. The mess they'd left in the living room this morning had put finding the next clue on the back burner.

"Good point." She swirled around, giving him another inadvertent glimpse at those shapely legs. "Okay, then, I'll see you after the library and food shopping. Make sure the animals don't get too rowdy. The fleece, you know."

Fleece was not uppermost on his mind this morning.

Because you're fleecing her?

He turned away to hide his guilt. "Good luck with the research."

He'd had a hell of a time figuring out what the damn

document had said, which explained some of his mood this morning. His dyslexia was severe enough that he'd known he'd had his work cut out for him. If only he weren't dyslexic, he'd be able to read the clues and be off and running, far ahead of Livvy. But no. He was stuck with plodding through various online translation programs and the text-to-voice feature on his tablet that had saved his sanity and his business many times. Thank God technology had caught up with his "issue."

He'd gotten a crude double translation from all the programs, showing that the document had something to do with a gift from Queen Elizabeth I for service from her "most loyal knight."

There was one thing in this house that was owned by a knight and was a "reward still standing."

Twenty seconds after Livvy clicked the front door behind her, Sean was staring at the suit of armor. He ought to be making some business calls, but this was the most pressing matter in his business at the moment.

Where would Merriweather have hidden the clue?

He cautiously slid a finger beneath the opening at the elbow. Nothing.

He tried the other elbow.

Nothing there, either.

A sound came from outside, and Sean jumped back. He didn't need Livvy to walk in and find him with his hands in the guy's pants or whatever they called that part of the armor.

He counted to twenty, then went searching again. He wasn't cut out for this subterfuge. Site plans and financial documents, yes. This? No wonder Bond needed a martini.

And a beautiful woman.

Sean shook his head, clearing the image of Livvy's legs from his mind. He had to hurry up. He still had to move the rest of his stuff from his old room, check in with his permit clerk to confirm everything was still moving forward on that end, touch base with the architect who'd been out last week to take measurements, make sure none of Livvy's animals had gone for a walk, and get enough work done on the barn that she wouldn't suspect him of doing what he was about to do.

Sean shoved the guilt behind a steel door in his mind and put a metaphorical lock on it. He couldn't let it get to him. Business was business.

Where would Merriweather have put the next clue? She certainly wouldn't want anyone taking the suit apart; the woman loved the trappings of the family name too much to destroy something so vital to it.

Sean tried the suit's neckline.

Bingo. There was a piece of paper wedged there.

Ignoring the bleats from the lambs outside the French doors in the makeshift pen on the patio, Sean slid the paper out and unfolded it.

More Latin graced the top of the letter and Sean groaned. English was bad enough. If Latin weren't already dead, he might just try to kill it himself.

Thankfully, it was only one line of Latin in scrollwork at the header of the page, then Merriweather's precise handwriting.

A half hour later, he listened to his tablet read it for the third time.

Brava, Olivia, for following the clues to this, the suit of armor worn by Henry Martinson III, gifted to him by Queen Elizabeth I for his service. It was from this man that the Martinson estates became a force to be reckoned with. He played the political games of the times, kept his head, and set this family on the road to greatness.

Now, in continuing your search, the next clue:

His father founded the family's fame
'Twas up to Henry III to secure their name.
It took two wives for the deed to be done
And bring forth that all-important son
When at last the heir was born,
The lord had it proclaimed that very morn
For such joy could not be denied
And he told all he spied.
Any way that he could.
I have preserved the deed in wood.

Sean stared at the screen, the letters making as much sense as the clue. Wood? He had to find a piece of *wood*? Like there wasn't enough of it in this place. Where the *hell* was he supposed to start looking?

The crash that came from the animals' holding cell might be a good place.

HOPE I'm not intruding, but you're Merriweather's granddaughter, aren't you?" The older woman standing across from Livvy's table in the library had a halo of silver curls framing her head, and the smile on her face lit up her sparkling blue eyes in a way that gave Livvy every reason to believe the woman was a friend of Dragonlady's, but not the reasons why. Livvy would have bet Merriweather had never looked so carefree and happy in her life.

"Um, yes. I'm Olivia—Livvy. You knew her?" She couldn't actually call Merriweather her grandmother, not when this woman looked exactly like what Livvy had always wanted her grandmother to look like. Soft, smiling, and approachable.

"Oh, Merri and I, we go way back." The woman's blue-veined hands rested on the back of the chair across from Livvy. "May I?"

Livvy cleared the stack of books she'd been looking through. "Please."

The woman sat down. "I'm Dafna Fine. Your grandmother and I played backgammon a few times a month." She interlaced her fingers and rested them on the tabletop. "Well, we liked to say we did, but actually, we just liked to get together to chat."

"Merri—my grandmother?" The woman played games? And chatted? Funny, the image Livvy had always had of her was either prune-lipped or barking orders.

"Oh, my, yes. Your grandmother was a fine card player, too."

Cardsharp if Livvy had to guess, but she wouldn't say it. Actually, she didn't have a clue what to say. She hadn't really known Merriweather. Not this side of her. "I, uh, guess you miss her."

Dafna's smile faltered. "I do. There are so few of us left."

"Us?"

"The girls. Surely she mentioned us?"

Was this where Livvy poked a stick in the inflated image Dafna had of Merriweather's largesse as a grandmother?

She couldn't. Not to those kind blue eyes. "I didn't see my grandmother all that much." That, at least, was the truth and surely something "the girls" would know.

"Yes, I know. Pity, but then, she wasn't the most flexible of people. She'd been incredibly hurt by your father. We told her not to take it out on you, but Merri did have her pride."

Merri? There was a misnomer if Livvy ever heard one. And she was glad "Merri" had had her pride. Livvy hadn't— nor much else either, but as long as Merri had hers . . .

"Who are the other girls?" Livvy stacked the papers. She'd found what she needed and there was no sense wallowing in bitterness; that would let "Merri" win, and Livvy wasn't about to allow that in any aspect of her life. With the information she'd collected over the last few hours, she was one step closer to beating Merriweather at this game.

"Just Hetta and I are left. Hetta Rothenberger. She lives in The Palisades, you know. Merri had the suite custom-painted to match her home because Hetta hadn't wanted to move. But when her husband passed, well, the house was too much for her. So Merri made a game of it. To see how much we could make the place look like Hetta's old rooms. We still smile about it today, Hetta and I."

Dafna blinked and looked away, brushing the corner of her eye with her pinky finger while Livvy tried to figure out what to say. What to think.

Her grandmother would do something like that? *Merriweather Martinson*?

Livvy shook her head. It was as if she'd just discovered that the woman she'd known all along was a figment of her imagination.

But those lonely years at boarding school weren't her imagination, and neither was that forbidding trip to the estate as a child. Or the utter lack of contact, warmth, and acknowledgment.

"Look at me." Dafna laughed. "Going all maudlin. I'm sure that's the last thing you want." She stood. "I just wanted to meet you. Merri rarely spoke of you, but when we found out she'd left you the estate, well, Hetta and I knew she wouldn't mind if we touched base. She was a proud woman, your grandmother. But she was loyal."

To whom?

Livvy didn't ask. It wasn't fair to this kind woman. *Merri* was in the past and it couldn't hurt to accept the olive branch Dafna was extending.

And maybe she'd know something about one of the clues.

Livvy shook the selfish thought from her head. She wasn't like her grandmother, using people for what they could do for her.

"Would you—and Hetta, of course—would you like to come out to the house for lunch some day? Say, next Wednesday? See if there's anything of my grandmother's you'd like to have."

Dafna's eyes sparkled even more, if that were possible. "Oh, my, that's so sweet. How thoughtful of you. Hetta doesn't get out like she used to." Dafna swiped at the corner of her eye again. "But thank you, Olivia. We'd love to come." She tucked the chair beneath the table. "It's been a pleasure. Your grandmother would think so, too."

Livvy didn't, but she smiled anyway and waved when Dafna turned back at the sign-out desk.

Livvy sat back. *Merri*? Backgammon? Cards? Decorating rooms for a . . . *friend*? Poems and hunky cleaning guys? There was a whole other side to the woman she'd never known.

Had never been *allowed* to know.

Livvy tossed her pencil onto the table. That's right. Merriweather had made it more than clear who was important to her. Livvy wasn't going to begrudge Hetta Rothenberger her painted rooms, but it stood as one more reason to find the clues and get away from this place and the memories she should have had but didn't.

She gathered her paperwork and books and stuffed them into her satchel. Enough dwelling. It was time to move on. Her dogs would be here soon.

That was her life. The dogs, the animals, and her bakery. This little sojourn at the family homestead was simply a means to an end, and no trip down Memory Lane was going to derail her from her goals.

Not Merriweather's goals, not Mr. Scanlon's advice, not even Dafna Fine's well-intentioned suggestions.

And no matter how much she hated to say it, not the hunky housekeeper, either.

Chapter Twelve

❧

WELCOME back, Ms. Barnum. The rest of your circus has arrived." Sean's sarcasm made Livvy smile.

She couldn't help it; he just looked so darn hot all disgruntled.

'Course he looked hot no matter what. If he could pull off the Manley Maids' mint green shirt and matching pants and still manage to be sexy, he could pull off anything.

Livvy arched her eyebrows (simultaneously, dammit) while juggling the bags of groceries and her satchel as she tried to shut the front door behind her. "Where are they?"

Sean grabbed the four shopping bags from her, the strength in his arms making her efforts almost laughable—though there was absolutely nothing laughable about his arms. Any part of him, actually. The man was actually better looking this morning than his rain-drenched self had been last night. Though she hadn't complained about his clothes being plastered to that physique.

"I put them in the Rose Room's master bath. I figured they couldn't damage the tile."

That snapped Livvy out of her pheromone-induced fog.

"You put my dogs in a *bathroom*?" She slid the strap off her shoulder and tossed her satchel onto the foyer table.

"The formal living room was taken, if you recall. By a herd of sheep. And a pair of amorous alpacas. What are you feeding those two, anyway? You might want to bottle it. You'd probably make a fortune putting little blue pill makers out of business."

"That's the plan." Her libido didn't need any thoughts of aphrodisiacs in it, thankyouverymuch. Not with him standing right there, looking like *that*. Man, those pants were tight enough to send her imagination in several directions, and as for the way his shirt hugged his chest . . .

Who needed little blue pills with Sean around?

"It feels like you spent a fortune," he said. "What's in here anyway?"

"Dinner." And that's all she'd say, still hung up on aphrodisiacs.

"Oh, about that. I won't be here. I, ah, have plans tonight."

"Plans?" He had *plans*.

"Yes."

Plans he wasn't sharing with her.

"Oh."

"So you're on your own."

Nothing new there.

Refusing to dwell on *that* lovely thought, Livvy ran upstairs to the Rose Room. She could only imagine what the poor things were feeling being away from her for so long, traveling here in the back of a delivery truck, and now being cooped up in a bathroom.

Thirty-two paws frantically shuffled on the tile floor as the dogs caught her scent. Then Ringo started barking. Paula joined in with her characteristic wolf-wannabe wail, then Georgia and John started crying. When Davy, Micki, Petra, and Mike joined in, it became a Beatles/Monkees medley in howl-minor.

Claws assaulted the bathroom door when she ran into the bedroom. Then they assaulted *her* when she opened the door and the assorted breeds bowled her over.

It took her about twenty minutes to give them all the loving they craved before they calmed down, but Livvy didn't begrudge them any of it. Each one was a rescue and still had abandonment issues no matter how much she tried to alleviate them, but she could relate, so she gave them all the attention she wished someone had given her.

Sean could call them her circus, Merriweather could spin in her grave, but Livvy didn't mind whatever chaos the dogs caused. They were her family, such as it was, and she loved each one.

Leading the now-behaved pack down the stairs, she bit her lip at the look of horror on Sean's face.

"Please tell me they're going to sleep in the barn, too."

She shook her head.

"The kitchen?"

"On that hard floor? Are you serious?"

He turned the color of his shirt. "Where?"

"Which room haven't you cleaned down here?"

"They've all been cleaned."

Darn. She didn't want to purposely ruin all his hard work, but the dogs needed a place to sleep.

"My room." Sure, why not? It's where they'd slept at the co-op. The only difference now being that they'd share a king-sized bed instead of a double. Winners all around.

Sean just shook his head. "You know what they say about lying down with dogs, right?"

"My dogs don't have fleas."

"Let's keep it that way. It's going to be a big enough job fumigating that living room as it is."

She grabbed her satchel off the foyer table and slung the strap over her shoulder, wincing as the extra weight banged against her ribs. "How's the barn coming? Anything interesting in the boxes?"

"It's coming. Slowly. Lots of dishes, knick-knacks, linens . . . So far there's enough to redo half the bedrooms in this place and there might be enough furniture to replace the goats' chew toys. I've cleared just enough room for the alpacas so far. With the way Rhett's been after Scarlett, I don't think he'll complain about them getting a room to themselves. I sure won't."

Livvy couldn't help it; she laughed at Sean's disgruntled look. But she had to hand it to the guy; he was being a good sport for a non-animal person.

Sean raised his eyebrow in that maddeningly sexy way of his, but it only made her laugh harder. Which was the perfect thing to dismantle the utter awareness she had of him.

Livvy hunched down and picked up Georgia, the pug mix, a clear cover-up for where her thoughts should not go. She was way too aware of the man. "I, um, had an interesting day."

"Oh?" Sean held out his hand. "Here, let me carry that for you."

She paused for a moment, but then handed over Georgia. If the guy was asking—

"Not the dog, Livvy. Your sack. I'll let you keep the dog."

"Oh. Right." She jostled Georgia—who wheezed her displeasure as she was wont to do when it came to movement of any kind—and worked the bag off her shoulder.

Sean swung it onto his and headed toward the study. "Have any luck?"

"Yes, actually. The Latin was an official document from what I could gather. A copy, of course. I'm sure Merriweather has the original locked up in an airtight vault."

"What'd it say?"

To his credit, he didn't say a word when he stepped back to let her pass and the dogs ran through first, dog hair soon marring the polished leather Chesterfield sofa. He did, however, groan when Davy popped one of the brass nail heads free from the wingback chair on his second attempt to jump onto it. The miniature poodle looked mighty pleased with himself as he curled around, even growling at Petra, his favorite, when she came over and licked his ear.

Livvy tapped the blotter on the desk as she walked around it to set Georgia in the executive chair behind it. "You can put the satchel down here. I'll show you what I came up with."

The dogs behaved themselves while Livvy explained her rough translation and the copies of similar documents she'd found. She pulled out Merriweather's note. "I think this last line is the clue. *A reward left standing.* Aside from this house, I can think of only one thing she could mean that has to do with nobility and service."

Sean's face was so close to hers as they examined the papers together that, when she looked up, all she'd have to do was lean in a few inches and their lips would meet.

The temptation was almost too strong.

So was the tug in her gut when he *did* lift his head and those blue eyes of his held hers.

And when those eyes glanced at her lips, well, Livvy couldn't really say what happened next.

Because, somehow, her lips were on his and her hands were in his hair and, oh, God, did all of it feel divine.

"Livvy." Sean's breathy way of saying her name only made her want to kiss him more.

But then she realized *she* was kissing *him. He* wasn't kissing *her* back.

Oh, God.

Livvy pulled back and spun around, grabbed Georgia, then the papers, looking for something, *anything*, any excuse to get herself out of this room and this situation without embarrassing herself any more than she already had. Oh, God, what had she been thinking?

"Livvy."

He was still there. Behind her. Next to the desk.

Within kissing distance.

She'd never been so mortified in her life. He had *plans*. Probably with some other woman who had more right to kiss him than she did. Not that she had any right but—

"Livvy."

Oh, God. Her shoulders drooped and Georgia grunted.

Livvy set the dog back in the chair and took a fortifying breath. She did not want to turn around.

"Look at me, Livvy."

"Do I have to?" she muttered.

Sean laughed. "Yes. You do."

That laughter was more compelling than any yank-and-turn would have been; the look in his eyes was even more so.

"I don't think this is a good idea, Livvy."

"You don't?" Oh, God, no begging. He had *plans*.

Sean shook his head. "No. You're my boss. We're living under the same roof. It could get complicated."

A voice of reason. Thank God *he* had one.

She took a shaky breath and worked very hard for the smile she stuck on her face. "You're right. I'm sorry. I shouldn't have put you in that position—"

His finger stilled her lips. "Hold on. I think you have the wrong idea."

"I do?"

Damn, he took his finger away. But that was probably for the best.

And then the backs of his fingertips brushed her cheek. No, *that* was for the best.

"Yeah, I do. I didn't say I didn't want to kiss you; just that it's probably not a good idea. Another time, another place, in any other situation but this one, oh, yeah. I'd be all over it." His eyes narrowed and Livvy shivered—and it wasn't from embarrassment. "I'd be all over *you*."

Well *there* was a way to get her to be able to walk out of this room—not. What was she supposed to say to that? And what about his *plans*?

Sean didn't seem to require her to say anything. "I'm going to leave you to whatever it is you need to do with your clues, and I'll move Rhett and Scarlett to their new suite. I'd offer to cook dinner, but I don't know what half that stuff you bought is, so I'll leave that up to you, okay?"

She nodded, still not trusting herself to speak—well, not trusting herself not to embarrass herself further when she spoke.

"Good. I'll catch you later."

He was certainly welcome to try—well, he would be if it weren't for his *plans*.

Still . . . she did watch every step he took as he walked away.

SEAN cursed himself, this situation, Merriweather, Livvy, the damn sheep, and most of all Randy Rhett as he led the pain-in-the-ass out to the barn. This whole thing couldn't be more screwed up.

He liked her. He *liked* Livvy. Even with her combat boots and gypsy clothing, her strange eating habits, and her animals, he liked her.

The woman had grit. She had tenacity. Goals. She was driven, she was resourceful, and she was sexy as hell.

And she was the enemy.

Damn Merriweather for pitting them against each other.

Damn his budget, too, for not being enough to do right by her and his brothers, and damn his ego for deciding that this was the property to make his mark. He had too much invested in this project to lose it.

But the sharks were already circling, wondering if Livvy was going to sell. He'd had to fend off six phone offers today; he wondered how many Scanlon was getting at the office.

God help him if Livvy heard the amounts people were offering. There was no way he could compete unless he brought in more investors, cut back on his vision for the place, or lowered the projections he'd given his brothers when proposing this deal. So either they'd make less or Livvy would. What a freaking choice.

The alpaca snorted and pulled back on the makeshift bridle Sean had fashioned.

"Not now, Rhett. I don't need you giving me trouble, too." His conscience was doing enough of that already, because the only way he could save his company and his brothers' money was to do the one thing that hadn't been a problem before he'd met her but now went against his very soul: swipe Livvy's birthright out from under her.

Chapter Thirteen

"YOU look awful pretty in green, Bryan. Matches your eyes." Sean couldn't resist ribbing his brother, the only one of them who hadn't changed for the dinner with Gran as they waited in the common area of the assisted living facility where she now lived.

"Don't push it, Scene."

Bryan had teased Sean about the spelling of his name their entire lives. As if it was *his* choice to have an odd spelling. That and the dyslexia that had made learning to spell it a bigger challenge than it should have been.

"Seriously. How does Mac expect us to call ourselves *Manley Maids* when we're wearing the most *un*manly pants in the history of work uniforms?" Bryan picked up the latest copy of *People* off an end table and thumbed through it. "See?" He held out the magazine. "Now *that's* a work uniform."

It was a picture from his last movie where he'd had bombs bursting behind him, a gun in each hand, and a woman clinging to each arm. Bikini-clad women.

"Hey, I'm up for giving Mac the money for new uniforms." Liam slapped Sean on the shoulder when he arrived. "I feel like a frickin' girl in those clothes."

"We could sing like one, too," said Sean, adjusting himself. "Who the hell designed them?"

"I did."

The three brothers shut their mouths when their grandmother walked into the waiting area. "I take it there's a problem?"

Sean felt about three inches tall. Another part of him did too after spending eight hours in the uniform *that his grandmother had designed.* "I'm sorry, Gran. We didn't know—"

"I realize that, Sean. I know you boys would never deliberately hurt me." She touched Bryan's arm and he bent down to kiss her cheek.

Sean was startled at how much Bry *had* to bend down. Gran had seemed to shrink as they'd grown, but he'd put it down to them growing so quickly. But now that they were all over six two—and presumably finished growing—she was still shrinking.

It didn't help that this new home dwarfed her. He'd never thought she'd leave the Cape Cod–style house that'd been too small for three rambunctious boys and the little sister who tried desperately to keep up. Gran had presided over her small old house where Mac still lived with such strict rules and fierce love that she'd seemed larger than she actually was. But now . . .

Gran was getting older. Sean sucked in a breath. She'd been the one constant in their life after their parents had been killed in the car accident. He didn't know what would've happened to the four of them if it hadn't been for her. Both of their parents had been only children, so Gran was their only relative. He didn't want to think about when she wasn't with them any longer, but seeing her here, so tiny and frail, he couldn't help it.

"So you boys tell me what needs to be done and I'll work on another design."

Sean didn't dare look at his brothers. He was not going to discuss *packaging* with his grandmother.

"They're a bit, uh, tight, Gran," said Bryan. The guy had always been fearless, which had given him the balls to go out to Hollywood and give the movies a shot. It was a good thing he hadn't worn the uniform then or his balls might not have been that big.

"Tight, how?" Gran asked as she led them down the hall to the private dining room.

"You know, Gran, *tight*." Bryan nodded to the residents they passed. This was probably the one place a movie star could go where he wouldn't be attacked by screaming hordes of fans.

Gran stood aside so Liam could open the door to the dining room for her, the manners she'd instilled in them now second nature. Not that that was the only reason they'd hold the door for her; they'd do anything for Gran. She'd held their family together, and nothing was more important than family.

Poor Livvy had had no one.

Sean wanted to groan. He didn't need to be thinking about her now. Or ever. He didn't *want* to think about her. He didn't *want* to want her. And he *certainly* didn't want to feel any sympathy for her. He couldn't. He had to get the estate from her; there was no other choice. He'd invested too much to give up at this point. Livvy had lived without the Martinsons for this long; she wasn't losing anything but the money.

He'd set up some sort of compensation for her. Maybe even give her a percentage of the resort's proceeds. Out of his take, of course.

Yeah, that's what he'd do. He'd make sure she never had to worry about a roof over her head or food for her zoo again.

"Sean, you bring the chicken over to the table. Liam, the potatoes. And Bryan, you can pour the wine. But not those Hollywood-sized drinks you're used to. I don't want any of you boys getting drunk."

"Yes, ma'am." Bryan rolled his eyes at them. Gran's bottle of wine wouldn't make a dent in any of their sobriety.

"And don't you roll your eyes at me, young man. You might think you know everything because you're a big movie star, but I can still take my switch to your behind if you get too big for your britches."

"That's what I'm trying to tell you, Gran." Bryan set the glass down in front of her. Half-filled as she deemed fitting. "I *am* too big for those britches."

"Bryan Matthew Manley, there's no reason to be crude."

Sean almost spit out his wine. Gran had understood Bry's sexual sarcasm? Since when?

Liam, too, looked like he was about to choke.

Bryan just looked flat-out shocked. "I . . . I didn't mean . . ."

Sean so wished he could inhale because he'd love to laugh at Bryan's expression. Instead, he whipped out his phone and snapped a photo.

"What the hell was that for?" Bry recovered quickly enough. But then, he always had around a camera.

"Insurance. Against poverty," Sean answered as he sat at the table. "I'm sure some magazine would pay big bucks for it."

"Sean Patrick Manley, you stop teasing your brother," said Gran in a voice he remembered too well from his teenage years. "Hand me that phone."

"Aw, Gran—"

"The phone." She wiggled her fingers.

Sighing, Sean handed the phone to Liam, who put it in Gran's palm.

"Bryan's your brother; you stick together. I will not have you sabotaging his career." She turned the phone around, peering at it. "Now, how do I delete that photo?"

Liam held out his hand. "Here, Gran, let me—"

"Oh, here it is." Gran pushed a button before Liam could take the phone back. "There. All gone."

"*All*?" Sean looked at Liam. "Please tell me she didn't delete *all* of them."

Liam held out his hand. "Gran."

Gran huffed. "I might be eighty-four, but I'm not senile, boys. I *have* worked a phone before."

"When?" Sean felt marginally better. Lots of senior centers had electronics; thank God Gran wasn't completely new to them.

"When Mildred's grandson came for a visit. He showed me how to take a picture of the two of them. It came out quite nice, too." She looked rather pleased with herself.

It should have reassured Sean, but Liam was frowning.

"Uh, Sean?" Lee held up the phone. "Sorry, bro, but they're gone. Something important?"

The clue. She'd deleted the clue. He'd wanted to get his brothers' thoughts on what it meant, but now it was gone and he'd left his tablet at the estate.

"No. Not really." No sense making Gran feel bad. It wasn't as if she'd done it on purpose. "Just some shots of the estate. I wanted you guys to see what you've invested in."

"Ah, yes. Mary-Alice Catherine mentioned something about a house you wanted to buy. I hadn't realized it was the Martinson estate. How's that coming?" Gran held her hand out for him to pass his plate to her.

"It's coming." Bad word choice.

"Coming, how?" Liam looked at him over the rim of his wine glass. "I thought you said there might be complications."

"I'm working on them."

"What kind of complications?" Bryan leaned forward.

Sean winced as he sucked up the courage to tell his brothers just where they stood. "Merriweather threw a slight wrench into the plans." He told them about Livvy's claim to the property.

"Son of a bitch." Bry tossed his napkin onto the table.

"Language, Bryan." Gran didn't even pause in spooning the chicken onto Sean's plate. She didn't raise her voice, either. She'd never had to. One sideways look or *tsk-tsk* from Gran reined them in faster than any switch she'd threatened to take to their backsides.

"Sorry." Bry grabbed his napkin and put it back on his lap. "What are you going to do, Sean?"

That was the question.

"As I see it, I've got three options. One, make sure Livvy fails and the sale can proceed as planned. Two, I was going to ask you guys if you wanted to cover the difference. For commensurate ROI, of course. "

"So you'd be the minor partner, then?" Liam asked.

Sean nodded and took his plate from Gran. "Obviously not what I wanted when I planned this, but we can work out the terms and I'll gradually buy you out. If you can float the money, that's my second option. The third would be to bring in outside investors, but that'll dilute everyone's take."

"That option's out." Liam rubbed his chin. "This is supposed to be a Manley Brothers project. We bring someone else in, we lose that edge, both in calling the shots and the publicity."

"But you have Bryan," said Gran, holding out her hand for Bryan's plate. "He's the best publicity you could ask for."

"No go, Gran." Bryan handed it to her. "I'm the silent partner. I don't have the background these two do for this business. We start plastering my face all over this and it'll become a circus. The media's great until it isn't. And even if that weren't an issue, Sean's got what I can afford."

"And you have my discretionary funds, too, Sean," said Liam. "I still need working capital for my business. There's nothing more."

So that was it then. He had to make sure she failed or he would.

"I'm sure you'll come up with something so everyone gets what they want," said Gran with the faith in him she'd always had. "Including Olivia. After all, it *is* her birthright. You'll have to treat her fairly; no taking advantage. Too many people in that family have done that to her." Gran's smile didn't hide the warning behind her words: *Don't steal from Olivia.*

"You'll do what's right, Sean. I know you will. That's how I raised you and that's the type of man you are. Remember what I've always said about cheaters never winning. You could always give your brothers their money back and forget about it."

Forget about it? His entire life plan? His future? His company? This was the *pièce de résistance* to what he was trying to build. This was the property that would put him on the map and put him in league with the big boys, proving that he had what it took to make it. And she wanted him to *forget about it*?

Hell. It wasn't bad enough he put pressure on himself, or that Livvy put a truckload on him unknowingly by virtue of just being, or his brothers' expectations brought their own load of stress, but now his grandmother had her own expectations to toss into the mix.

All he wanted to do was buy the property, get the construction team working, and open for business in ten months. Was that too much to ask for?

"So." Gran smiled a different smile at him. This was one he recognized. It said she'd gotten her way and everything was right in her world again.

If only that translated to his.

"Has Olivia baked you her pepper loaf yet?" She handed

Liam his plate. "It's delicious. Mildred brought some on her last visit. I think it's still in the bread box. If you'd get it, Liam."

It wasn't a request.

Liam brought the sliced bread back to the table. Sean looked at it. On a good day he wouldn't be able to eat it—peppers didn't belong in bread, they belonged on a burger—today, he definitely couldn't. "Thanks, Gran, but I—"

"Try it. Your Olivia works hard at her business. The least you can do is try it."

Especially if he was going to steal her inheritance out from under her. The words weren't said, but they didn't have to be. His conscience was shouting them from the rooftops.

He took a bite. So did his brothers.

Damn. The woman could cook.

"It's good." Bryan helped himself to another slice.

Gran slapped his fingers. "Don't reach, Bryan. Is that how you behave at that Mr. Spielberg's dinner parties?"

Bryan raised an eyebrow. "I don't know, Gran. When I go to one, I'll let you know."

She slapped his fingers again. "Wrong answer, young man. Don't be flip with me."

"Yes, ma'am."

Sean bit his lip. Here they were, all over thirty, and Gran was treating them as if they were three.

He wouldn't have it any other way. Thank God for family. *Which Livvy didn't have.*

Jesus. He had to stop thinking about her and her life and what she did and didn't have. This project put enough pressure on him; Livvy and that dilemma only upped it.

On second thought, maybe he would have that glass of wine.

"So how are your assignments coming, boys?" Gran finally served herself the best smelling rosemary chicken Sean had ever tasted, her signature dish and a reminder of home.

"How's it *going*?" Bryan's fork clattered to his plate. "I seriously have no idea why people procreate. You ought to see these five kids. I get the place all clean and nice, and by the time I've finished the last room, I have to start all over again. It's like each kid is their own tornado. Inversely proportional to their size, too. That little one . . . *whew*. She can create a mess of epic proportions."

"She's hurting, Bryan. Acting out. Have patience." Gran looked at Sean and Liam. "Her father was the pilot of that plane crash a few years ago. Sad."

Bry took another slice of bread. "I know *exactly* what she's feeling, Gran."

They all did. Only Mac hadn't been old enough to remember that awful day they'd gotten the news about their parents.

"I know you do." Gran squeezed Bry's hand. "Liam? How's Cassidy?"

Liam shook his head. "She's Cassidy."

There was only one *Cassidy* in town who anyone meant when they said, "Cassidy."

Cassidy Davenport: spoiled socialite daughter of their town's version of Donald Trump.

"Now, Liam, don't judge her by what everyone says about her. I mean, look at Bryan. Do you really think everything they've printed about him is true? He hasn't dated all those women."

Sean and Liam didn't look at Bryan. Because he had. Bry was definitely enjoying the fruits of his labor.

"Don't worry, Gran. I'm letting Cassidy prove herself." Liam glanced at Sean and arched an eyebrow.

Sean shoveled another helping of potatoes in to keep from laughing. Poor Cassidy was hanging herself just by breathing. Liam had been through a rotten breakup with a woman like her who'd only seen dollar signs when she'd looked at him and hadn't dealt well with the reality that Liam's bank account hadn't matched her father's. He'd been crushed, at first, and it'd shaken all three of them.

"Good. I'm glad to hear it." Gran waved her glass around for a little more wine.

Sean almost choked on another helping of potatoes. Gran *never* had two glasses of wine. He handed Liam the bottle. "You okay, Gran?"

"I'm fine, why do you ask?"

"No reason." He was *not* about to accuse her of drinking too much. She'd caught him more than a few times in high school with beer he shouldn't have been able to buy but had. She'd never found his fake ID, though, thank God. It had served him well for the four years he'd used it.

"I hear the estate is lovely inside." Gran spooned another helping onto his plate.

If one didn't mind bird feathers and alpaca sperm. Seriously, he'd caught Rhett making a go of it *again* the moment his back had been turned in the barn this afternoon.

Lucky bastard.

"It is, Gran. I could bring you out one day." When it was well and truly his.

"Wonderful. How about next Wednesday?"

Sean snorted on the mashed potatoes. "Wednesday?" He'd been thinking more along the lines of next year once the place was up and running. And his. He wanted to own it before he brought her out. Wanted to make her proud of him. Prove her faith in him. She'd always told him he could do anything he put his mind to. Considering he'd grown up thinking his mind was screwed up, her faith had meant a lot. Yeah, there was a lot more at stake than money on this project.

"Yes, Wednesday. That's when Hetta and Dafna are going. We can make it a group outing."

"Hetta? Dafna?"

"Merriweather's friends. Hetta lives across the hall here, and Dafna stops by all the time. We've gotten to be quite friendly."

"Why are those women going to the estate?"

"Olivia's offered them whatever they want from the house. Isn't that generous? She's such a nice girl, that Olivia. I don't know why her grandmother never saw it."

Because her grandmother was a hard-headed, prejudiced old cow who didn't care who she hurt with her hollow promises.

And now he had to deal with three *other* senior citizens with their own agendas because Livvy *couldn't* give the women whatever they wanted from the estate. What if it had a clue in it?

Sean cursed under his breath. He really needed to get a

jump on her and figure out where that next clue was, because with Gran erasing that last one from his phone, he was back at the same starting place as Livvy.

"So what do you think about switching, Sean?" asked Bryan.

Sean shook his head and looked up. His grandmother and brothers were staring at him. "I'm sorry, what'd you say?"

"Your assignment. She must be a babe if you haven't even told us word one about her," Bry said with his smart-ass smirk that the media called *smoldering,* but Sean called *annoying.* "I'm thinking I might have to check her out if you're not calling dibs on her. Maybe we can switch jobs."

Sean refrained from flipping him off only because Gran was sitting at the table. "You have your own client to deal with."

"And she's quite lovely if I remember correctly from the newspaper," said Gran.

Bryan shrugged. "Yeah, she's hot, but she's got five kids. Nothing destroys a woman's attractiveness faster than a bunch of kids hanging around."

"Ahem." Gran cleared her throat.

Way to go, idiot. Sean wanted to kick him. Gran had had a bunch of kids hanging around for years and, as far as any of them knew, she'd never dated. Maybe it hadn't been by choice.

Liam's glare said everything Sean didn't. And more.

Bryan looked sick. "I'm, uh, sorry, Gran. I, uh—"

Gran raised her hand. Such a tiny movement. Such a tiny hand. And yet so very effective. The three of them looked at her.

"I raised you better than that, Bryan Matthew. That woman has a lot to offer someone, and those children are blessings. You should be so lucky to have her even *think* about going out with you. With comments like that, you don't deserve her."

Bryan winced. Gran didn't pull any punches when they were wrong and this time was no different. Bry really shouldn't be down on the woman. It wasn't as if she'd wanted her husband to die in a plane crash and leave her to raise all those kids.

Just like it wasn't Livvy's fault that her grandmother was pitting them against each other.

Hell. If Gran could wither Bry's inflated self-importance with just a wave of her hand over one comment, she was going to have a field day when he sabotaged Livvy's search.

Wednesday promised to be a banner day.

Chapter Fourteen

IVVY tapped the eraser end of her pencil against Merri-weather's latest joke, er, clue, as she sat at the breakfast bar in the kitchen. *Wood.* The woman wanted her to find a piece of wood. If that wasn't a needle in this mausoleum's haystack, she didn't know what was. The house was *made* of wood. Corbels, lintels, mantels . . . so many "els" that she didn't know which one she should start investigating first.

She'd been up since six taking care of the menagerie, once she'd shoved the snoring pack off her bed. She should have banished them last night; they'd sounded like a chorus of foghorns as they slept and it'd woken her up early.

Her neck had a crick in it, and Georgia, the pillow hog, was the reason. And her *real* hog had taken exception to that fact. He'd been the one to steal her pillow back at the co-op, so when he'd sniffed her hand this morning, he'd turned his snout up, practically pirouetted on his hooves before prancing off to his oversized dog bed to glare at her while she filled his trough. It'd taken her three apples to coax him over to eat.

God, what a pitiful testimonial to her love life. Forget sleeping with fleas; what did it say when she slept with a pig?

She took another bite of her asparagus and sundried tomato egg white omelet with a schmear of homemade pesto on top before starting off on round two of this wild goose chase. Hmmm, maybe she ought to get Calliope and Callista in on the act. Nah, Sean would have a fit about their feathers being all over the place.

Sean.

Her cheeks heated at the thought of what'd happened in the study yesterday. The rest of her body did, too, and Livvy couldn't find it in herself to regret it.

She did, however, regret listening for him to come home last night.

No. Not *home*. He'd come *back*. This wasn't anyone's home.

She'd tortured herself for hours wondering what he'd had to do, where he'd gone, what his *plans* were. Had he had a date?

Why did she care?

She shuffled her foot that Paula was using as a pillow. She *didn't* care. Not really. She was curious. Yes, that was it; she was curious. He was a good-looking man and he'd kissed her (before she'd kissed him), so, yes, she *could* wonder if he was kissing anyone else.

Although . . . he'd said that it wasn't a good idea for anything to happen between them, so maybe there was someone else.

And maybe she was reading way too much into the situation for a guy she wouldn't see after a few weeks.

Or . . . could she?

Well, look at her. A possible turnaround in her fortune and she was considering turning a few other things around. Wow. You just never knew what life would throw at you.

She was more than a little glad it'd thrown Sean her way.

SEAN checked the back of the last wooden picture frame in the foyer that he could reach without a ladder. He thought about getting the ladder off his truck to check the rest because he wouldn't put it past Merriweather to have hired someone to glue the next clue on the back of the highest, farthest portrait in the room, figuring Livvy would give up at some point.

Except that Livvy had enough fire in her to *not* give up.

And maybe that's what Merriweather had counted on.

Livvy had been up early, the dogs following her as if she were the Pied Piper while she ran her hands all over every wood surface she saw, pressing on the paneling as if a secret door would spring open; all the while a certain part of *him* had sprung to life at the thought of her hands doing the same thing to him.

He exhaled and once more adjusted himself in the stupid thin pants. *Focus, Manley.*

Right. The clues. Where the hell would Merriweather have hidden the next one?

He almost tripped over one of the dogs that'd elected to stay behind instead of following Livvy out to the barn. What was the thing's name? Peter? Peta? Pickle? He'd never had a dog growing up. Gran hadn't needed to feed or pay for one more thing, so he wasn't used to having anything trail after him.

But this little guy—or girl—didn't seem to get that. It looked up at him with soulful eyes, a little droopy in the corners, its stubby tail thumping the wall with a rhythm all its own.

"I'm just going over here, you know. You don't have to follow me."

Nope. The thing lumbered to its feet—Livvy's organic diet was obviously agreeing with this guy a little too much—and followed him over before plunking back down onto its roly-poly belly with a wheeze.

Sean gave it a pat on its head, then looked around. Where could the next clue be? He'd checked the corbels. He'd run his hands over the lintels. Where the hell could she have put it? What was he missing?

He walked past the salon the animals had destroyed. Just his luck she'd have hidden it in there. No place was safe from the gnawing teeth and curiosity of a group of young goats. Well, not unless she'd drilled a hole in the furniture and stuffed the clue inside . . .

No. She wouldn't have.

Would she?

Sean discarded that idea. She wouldn't destroy an heirloom. Not when she wanted Livvy to appreciate them.

But what if a piece already had a hole in it?

A desk. There had to be a desk somewhere. One with little cubby holes and hidden drawers . . . Didn't those old English aristocrats have a thing for desks like that? Spy desks or something?

There was a desk in the master bedroom.

Merriweather's bedroom.

T took Sean ten minutes to realize there was nothing in the desk. Merriweather had cleaned out every drawer and slot, and had conveniently left hidden compartments open.

Damn.

He slumped onto the bed and picked up his little four-legged stalker and set it on the bed beside him. Where would she have hidden the clue? It had to be somewhere significant; this wasn't something she'd just stuff behind a baseboard somewhere. It was too important.

He replayed the clue. *All-important son* and *the heir was born.* Two comments, one idea. The son was important. His birth was important. What was wooden that had to do with his birth? A crib? Bassinet? Sean hadn't seen either of those anywhere.

He gripped the bedpost. *Think, Manley. What would be significant enough for the birth of an heir and made out of wood?*

He tapped the post, a solid *thump thump* under his fingers. This thing was sturdy. Old, too.

Sean looked at the post. It was made of wood. It was an heirloom. And babies in the eighteen hundreds, especially aristocratic ones, were typically born in style. Like in a big, four-poster estate bed.

Sean stood up. Each post had a finial. Which meant each post had a hole in it.

The dog followed him to each corner, its tongue lolling out of the side of its mouth in a cockeyed smile, a little hop every so often of its front paws as if the clue was a big deal to him, too.

"Probably expecting it to taste like bacon," Sean muttered as he replaced the second finial. He hoped he wasn't wasting his time with this.

The third finial gave up the clue.

Sean quickly snapped a picture of it, vowing that Gran was *not* getting her hands on his phone again, and emailed it to himself just in case.

It looked like another poem.

He ought to destroy it. Cut Livvy off right now so she couldn't find any more.

The dog yipped, which was about the length of time Sean considered it. It was one thing to beat her to the finish line, another to sabotage her.

And his damn conscience wouldn't let him flush the clue down the toilet.

"I know I'm going to regret this," he said to the dog. Another thing he'd probably regret, but at least no one but him and the dog knew he talked to it. "But it's only fair."

He screwed the finial back in place and was going to help the dog down from the high bed just as Livvy showed up with a singing shoulder ornament and the rest of her motley pack of dogs—who immediately took possession of every chair, ottoman, and accent rug in the room, the one saving grace being that none jumped onto the bed where the little pug thing rested with its paws crossed like some royal dignitary.

Orwell's rendition of "Every Breath You Take"—especially that last line about watching him—upped Sean's guilt.

"I think I figured it out, Sean." Livvy set Orwell on *that* post, of all places, then ruffled the dog's ears. "So this is where you got to, Georgia. Were you keeping Sean company?"

Georgia. That was the little guy's, er, girl's, name. "What'd you figure out?" He kept an eye on the bird. Livvy really needed to get diapers for her pets.

"I think it's in this room. Noble babies were always born at home in the ducal bed, so Merriweather probably had a plaque or something made up and hung around here to proclaim the joyous occasion. Help me look."

He set the dog onto the floor with the others and was once more tortured by the sight of Livvy running her hands over every surface. Her small, delicate, graceful hands that had felt so good bunched up against his skin and threaded through his hair and scraping down his back and . . .

Damn pants.

He ought to just give it up and tell her where the clue was, because he didn't know how much more of this he could take. She kept bending down to check the molding. Stretching to feel around the tops of pictures. Murmuring to herself as she discovered a new possibility, with the sexiest little catch of her breath as if he'd just discovered some secret place on her body—

Head in the game, Manley.

But then she moved to the headboard, leaning over the mattress—lying *on* the mattress—and Sean finally *did* give it up. He held out his hand for the parrot to climb onto his hand and was reaching for the finial when Livvy rolled over on the bed.

"Aww, Sean. I didn't know you cared," she said looking at him and the bird.

Oh, he cared. But not about the bird.

What he cared about was that she was on the bed with her arms over her head, gripping the headboard, her skirt hiked up over those amazing legs, and she was smiling at him as if she was damn glad to see him.

It was very obvious in these completely useless pants that he felt the same way.

And she noticed.

Her breathing changed. Her eyes widened. Her lips parted in a soft O that he wanted to taste.

"*I'll be watching you.*" Orwell's mimicry was perfectly timed.

Sean shook off his arousal as much as possible and tried to draw some clear, innocuous, safe thought into his head. "He uh . . ." He raised the hand that was Orwell's perch. "Poo."

She giggled. "I would've bet money you'd never have said that."

"Why?" He winced as Orwell shifted on his fist. Those claws were sharp—and at this moment, very welcome.

"I don't know. With how indignant you get about my animals, I would have thought such bodily functions were beneath you."

There were *some* functions that he definitely wanted beneath him.

"Hey, I've been watching that dog all afternoon." Georgia yipped at him as if it understood what he was saying. "And I'm concerned that parrot, er, droppings have enough acidity to peel the finish off the wood and he, you know . . . where you perched him."

He grabbed the rag out of his back pocket—the one he was now going to keep in his waistband, draped over one area in particular—and started wiping away the offensive matter.

Which was enough to wobble the finial on the post.

Shit.

No pun intended.

"Is that loose?" Livvy sat up on the bed, her hair all mussed up, her skirt all hiked up, and his libido all *jacked* up.

"I wonder . . ." She walked across the bed on her knees and Sean mentally undressed her while she did so.

He was a dog. Worse than any of those snoozing in this very room. Why the hell couldn't he focus on what was important?

You are.

Yeah, his conscience could go take a flying leap. Women were a dime a dozen; Livvy wasn't so special. Certainly not worth giving up potential millions of dollars and his brothers' faith, trust, and respect.

Keep telling yourself that.

Livvy wrapped her hand around the post, her fingers brushing his.

He was in so much freaking trouble because he *couldn't kid* himself. There *weren't* any other women like Livvy.

She unscrewed the finial.

"Oooh! Look!"

He was and it was a beautiful sight.

He didn't mean the clue.

Livvy's eyes lit up and her smile slid through him like sunshine on a spring day. She was everything good and light and right with the world.

And now he was sounding like Merriweather and her blasted poetry.

Livvy pulled out her grandmother's latest installment. Sean stuck the rag into his waistband and pulled out his cell phone. He hit the microphone app. It'd save on translation time.

She read:

> Lord William Martinson the first,
> Lost three babes as if cursed
> The last, yet another son,
> He declared to be the one
> To raise the profile of their family
> From gentry to noble dynasty.

She folded the clue and tapped her lips with it, tilting her head to the side, exposing that soft curve of her neck that he hadn't had nearly enough time to explore on the two short kisses they'd shared, and Sean could only imagine the hidden delights he'd find there—

"*Watching you.*" Orwell wasn't one to let silence go to waste.

"So what's it mean?" He hit the off button on his app and stuck his cell back in his pocket, more to give himself something to do so he wouldn't stand there and moon over her.

"I don't know, but it's all so pretentious," said Livvy. "Who cares, really? We're not in feudal England anymore. The serfs now work at Microsoft and some of them earn more than a lot of the outdated royal houses these days. The American dream. Yet my grandmother persisted in perpetuating this monarchical ideal that she now wants to pass on to me. I don't get it."

"But do you get this?" Sean tapped the clue, trying to keep the focus on business, not how wistful she looked.

Livvy flicked the clue between her fingers. "I guess we have to find out who Lord Martinson's fourth son was. Then figure out what he did that was so wonderful."

She swung one leg off the bed, bobbling a bit as she gained her balance, using his arm to do so, and as far as Sean was concerned, the most wonderful thing William's son had done was to keep the family tree going, right down the line to Livvy.

Chapter Fifteen

"YOU'RE sure you're not hungry? I can make you some lunch." Livvy leaned against the back door in the kitchen after letting the dogs out and looked at Sean.

He looked really good. Too good.

And he'd thought the same thing about her.

Eyes above the waist, Carolla.

Right. She kept them firmly planted on his face—not that that was a hardship, but she'd seen his reaction upstairs in the bedroom. Kind of hard to miss, since she'd been practically eye level with it and those pants couldn't keep a secret.

"No, I have to finish the last few stalls in the barn. The goats are a little too energetic for just one and Reggie has been bothering the geese, so he needs a place."

"Yeah, but you have to eat something. And I did do all that food shopping." She should stop begging. It wasn't attractive—not that she was trying to be attractive. She wasn't.

Was she?

Livvy bit her lip. He really was good-looking, and the chemistry between them . . . *phew.* Had Merriweather seen that coming when she'd put in this stupid stipulation? Surely, her grandmother couldn't want her to mingle with *the help*? How *de trop* that would be . . .

The perfect reason *to* mingle with him. If she needed another reason, that was.

He stood in the doorway to the kitchen after she walked in. "What did you have in mind?"

For a second, Livvy just stared at him. She ought to tell him what she had in mind.

"I *am* kind of hungry. Do you have anything, you know, normal?"

Oh. Food. Lunch. Right. Livvy got her brain back into this room and not the little trip down Sexy Lane it'd gone on.

"Normal? What, exactly, constitutes *normal*? 'Cause those phosphates and tri-whatever-o-cides aren't normal. *Those* are man-made. What I make is organic. Good for you. As *nature* intended, not big pesticide companies." She grabbed the grass-fed cow's milk cheese she'd been thrilled to find, and a loaf of her favorite bread, some brown sugar, pecan mustard, the jar of organic pickles, a tomato, and a mango. "Sit. It won't take me long. I guarantee you'll love my grilled cheese."

She loved watching him set the table. So much so that she almost burned the sandwich, all those muscles flexing and bunching and tightening . . .

A few things of her own were tightening.

She hadn't been able to get him out of her mind all last night. That moment when they'd been in her grandmother's bedroom earlier—on the bed—he'd looked at her *that* way. She'd known exactly what that look had meant and her blood had started to boil. Her nerve endings had gotten all tingly and her breathing had gone for a hike.

Livvy squirmed a bit as she carried the sandwiches over to the table.

He ran his tongue over his lips. "Wow, that looks good."

He had noooo idea . . .

The dish rattled as she went to set it on the table. Luckily, Sean took it from her and set it down gently. "What can I get you to drink?"

A bucket of ice water and pour it over me. "Um, the iced tea is fine. I steeped it overnight." She'd liquefied the raw sugar crystals this morning and mixed them with some fresh-squeezed lemon, then added mint extract in her own secret ratio. A line of herbed teas was going to be her next venture.

Sean brought two glasses back to the table. "You even make it look nice," he said, handing her her drink as he straddled the chair beside her.

"The presentation should be as good as the food." She alternated the tomato slices with mango and pickle for a bit of sweet, a bit of tart, and a bit of spice, the perfect complement to the sharp cheese. *"Bon appétit."*

She watched him take a bite. She loved watching people's reactions to her food. Most were so ingrained in their normal rigmarole that they couldn't see outside the box to appreciate what she'd come up with. But when they did, when they tried her creations, they were usually very pleasantly surprised.

She had a feeling Sean was one of those people, so into his daily routine, doing everything the way he'd always done it, that having her around rattled his cage a little.

It certainly rattled hers.

"My God, Livvy, this is amazing."

So was the way he licked a spot of mustard off his bottom lip.

She wanted him.

Plain and simple, she wanted Sean. And if that rise in his pants earlier was anything to go by, he wanted her, too.

And what was wrong with that? Two consenting adults . . .

Though it wasn't as if she could just lean across the table and plant one on him, then sweep everything to the floor and make mad, passionate love on this three-hundred-year-old oak table—

And why not?

"So," said Sean, taking a bite, "I was thinking we ought to check the family bible again and see who this fourth son was. Maybe it will spark an idea of where she would have hidden the clue."

Oh. Right. That's why not. She was on a deadline.

"Livvy?"

"Thinking." But not about the clues. "You're right; the bible is probably a good place to start. Looks like anyone who's anyone in the Martinson family is listed, so it should tell us something."

"Is your name in there?" He took another bite and the muscles in his cheek clenched, giving him a very square jaw that was more than a little manly.

He was so well suited for this job. "My name? I doubt it. I'm not a Martinson."

"On paper, no, but by blood you are. I would think Merriweather would have put your name in there, even if it was only after she wrote her will."

Livvy picked up her sandwich and stared at the melted cheese oozing from beneath the crust. "You obviously didn't know her well. I wouldn't be surprised if they never served olives at any function here just so there'd be no chance my name would be uttered. I mean, did she ever mention me to you?"

"No."

"And how long have you worked for her?"

"Uh . . ." He took a bite of his sandwich. Then a long drink of the tea. Then a few mango slices. Crunched on a pickle.

"Must have been quite the experience if you don't want to talk about it," she said, scooping a couple of her mango slices onto his plate.

"Definitely an experience knowing ol' Merriweather." He swirled the tea around in his glass. "This is really good. You ought to bottle it and sell it."

"That's the idea. But it's a big start-up expense with all the bottling and the labeling and keeping it chilled, plus the tea is a bit pricey. But once I sell this place, I'll have that money."

Sean choked on the sip of tea he'd just taken. Nothing like making her feel guilty. "Oh, don't worry, Sean. I'll think of something to do with you when I do."

Sean coughed. "*Do* with me?"

"Well, yeah, you know, if I sell, you could be out of a job. But I figure anyone who can afford my asking price is going to be able to afford the monthly operating expenses as well, so they can keep you on as a condition of the sale. Or, if you'd like, I'll roll your salary for say, what, two years, into the asking price. That way you don't have to worry. I know how hard it is having your income pulled out from under you."

He choked on the next swallow of tea.

Livvy hopped to her feet and pounded him on the back until his airway cleared. "You okay?"

He coughed, then coughed again, then swiped a hand across his mouth. "Uh, yeah. I'm good."

He certainly was.

Livvy sighed as she sat back down in her chair. There. She'd told him. Now to get potential buyers to agree.

"How'd you come to be in this line of work?"

Sean looked up. "What?"

"I asked how you came to work as a maid. Lose a bet or something?"

There he went with the choking again. He downed his tea, coughed a whole bunch, and stuffed the rest of his sandwich into his mouth—probably not the best idea given all the choking, but he was still chewing as he stood up and carried his dishes over to the sink. "We really ought to get a look at that bible. I have a feeling this clue is going to take a lot more effort to figure out than the others."

A S they headed back into the library, Sean tried not to be impressed. He tried not to like her. He tried to look away and put her out of his mind.

But he did none of those things.

Because, yeah, she impressed the hell out of him. She was so fiercely independent, so determinedly self-reliant, and so sweet to worry about him that he couldn't help but admire her. As a human being.

As a woman . . . well, that was a whole *other* level of interest.

This was not going to end well. It couldn't. By its very nature one of them would lose. Sean was torn between praying that, whichever way it shook out, *he* wasn't the biggest loser, but that would mean Livvy would be and . . . shit.

The bible gave them a name—and, no, Livvy's name wasn't in there—but it didn't give them anything else.

They pulled out a history book from her ancestor's lifetime, but for the guy who was to raise the family to dynastic proportions, there was woefully little about him.

"So is there something on the property with his name on it?" Livvy asked as she set the book back on the shelf. "A statue or plaque or monument or something do you know?"

Sean had been over most of the grounds and the only statues he'd seen were of Greek or Roman gods. "Only thing I've seen honoring your ancestors is the hall of portraits. Maybe it's there."

So much for Livvy's assertion that Merriweather didn't want her to find the clue. This one was attached to the back of the portrait of Lawrence Martinson I, Livvy's father's namesake, whose only claim to fame was to have twelve children. Eleven of whom were girls.

"You'd think my grandmother wouldn't have named her son after someone who'd let the family name down by not producing enough male offspring," said Livvy, tapping the next clue that was sending her back to the public library again tomorrow. "But then, I guess she never expected him to fail the family so spectacularly by choosing my mother and, worse, producing me."

As far as Sean was concerned, Livvy's father ought to be commended for that. "The failure was Merriweather's, Livvy. Maybe that's *why* your father chose your mother. He wanted to live his life on his terms, not Merriweather's. Just like you."

He knew it was the wrong thing to say the moment it left his mouth. Livvy had worked too hard to establish herself without the backing of the Martinson name. To compare her to the epitome of what she didn't want to be . . . Sean braced himself for a rant.

Instead, he got a straightened backbone, a pair of narrowed eyes, and the most clipped voice he'd ever heard.

"I am *not* like my father and I never will be. I am *not* a Martinson."

Chapter Sixteen

❧

LIKE her father? Livvy was still stewing about that conversation the next morning in the barn while she mucked out the stalls, the analogy for her life a little too close for comfort. She was *not* like her father. She was as far from being a Martinson as . . . as . . . as Reggie was.

Who was also a little too close for comfort, butting her in the butt when she went into his stall.

"I know, Reg, but you can't sleep in the house. Sean's right. I can't let you guys destroy it in a fit of pique. I want to get as much money as I can for the place. I'll give you your own room when I redo our farm." She petted his cheek. He liked that. He also liked her to scratch under his chin, too, but he was usually too "drool-y" and she didn't have anything to wipe it off with. He purred as well as a pig could purr as he leaned into her hand.

Livvy had to sidestep to keep her balance. Reggie had gotten a lot stronger as he'd gotten bigger. This barn would be the perfect place for him. For all the animals. The peacocks apparently thought so. They'd even deigned to "accept" the chicken's food.

Livvy shook her head as she shooed them away. She wasn't

staying. She had to get that out of her brain. Had Merriweather hoped the place would grow on her and she'd make it her home? Well, she had news for Merriweather Martinson, who, for all her money and her plans, didn't *get* that timber and shingles didn't make a home. Home was where she could feel safe. Rooted. It was her haven. Her spot in the world. This had never been and could never be that.

"Hello? Ms. Carolla?" A woman's voice echoed through the barn accompanied by the excited snuffles of her so-*not*-watchdog dogs.

Livvy brushed her hands off. "Be right there."

She hoisted the pitchfork onto a hook on the wall where Reggie couldn't reach it and let herself out of his pen. A woman stood in the doorway, surrounded by the pack that were obviously willing to let her in with wagging tails. Livvy had always considered the dogs good judges of character. After what many of them had survived—neglect, cruelty, abandonment—they didn't welcome strangers readily. It spoke well of this woman that they'd accepted her.

And Sean. They'd accepted him right away. Georgia even had a little crush on him.

Livvy could so relate.

Hello? Mind back on the matter—person—at hand.

"Um, yes?"

"Hi. I'm Mac Manley." The woman walked toward her, hand outstretched. "I own Manley Maids."

And here Livvy had thought *Sean* was the reason the company had that name. Still, a good marketing strategy to have manly maids.

"Nice to meet you." Livvy shook her hand.

"I wanted to stop by to see how things were going. I always like to say hi to new clients, even though, technically the Martinson estate isn't new, since we've been contracted for the last year. How's Sean working out for you? Are you satisfied with his performance?"

Not yet . . .

Livvy coughed. Hmmm, she seemed to have caught his coughing bug. "Uh, yes. He's doing a great job."

"Good, I'm glad to hear it. I pride myself on giving my clients excellent service. So Sean's everything you'd wanted?"

She was *such* the bad person for twisting this woman's comments into something hot and sexy.

Livvy gathered the sides of her unbuttoned blouse together and overlapped them across her camisole before crossing her arms. "Uh, yes. It's—he's—fine." He certainly was. In so many ways. He made her smile, and made her laugh. And he looked damn good doing so. "Has he worked for you long?"

Mac laughed. "Sean? Not long, but he's good. I wouldn't let him work for me otherwise. My clients' satisfaction is my top priority." She propped her hands on her hips. "So, are there any other needs you have that Manley Maids can fulfill?"

Livvy seriously needed to get her mind out of the gutter because she was ready to spout off a list that one certain Manley Maid *could* fulfill. "Uh, no. I think I'm good. Sean's, uh, handling all aspects of the job just fine. He's even helping me with a few extra projects."

"Oh?"

Darn, even *she* could raise one eyebrow. "I'm planning to sell the place and he's doing things like cleaning out these stalls to help me get it ready. They were packed with boxes and I didn't have anywhere to put my animals." She told her about the incident in the salon. "He was more than a little put out."

"I can see how he would be." Mac crossed her arms and tapped her fingers on her arm.

"He's very conscientious."

"Isn't he, though?" Mac looked around.

"And he's helping me with a scavenger hunt."

"A what?"

Livvy explained about Merriweather's bizarre idea of a joke. "So if I don't get all the clues to Mr. Scanlon in the next two weeks, I lose the estate."

"And Sean's helping you look?"

"Yes. It's really nice of him."

"Isn't it just?" Mac pulled a business card from her pocket and handed it to Livvy. "Here's my card. If you need anything, please don't hesitate to call me. I like to keep my customers happy."

Livy wanted to say that Sean did, too, but she was worried

that she'd gushed a little too much about him. She didn't want Mac getting the wrong idea about her and Sean.

MAC had a damn good idea what Sean was up to with Livvy. And she wanted to kill him. No *wonder* he'd jumped on the Martinson estate the minute she'd mentioned it.

She'd thought she'd have to convince him, but no. *This* was the place he was planning to buy. She knew all about the big property he was in negotiations to turn into his luxury resort. Knew, too, that Liam and Bryan were in on it. She'd been a little bummed that she hadn't been able to get in on the action, but her bank account couldn't compete with theirs, which was why she'd had to resort to cardsharping at the poker game.

But this made sense. Sean had been a little *too* accepting of one of her biggest clients. She'd come out today to check in, to make sure everything was okay, and talk to the two of them about publicity shots, both for the estate and for Manley Maids.

But with Sean trying to sabotage Livvy, that option was out.

It wouldn't look good when it came out that Manley Maids had put him in the position *to* sabotage her. If he succeeded, Manley Maids' name would be dragged through the mud. Suddenly her little poker bet took on ramifications of epic proportions.

Winners never cheat and cheaters never win. Gran must have said that a thousand times during her childhood.

But she *hadn't* cheated. Not really. Counting cards was a talent; it wasn't as if she'd palmed any of them. She'd just known with a reasonable certainty that she'd had the high hand that last round. She wouldn't have bet her company, her future, on a whim unless she'd been reasonably certain of winning.

But she'd never seen this coming.

She parked at the back entrance to the house and strode toward the door, stubbing her toe on a dislodged brick in the walkway. She made a mental note to tell Sean about that. He could add that to his other "special projects" list.

She found him in the salon, rolling up the rug that must be the one the goats chewed.

"I hear you've got ulterior motives."

"Hey, Mac." He looked up, his hair mussed and his face a bit sweaty. Damn, he was a good-looking man, and if she could only advertise him like that, she'd have women offering double for his services.

The jerk.

"Don't *hey Mac* me, Sean. I know what you're up to and I'm telling you to stop. You don't get to sabotage Livvy's inheritance and my company for some stupid resort that people with too much money don't need. They can go to the Catskills if they're so hell-bent on roughing it in luxury."

"Mac, calm down."

"No I will *not* calm down. This is *my* business. *My* livelihood we're talking about. How *could* you? How could you do this to me? I trusted you."

"You think I *like* the idea, Mac? Trust me, it's the last thing I want to do." He didn't deny it, thankfully. Not that she would have believed him, but at least he wasn't lying to her face. By omission, yes, but the pot couldn't really call the kettle black on this one.

"The project's too far along at this point. I've invested almost everything I have in this. I have money out for inspections and architecture and engineering reviews. Design fees and interest and a whole bunch of other expenses I'll lose if this deal doesn't happen. Business is business, but I'm trying to come up with a way so no one gets hurt because it'll break me if it doesn't happen."

"You're not the only one, Sean. This is *my* business. If you do this, if word gets out, I'll be finished."

"I'll give you the contract here. Nothing will change."

"*Everything* will change. First of all, nepotism is as dirty a word as some others I can think of and I shouldn't need nepotism to keep a contract I got on my own in the first place. I've worked hard to keep it. And what about Livvy? What do you think she's going to do when she finds out?"

"It should never have been an issue, Mac. Everything was falling into place until Merriweather had a last-minute change of heart and pulled a fast one. I had to react. For all of us: you, me, Liam, Bryan. Gran."

"Don't you bring Gran into this, Sean. Don't you dare. She's completely innocent of any of this." Mac bit her lip. That wasn't exactly true, but Gran hadn't been the one who'd counted the cards. "And if you think this was last minute on Merriweather's part, you obviously didn't know her very well. She never did anything last minute. If she was going to change her will, you can be damn sure she knew exactly *what* and exactly *why* she was doing it, and she definitely knew *how* she was doing it. For some reason, she led you on. Promised you things she might have had no intention of delivering. But she'd also been working the Livvy angle. This was no fluke. That woman didn't make fly-by-night decisions. Ever. Trust me. She had a plan."

Sean sat on the rug. "Okay. Fine. Whatever, but the fact is, I need this place. I've got a lot of money tied up in it."

"So buy it like anyone else would."

He cocked his head. "The budget's not there."

"Then you shouldn't have bitten off more than you can chew."

"I didn't. All my plans were based on numbers she gave me. The numbers I still have a chance of hitting if Livvy doesn't inherit. Then the property's mine."

"How can you do that to her? Hasn't she been through enough with this family? Now you're going to steal the one thing they've finally given her? How can you live with yourself, Sean?"

He swiped a hand over his mouth. "It's complicated, Mac."

"Yeah, no kidding. And you're dragging me down with you." She put her hands on her hips. "I'm sorry, Sean, but you're fired."

"You can't fire me."

"I just did."

"I could tell her you knew all about it."

"You're blackmailing me?"

"No. But I could."

"So you are."

"No, Mac, I'm not. I'm trying to salvage this for everyone,

but if I leave now, that's it. It's done. Over. I lose. Guaranteed. Give me until Livvy's deadline. I'll come up with something."

Mac stared at him. She shouldn't. She really shouldn't. She needed to think of her company. Of her reputation.

But she also thought about all the times her brothers had stood up for her. Had protected her. Had helped her and Gran. They were good guys. All of them. If Sean said he'd find a way for it to work for everyone, she had to give him that shot. How many times had they cut her some slack? "Fine. But only if you can find another way."

"I'm working on it, Mac."

She exhaled and turned around. She had to get started on Liam and Bryan's promo because Sean's was a lost cause. "I can't believe I—"

"You what?"

"Nothing. Never mind." No way was she going to spill *The Plan*. The one she'd started and Gran had joined in with.

She'd wanted to use her wealthy, good-looking brothers as promotional tools, totally capitalizing on the play on their last name and how good they looked in those uniforms. Gran had wanted to find them women to fall in love with, and what better way than putting them in those women's homes? Mac had seen the instant benefit to herself: Gran would be busy with her brothers' love lives and stay out of hers.

It'd been perfect. So when Mr. Scanlon had called her to discuss Manley Maids' contract and had mentioned Livvy would be arriving, she'd done her research. When she saw Livvy's picture, she'd figured Sean wouldn't be able to resist. *That* was why she'd offered him the Martinson estate. If only she'd known this was the place he was planning to buy, she would have done things differently.

Karma was paying her back in spades for those five hearts she'd thrown on the poker table.

Sean exhaled. Long and loud. "Look, I'll come up with something, but I'm not going to lose Lee and Bry's investment. They believe in me; I *have* to deliver."

Her heart ached for him. He'd always had it tougher than the other two. Middle child, second son, learning problems in school, always acting out . . . Sean had had to claw and scrape for everything he had, unlike Liam, who things came easy to, or Bryan, who'd had that face since birth and women coming on to him shortly thereafter. Things came easy to those two, but Sean? He'd had to work as hard as she did.

And with what she'd pulled at the poker game, did she really have any room to call him on what he was thinking of doing?

"You can't leave her high and dry, Sean. She has to get something out of this. It's not fair."

"I know, Mac. And I don't want to hurt Livvy. I have two weeks. I'm working on finding a solution. I have no intention of letting her walk away with nothing. I'm not a heartless bastard, just a desperate one. You think I like doing this to her? She's a nice person. Merriweather caused this, not me. But I can't walk away from the millions of dollars in earning potential, not to mention the money I've already invested."

"And Manley Maids. You have to make sure my reputation is intact."

"I promise. I'll do what needs to be done to make sure your name isn't harmed."

"I don't like it."

"That makes three of us because I can guarantee you she's not going to, either."

Chapter Seventeen

❧

SEAN stared at his laptop screen again. The numbers didn't lie. They also didn't add up. No matter what he'd promised Mac, he couldn't hit the benchmarks he needed to if he paid Livvy more money—if he could even come up with it. Maybe she'd be willing to sell it to him for Merriweather's price.

But why should she? She didn't owe him anything.

He skimmed the list of potential investors he'd compiled. It was either them or asking Livvy to take the lesser amount, and he really didn't want to risk showing his hand in the event she said no.

God, he was so sick of the poker reference.

He shut down the computer and pulled on a T-shirt, damn glad to be out of his uniform, and headed to the racquetball court with Liam. He'd research the clue he and Livvy had found when he got back, because if he had to stay in this house one more minute, he'd go nuts.

This whole scenario was driving him nuts.

And so was Orwell, who swooped into his room and landed on his shoulder. "*Oops, did it again!*"

The bird was either mimicking a pop star or it'd done

something Sean really didn't want to know about. But, of course, in morbid dread he asked, "What did you do, Orwell?"

The bird's answer was the next line about playing with someone's heart.

Not the song Sean needed right now. Wasn't there a line in it about getting lost in a game?

Sean transferred the parrot to his hand and strode down the hall toward Livvy's open door to return Orwell to his rightful caretaker.

He was already through it when he realized he should have knocked.

She walked out of the bathroom in a towel before she realized he was in the room.

Orwell went into a rendition of Donna Summers's "Bad Girls" that Sean did not need to hear.

"Orwell!" Livvy's face turned as red as her hair and she held out her hand for the parrot. The movement loosened her towel and she had to scramble to keep all parts covered.

Talk about a shame.

Sean finally remembered to turn around. "Oh, sorry. The door was open and I didn't think . . ."

"Actually, it was closed. Orwell hates to be caged in, but I didn't think he'd see the room as a cage. And I certainly didn't know he knew how to operate a latch. That's going to make things, um, interesting."

"Okay, then, I'll leave you to . . ." He waved his hand behind him. "I've got a racquetball game tonight, so I'll see you later."

"You play racquetball?"

Keep moving, Manley.

Of course he didn't. "Yeah."

"I haven't played racquetball in years."

Walk out now, Manley. "You play?"

"Not very well. But we had a court at school and I enjoyed it."

Sean squeezed his eyes shut for a second. He didn't need this temptation. He so didn't.

But he turned around anyway. "You want to come?"

"You sure you wouldn't mind?"

Oh, he'd mind. The entire time she was running around

the court in shorts and a T-shirt that wouldn't hide a single thing, with sweat running all over her body, her skin pink from the exertion, he'd mind. A *lot*.

He'd mind that all that exertion wasn't for him, and that he couldn't peel her T-shirt and shorts from her body and slick his hands over her silky skin—

"No. Not at all. I'll call Liam and see if he can find someone else for a foursome."

There was a word—and an image—he didn't need.

He was going to have to wear an athletic cup for tonight's game because nylon shorts wouldn't hide his reaction to her any more than those stupid work pants did.

He had a feeling nothing would when it came to Livvy.

YOU brought *Cassidy*?" Sean didn't know whether to laugh or be horrified. Cassidy Davenport, Liam's client, was the only person he could imagine who'd be more out of place on a racquetball court than Livvy.

Liam unzipped his racquetball bag, then put on his glove. "It's not like I had a lot of time to come up with someone else, and she overheard."

Sean looked over to where the girls were warming up. "She's in pink. Rhinestones."

"Tell me about it." Liam rolled his eyes.

Sean decided to laugh because poor Lee hated pink as much as he hated rhinestones. Probably more than any guy alive. But then, he had reason to.

"She does know that this is a sport, right? That you get hot and sweaty and the makeup will slide off her face?"

"If she doesn't, she soon will. That could make this whole thing worthwhile." Liam slung his racket over his shoulder. "Any progress with the gypsy chick?"

Sean had to laugh at himself this time. He'd thought he'd have to worry about Livvy in tight shorts and a T-shirt, not some skirt thing that flared over her hips with beads dangling from it and a flouncy shirt that he was half afraid was going to fly up if she switched direction too fast. A workout outfit only in Livvy's world, but she said she hadn't been planning to need one during her sojourn at the estate, so this would have to do. Thank God, she'd at least had sneakers; those combat boots she was so fond of would have had her breaking an ankle on the first play.

"We're following the clues. Tomorrow we're chasing down baby cradles."

Liam arched an eyebrow. "You realize that's a dangerous line of thought around any woman, right?"

Sean ignored the stirring in his dick. "Trust me; it's not an issue."

"Famous last words." Liam exhaled. "Come on. Let's get this torture over with."

And torture it was. Sean found himself looking at Livvy's backside more than he did the ball. And Liam, for all his disgusted attitude with the tall, pink, frothy milkshake that was *his* client, was just as easily distracted, missing the return to Livvy's serve.

"Woo hoo! Score one for me!" Livvy came bouncing over to Sean to high five him in all her bouncy glory.

Good lord, to hell with the cup he should have worn; she needed a sports bra. Several of them. Because the one she had on might as well not even have been there, and that's if she even had one on. He could see her nipples beneath her shirt.

"Sean?"

He shook his head. "Yeah?"

"Aren't you excited?"

Like she wouldn't believe. "Sorry?"

"We're winning."

"Oh. Right." He smacked her palm with his. "But it's still a long way to go to fifteen."

"And don't get too comfortable with a one-point lead. Cass and I will have you eating our dust," Liam grumbled as he tossed Sean the ball.

"Cass-i-dy, Liam. I don't like Cass." *Ms.* Davenport tucked her already tucked-in, figure-hugging, baby-pink T-shirt into her white shorts. She ought to be more concerned with the rhinestones ringing the neckline because Sean could just see them bouncing all over the floor if someone ran into her.

The look on Liam's face as she corrected him said Lee might actually do that. "Serve, Sean," he said between gritted teeth.

Yeah, it was going to be a long game.

A sweaty one, too. The girls were, for all their inappropriate clothing, pretty athletic. Livvy made those beads bounce and sway as she covered the court, returning the rally before there was a second bounce. He was suitably—and surprisingly—impressed.

"You need a break, yet, Cass?" Liam had been using that nickname ever since Cassidy said she didn't like it. Sean could have told her that would happen. Cassidy was the exact type Liam had learned to *not* appreciate, and shame on Mac for pairing him up with her. His last serious girlfriend had been just like Cassidy: a woman who'd looked to the men in her life to take care of her. They'd all wondered why Liam had been so whipped but hadn't said anything to him. It was the Bro-Code. Unless they caught a girlfriend cheating or something equally as awful, they supported their brother's choice. So when she'd turned out to actually have someone on the side that they all hadn't realized, it'd come as a huge blow to Lee, and he'd sworn off women ever since. It was just cruel of Mac to give him the most high-maintenance client she had.

"Sean, you gonna serve it or stare at it? I don't have all night, you know."

Liam was lunging from side to side and twirling his racket handle in his palm as if this were a high-stakes game.

"Come on, Sean. I'm ready." Livvy smiled at him and Sean wanted to show her just how ready *he* was—

Okay, so maybe there were some pretty high stakes.

She looked so damn adorable. And sexy as hell. And that combination was guaranteed to suck his brain out through his—

He served.

And fell short.

"One more, Sean," Lee growled triumphantly behind him. "You lose the serve, you can kiss this game good-bye."

Sean didn't, managing to get his head in the game just enough, and he and Livvy scored another two points before the serve changed teams.

"Ladies first." Liam swept his arm wide toward Cassidy and bounced her the ball. "Let's show these two how it's done, *Cass*."

She glared at him through her rhinestone-studded—of course—protective glasses.

But she had a wicked serve and Sean had to concentrate on returning it. Then Liam got in on the act and suddenly the game became cutthroat. Sean might have been amazed the girls were keeping up if he had time to be amazed. The rally came at him fast and furious. Cassidy was no slouch in the racquetball department, but poor Livvy was out of her league.

"I'm sorry," she muttered as she cost them their fourth consecutive point. "I guess I'm a lot rustier than I thought."

Sean patted her on the shoulder. "Buck up. We're only two points down."

"Yeah, but we were up four."

"We'll come back."

"If you say so."

He tried to get them within a point or two, but Liam-on-a-mission and country-club-racquetball-team-member Cassidy barely gave up the serve. The third time they did, Sean could swear a look passed between them—and it wasn't the antagonistic ones they'd started out with.

"Come on, Liv, perk up," he whispered as he walked behind her to take his spot on the backcourt. "You're doing great."

She raised her eyebrows at him. "I'd hate to see your definition of *bad* if you think this is great."

He had to hand it to her, though; she didn't give up. She kept running all over that court, taking a couple of shoulders to the wall when her momentum kept her moving forward. She was going to have some nasty bruises.

And he wanted to kiss each one.

"Score!" Liam raised his arms and whooped it up when Sean missed the rally. Cassidy was jumping up and down, something he'd normally enjoy if a) he wasn't losing, b) Liam wasn't looking so interested in that jumping, and c) Livvy weren't so down about their point count.

He dropped an arm around her shoulders. "Come on, Liv,

we can do this. Think back to what we did at the beginning. We were on top. Let's go back to whatever it was we were doing then and turn this thing around. I know we can."

She looked up at him under her lashes and Sean was struck by how long they were. And that they weren't brown like he'd thought, but more of a rust color. No, not rust. Wine. Yes, that's it. They were wine colored. Just like her hair. It wasn't your typical shade of red; it had some brown and some orange and maybe even some blonde through it. It looked like a shimmery mass of wine-colored curls pulled back into a ponytail with a few errant ones that escaped to twist damply against her jaw. Her throat. The back of her neck . . .

"*Can* we do it, Sean?"

They could do *it* and whatever else she wanted anytime she wanted—

"Uh, yeah." He dropped his arm. "We can beat them." Right. Them. Cassidy and Liam. The other team. In the game. Racquetball. "We just have to focus."

On the game. On the racquet. On the ball. Nothing more.

"You're going down, Sean." Liam had a wicked gleam in his eye and a cocky grin on his face. "Ready to cry like a baby?"

"Bring it on, bro." He braced his feet apart, put some bend in his knees, and waited for Liam's serve.

It was fast and it was powerful and Sean relished the chance to smash something. He drove the ball into the back wall with enough force to shoot it between Liam and Cassidy with so much momentum that he was glad one of them hadn't been in its path.

Cassidy hit it after the bounce with just enough power to almost put it out of Livvy's reach.

Livvy lunged, saving the rally at the last second as she took a dive to the floor.

Sean wanted to run over at her *oomph*, but Liam wasn't backing down. Of course, none of the brothers ever did when it came to sports, but Lee seemed to have forgotten that they were playing with women this time, and spiked that ball so hard, it whistled as it flew toward him.

Sean took the shot, feeling the power reverberate up his arm despite the give in the racket and the absorption of his glove.

Then it was Cassidy's turn and once again, she returned it smoothly. Even looked good doing it. Did they teach that at boarding school or finishing school or wherever it was that girls like her went to learn the nonessential things in life like flower arranging and dinner table setting?

Livvy lunged again, this time her palms smacking the floor when she landed. Sean winced, trying to make sure she was okay out of the corner of his eye while still trying to watch Liam.

Liam wasn't giving anything away. He smashed the ball again. Sean had to make a quick half turn to get into position, losing the momentum behind his swing, but luckily managed to get it back to the wall for Cassidy's turn.

She lobbed it beautifully. Classic swing . . . *if* she were playing golf, one leg on-point, knee turned in, back gracefully arched.

Poor Livvy reminded him of Reggie after that storm: soaked hair clinging to a face that was red with exhaustion, her nose even redder from where she must have smacked it on the floor on one of her lunges, her clothing askew and sticking to her in sweaty patches, the hem of that ridiculous skirt cockeyed, the beads clacking loudly.

She looked utterly beautiful to him.

And that's when Sean missed the next rally.

"Winner!" Liam's racket went clattering to the floor as he swept Cassidy up in his arms and twirled her around, their heads thrown back laughing. Gloating.

Sean rubbed his triceps. Damn ball hurt. He was going to have a bruise. Not that he was vain enough to care, but it'd linger—which meant Liam would draw out his crowing about the victory for at least that long, and the story he'd invent would become consecutively inversely proportional to the color of the bruising.

"Sorry." Livvy brushed her shoulder against his other arm.

The sizzle that accompanied it hit him harder than the ball had. He ran his hand over her shoulder. "Hey, don't take it so hard. It's just a game." If this had just been between him and Liam, he would have choked on those words.

"I know, but I wanted to win. You did, too."

"We'll get them the next time." Oh, great. He'd just signed himself up for another round of torture.

Needing a distraction from that thought, Sean turned around. "So Lee, you and Cassidy want to—"

Sean shut up. Lee and Cassidy did *want to* if that long slow slide she did down his body was anything to go by. And Lee wasn't letting go.

But then he was. Quickly. And so was Cassidy, practically stumbling to get away from Liam.

This wasn't good. Liam had gotten burned once already by a woman like Cassidy Davenport.

"You guys want to go grab something to eat?" Sean asked. Forget the rematch; Liam driving Cassidy home alone right now was *not* in his brother's best interests.

Surprisingly though, Liam did manage to tear his gaze away from the tall, sexy definition of a bad idea.

Good. Maybe he wasn't as into her as it appeared.

"Thanks, but I have to go to the office."

Lee did a hell of a good impersonation of someone not giving a damn—unless someone *knew* that someone. And Sean knew Liam.

Shit. This wasn't good.

"Billing's backing up with my assistant out on maternity leave, and if the bills don't go out, money can't come in." Liam looked at Cassidy with more of the sneer that Sean was used to seeing. "That's how businesses work."

Pain slashed across Cassidy's face for a second. "I'm well aware of how business works. I did work with my father you know."

"How could I forget?"

"Okay, then." Sean tossed Liam's racket to him since the status quo had been reestablished. "Give me a call after you drop Cassidy off. I need to go over a few things with you."

He'd come up with something—maybe get Lee's perspective on where to start looking for odd-looking baby cradles so he could get the jump on Livvy—instead of jumping *on* Livvy—and to keep Lee from doing the same thing to Cassidy.

Yeah, it was going to be a long two weeks.

Chapter Eighteen

❧

LIVVY stared at the baby cradle in the wing of the museum her grandmother had endowed. It was the same one as in the picture, and the plaque beside the cordon rope said that generations of Martinsons had used it.

Olivia Martinson was the last name on the list.

Olivia *Martinson*?

Livvy didn't think so. That name wasn't even on her birth certificate, and as for sleeping in that thing . . . When? As far as she knew, she hadn't been under Martinson guardianship until she'd been five. Was this the old lady's push for dynastic excellence?

Livvy stared at it, trying to imagine herself in that ridiculously overdone curlicue Victorian design. She'd probably had nightmares—nothing new when it came to her father's family. Present scavenger hunt included.

Livvy shook off her bad mood. Water under the bridge, spilled milk, all the clichés. She was an adult, get over it already.

Right. So where was the next clue?

It had to be something on the plaque because the museum curator would surely have found any note or carving on the cradle itself, and her grandmother had to have known it'd be cordoned off from the public—including her.

Then again, why should she expect Merriweather to make this easy? She still didn't get why the woman was making her jump through these hoops. Did she just want to be known for giving her prodigal granddaughter the opportunity? Or was it because she *knew* Livvy would fail and wanted to pay her back for having the audacity to be alive?

Livvy sat down on the bench beside the display. *Would* her grandmother have been so devious?

It was possible. Merriweather had certainly never made the effort to welcome her into the family while she'd been alive; why should she be any different in death?

Livvy stood up, ready to leave. She was not going to dance to her grandmother's tune any longer. She didn't care what the next clue was or where it was or what it led to or anything. Let the old woman roll over in her grave, agonizing that Livvy wasn't following her orders. Livvy didn't care. She'd done well enough without this place while the woman had been alive and she'd do just as well now with her gone.

She turned to leave and banged into one of the poles holding up the ropes designed to keep the public out. And her. They were keeping *her* out. Just like Merriweather wanted.

Livvy fought off the sting of tears. Why hadn't she been good enough for the woman? How could Merriweather have visited the sins of the parents on her, an innocent child? All her life, she'd kept a low profile, trying to keep from ruining the Martinson name because she'd never wanted to feel the full wrath of Merriweather.

Why? What had she done? What was wrong with her that her own grandmother hadn't even wanted to know her?

Tears blurring her vision, Livvy knocked the pole yet again, this time making a mad scramble to keep it from hitting the floor. That's all she'd need: to bring attention to herself right now while she was an emotional mess.

But shame on her. Shame on her for letting Merriweather's inattentiveness get to her. She wasn't a kid anymore. She knew the ways of the world and the workings of a nasty old woman's small mind.

A slow burn started in the pit of her stomach. The woman

wanted her to fail? Well, hell no. She was going to find these clues and inherit the mansion and enjoy every moment of selling it off to the highest bidder. Let Merriweather roll for *that*.

Livvy righted the pole, swiped the corners of her eyes, and rolled her shoulders back. She wasn't about to let the old battle-axe win.

She reread the plaque. *Generations of Martinson family members slept in this excellent representation of every child's dream. The Victorian design was commissioned by Albert Martinson to coincide with several revisions he was having craftsmen make to the Martinson estate.*

Every child's dream? It hadn't been hers. The thing looked more like a nightmare. She certainly hadn't dared to dream anything when it came to the Martinsons.

But now she was dreaming about the Martinson maid. Wouldn't *that* get old Merriweather's goat?

Goat. Oh, crud. She was supposed to stop at the feed store to pick up a special blend of grain products for Dodger and his brothers to counteract the wool fibers they'd recently added to their digestive tracts.

She reread the plaque once more, then took a picture to show it to Sean later to see what he made of it.

SEAN moved the sofa back into place in the third seating area on the upper floor in the west wing after vacuuming the rug beneath it. How many places had people needed to sit and chat in Merriweather's day? And on the bedroom level? He shook his head. Who understood the super rich? But it was not his place to complain; he was just glad this little area and the others like it existed. His architect's plans called for them to be converted into meeting rooms for another source of revenue.

Sean repositioned the coffee table in front of the sofa and replaced the ornate crystal knickknacks that'd taken him the better part of a half hour to dust. If he never saw another nook or cranny ever again it'd be too soon for him.

The grandfather clock in the niche behind him chimed. Noon. The dogs had woken him at five when Livvy had taken them out. So he'd gotten up and used the time to clean out the nursery on the third floor, though he'd really been searching for the next clue, even checking for loose floorboards for a hiding spot. If yesterday's racquetball game had shown him anything, it was that Livvy didn't give up and she hated to lose. They had that in common.

Among other things.

He shifted uncomfortably, remembering the torture that had been yesterday. Her silly froufrou skirt had kept him guessing what was beneath it; her shirt hadn't—and those lips of hers had made him want to taste every curve of her smile. He really needed to keep his distance and stop kissing her.

The problem was he didn't *want* to stop kissing her. Kissing Livvy was unlike kissing any other woman, and while he liked that—more than liked it—it also bothered the hell out of him. Why her? What was so special about *her*? If anything, this whole nightmare with her and the house and the money ought to have him so put *off* her that they could be naked in the same room and it wouldn't have any effect on him.

Except that wasn't happening. Just thinking about her naked got him as hard as this damn table and clouded his judgment, removing his focus from where it ought to be, making him rethink his investment. His business plan. Even his life.

Wait—his life? Was he out of his mind? His *business* was his life. This place. *This* was the dream. The one he'd decided on when Liam had made his first hundred K. When Bryan had gotten that big movie role while Sean was still cleaning out moldy old B&Bs to get them into "quaint" shape to build his company. He wasn't about to give up on all his hard work. All his determination. Hell, he'd even put dating on hold, electing to end relationships before they'd gotten too serious so that he could achieve his professional aspirations. He wasn't about to let some bohemian-clothing-wearing free spirit with a penchant for barnyard animals over regular social niceties tear down what he was working so hard to create. He needed this estate. It would make all the hard work, all the sacrifice, all his principle-compromising worth it.

He needed that damn clue.

Sean set the crystal pyramid down, taking care not to ding

the mahogany table. *Baby cradle.* What in the hell could Merriweather have meant by that? He hadn't found anything in the nursery, and if there was a playground on this property, he had yet to see it. All his internet surfing had gone nowhere. He was going to have to see what Livvy had come up with once she returned home.

Which she did while he was eating lunch, flouncing through the kitchen door with a flash of midriff that all but dried up his mouth and sucked every bit of breath from his lungs. The memories of her creamy, toned skin had kept him up—and hard—half the night. The woman was a menace on so many fronts.

"Hey, Sean! How are you?" she asked, her hair billowing out around her in the sunshine spilling in through the glass panes like a corkscrew halo. "Where are the dogs?"

He took a gulp of his iced tea. How *was* he? Hard as hell and frustrated to match.

Then there was the whole nightmare of this situation and what he was going to do about it, not to mention sounding like Merriweather's stupid poems.

"Uh, good," was the safer answer. "And I let them out. I'm surprised you didn't see them. Ah, shit. Maybe they ran away?"

Livvy shook her head. "That's the thing with rescues; they're grateful for the home you give them. They won't go anywhere. Probably just scoping out their new territory. They'll be back."

Good. He didn't need to take her four-legged family away from her, too. "So, any luck?"

She shrugged and there went that midriff peeking again. The woman needed new clothes. Preferably something drab like a burlap sack. Though she'd probably look gorgeous in that, too. Livvy *was* gorgeous, and her sunshine personality only made the outer packaging more appealing.

"I found the cradle. My grandmother claims I slept in it, but that's not possible. I'm wondering if her mind was going at the end."

Sean had his own reasons for questioning the workings of Livvy's grandmother's mind, but her having lost it wasn't one of them. "Merriweather seemed pretty sharp to me." And

pretty *shark*, too. She was driving *him* out of his mind, but
Mac was probably right. Having dealt with her one-on-one
while making his plans, Sean could attest to Merriweather
being a savvy businesswoman. He'd bet she'd known exactly
what she was doing by changing her will yet still letting him
believe the place was his.

Then again, betting hadn't done him much good recently.

Livvy hiked herself up onto the countertop next to the
barstool he was sitting on, smelling too damn good for his
liking, and he rethought that bet thing.

"The cradle was cordoned off so I couldn't get close, but
I doubt there was anything in it or on it for me to see. My
grandmother would have known how the museum would treat
it, so she couldn't have expected me to be able to inspect it
all that closely." She pulled a digital camera from the sack
that functioned as her purse. He'd never seen such a sorry
excuse for a bag, but then, things around Livvy were always
skewed a little left of center. "Here, read this. Tell me what
you think it means." She zoomed in on a plaque.

Read it? He didn't think so. Sean picked up his glass and
stood. Trying to make sense of the letters was too humiliating
to do around other people, even his own family. He hated
showing that weakness, and he'd be dammed if he'd let Livvy
see it. And he sure as hell wasn't going to pull out his tablet
to have it read to him. Over the years he'd learned tricks to
keep people from learning about his "issue." He'd had to;
they'd look at him pityingly once they found out and it'd taint
their opinion of him. If there was one thing Sean hated it was
to be pitied. "Sometimes it makes more sense when you read
it aloud." He made a big production of getting more iced tea
from the fridge. "Why don't you read it to me?"

Livvy nibbled on her bottom lip—damn her—then cocked
her head to the side, those gorgeous auburn curls cascading
down her arm and over her breast, the ends almost reaching
the countertop, and Sean had to swallow a groan trying *not*
to imagine what they would feel like trailing across his skin.

Damn stupid pants.

He slid back onto the barstool before the thinness of the
fabric became any *more* evident, but then he was treated to
the site of Livvy's perfectly shaped calf as she swung it over

the other in a rhythm only she could hear, her silly combat boot making the slightest contact with his arm and Sean wasn't about to move.

Pitiful. So damn pitiful that he had to struggle to focus on what she was telling him instead of the sexy way her lips moved *while* she was telling him.

"I think the clue has something to do with whoever made the cradle. The plaque mentions work a craftsman was doing around here." She tucked the hair behind her ears, which made it swish against her breast again, and Sean's cock jerked at the movement.

Really damn stupid pants.

"With the size of this place, that could take a lot longer than two weeks to figure out." She held out the camera again and the scent of her perfume or soap—or with his luck, her normal, everyday, drive-him-out-of-his-mind scent—circled around him like a net, reeling him in. "What do you think?"

He was thinking more about the act that *filled* cradles than the cradles themselves. "I think you might not want to sit so close."

She cocked her head some more, looking way too cute. "I won't? Why?"

She really had to ask? Sean's confidence shrank a little at that—but that was the only thing that did. Man, she looked amazing with that wild hair and her bright eyes and those breasts that were straining against her top so much he could see the outline of her nipples.

Especially when they perked up right before his eyes.

The mood changed in an instant. He felt it before he saw the way she was looking at him. At his lips, specifically. Which was fine with him because he could then look at hers and wonder how the sheen of moisture her tongue left behind when it slicked across them would taste. And he could stare at the flutter of her pulse at the base of her throat and allow himself to imagine it against his tongue. Or how those nipples would feel against—

Back off, Manley.

He didn't listen to his voice of reason. He couldn't. Not with the wide-eyed look Livvy was giving him and the way she put the camera on the countertop, then leaned back onto her palms, her breasts changing angle just enough so those temptingly perky nipples were trained on him like a heat-seeking missile and, yeah, that was exactly what he had inside these damn stupid pants. She really shouldn't be sitting so close.

"Why?" Against his better judgment, he stood. "Because of this."

He dragged her the ten inches across the countertop until she was right in front of him, her legs on either side of his hips, his hand clamped firmly to the perfect muscles of her insanely delectable ass, with her heat inches away from where he wanted it to be.

"I'm going to kiss you, Livvy." He threaded his fingers through her hair like he'd been itching to do since he'd first seen her looking so imperiously sexy in the foyer. "And you're going to kiss me back."

"I am?" She licked her lips again.

He didn't answer. Well, not with words.

He spread a palm against the curve of her waist, caressing the skin that had been teasing him since she'd flounced in, sucking all the oxygen from the room. Her skin felt so damn silky good beneath his fingertips. Her fluttering breaths ratcheted up his own until the next thing he knew, he'd speared both hands into that wild, frothy concoction she called hair but he called heaven, and his tongue was discovering all those sweet secret places in her mouth. Her hot breath seared fire through him and surged to that one part of him that was against that part of her he wanted to get to know better, and her hands clung to the damn flimsy pants that suddenly weren't flimsy enough because he wanted to feel every clench and tug she made. God, he wanted to lay her back on the counter and take her until neither of them could think straight.

Hell, if he was considering doing that, he *already* wasn't thinking straight.

Which was the perfect excuse to do it.

He sank down onto her, pressing her against the granite, shifting so her legs could wrap around his waist and her amazingly, wonderfully soft breasts were cushioned against his chest, her head angled to take the kiss deeper while she moved against him. Sean had to focus on not coming in these stupid pants, which wasn't easy to do when his hands were skimming surfaces he'd only dreamed about—recently—hugging curves he'd fantasized over, and the temperature spiked in the kitchen faster than Merriweather's seven-thousand-dollar professional convection oven.

"*Big mistake. Huge.*" Orwell punctuated his commentary with a set of talons to the shoulder blades.

"Sonofabitch!" Sean shot up.

"*Sonofabitch! Sonofabitch!*" Orwell even had his voice down pat.

"Oh, no!" Livvy raised herself up on her elbows. "You have to watch what you say around him, Sean."

"*Sonofabitch!*" Orwell flapped his wings, sending feathers scattering all over the countertop.

Sean took a deep breath, willing his body to calm the hell down. Jesus. One two-minute kiss and all the blood had left every cell in his body except the ones in his groin.

He stepped away from the cradle of Livvy's thighs.

Bad idea. Gravity had done what his hands had wanted to do to her skirt, draping it around her hips, revealing, holy hell, the skimpiest triangle of baby pink fabric between her legs. Something so utterly feminine against the camo skirt, those chunky boots, and the drab olive green shirt that, on her, was incredibly sexy, and Sean felt all those southern blood cells go on the march.

Orwell fluttered onto Livvy's belly. "*Sonofabitch.*"

Sean could have sworn the damn bird winked at him. "Sonofa—"

"Okay, now that we've established *that* particular bit of profanity firmly in Orwell's vocabulary, I think it's time for him to learn something else." Livvy sat up, managing to pull her top down and her skirt back into place in one fluid motion that was as effective as slamming a vault door closed. She transferred the parrot onto her shoulder where it looked at him with a smirk.

"Livvy." Sean put a hand on her arm.

The bird swiped at it.

Sean yanked it away just in time. But it was going to take more than that to deter him. "Livvy, we need to discuss what just happened."

"Why?"

She cocked her head and her curls tumbled over her breasts, and Sean had to tuck his hands into his pockets to not only keep them off her, but also to gain some margin of dignity so that his raging hard-on wasn't outlined against the stupid fabric.

"Because we can't pretend it didn't."

She tucked some curls behind her ear. "Were you going to? I wasn't. I like kissing you."

Her candor was so unexpected, so disarming, that Sean didn't know what to say. He went with "You do?" which almost had him crawling under the counter in mortification. She made him feel like a teenager again.

Though that wasn't necessarily a bad thing.

"You couldn't tell?" The corner of her mouth curved up, highlighting the sparkle in her amber eyes.

Once again desire socked him in the gut and stole his breath.

"Sean? You okay?"

Actually, he was a little put out that she was able to breathe. And to joke. And to hold a conversation. He obviously didn't affect her like she affected him. "I should apologize. I don't normally go around kissing clients or—"

"Maybe you should."

"Huh?"

She set the bird on the overhead wagon wheel with the pots hanging from it, and the damn menace climbed around it like it was a jungle gym. Sean just *waited* for it to christen him with his reconstituted morning meal—for all of about a second because Livvy hopped off the counter in front of him.

Right in front of him.

"I said, maybe you *should* go around kissing your clients. You're quite talented in that area. Not that you aren't in the cleaning department, but I don't see why we can't combine the two. It's not as if we're going to be able to ignore what's between us, and unless you quit or I fire you, we're stuck here together. And I'm pretty sure if I fire you, that'd be grounds for a lawsuit."

Sean got breathless just from listening to her. Among other

reasons. "You seem to have given this a lot of thought." He didn't know whether to be flattered or insulted.

She shrugged and it brought his attention front and center to those gorgeous breasts that shifted so provocatively beneath her shirt.

He was going with *flattered*.

"Yes, some thought." She tucked her hair behind her ears. Which were adorable.

Jesus. He had it bad.

"I mean," she went on, oblivious, as if they were discussing the weather forecast, "it's not as if I can ignore you or your effect on me. Plus, I don't want to."

"Are you always this candid?"

She shrugged again. An added bonus. "Pointless to beat around the bush. Life's too short. We're attracted to each other. Nothing wrong with that." Her fingers made a little foray up his shirt and Sean felt every touch clear down to his toes. "So if you want to kiss me again, I'm not going to complain."

Did she have to make it so freaking easy for him? Which only made it so freaking hard. It made a *lot* of things hard, but Christ. He was trying to take her million-dollar inheritance out from under her. What kind of guy would he be if he took her up on her offer, and then did that?

She stood up on her tiptoes, put her hands behind his head, angled it down, and pulled him into another kiss.

He'd be a foolish, desperate guy who wanted just one more taste.

Her tongue sought out his, her fingers threaded through the hair at his neck, her nipples tightened against him . . . and Sean was lost.

It was a lot more than one taste.

GOD, he tasted so good. He *smelled* so good. He *felt* so good.

Livvy couldn't get close enough to Sean. She ought to be worried about how inappropriate this was, but hanging out with him, playing racquetball, being with him . . .

She was lonely. Her co-op family was nice, but they weren't *this*. She hadn't had *this* in far too long and she missed it. It wasn't as if she had this spark with everyone and hell, what was the reason not to act on it? She wasn't moving in here forever, so it wouldn't cause awkward complications for the rest of their lives.

Yeah, but is it a good idea? Like, what do you really know about the guy? Maybe he's only into you so you'll be his sugar mama. Gotta admit, this house is good incentive.

No she wasn't going to admit it. It wasn't as if they were going to pledge their undying love to each other. . . Sex wasn't happily ever after. They could just enjoy their time together. If there was one thing she'd learned from Merriweather, it was that she couldn't count on anything or anyone, so she was living in the moment. The here and now. Which consisted of his arms and his lips and oh, God, his hands . . . They'd migrated to her backside and were igniting a thousand sparks beneath her skin, so her conscience could just take a hike and let her enjoy this.

She rubbed her belly against his erection. It'd been a lot longer for *that*.

"Livvy, we need to—"

She stuck her tongue back into his mouth. That way he couldn't speak. She didn't want him to speak. She wanted him to moan. And groan. And maybe even call out her name on a long drawn-out cry. But no speaking. No reason to say *no* or *stop* or *wait* . . . She didn't want to wait and she *definitely* didn't want to stop.

"I want you, Sean."

Three words and the floodgates opened. Whatever protest he'd been about to utter disappeared into her mouth as he thrust his tongue inside and took over the kiss.

She was more than willing to let him.

One hand cradled her butt, and the other trailed the sweetest bit of heaven up her spine and knotted in her hair, tugging it back with just the right amount of *want* and *sexy* that Livvy almost melted at his feet.

"This isn't a good idea," he muttered against her throat. But he didn't stop kissing it.

"I disagree," she gasped amid the effects the swirls of his tongue were causing.

"We have to live together." He nipped the cord in her neck and Livvy wanted to swoon.

But she didn't. Swooning women missed out on the good stuff. "So the issue with this is . . . ?"

She got the groan then. And a moan. And a hike back up onto the countertop, this time with both of his hands spearing through her hair, and his hard body—*all* of it—pressed against her just where she wanted it to be.

But she wanted it naked.

So she tugged the bottom of his shirt from his pants and ran her palms up the smooth, sleek muscle there, every toned, fit inch of it setting her nerve endings to shiver.

He had the perfect amount of hair on his chest, enough to tease her fingertips—and her nipples—and she combed through it, aching to nuzzle her cheek against it.

She pushed his golf shirt higher, and then suddenly, she didn't have to worry about it as Sean took over, drawing it over his head from the back and replacing his hands in her hair in one solid, sexy, masculine movement that had her tummy sighing with need.

He nipped her bottom lip.

She licked his top one.

He groaned.

She smiled.

"Proud of yourself?" he growled, hiking her closer to his chest, cradling himself between her thighs where her panties were already useless against the desire he was creating in her.

"Proud? No. Desperate? God, yes." She wiggled against him. "Touch me, Sean. I need your hands on me."

"Ah, Livvy. This is such a bad idea." But he did it anyway.

His hands slid from her face to trace over her shoulders, his thumbs dabbling along her collarbone, every point of contact an ignition switch for her libido.

He slid his palms down her arms and intertwined their fingers, all the while keeping up the seductive sweep of his tongue in her mouth, along her lips, over her jaw, nuzzling into the sensitive area of her neck.

He drew her hands up her body, both of them fitting over her curves, rubbing spirals around her nipples, never actually touching them, but oh so close. She turned slightly, but Sean moved their hands away before she got them where she wanted them to be.

Instead, he did something almost obscenely sexy, bringing their fingertips to where their lips met, the soft brush-by as erotic as any intimate caress, the quick lick to her fingers almost sending her over the edge.

She whimpered, wanting more, but knowing he wouldn't give it to her. He was teasing her and he was damn good at it.

But she was no slouch in that department either, so she slid her fingers from his and tucked them beneath the waistband of his pants just above his backside, flexing against the amazing muscles beneath his skin.

"God, Livvy, careful."

"Am I hurting you?"

He took another long, mouthy kiss along her jaw line, ending just below her ear, sending shivers all through her. "Not in the way you mean, but you definitely have me aching."

She smiled then. She felt the ache he was referring to, and yeah, it was growing by the nanosecond.

"Let's get naked, Sean."

She felt the breath leave his body. Felt the shivers that wracked him. Good.

"Livvy, you can't just say that with your legs wrapped around me and not expect me to act on it. Even if you are on the kitchen countertop."

She ran her hands over his chest, swirling the hair with her fingertips, then tugging on it ever so gently. "Why do you think I said it?"

He went willingly into her, groaning again, his lips fastening on hers as he once more laid her back against the granite, what was rocking between her legs just as hard. Livvy wanted him. Badly. Or, *goodly*, actually. Though he could be bad if he wanted. Whatever he wanted, she was as up for it as he was.

And that was quite a lot.

She wrapped her arms around his shoulders, wanting to

absorb him into her, returning each thrust of his tongue with one of hers, answering every grind against her pelvis with a give-and-take of her own.

"I want you, Sean," she gasped when he let her come up for air—only to steal it by gently biting the curve of her neck.

"I want you, too, Livvy," he whispered, his breath hot against her skin.

Sean was hot against her skin, in all facets of that word.

"*I want you, too, Livvy*," came a squawk from above them.

Great. Orwell added something new to his repertoire.

Then he dropped a present on the countertop next to her. Way to kill the moment.

"Sean." Livvy didn't want to end this, but while she was all for being in the moment with hot sweaty sex, she wasn't up for rolling around in bird *presents*. "Sean." She tugged his head back. "Sean, we have to stop."

*S*TOP? Sean stared down at her, her eyes wide, her skin flushed, with a just-kissed puffiness to her lips that grabbed him by the gut and twisted. Holy hell, she was gorgeous. He didn't want to stop. And neither did she.

She wanted him. Laid out before him, her nipples let him know just how much she wanted him, her chest fluttering with the shallow breaths she was making no attempt to disguise . . . she didn't want him to stop. She was as into this moment as he was.

And then Orwell broke into the moment with another inappropriately timed, "*I want you, too, Livvy*."

Damn bird.

Sean might have ignored the stupid thing, but he saw what was on the counter next to Livvy's gorgeous hair, and well, yeah. That was kind of a mood killer.

And then there was a whole bunch of scratching on the back door, which *totally* wiped out the moment.

And then the howling started.

Howling?

"Ringo!" This time it was Livvy who pulled away, swinging her leg up and around in front of him so that, if he'd been prepared for it, he would have gotten quite the show, but because he wasn't, it was over before he knew it. Her skirt fluttered around her thighs as she twisted on the counter, did some sort of gymnastic move, and ended up beside him for the space of a heartbeat before flouncing—*again* with the flounce—over to the door. She flung it open, catching it just before it smashed into that triple-thick granite countertop, then flung her arms open to receive the biggest, wettest kiss outside of the one he'd just given her.

The dogs came barreling in, the rottie practically trampling Livvy to get in her arms. Great. An even more effective buzz kill than Orwell's little "gift."

"Hey, Liv. Quite the welcoming committee you've got there." A big guy walked in the back door.

A big, *good-looking* guy who was familiar enough with Livvy to call her *Liv,* who carried yet another dog with him. Not that that thing could really be called a dog. It was more of a dust mop with legs. With a bow on its head. A purple one. It looked like it ought to belong to the over-accessorized Cassidy Davenport instead of bohemian Livvy Carolla.

"Sorry about that, Kerry. I'm sure they miss you." Livvy ruffled the rottie's steam shovel–like jowls.

The little puff ball in the guy's arms growled and wriggled around. Sean put on his shirt, taking the opportunity to smile. The puff ball reminded him of Livvy: inappropriately dressed for the situation and too small to make a difference, but going at it full force while packing a growl or two.

Like the ones he'd gotten out of her a few minutes ago.

"Kerry, you forgot Mr. Choo's booties. I just had his nails done." Another guy walked in and plucked the puff ball from Kerry's hold. "Mr. Choo, you settle down this instant or I'll let John have his way with you."

The doglet must have understood because it shut up mid-squeak.

But then Orwell decided to join the party. "*I want you, too, Livvy.*"

Kerry, the other guy, and Livvy just blinked at the bird. Sean wanted to fricassee it.

"*I want you—squawk!*"

Instead, he settled for scooping the thing up and walking it across to the disaster zone across the hall. He tossed the

parrot into the air and the damn thing flew to the highest
perch in the room where it'd be impossible to get it down
from. *Of course.*

"*I want you, too, Livvy.*"

Great. Now the words reverberated along the high ceiling.

Sean closed the French doors and returned to the kitchen.
Damn bird.

The three of them all looked up guiltily from where they'd
huddled over the end of the island.

"Am I interrupting something?"

The other guy nudged Kerry. "I think that's our
question."

Livvy blushed, and the sight dug into Sean's psyche and
started growing roots.

He brushed the parrot feathers off his hands and held one
out, walking toward them. "Hi, I'm Sean."

The other guy took it. "I'm Sherwood. But you can call
me Sher." He said it as if it began with a *C* instead of an *S*.

Kerry rolled his eyes and tapped *Sher* out of the way. "I'm
Kerry. We live with Livvy."

"Live . . . with?" Sean couldn't stop the words, nor the
sinking feeling in his gut.

"He means at the co-op." Sher swatted Kerry in the stomach. "We're the next plot over. We were out antiquing today
and thought we'd make the drive to see the place."

Why should it bother him? He didn't *want* it to bother him.
Then again, he didn't want *her* to bother him, but he wasn't
getting what he wanted on that front, either.

"Welcome to the Martinson estate." He got his head out of
the damn clouds and shook Kerry's hand, even if he did practically choke on those words. *Martinson estate.* That was going
to change the minute the place was his. *If* the place was his.

"Quite the snazzy set-up here, Livs." Sher trailed a hand
along the countertop and walked around the edge of the bar.
"Care to give us the grand tour?"

"*I want you, too, Livvy.*"

Damn bird was loud.

"Sure!" Livvy said almost as loudly, and way too brightly,
keeping her gaze firmly averted from Sean's while she tucked
another strand of hair behind her ears.

She was doing that a lot lately and Sean found it endearing. Of course, the more time he spent with her, the more he found endearing. As Orwell was attesting to like a broken record.

He ought to put some distance between them. Keep it professional. Remember the ultimate goal. Stay far, far away from her.

It worked in theory.

Livvy headed back toward the doorway that led into the foyer, and her pack of dogs jumped to their feet to trail after her like, well, puppies.

Thankfully, she stopped in the doorway, held her hand, and said, "Stay."

And just like that, they all plunked their furry butts down, tongues lolling out of their mouths, tails thumping on the floor, and didn't take even one whiney, groveling belly-crawl toward her. Though the looks in their eyes were hopeful.

But Livvy spun around, that ruffled skirt sailing around her legs, and headed into the foyer.

Kerry patted Sean on the shoulder as he passed. "Don't try to rationalize it. Animals just *get* her."

"What is she, the dog whisperer?"

Kerry shrugged. "There's just something about Livvy that makes animals want to do whatever she tells them to."

Considering he'd felt like one when she'd been on the countertop, Sean got it, too.

Chapter Nineteen

"SO do tell about the treasure hunt, Livs." Sher hefted Mr.
Choo under one arm and tucked his other through hers
as they headed up the front staircase. "Kerry mentioned your
grandmother is a poet?"

Behind her, Sean snorted.

Livvy smiled. "I don't know that *poet* is the right word,
but she did seem to have a penchant for rhyming."

"To what end? I mean, why not just come out and tell you
what you're supposed to know or find or look for or whatever?
What does she get with you running around like a pretty little
chickie without a head? She's never going to see it since she's
dead."

"Sensitive," muttered Kerry. But Kerry of all people should
know that no sensitivity was required when it came to the Martinsons. Livvy had been done with them ages ago.

She ran her hand along the banister she'd slid down the
other day. "Who knows? I didn't understand her while she
was alive and her death hasn't made things any clearer. All I
know is that the lawyer said I can't inherit this place unless
I present him with the last clue."

"So you don't have to give him all the others? Then we

ought to be looking for the last one and be done with this interim nonsense."

"This interim *nonsense*," said Sean, who'd been way too quiet since their kiss earlier, "is leading us to that clue."

Kiss? Be real. That wasn't just a kiss. That was an interrupted prelude to something she hadn't had in a really long time. Like maybe, never. Sure, she'd had sex before—hot sex, too— but losing herself in the act as she'd done with Sean, and they hadn't even *had* sex. Um, no. Nothing had ever been like that before. No *one* had ever been like that for her before.

She tried to stop the blush that blazed across her cheeks, hating that she couldn't. Blushes didn't go well with her red hair and pale skin. She always thought she looked like she had a fever when she blushed, and no one looked good when they were sick. And, yes, she did want to look good for Sean because he brought something to life inside of her, something Livvy was afraid to examine. Examining it would make it real. It'd define it. *Name* it. She didn't want to do that because the minute she defined something, be it a friendship, acquaintance, roommate, family member . . . it all disappeared. She'd spent way too many holidays alone to not learn that forming bonds with people only led to heartache.

That's why she adopted animals. That's why she lived on a co-op. The people she lived with, like Kerry and Sherwood, and Jenny and Sheila and Marci; they were all on the same wavelength. All geared toward a common goal. It wasn't a goal that had to do with personal relationships, but rather a means of survival. A you-scratch-my-back-I'll-scratch-yours existence. And that was okay with her. She could depend on that. She could live with that. Everyone working together meant that everyone did what they said they were going to do. They made the commitment and they lived up to it. Because if they didn't, if they didn't bring anything to the table—literally and figuratively—they were voted off. It was one big reality show without the cameras. Or the monetary payoff. But some things were more important than money. That place proved it.

"Leading *us* to the clue?" Sher looked over his shoulder at Sean as they reached the second floor. "Treasure hunting is part of your duties? My, you *are* a jack of all trades, aren't you?" He peered into Livvy's room. "Nice bed you got there, sweetie. A little too big for one, though, isn't it?"

He raised an eyebrow at Sean.

She knew they cared about her, but Livvy could only take so much innuendo given what he and Kerry had interrupted. She'd reached her quota for the day. Possibly the year. "The dogs sleep with me."

"Pity."

No kidding.

"Anyhow, this is my room and Sean's is over there." She pointed across the hall two doors down. Not close enough, yet not too far. It epitomized their relationship—well the one they'd had up until the interrupted *kiss.*

Sher was noncommittal as he crossed the hall to look inside. Even more noncommittal when he walked away. She understood why, too: Sean's room was just that: a room. It didn't have any of his personal effects other than two duffel bags, his Manley Maids uniforms, a couple of sets of workout clothes and jeans, some sneakers, his toiletries, and a book on his bedside table. It was an old thriller, but a good one. He must be one of those people who kept favorite books to read over and over again.

And no she hadn't been snooping through his things; she'd been searching for clues. Just like Merriweather wanted her to do.

That was her story and she was sticking to it.

"The rest of this hall is filled with bedrooms if you want to take a look," she said, wanting to get them all away from Sean's room—herself especially. Again, quota met. "Or we could go to the nursery on the third floor."

"Nursery? As in babies?" Sher raised both eyebrows this time.

He got a smile out of her, which she was sure was his intention in the first place. *He* wouldn't mind if she started popping out kids. He wanted to be a favorite uncle; he'd told her that every time she'd said she was never having children. Her own childhood hadn't been a sterling example so what reason did she have to think she could do a better job? Though she certainly couldn't do worse.

"So where are these clues?"

"If they knew that then it wouldn't be much of a treasure hunt, now would it?" Kerry ran his hands over the wallpaper. "Nice. Damascene, I believe. Costly but elegant."

Of course it was. "Merriweather could afford it."

"The old girl could afford a lot of things." Sher picked up a piece of crystal from one of the pointless little tables that lined the hallway. Livvy had already checked the drawers for clues, but nope. Not even a match book or stray rubber band. Completely pointless. Just like the other twenty-seven rooms in the place.

Of course, Sher didn't think so. He was all for claiming one as his own personal boudoir for visits, another for his study, still another for an office . . . The list went on. Livvy actually started to enjoy herself as they walked down the long hallway, playing lady of the manor and almost forgetting her real purpose in being here.

But then she'd see Sean checking a piece of furniture, or running his hands over the lintel, peeking behind the picture frames, and the bittersweet reality would come roaring in. Sure, she could own the place, but she'd have to prove herself yet again. Would she come up lacking once more?

"So how many more do you have to find?" Sher asked as they headed back to the kitchen.

"I don't know. Merriweather didn't say. Typical." She pushed open the door and was immediately bombarded by puppy love. Big puppies, pushy puppies, some not-so-puppies . . . This was why she had the dogs and the other animals. This universal, undemanding, totally accepting love.

She plunked her butt onto the closest chair and hugged as many of the wiggling furry bodies as she could while dodging the slobbery kisses they were intent on bestowing. There was only one person's kisses she wanted and he was standing across the kitchen, smiling and shaking his head at her.

"Is that a Hodgeson?"

"A what?" Livvy asked, looking where Sher pointed.

"A Hodgeson. That tea set. They're pretty rare."

"If they're rare and worth something, I'll go with a yes. Merriweather would have only the best."

Sher handed Mr. Choo to Kerry then picked up the creamer. "It is." He showed it to them. "From the mid-eighteen hundreds is my guess. The company created custom pieces for members of the *ton* and did commemorative work for the Crown." He picked up the sugar bowl. "Very *chi-chi* to have one of these hanging around. Someone must have done something important to get one of these. You come from some pretty upper-crust stock, Livs."

"Which has gotten me all of where?" She took the sugar bowl from him and set it down.

"Well, here for starters."

"And the plus in that is . . . ?"

"Because you ended up next door to us, and Kerry and I want to take you away from all of it this weekend." Sher took Mr. Choo back from his partner and tightened the top-knot bow.

"I'm kind of on a deadline, Sher."

"I get that, sweetie, but you're going to die when you hear why."

"Okay, I'll bite."

Sherwood fluttered his eyelashes, put a hand to his chest, and only needed that gold dress and a subway vent for his Marilyn Monroe impersonation. "*We* have a booth at the Tri-State Farmer's Market this Sunday."

He might be a bit of a drama queen, but in this instance, Sher was fully justified.

"How? I thought they were booked solid like eight months ago." Back when she'd been struggling to come up with the funds to pay for the leaky roof and hadn't had any extra cash for the registration fee. The Tri-State Market was the largest in the area, and sales from even one day could pay her rent for months. If she failed Merriweather's *little test*, she'd need that money.

"They were booked. But Philip Johnson knows a girl named Mary who works for a guy whose sister-in-law runs the whole shindig, and when they got the cancellation, Mary overheard and was on the phone to Philip. He already has his booth, but he knew we were interested and voila! We're in. We want you to join us. Think of the crowds. The business we could do. I'm planning to unload our entire inventory."

She'd always done well at the market. Lots of referral business for the rest of the year and the exposure helped build name recognition. She'd been bummed to miss it this year. "But it's a two-night trip. Who will I get to take care of the animals on such short notice? Richard signed up all the college kids for his place, and you guys are going with me. That's why I brought them here in the first place."

"I'm sure we can find someone." Sher tapped his lips. "There is that new guy, what's his name? Matthew, Mark, Mike . . . Something with an *mmmmm*."

Kerry rolled his eyes. Livvy hid a giggle. For all Sher's flirtatiousness, he was utterly devoted to Kerry and they all knew it.

"Well, no matter. I'm sure we can come up with someone."

"Uh, hello?" Sean set down the spray bottle he was using to clean up after Orwell. "I can do it."

"But you don't even like my animals," said Livvy.

"It's not that I don't like them; it's just that there are so many of them."

"And they eat antiques."

"Well, yeah." He smiled and it did funny little flippy things to her stomach. "There's that."

"And they leave presents all over the place."

"That, too." His smile got bigger—and so did the flippy things.

Not optimal with Sher and Kerry staring at her so intently—and her hormones reacting so intensely to the memory. And to his smile. "But it's not in your job description."

"Oh, I'm sure a little bonus in his pocket would eradicate that worry, Livs," Sher piped in with enough innuendo that even the dogs knew what he meant.

"Watch it, Sherwood." Sean put his hands on his hips, the action stretching that shirt he'd had off an hour ago over the abs and pecs she'd run her hands all over and, oh, the memory—

"I'm *offering* to help, so you can keep your insinuations to yourself."

Blush number two hundred and thirteen started. How sweet was it that Sean rushed to her defense? How strange it felt, too, because no one had ever done that for her before. But sweet won out over strange, and she let the warmth of his action spread through her. If that caused another blush, so be it.

Then he leaned onto the countertop and her blush happened for a whole other reason.

"The hell with the job description, Livvy," Sean went on as if he weren't leaning over the *very same spot* he'd been leaning over her before Sher and Ker had shown up. "We pretty much shot that when the animals ate the rug and I made that pen for them. And then there's the barn clean-out." Not to mention the kissing-on-the-countertop thing. "I think we're redefining my job as we go along."

"This sounds interesting." Sher leaned a hip against the ice machine and crossed his arms.

Kerry swatted his shoulder.

Livvy brushed her hair back. "But it's in less than two days. I don't have anything ready."

"Sweetie," said Sher. "I've seen you work. You're a whirlwind in your tiny kitchen; imagine what you can do in this place. You've got all day tomorrow, and Mr. Volunteer here can help out with that, too, since he apparently can do anything."

Sean raised an eyebrow at him. "Uh, yeah. Sure. I can help."

"There, see? It's all settled." Sher straightened and swatted Kerry back. "Let's get going so these two have time to strategize tomorrow's baking extravaganza. Plus, I need to price out those corkscrews we found. I have a feeling they're going to be big sellers."

Kerry rolled his eyes as he followed Sher toward the door. "Pirates," he said to her and Sean. "He bought *pirate* corkscrews, with the screw part in an, um, interesting location. I think he's going to have a harder time passing them off as a 'family friendly' item than meeting any big demand, but if it makes him happy . . ." Kerry pulled the door behind. "See you tomorrow, Liv. About five." He looked at Sean. "Nice meeting you."

Sean nodded back.

And then they were alone.

Well, as alone as they could be with eight dogs looking at them expectantly.

Livvy had a funny sensation that's how she looked at Sean, too. "You didn't have to do that you know. Volunteer."

"If that's what you call it." Sean removed his palms from the countertop.

The countertop.

"Sherwood can be a bit of a steamroller."

He walked around the island. "You think?"

"I don't really have to go."

Sean closed the distance between them. "Do you want to go?"

Hell no she didn't. She wanted to stay right here and pick up where they left off. "I—"

"You should go."

"What?" Okay, he obviously wasn't on the same wavelength as she was when it came to picking back up . . .

"Even *I've* heard about the market. It's a big deal and from what I gathered from that conversation, it could be important to your business. Go. I can hold down the fort here. It's only one night."

So many things could happen in a night.

"It's two nights." Even more could happen in two nights.

"Okay, that's fine. I'm a big boy; I can handle a few animals."

Not thinking of him and *big* in the same sentence . . .

"Plus, I think it's a good idea."

"You do?"

He nodded and reached out to touch her, but then pulled back. "It'll give us some perspective."

"Perspective?"

"On what happened earlier."

"Oh."

"Yeah. Oh."

He looked at her.

She looked at him.

Was it wrong to want to kiss him? To go back to earlier? And if so, why?

Ringo started to whine. Yeah, she could relate.

But then Mickey joined in, followed by John, and when Georgia added her high-pitched *yowl*, well, there went *that* moment.

"What's wrong with them?" Sean stepped away from her, looking as confused as could be.

And he wanted to take care of them? He didn't look like he was handling this well with her standing right here, let alone doing it on his own.

Of course, she doubted the dogs would be picking up on raging pheromones when she wasn't here.

Davy stood up on his hind legs and joined in the ensemble, twirling like poodles do. Give him a tutu and he'd be a circus performer.

Livvy had to smile. They wanted her attention. He always did that when she was sad or upset, somehow knowing it'd make her smile. Even the way his tongue drooped out the side of his mouth made him look as if he was smiling.

"Livvy? What do we do?"

She took pity on him and the dogs and knelt down. Instantly, she was inundated with eight wet noses and snuffles of joy. "It's simple, Sean. They just want some loving."

SEAN could totally relate. And hell, if all it took was a few pitiful whines and some twirling on his toes, he might go that route.

Not.

Livvy was trouble. He'd followed her up those stairs and into her bedroom, then his own, and all the others down that god-awful long hallway and all he could think of was hauling her into one, slamming the door, and finishing what they'd started in the kitchen. God, he wanted her.

And, *God*, he so couldn't have her.

He needed her to go on this market trip. He needed perspective. He needed to be able to think clearly and figure some way out of this mess, and with her around, clear thinking was nonexistent in the haze of sensuality that governed her every move. From the way she slipped those wispy curls over her ear, to the sexy little nibble on the corner of her lip and the way she flounced and bounced and breathed life into every movement she made, even the way she turned her head to accept the slobbery kisses of her dogs, something in Livvy reached out to him, wrapped itself around him, and reeled him in.

He shoved his hands into his pockets and walked back around the counter. *The* counter.

Christ.

He backed away. He didn't need any reminders of how she'd looked there, wanting him.

He opened the drawer where he'd found pens and paper on one of his forays through this room for clues. "I'm assuming you're going to need some baking supplies for tomorrow. Give me a list and I'll go shopping." It spoke to his level of frustration—both with the situation and with his pain-in-the-ass libido—that he was willing to not only go shopping, but also write it down in his pictographic shorthand. In his world, writing was second in torture only to reading aloud.

Livvy looked up at him, her gorgeous amber eyes framed by those rust-colored lashes, like a sunflower in the fall.

There he went with the poetry again.

"I do need certain things, but I just wing the other stuff when I get there. Plus, you won't know which brands, so I'll have to go with you."

He almost whined like the dogs. The purpose of making this list was so that she *wouldn't* have to go with him. Sean exhaled. He just couldn't win.

Chapter Twenty

❧

SHOPPING with Livvy turned out to be a pretty winning experience, surprisingly. The free spirit-ness of being with her was contagious. She was like a ray of sunshine in a dingy world—oh, hell. There he went again.

Sean had to chuckle at himself. Livvy created a perpetual state of *happy* and no one, not even he, was immune, so he ought to just stop fighting it, and go along for the ride.

She smiled at everyone, and everyone smiled back. It was a gift, actually, how she could turn someone's bad mood around as if she were sprinkling pixie dust on them.

Pixie dust? What the hell happened to his brain? To his vocabulary? He'd never said *pixie dust* in his life, not even to Mac when she'd been a kid. Of course, he hadn't been the one reading her any bedtime stories where there could have been mention made of pixie dust, and why was he going on about this?

"I was thinking I'd make scones. What flavors do you like?"

Weren't scones those tasteless flaky things the Brits loved? "Doesn't matter to me. I'm easy."

She slid him a look that heated his blood.

"I mean, whatever you want to make is fine with me. What are your best sellers?"

"I don't have any but—"

"What do you mean you don't have any best sellers? Livvy, you want to find out what your clientele wants and cater to them. You can't just make whatever you feel in the mood for. Customers drive your business, and if they can't get what they want from you, they'll go elsewhere. Successful businesses tap into customer's wants and needs, and back it up with excellent service. If you don't provide what people want, you will have no revenue, and therefore no means to continue the company or your employment with it."

"I'm not an idiot, Sean. I know how businesses work. How do you think I've managed to keep mine running for so long? *And* managed to get the time off to come here for my grandmother's little whim? Cash flow might be tight, but it's been flowing. These guys don't eat grass, you know. I was asking your opinion for personal interest. I wanted to make sure we'd make something you liked, too. And I don't have any best sellers because *all* my scones sell well. I make a mean scone." She raised her chin and stood a little straighter.

And knocked Sean sideways. Metaphorically. She was too tiny to do much damage physically. But otherwise . . .

Was it silly of him to get all warm and fuzzy inside that she'd wanted to make something he liked? That she'd asked because she wanted to do something nice for him? To include him? For too long he'd been running this tightrope of budgets and contingencies and stress and worry and now subterfuge . . .

Her honesty was as refreshing as it was guilt-plaguing. She was going to hate him when she found out.

If she finds out. You could still pull this off, Manley.

"Uh, okay." He swiped a hand through his hair and kneaded the tight muscles in the back of his neck. Today had been one big lesson in torture and it showed no signs of letting up any time soon.

Then he heard a crash, followed by "Scene!"

Enter his brother, Bryan. The fun just kept piling on. "Hey, Bry."

"Is that . . . Oh my God. Is that *Bryan Manley*?"

Of *course* Livvy would know who his brother was. Was there a woman on the face of the planet who didn't? Sean was shocked there wasn't a harem trailing behind him as usual—though the two kids with him who were kicking the mac-n-cheese boxes they'd knocked over might have something to do with it. No one would expect *the* Bryan Manley to be food shopping with kids in tow. Probably the best cover his brother had ever had in public.

"Yeah, that's Bry."

"Bry? That sounds awfully familiar."

"Because he's my brother." No sense in keeping it from her. The truth was bound to come out. He couldn't be around Bry for more than five minutes before someone snapped a picture and it was on every social media site in under twenty seconds. If he kept it from her, she'd get suspicious.

"So that makes you Sean . . . *Manley*?"

"That's usually how it works."

"So you *own* the cleaning service?"

"No, my sister does."

"Mac is your *sister*? How did you come to work for her?"

He wasn't going there. "Long story." He didn't elaborate, choosing to wait for the conversation to turn back to Bryan. It always did.

"So Bryan Manley is your brother."

This time, though, it bothered him more than it ever had. "Yes he is. And, yes, he's single. But he's not exactly ready to settle down."

"Wow. Talk about jaded."

"No. Just used to it." And he was. He had to remind himself of that fact. And the fact that Bryan *wasn't* ready to settle down. Never would be to hear Bry talk.

"Hey, Scene." Bryan patted him on the back when he walked over. "And you must be Olivia."

Sean really hated how Livvy blushed. Her blushes should be reserved for him and him alone.

Which was totally irrational.

"Yes, I'm Olivia."

Olivia? What the hell happened to *Livvy*?

"Bryan! Take us to your leader! We want soda!" The twin boys beside him brandished their lightsabers.

Bryan nudged them aside with a finger. "Watch it, guys. You'll poke your eye out." He winked at Livvy.

Winked.

If they weren't in a public place, Sean just might punch his brother for being too damn charming. Especially when Livvy blushed again.

"What are you doing here, Bry?"

"We. Want. So. Da!" The lightsabers were now doing circles in the air, complete with mechanized sound effects.

"Guys! Chill! I know your mother didn't teach you to be rude, so pipe down, will you? We'll get what your mom said we should get and not a thing more." Bryan exhaled. "Why do people have kids again?"

Livvy knelt down to the boys' level. "Guys, you know what you want to try? Put a hard-boiled egg in your favorite cola and wait to see what happens."

"Why, what happens?" The boys were just as enthralled with Livvy as their grown-up counterparts.

"You'll have to try it and see. But when you do, you're going to think twice about ever drinking soda again."

"Cool! I love soda!"

"Me, too!"

"So can we get some, Bryan? Please? It's in aisle number twelve."

Livvy stood up. "How about you guys pick up the display you knocked down with your swords and I'll talk to Bryan about your soda."

"Really? You're cool!"

"Yeah, much cooler than Mom."

Sean just shook his head. At least he couldn't blame himself for the effect she had on him; she had it on every member of the male species, young and old alike.

Livvy ruffled one of the twins' hair. "That's because she's your mom. Moms have to be tough, so they can't be cool. But she loves you, you know."

"That's what Bryan says."

"That's because she's the only one who *could* love them," Bryan muttered.

Sean hid his grin. All in all, it sounded as if Bry had gotten the worse deal of all of them. Sean would take bird droppings and alpaca sperm over sword-fighting eight-year-olds any day.

The boys ran to the end of the aisle to restack the food they'd knocked down.

"Soda's not on their mother's list," said Bryan. "She's not going to be happy if I come home with it."

"Trust me. You do that experiment and I guarantee you they'll never want to drink soda again."

"Why? What happens?"

"Twenty-four hours will make the eggshells thinner and turn brown. The correlation, of course, being their teeth. It erodes enamel. If you leave the egg in longer, it dissolves the shell. I haven't had a soda since ninth grade when we did this on the first day. By the last week of class, I was off soda for good."

"Wow. Beauty and brains. You free for dinner?" Bryan gave her the patented Bryan Manley smolder.

And Sean wanted to give him the Manley Brother back-the-fuck-off punch.

"That's awfully nice of you to ask, but Sean and I are on a deadline. We can't have dinner with you."

And he'd like to kiss her for including him in the invite.

Especially when Bryan scowled.

"Yeah, Bry. We've got plans." Let his brother make of that what he would.

Then Sean wanted to smack himself. Seriously. How old were they? Twelve? Fighting over a girl . . .

Bry raised an eyebrow. "Plans, huh? Well then. I guess I'll leave you to 'em. What are they again?"

"Plans." Bry could *stick* his innuendo.

"I'm baking and Sean's going to help."

Sean knew the smirk would be on Bryan's face before it actually was.

"Don't." He held up his hand to stop the dumb-ass question he knew Bry would ask—just because he could—but Bry wasn't reading the same playbook.

"You're going to be cooking in the kitchen together?"

He did love Livvy's blushes, though. Especially since they actually *had* been *cooking* in the kitchen.

"Don't you have twins to take care of or something?" Sean pointed to where the boys were restacking the boxes, only this time in the shape of a fort. Around themselves.

"Oh, hell." Bryan sighed. "Nice meeting you, Olivia." He headed toward the rambunctious pair. "Boys! This isn't a playground."

Sean laughed. Bryan sounded like Gran.

"Looks like your brother's got his hands full. I didn't know he had kids. Is this his weekend or something?"

That made Sean laugh louder. "Bry? A dad? That'll be the day." As in *never*. Bry had been vowing for years he'd never have kids; it really was Karma that he'd gotten the assignment with them. "No. They're, uh, a friend's."

Sean wasn't too keen on mentioning the poker bet. Livvy had to believe in him as a professional housekeeper. She had to believe that Mac was sending out her best, and he wasn't going to be the one to burst that bubble.

"Yeah, I can relate. I mean, they're cute and all, but raising them? So not me."

She headed off in the opposite direction while Sean replayed what she'd just said. What she'd revealed. He did want kids some day. When he could provide for them. The way he and his siblings had grown up made him want stability. A home to call his own and the means to pay for it. Which was the reason this business had to succeed. He had to remember they wanted different things out of life . . .

It ought to be a relief, but instead, it made him sad. For her. What her childhood must have been like growing up. On the outside, it looked great: She'd had the boarding school and Martinson money behind her. But inside it . . . she'd had no one to love her. He'd had just the opposite and he'd been richer for it.

T was late when they got home, even later once he'd helped her feed and water the menagerie. And muck out the stalls.

"Tell me why you want to do this day after day," he said, dodging the gonad-seeking ram to hang her pitchfork on a hook on the wall that looked more like a trophy case than a place to store farm instruments. Someone had even decorated it with crown molding and other non-barnlike plaques and stuff. Livvy was right; the Martinsons were pretentious.

"All sorts of reasons. The alpaca wool is an investment because of the price it can bring, and the sheep's wool is our daily bread and butter. Then there's the milk from the goats and eggs from the fowl. All things I can use or sell."

"And Reggie?"

She smiled when Reggie snorted at hearing his name. "Reggie is just for companionship. A guy had been trying to sell him for bacon. I couldn't let that happen."

"Of course not."

He could see her being horrified at that and picking up the little pig, cuddling him to her like a baby, crooning that he was safe with her. Her. The woman who didn't want kids.

She had more maternal instinct than she knew what to do with.

"Plus, I sell off the pullets and lambs for more income. I'd love to keep them all, but it's not possible. Although, once I sell this place, I can build a bigger barn and keep more of them."

"Which means more mucking out."

She shrugged, a stray curl falling over her shoulder to disappear inside her camisole . . .

What was it with her and camisoles? At least she had a shirt on over it this time, but those things hugged her curves in a way that wasn't fair to the male population.

"Mucking out their stalls is a small price to pay for the companionship, love, and acceptance they give me."

"Acceptance?"

Livvy tucked that stray curl behind her ear. Again. One of these days he was going to do it for her.

"Animals don't judge you. If you take care of them, fulfill the promise you made to them, they'll be your best friends. They even cut you some slack if you fall down on the care-giving so long as you aren't cruel to them. People could learn a lot from animals."

There was a century's worth of pain laced through her words. He propped the pitchfork against the goat's pen. "Do you want to talk about it?"

"Talk about what?" She busied herself with picking the hay off the wall dividing the pens.

"Livvy."

It took a good ten seconds before she stopped and looked up at him. "I'm okay, Sean. Thank you, but there's no need. I learned a long time ago to depend only on myself. Sure, I'm angry at Merriweather, but in the end, anger benefits no one. It sucks you dry. Moving forward, focusing on the next step, the big goal, what you need to do to get there . . . *that's* productive. Dwelling on might-have-beens is counterproductive."

They both noticed that word. *Counter.*

He took a step toward her. Saw her lean in just a bit. It'd be so easy to pull her into his arms and finish what they'd started earlier.

But her words replayed like a loop in his head. *They don't let you down.*

Like he was going to do.

He had to crunch the numbers again. *Had* to figure out some way to make this project work for both of them.

So he stepped back. Didn't act on the temptation. On the knowledge that she wouldn't refuse him.

It was probably the hardest thing he'd ever done in his life.

Chapter Twenty-one

ᵔᷛᕙᕐᑅᕗ

TRYING to fall asleep last night had been one of the hardest things Livvy had ever done. Her body had still been on "burn" from being with Sean and she couldn't understand why he'd backed away. She'd made her intentions—desires, wants, preferences—pretty damn available last night. And in the kitchen before Kerry and Sher had interrupted—

Oh crud. Kerry and Sher.

Livvy leapt out of bed, jostling Georgia, who'd decided that Livvy's head was the perfect thing to rest her warm full belly against, so she grumbled when it was taken away.

The pug rolled down into the depression Livvy left behind, her back legs kicking Petra in the shoulder. Which caused Petra to whine, and John to growl, which woke up Mike, who rolled over with a yawn, practically squishing Davy in the process.

Within minutes, the entire group was awake and demanding to be fed and let out. And not necessarily in that order.

She rubbed her eyes after setting them free in the backyard and turned on her iPod. Maroon 5's *"One More Night"* was a sufficiently danceable start for a day spent in the kitchen. She bebopped over to the Sub-Zero for a glass of OJ. No caffeine for her; she'd told those boys in the supermarket the truth. One twenty-four-hour period of the soda/egg experiment had been enough to convince her to stay away from the stuff; the full year of shell-dissolving had solidified that resolution.

The eggs were there. The eggs she and Sean had bought yesterday at the store. The ones they were going to use to bake her signature scones with today. Together.

She took a deep breath, not surprised to feel a flutter in her stomach at the prospect. She'd been doing a lot of stomach-fluttering in the last few days. And skin-shivering. And then there was the blushing.

But not nearly enough kissing.

She felt the heat travel up her chest and into her cheeks again, but not due to any blush this time. Sean was just . . . well, he was pretty darn near amazing. Perfect almost, if such a thing existed. Smart, funny, good-looking, a good sport, tolerant, willing to pitch in . . .

She sounded like she was advertising for farm help instead of listing the qualities of the man she . . . what? What was Sean to her?

"Is that what all the best-dressed chefs are wearing these days?"

Speak of the devil; he showed up in her kitchen looking deliciously sinful in a pair of shorts, a T-shirt, and flip-flops.

Lusted after. Yeah, that was as good a term as any. And a lot safer than some.

She stopped dancing mid-bebop and tucked her hair behind her ears. "Um, good morning. No uniform today?" It was a definite improvement.

He shrugged and helped himself to the pomegranate juice she'd bought. Maybe he wasn't as opposed to anti-high-fructose-corn-syrupy food as he'd let on.

"I figured since we were going to be in a hot kitchen all day, I ought to dress for it."

Or undress . . .

Livvy licked her lips that had suddenly gone dry and looked down at her attire: white camisole, and Capri-length silk pajama bottoms. "Well I'll be wearing my apron, so it doesn't really matter what I wear."

He raised an eyebrow again. "If you say so."

Pitbull's *"Give Me Everything Tonight"* segued onto the iPod. Yeah, not really the song she wanted right now.

Livvy jerked the apron off its hook and busied herself filling the eight dog bowls with breakfast, trying not to listen to the song's lyrics. Then she pulled out the baking sheets, mixing bowls, and cooling racks they'd need for scone baking.

Then she spent a good couple of minutes searching for a walnut crusher, and lined all the dry ingredients up nicely on the baking prep counter before finally running out of things to do besides look at him. Which was what she'd wanted to do all along anyhow.

Leaning against the sink, he had his arms crossed over that amazing chest and one foot crossed over the other in such a masculine pose that it made her mouth water.

Sean *Manley*. There'd never been a more perfect name.

"So would you like to eat before we start, or are only the dogs getting lucky today?" he asked.

He could get lucky anytime he wanted— "Um, sure. I can whip something up." She nodded at the items he'd accumulated on the counter while she'd been searching for what she'd need.

He pushed off from the sink as Jay Sean's *"Down"* started playing. "I wasn't asking for you to make it. I was asking if you wanted it. I'm more than capable of rustling up some breakfast for us, you know."

"No, actually, I didn't."

He grabbed a skillet from the overhead wagon wheel and turned on the burner. "Hmm, I guess you're right. You haven't really seen me in action in the kitchen."

Oh. yes she had, and she used five of the song's downbeats to remember it.

So, apparently, did Sean, since he dropped the pan onto the flame with a clatter, then fumbled with tossing a couple of slices of multi-grain bread into the toaster. "So, uh, why don't you take a seat and I'll throw something together. You bought extra eggs, right? And did I see pork roll or something?"

"Pork roll?" Livvy shuddered. "Hardly. Reggie would never forgive me."

"I thought elephants were the ones with long-term memories." He flicked some butter into the pan, where it started to sizzle.

Just like Livvy was doing. The guy was *hot*. "Pigs are smart, too. If I were to go anywhere near Reggie smelling like one of his relatives, he'd never forgive me." She'd done it once. The pig had stayed in his bed for a day and no amount of dog biscuits would coax him from it. He'd even turned up his snout at her when she'd tried to pat him.

"Your diet must be very limited if you don't eat any of your animals' relatives."

"Only Reggie is sensitive. I eat chicken and eggs all the time. Though I do try not to eat them around Orwell."

"Speaking of which . . . where is the little one-bird wrecking crew?"

The forty-five minutes it'd taken them to finagle the bird off the curtain rods last night hadn't been fun, so this was a welcome respite. She loved Orwell, but he was a lot of work. "Sleeping. He isn't an early riser."

"Must be nice," said Sean, cracking two eggs in one hand simultaneously over the skillet.

"Pretty neat trick."

He raised an eyebrow.

"That. The thing you did with the eggs. How'd you learn it?"

"Growing up with two brothers and no video games, you learn to amuse yourself. We used to have contests to see how many we could do without getting shells in the pan."

"You won?"

Sean smiled and it took her breath away. The guy was flat-out gorgeous.

"Yeah, I kicked their—butts. I did five once."

"You must have really big hands."

It wasn't a blush that roared over her skin. It was a full-on scarlet cloak, and she ought to wrap herself in it and die of embarrassment because they were both thinking of what hand size supposedly correlated to.

She looked at his hands. They weren't too big. Just the right size with just the right shaped nails and just the right amount of hair on them, and just the right amount of strength and muscle and OMG, was she really describing his hand to herself? "What can I do to help?"

Wrong question to ask. His eyes darkened, and the look he gave her pierced right through to her belly, igniting a fire there that had nothing to do with what was happening on the stove.

"Nothing. I'm good."

Yup. He was.

"Is there something you need to get ready for baking?"

She shook her head, both as an answer and as a *Get-Over-It-Livvy* mechanism. Scones had to be made individually. At least hers did to achieve the perfect amount of flakiness. If she let the dough sit too long, the scones would fail. With the amount she was planning to make today, she needed to get her head into the project.

Sean pulled the bread from the toaster, slathered it with the apple butter she'd bought, poured two more glasses of pomegranate juice into a pair of ornate wine glasses from a shelf she couldn't even see into let alone reach, then plated the eggs as if he were a chef.

"Did you ever think about becoming a personal chef instead of a maid? You're really good at it." She took the juice glasses from the counter and set them at the table, catty-corner to each other. She didn't need him sitting beside her— too much temptation—but she didn't want him sitting too far, either.

Too much disappointment.

He brought their plates to the table. The over-easy eggs were done to perfection, the toast was just the right amount of toasted and buttered, and the slices of orange he'd included were an added bonus.

Just like him. An added bonus she never could have fore-seen when she'd learned about her grandmother's death.

"How's this going to work today?" he asked. "What do you need me to do?"

So many things . . .

She set her fork down, dabbing at her lips with the linen napkin he'd found in one of the drawers, and reined in her happy hormones.

She made a mental note to turn off her iPod as yet another round of inappropriate lyrics filled the room.

"I make each batch individually," she said, trying to ignore the vocalist singing about not being able to keep his eyes off a woman. "To get enough layers in the bread, I have to knead the dough to the right consistency, which takes time. It can't be done production-line style. But we can do that for the setup and cleanup. I'll line up rows of bowls for several batches, then you can measure all the ingredients into them and I'll come along after you, mixing them together one at a time. Work for you?"

"Sounds like a plan." He raised a forkful of egg. "So? What do you think? Good enough for you?"

He was talking about the food he'd made, right, and not himself because, yeah, he was good enough for her. Too good actually. There had to be a catch. Sean couldn't possibly be as good as he appeared. Good-looking, hardworking, loved his family, funny, kind, helpful, able to do pretty much anything—*and* clean—and he'd stopped complaining about her animals. Had even helped her take care of them.

For the first time in a long while, Livvy let hope trickle into her vocabulary.

"Livvy?"

"Oh, um, yes. Great. You really are amazing in the kitchen."

She *so* did not just say that.

"Speaking of . . ." Sean set his fork down. "Not addressing it isn't going to make it go away." He covered her hand with his and forget the flames on the stove or the temperature of this room once they had all the ovens going today, or even how delicious he looked in something as nondescript as shorts and a T-shirt; nothing could compare to what Sean's touch did to her.

Hope roared back in, swirled around inside of her, touching every part, and, planted itself firmly into her soul, and suddenly the song lyrics were totally appropriate.

"Livvy, we can't have a repeat of yesterday."

Until Sean said that.

"It's really not a good idea."

"Okay. Fine." There was only so much rejection she could take and, frankly, she was over her quota for that for, like, *ever.* She wasn't about to beg. Nope. Not her. She hadn't begged for anything from her grandmother, and she certainly wasn't about to beg for anything from a guy who wasn't smart enough to want her.

She crumpled her napkin and tossed it on top of the now-unable-to-be-eaten eggs, then gathered up her place setting and stood. "We ought to get started on the baking. I have a lot to make and, while the breakfast was nice, there really isn't time to sit around and gab." She slid the plate to the edge of the table, her napkin dragging the tea set's sugar bowl with it.

"Livvy—" The lid clanged to the floor, but Sean managed to grab the bowl before it went after it, staring at it as if he didn't know what it was.

"Can you let the dogs back in, please?" They'd started whining the minute she'd stood, and Livvy was never so glad for their demands as she was this minute. She needed time to compose herself from the electricity thrumming through her, the disappointment of yet another round of hope being dashed, and the embarrassment of him knowing how much she wanted him and being turned down.

And she'd had such hopes for today.

S O much for breakfast.
     Sean gathered his plate, not really caring about the food as much as the conversation. He'd tossed and turned most of the night, desire keeping him awake as much as the guilt. Around four A.M. he'd resolved to put an end to it once and for all. Whatever *it* was. He needed to discuss it with her. Make her see that it wasn't as cut-and-dried, let's-sleep-together as she'd made it out to be. Not without telling her the true reason.

Or that there was a clue in the sugar bowl.

God, he was a shit. It was poetic justice, karmic law, the universe laughing at him, that he was turning her down. He wasn't on Bry's level when it came to getting women, although he'd never been a slouch in that department, but the one woman he wanted more than any other was the worst possible one for him to hook up with.

Except this wasn't about hooking up. A night of mutually pleasurable sex could be a good thing if it didn't come with the rest of the stuff that came with wanting Livvy.

The howling started again at the door, and Sean could totally relate. Besides having to put the brakes on this run-away train–like attraction, *there was a clue in the sugar bowl.*

What the hell was he going to do about it?

The scratching came next. Sean leapt to his feet, scooped up the eight food bowls and headed out to stop yet another disaster from encroaching on his world because he didn't need to pay for someone to repair the door as well.

Surprisingly, the dogs were well-behaved for a pack of hungry animals. Their thumping tails and the hyper dance the little ones did were the only signs of how much they were looking forward to the food. Ringo didn't even growl at him.

Maybe his luck was changing.

The thought held when he went back into the kitchen and found Livvy had tied an apron around her waist—and the bib on it covered a lot more of her cleavage than her camisole, thank God. If he couldn't touch her, he didn't need the temptation.

Unfortunately, the universe wasn't listening. Temptation swirled around him all morning. Every time Livvy danced— she *danced* constantly—past him, or reached around him, or slid a bowl across the counter, or bent over to take the scones out of the oven, or licked her fingertip when she accidentally touched the hot baking sheet, it was as if someone Up There was laughing at him.

Give him the mess in the living room any day over this. At least he'd be sweating from exertion and honest effort, not frustrated desire he couldn't act on.

He checked the clock on the wall. Too many hours until she left.

The song changed and Sean winced. "*Any Way You Want It*" was *not* what he needed to hear right now. Especially when he heard the chorus echoing down from upstairs. "Sounds like Orwell's awake."

Livvy looked up from the kneading board, a spot of flour on her nose. And her cheek. And her shoulder.

"He loves this song. I think it's the only one he knows all the words to."

"How about we change it, then?" Perfect excuse not to have a little red Steve Perry devil sitting on his shoulder tempting him for the next three and a half minutes, or however long the damn song was. He pushed the advance button on the iPod.

Bruno Mars. Seriously, could he *not* get a break here when he was trying to do *something* right and good?

Upstairs, Orwell was still into Journey, trilling out Perry's classic, "Ooooooooh."

"Maybe I should get him. Bring him down into the action." And get himself out of it, even for a little bit.

Livvy shrugged her shoulders and, interestingly, the bib on her apron stayed in place but the breasts behind it . . . They peeked out a little more over the top and oh, shit, he was in trouble.

At least, he didn't have those damn pants on and his shorts hid his reaction better.

He headed out the door for Orwell. He'd never have bet he'd see the day when he'd pick a parrot over a woman.

Apparently he would have lost that bet, too.

Chapter Twenty-two

THE twelfth batch of scones came out of the oven, and Sean was ready to call it a day. There were scones everywhere and the damn parrot knew it, too. If Orwell said, *"Polly wants a scone"* one more time, Sean was going to bake him *into* one.

"He's got his clichés mixed up."

"He does that." Livvy brushed some crust flakes off her nose. The woman was too utterly adorable for his liking on *top* of being sexy, and the combination was making mincemeat of his resolution to stay away from her. She couldn't leave here fast enough.

Which meant, of course, that she ended up hanging around.

She pulled the oven mitts off and plunked herself on the barstool next to his, swinging her bare foot against the rails. Her toenails were pink.

He didn't know why that should surprise him, but it did. Maybe because he'd expect her to have painted them blue. Or green. Or brown. She was the biggest dichotomy in a woman he'd ever met. Most wouldn't be caught dead wearing combat boots and gypsy skirts like some throwback to the seventies, but on Livvy it all worked and she was completely unselfconscious of how well it did. He had a feeling she was oblivious to exactly how she looked. In anything.

He'd like to see her in a dress. A real dress. Something sexy and form-fitting, but not too revealing. A bit of sparkle at her wrists, but nothing more, letting the beauty that was inside of her do the shining for her.

Once more with the poetry, Manley. Seriously?

He seriously needed to get over her. He seriously needed to move forward with the plan. And he seriously needed to get to that clue. Without her.

"So what time are the guys picking you up? Do we have much more left to do?"

"Are you trying to get rid of me?"

"Of course not. It is your home, after all." More a reminder for him than her.

"Not yet, it's not." She pinched the bridge of her cute little nose. "You knew my grandmother better than me. Any idea why she did this?"

He didn't know Merriweather at all. He'd thought he had, but not after this. "Not a clue. Maybe she just wants to give you a feel for the family history."

"It wasn't enough that I had to live it? The woman endowed half the school, for Pete's sake. I couldn't *not* know about the family."

"I'm guessing you weren't thrilled being there?"

"If I'd wanted to go there, then, sure. I'd have been thrilled. But I didn't. I didn't want to leave here. My home. My mom. She was still alive when Merriweather got custody. So was my dad. Yet neither one did a thing about an old woman stealing their kid. As if they couldn't *wait* for their little *problem* to go away. Out of sight, out of mind."

Her voice broke and she looked away.

Sean wanted to wrap her in a hug and squeeze the hurt out of her. But he didn't. Because that would only make what he was trying to do all that much harder. For both of them.

"They were just kids, Livvy. Probably too freaked out to know what to do."

"Nice argument *if* she'd taken me right away. But I was with my mom for five years. Just the two of us, since her parents tossed her out the minute they found out about me. And *Daddy* didn't do jack. Not one penny. Not even a card. I'm surprised Merriweather ever knew about me, though not for Mom's lack of trying."

"Don't be so hard on her, Livvy. She was probably scared about taking care of you. Once your other grandparents threw her out, I'm sure it was really tough for her. Perhaps giving you to Merriweather was her attempt at giving you all the things in life she'd never have."

"And then she drank herself to death with the kiss-off money."

This time he did reach out to her. He covered her hand. Sometimes simple human comfort was bigger than anything else, and Livvy was hurting. "You can't know what was in her mind. She might have regretted giving you up. It might have been the hardest thing she'd ever done. Who knows where you'd be now if she hadn't? You can't change the past, Livvy. But you can make your future what you want it to be. Don't let your bitterness over those events color who you are today. Because I think . . ." And here he went veering down a path he had no business going. "I think you turned out all right. More than all right." He watched his thumb caress her soft skin.

Watched her shift her hand just slightly so she could capture his thumb with hers.

Watched her raise her eyes to meet his. "What are we doing, Sean?"

Hell if he knew. The love song emanating off the damn iPod wasn't helping, either.

Thankfully, a horn honked outside and the dogs started barking.

The moment was lost.

But not forgotten.

TEN seconds after she drove away, all hell broke loose.

The dogs were no longer his friends, Orwell traded in his nasal singing voice for a full-on, jungle-level parrot screech, and Sean's phone wouldn't stop ringing.

The architect had questions. His attorney had questions. Gran had a few. Then there was Mac asking for his help the next day, all of which meant it was well after dark before he had the chance to sit down and decipher the clue he'd taken from the sugar bowl.

You're going to put it back, Manley.

He would; he didn't need his conscience reminding him. No matter how badly he wanted this place, he'd never be able to live with himself if he sabotaged her.

Sabotage, beat her to the punch . . . What's the difference?

Yeah, he was still working on that part. But until he figured it out, he was putting the clue back. After he'd figured it out.

> *The battle was complex, but so was he*
> *And for it, he earned the family's heraldry.*
> *Under the banner of an eagle*
> *This knight so regal*
> *Claimed victory with his force*
> *From astride his horse.*

Another poem, another riddle. The woman was driving him nuts.

Sean tapped his tablet again, replaying the clue for the key words. An eagle banner, heraldry, a knight, and a horse.

God, he hated puzzles.

Eagle, knight, horse. He had no idea on the eagle thing, but horses would've been kept in the barn.

Sean swiped a hand over his mouth. It was a long shot, but at least it was something.

He stuck the tablet in his pocket, praying he'd get lucky and find the next clue, then headed out through the kitchen.

Big mistake. The dogs were waiting to go with him. Yeah, that's all he'd need, them stirring up trouble with the barn animals. No way.

"Sit," he said as they followed him en masse to the door.

Of *course* that only worked for Livvy the dog whisperer.

"Stay." He put his hand up like she'd done.

Nothing. Tongues lolling, tails wagging, the clatter of nails on the wood floor . . . The dogs wanted out.

Then Ringo whined. So did John. Or maybe that one was Paul.

The little Pomeranian rolled over onto its back, waved its paws, and cried pitifully.

Great. Sean pinched the bridge of his nose. He didn't know how to deal with mass animal hysteria.

He backed into the screen door, pulling the interior one with him. "Guys, look. You can't come. Just hang out for a little bit and I'll be back."

The poodle, obviously not on board with that idea, wormed itself between his feet, nudged the door open, and took off across the lawn.

Sonofabitch! Livvy would kill him if he lost her dog.

He locked the others in the kitchen, then ran after the little annoyance.

Tiny legs, but that thing could *move*. It darted left and right, trying to evade him, and Sean was embarrassed that it was winning.

"Get back here!" He lunged, but the poodle zipped around him to make a beeline for the barn.

Sean ran after it, thankful there was moonlight so he could at least *see* the black animal, catching up just as the dog nosed its way inside.

As expected, all hell broke loose in there, too. Could he *not* get a break?

Sean turned on the lights to see the ram butt its head against the stall door, bleating as the baby goats hopped the dividing walls between the stalls and jumped down to circle the dog in a reverse prey-hunter stance, their parents up on their hind legs, front legs draped over their stall doors as if they were at a Little League game.

"Stay!" he called to everyone.

No one listened.

"Sit!"

Not to that, either. The dog yipped at him and moved closer to a baby goat that lowered its head and pawed the ground as if it was going to play bullfight.

He'd have to clue the little thing on how well those *didn't* end for the bulls.

"Heel!"

Again, no one paid any attention.

"Look, John, Paul, George, Ringo, Yoko . . . Whatever the hell your name is, come here!"

No dice. The dog yipped again, this time dashing between two of the kids.

The goats ran after it.

The parents jumped the stall door and ran after them.

The geese scattered, honking and waddling all over the place. A pair of them smashed into each other and practically knocked themselves out.

Rhett started kicking the stall door. Poor Scarlett just looked over it with her soulful eyes as if she was wishing Sean would get her her own stall.

"I'll talk to Livvy about it, Scarlett." He reached out to pat the alpaca's neck to calm her, but Rhett spit at him.

"Alrighty then." Sean backed away, hands up.

Reggie lumbered over to his stall door, his grunts getting louder with each step.

Sean tossed him a few dog biscuits from the bag hanging on the outside of the stall. Reggie did a little jig back to them, rooting them onto his bedding, the sound he was making more of a purr than anything remotely resembling a pig.

The chickens came flying—metaphorically—out of their supposedly enclosed pen, feathers everywhere, squawking as if the sky was falling, and the ram started *kicking* the stall now. The lambs started bleating, which got an answering cry from the baby goats, and pretty soon Sean couldn't hear himself think, let alone make himself heard over the noise.

The poodle zoomed by him and Sean tried to grab it, only to end up having three kids and a parent goat smash into him, taking him down onto the cold, hard, unforgiving concrete floor.

He managed to not land on his tablet, thank God, and avoided having it broken by the goat that climbed onto his back. But with two near-misses avoided, Sean didn't want to risk a third. His luck couldn't hold forever.

He rolled over to dislodge the little mountain climber. One of the geese went waddling around his head, a chicken fast on its heels.

Sean had to laugh at that. He was pretty sure that was a first in the annals of barnyard history.

And then a lamb landed on his gut, knocking the wind out of him.

"*Baaaaaa.*"

He dropped his head onto the concrete. Ouch. That wasn't the best idea.

Two of the kids jumped over him, then the dog went sailing by. With a swift kick to the groin.

His groin.

"Ooooph!" Sean curled into a ball, grabbed himself, and tried to breathe through the pain. Oh, sure. The *ram* he managed to avoid but this little bit of fluff . . .

God, if his brothers saw him now . . . Laid low by a baby goat and a stuffed animal brought to life. It'd be funny if it'd happened to anyone but him. He'd love to see Bry in this position.

The dog came back, its little eyebrows quirking up as it cocked its head.

"Oh sure. *Now* you show up. All I had to do was get kneed in the nuts for you to listen? Great, dog. What's your name anyway?"

The thing wagged its stubby tail as if this were the first time he'd seen anyone all day and licked Sean on the nose, then sat down and looked at him expectantly. Hopefully. Trustingly.

Ah, the loyalty and love of an animal, just like Livvy had said. Given the lack of it in her life, he could see why she had so many.

Hell. He didn't need this. He didn't want to understand her. To feel bad for her. To want to make it all go away for her.

Millions of dollars, Manley. This place could be your gold mine. Isn't that what you want?

Yes. It was.

Except now he was out of commission, kneed in the nuts by a *poodle*. Not the ram, or Rhett or even Ringo, but a *poodle*. His brothers were definitely *not* going to find out about this.

A flash of pain shot through him. Sonofabitch. He needed an ice pack.

And he'd get one—as soon as he could walk again. And breathe. Breathing was a good idea.

He inhaled, sucking every ounce of oxygen he could into his lungs, focusing inward, ignoring the pain.

He did it again, and this time, the pain began to dissipate. Thank God.

He took one more deep breath and opened his eyes.

To see an eagle.

Right there. In front of him. Well, about fifteen feet above him, but still, it was an eagle. An emblem of sorts. On a plaque. Like the presidential seal.

Under the banner of an eagle.

Thank God *something* had finally gone his way.

The dog licked his nose again. Okay, make that *two* things.

Sean raised himself onto his elbows and ruffled the dog's ears over. "Did you plan this?" He was rewarded with another lick.

A couple more minutes—and several goose nips to the shoulder—later, Sean had recovered enough to climb the ladder to what would normally be the hayloft, but was, here, used for storing boxes. *More* boxes. Lots of boxes. All over the place. He wouldn't relish going through those, but God, the lawyers, and fate willing, he'd like to get the chance to.

Just off the edge of the loft, the eagle was mounted on a wooden plaque cut in the same shape. And there, between the two layers, was another clue. No note from Merriweather this time, but the clue said it all.

> *Sir Frederick's strategy, a puzzle for the enemy,*
> *Ensured our family's legacy.*
> *His reward, commemorated in lands and silver*
>   *plate*
> *Had been hard-earned, not left to Fate.*
> *So with this font of knowledge, Olivia, I request*
> *That you find six more clues to claim what I*
>   *bequest.*

Below him, the poodle—whose name he still couldn't remember—was running circles around a goat who'd decided it'd had enough and had plopped onto the floor and started bleating. Her mama came trotting out from the chicken area

and bleated back. Which got an answering call from the rest
of her kids and a headbutt by the ram into the post supporting
the center of the loft.

Sean's tablet went sailing out of his hands and shattered
on the concrete floor below on impact.

Great.

Sean exhaled and leaned against the wall that spanned the
front of the barn, looking out through the bank of windows
along the back until the post stopped shaking.

Hell of a view. Or it would be if he could see. Sean turned
off the light switch they'd conveniently included up here.

The animals quieted down, which was a win as far as he
was concerned, but an even bigger win was what was out
there.

Moonlight shone across the vast expanse of Martinson
lands. *Lands*. One of the words in the clue.

Another one was *puzzle*. Like the answer to this one that
was right out there.

The maze.

Mazes were puzzles. And *font* was another word for *fountain*. There was a fountain in the middle of the maze. He
knew because he'd had someone give him an estimate to up
the power on the plumbing so the waterfall would show above
the hedgerow.

He'd learned that it'd be less costly to cut the hedges down
enough for the current plume height, and Sean was still debat-
ing which avenue he'd go when the time came, because that
was years' worth of growth on those hedges.

He had to hand it to Merriweather; this clue was pretty
clever. Which meant her mind was working right up until the
end and she'd known exactly what she was doing.

Sean got a sick feeling in his stomach. She'd led him on.
Promised him things she'd had no intention of delivering. Or
maybe she wanted to see which one of them wanted the estate
more and was willing to do whatever it took to get it.

Yes, Merriweather would appreciate that sort of
reasoning.

Sean climbed down the ladder, cleaned up the broken tablet, and whistled for the poodle. "Come on, dog. Time to be

getting home. You can see your"—he checked under the goat—"girlfriend tomorrow."

While he was checking out the maze.

His cell phone rang. Sean didn't recognize the number, but with all the calls he had out to potential investors, he wasn't about to ignore it. "Hello?"

"Sean? It's Livvy."

Silly that his heart thudded. "Hi. Is everything okay? How'd you get my number?"

"Your sister. I called the office and asked to speak to you."

Mac was way too obvious. She'd never give out employees' phone numbers if they were real employees. He knew exactly why she'd given Livvy his. "Is everything all right?"

"That's what I wanted to ask you. I wanted to see how you were making out."

He knew what she'd said, realized that she'd added a *how* in there, but all Sean heard was *making out* in Livvy's voice and he was hard in an instant. Seriously, Livvy needed to brand her unique whatever-it-was that turned him into an eighteen-year-old and sell it. She'd make a killing and wouldn't need this place, thereby solving everyone's problem.

". . . because Davy doesn't like when I leave."

Davy. That was the poodle's name.

"And Reggie could use a kind word or two. I know he doesn't understand it, but if you use a pleasant tone and maybe give him a few extra dog biscuits, he should be good for the night."

"One step ahead of you." Sean looked into the pig's stall. All of the biscuits were gone and there were crumbs sprinkled on the bedding around him as he snored away contentedly.

"Oh. Well that's good. And what about the geese?"

Sean made a quick count. He thought there were only three of them. "They're, uh, fine." Except for the one who was limping . . .

"Oh. Okay."

"How are *you*, Livvy?" There was something in her voice that made him ask. Her *oh*s were a little surprised, her questions tentative, and her tone way too soft. "Are *you* doing okay? The animals are fine." He crossed his fingers, both to ward off the lie and praying it was true.

Her laugh was self-conscious. "I know, it's just . . . Well, it's just that they don't know you. You're a stranger to them and this is the first time I've ever left them with someone they don't know."

"They know me. Scarlet even let me pet her. *Rhett* even let me pet her." Well almost. "Everyone's watered, fed, and bedded down for the night. They'll still be here when you get back."

"Oh."

Yeah, *oh*. *Oh* that they were on opposing sides and she had no idea. *Oh* that he did. *Oh* that it was eating a hole in his gut.

And while he was at it, he might as well own up to the *oh* that she hadn't called to talk to him about what was going on with them, or the *oh* that he'd *wanted* her to have called to talk to him about what was going on with them.

And then there was the *oh* that no matter how much he tried, he just couldn't get her out of his mind.

Chapter Twenty-three

❦

So have you given any thought to our conversation last night?" Sher tapped Livvy's shoulder in the booth at the market the next morning during a break between customers.

"Yes." It was *all* she'd been thinking about. He and Kerry had tried to convince her during the drive here that she shouldn't sell the estate. They'd argued every angle: The kitchen was perfect for her, the barn and the lawn were perfect for the animals, the house could be turned into a fancy B&B—which they'd graciously offered to move into and run for her so she could have the last laugh on her grandmother.

Which would be fine if she wanted a last laugh. She didn't. She just wanted what was due to her, and then she'd be outta there.

"Livs?"

"I don't want it, Sher. It's not my home. It's not even *a* home. Home is a leaky roof. Home is a barn three stalls too small and having Reggie sleep in the living room. Home is having you guys next door, and all the others. Richard and Marci and everyone. You're all my family. *You're* my home. Why should I leave?"

"Sweetie, you know we want what's best for you, but it *is*

a pretty impressive place. There's so much you could do there."

"I can do those same things elsewhere with the money the sale will bring. Don't, Sher." She put a hand on his lips when he took a deep breath, a sure sign he was about to go off on one of his lectures, er, suggestions. "I know you mean well, but if I have to live in that house day after day, being reminded of how unworthy I am to carry the Martinson name, I'll be miserable."

"Don't let that woman's idiocy ruin this for you. She owes you this place. She owes you a hell of a lot more, but the estate is a good start. It's not your fault that the woman wasn't smart enough to see the real treasure right under her nose, all gift wrapped in the most gorgeous package any grandmother could ever *hope* to receive. Get mad at that. That she threw away what you two could have had. But never, and I mean, *never* consider yourself unworthy. She was the unworthy one. To have treated you like she did . . ." Sher shook his head and blinked a couple of times. "It's disgraceful and she ought to be ashamed."

She hugged him. "Thank you for saying that. I needed to hear it."

"That's why you deserve the house, Livs. Take it. Do with it what you want. You don't like the décor? Change it. You want to make the salon an indoor/outdoor barn? Your prerogative. You want to change all the bedspreads to camouflage? Be my guest."

That got a giggle out of her. Sher always could. "I think I'll pass on the camo."

"Point being, it's up to you. Just make sure you're giving up the estate for the right reasons, *not* to spite her. Spite never solved anything. It feels good while you're doing it, but you have to live with the consequences."

She rearranged the scones, putting the chocolate ones closer to the front of the table. Kids typically liked those the best, and if she could tempt them to stop, the parents usually ended up becoming repeat customers. Bait and hook; she'd always let her food speak for her instead of allocating a portion of her meager budget for advertising. In this business, word of mouth was the best way to pull in new customers. Which would be the only reason she'd even considered what

Sher and Kerry had said last night. It *had* been amazing working in that kitchen.

Maybe because Sean was with you?

"And what about hunky maid guy?"

"Huh?"

"You know, Tall, Dark, and Delicious. You keep the place and you'd have the added bonus of having him around. After what Kerry and I almost walked in on, you can't say that would be a bad thing."

The blush blazed up from her toes, covering every part of her. *Heating* every part of her. "It wasn't what you think."

"Sweetie, I may not play for the same team he does, but I know what I saw. The man wants you."

Except he'd *stopped*.

She shouldn't have called him last night. She hadn't really been worried about the animals. It was just that she'd . . . What? Missed him? Had been thinking about him? Wanted him?

Yes to all three. Which was why she shouldn't have called him. Shouldn't have let him in. She knew better than that. Knew better than to get her hopes up. They always got dashed.

"And, BTW, I want deets. With what Orwell was spouting, I'm guessing they're juicy."

"There's nothing to tell, Sher." Damn talking bird. Whenever she'd dated anyone before, she'd immediately gone to Sher and Kerry's afterward to dissect the date. Discuss the pros and cons of a guy, if the relationship was worth pursuing, what they'd done, had she had fun, that sort of thing. Girlfriend chat. But this time . . . *this* time, she didn't *want* to dissect it. She didn't *want* to put this relationship through Sher's wringer.

What relationship?

She exhaled and looked around for a customer. *Any* customer. Just one. One would be fine.

Nope. Nothing. Nada. Zilch.

Figured.

"No one's going to ride in on his white horse and save you from me, Livs, so spill."

She exhaled again. "Fine." She brushed her hair back. "Yes, something was going on when you walked in. I mean, can you blame me? Sean's hot. Even in a maid outfit."

"*Especially* in a maid outfit." Sher fanned himself.

"Aren't you married?"

"I'm not dead. And neither are you, thank God. So, what's the plan?"

"Plan?"

"Yes, sweetie. To reel this guy in. You don't think it happens by itself, do you? You want him, you have to go after him."

"Why doesn't he have to go after me?"

"Livs, please. It's not like that anymore. We have to make them want us. Make them think they can't live without us. Pique their interest enough that they keep coming back."

"Sounds like an awful lot of work."

Sher shrugged. "But worth it. Look who I ended up with."

They both watched Kerry heft another container of wine bottles onto the table, muscles flexing nicely beneath his golf shirt. Kerry worked out religiously and it showed.

"You're a lucky man, Sher."

"And I know it. So is Sean if he lands you. Are you going to let him?"

"Let him? I've practically thrown myself at him, but he wanted to stop."

She hadn't meant to mention that. Let her personal shame remain hers. But this was Sher and he cared about her. And frankly, she was just a little annoyed that Sean *had* stopped.

"Wait. What?"

"Exactly. There we were in the kitchen, in the heat of the moment, and he said we should stop."

"As in cold turkey? He pulled back and refused to go on?"

She waggled her hand. "Not quite refused, but he kept saying it wasn't a good idea."

"*Was* it a good idea?"

She felt her stupid blush flare across her face. "I thought so."

Sher flicked the end of her nose and laughed. "Then I'm going to go with a *yes* to that question. Especially if he said it wasn't a good one but didn't stop completely."

She flushed again, remembering. "Well, he slowed things down. Just stopped, um, kissing me in that way that, you know . . ."

"Yeah, I know."

They both sighed and looked at Kerry again. He must have

felt their stares because he looked up and gave them a quick wave and a smile.

She knew that smile. Knew what was behind it as he looked at Sher.

Livvy sighed yet again. What they'd found together was beautiful. Special. She wanted that. That feeling and that secret look and that knowledge that they had someone in their corner. That no matter how bad it got, no matter what Life threw at them, they had each other.

"Okay then." Sher cleared his throat and turned back to her. "So the question is, how do you get Sean to *start again*?"

"That *is* the question." The other one was whether she was willing to risk her ego again, but Sher couldn't answer that one for her. Only she could, and right now, she wasn't so sure of her answer. She ought to just focus on finding the clues and put this idea on the shelf.

Kinda hard to do when you're living in the same house.

"It shouldn't be that hard." Sher raised an eyebrow. "Scratch that. We want it hard."

She had to laugh.

"Good. There's the smile you should always be wearing." He tapped the tip of her nose. "Anyhow, as I was saying, I saw how he looked at you. If he's not married, gay, or carrying something communicable, there's no reason for him to stop. Any of those things happening?"

She shook her head. "Not that I know of."

"Great. So what you need to do is get him all alone, preferably someplace more romantic than a kitchen—oh my God. Olivia Marie Carrolla, do *not* tell me you got funky on the kitchen counter."

Livvy tucked her hair behind her ears and looked around again for another customer. "Okay, I won't."

"Oh my God, girl, are you nuts? Those countertops are *hard*. And not in a good way. That's not where you want your first time with someone to be. A kitchen is the place for quick, raunchy sex with your significant other, wearing only an apron and—"

Thankfully, *he* stopped. Livvy didn't want to know that much about her neighbors.

"Uh, yes. Well." This time, Sher was the one looking around for a client. "What I mean is, you don't want your first time with him to be a quickie on the counter. You want seclusion, some romance, somewhere where you can't be interrupted by people showing up at your back door. And for God's sake, keep Orwell away. I do *not* need a play-by-play of your lovemaking session."

If there *was* a lovemaking session, she'd be sure to do that.

"So let's figure this out. What's the best place in that house and how can you lure him there?"

"I'm not luring anyone. If he wants me, he's going to have to let me know. I'm done throwing myself out there for people to trample all over. I'm worth more than that, and if Sean doesn't see that, then it's his loss. I can't keep putting myself out there only to have my hopes and feelings dashed. You and Kerry are the only two important people in my life who haven't rejected me. Besides, it's not as if it's going to lead to anything. Two weeks and I'm gone."

Sher wrapped his arms around her. "Ah, sweetie, come here. I know it's hard. I do. But he's obviously got issues with wanting you if he stopped. But he *is* into you. You just need to give him the opportunity to finish what you started. It's not as if you live so far away; things could happen. But you have to be open to any possibility that presents itself. If it's meant to be, it'll be." He kissed her on the temple. "Just don't be afraid to take a chance, and don't be so afraid of the future that you forget to live in the present."

Chapter Twenty-four

꧁⋙❀⋘꧂

SEAN looked at his cell phone every fifteen seconds on his drive back from Mac's. A whole day, wasted. Well, not wasted. Mac got her stuff moved and it was good to see Jared, Gran's friend Mildred's grandson, but, man, the tension between those two had made the day seem longer than it actually had been. He hoped to hell they could resolve whatever the issue was between them, but then, they'd always been oil and water together. It was probably just their normal inter-action and he was projecting *his* frustration onto their dynamic and what the hell did he care anyway? The day was over and Mac's love life was her business.

Hell, he didn't even want to think about his little sister *having* a love life. Especially not if it included Jared Nolan. The guy was almost as big a player on the women scene as Bry.

Sean tapped the signal key on his dashboard that opened the estate's wrought iron gates. He'd been planning to research key manufacturers this evening to find ones that could incor-porate gate access into hotel keys for his guests—if he had guests—but the maze was the more important item on his to-do list.

He glanced at the low-hanging sun. One, maybe two hours at best before searching the maze would be pointless. He drove the truck a little faster to the parking area by the kitchen entrance.

The Howl-o-lujah Chorus greeted him the minute he turned off the engine.

Damn. He had to deal with the animals before he could check out the maze. He didn't need a mess to clean up when he got back.

He filled the dinner bowls while the dogs took care of business in the yard, then had to corral them into the house to run after Davy, who'd taken off for the barn again. "Geez, dude, show some restraint," he muttered as he scooped the little dog up. "She'll still be there when we get back."

Words to live by.

Sean shook his head as he entered the barn. After another round of chores and mucking out—that had really lost its appeal—he turned around to find *Davy* was the one running along the wall above the goats' stall this time.

"How the hell did you get up there?" Sean unlatched the door to get the little bugger.

The dog yipped at him and danced across the two-inch wide rail as if he were a cat.

"Get back here."

Of course the animal wouldn't listen.

Sean went into the goat pen. The kids were hopping onto their parents' backs as a stepping stone to the top of the wall.

The first one made it up before Sean could get to it. He caught the second one mid-jump, and thwarted the third from making it onto the ram's back. For the first time since they'd met, the ram didn't try to prod him in the nuts.

The fourth one made it onto the rail and ran after its sibling who was tap-dancing behind the dog along the top of the next pen, all of them headed straight toward Rhett.

The alpaca looked like he was working up a good wad to spit at them, his eyes trained on every movement they made.

"Davy, come!"

The dog didn't even make the effort to look back as he kept scampering toward Rhett.

Sean left the goat pen, dropping a handful of carrots into

their feed bowl to keep the remaining kids occupied, then ran to Reggie's stall where Davy and his followers now were.

Rhett was working the wad faster.

"Damn animals. All I want to do is check out the maze, but instead I'm playing tag with a bunch of four-legged kids who ought to be in bed for the night." Sean unlatched the door. "This is the last time I bring you with me, mutt," he muttered just as Rhett let loose with his ammo.

It hit the poodle broadside, sending the thing toppling over the edge and headed straight to where Reggie was resting peacefully.

"Sonofabitch!" Sean forgot about Rhett's stall and lunged through Reggie's door to catch Davy so he wouldn't wake the sleeping pig. While catching Davy, he tripped on a dog biscuit, twisted around, and landed flat on his back on top of Reggie—who merely grunted and rolled over in his sleep, depositing Sean and the dog onto the floor.

"Sean? What are you doing?"

He looked out through the open stall door to see Livvy standing in the barn doorway, backlit by the moonlight that seemed to have sprung up as if someone had lowered a backdrop for the express purpose of driving him insane.

The gypsy skirt was gone. In its place was a pair of cut-off jean shorts with ragged hems, threads trailing along her thighs.

She had great thighs.

Great knees, too. And her calves . . . He wanted to run his tongue along her calves.

"Catching your dog before he breaks a leg." His voice was tight because his damn shorts suddenly were. And these were the baggy nylon kind.

Then a goat leapt onto his lap.

"Ooooph!" he wheezed, rolling onto his side to avoid taking a hoof to the balls.

"Oh, no!"

Livvy took the dog from him, then ran her hand over his side. "Are you okay?"

He would be if she kept doing that.

"Fine," was all he managed to get out. Part of him wanted to say *no* so she'd keep doing what she was doing, and the other part . . . The other part wanted to grab her, pull her beneath him, and make them both forget about dogs and alpacas and goats and inheritances and clues and all the other baggage for the next few hours right here on the barn floor.

Classy, Manley. Way to show a woman a good time.

He sucked in a breath and sat up. "I'm . . . good." In a breathing-is-highly-overrated sort of way.

Damn goat.

Davy yipped as he leapt from her arms, then stood on his hind legs to plant a slobbery kiss on Sean's shoulder.

"Aw, he likes you." Livvy petted the dog.

Sean wished she'd pet him— "What are you doing here? Don't you have your market thing?"

"We sold out, so we decided to come home early. Saves on hotel fees. Plus, I thought you might need a break."

He did. From her. "You mean from all this? Are you kidding? I'm on top of the world when mucking out alpaca poo."

She smiled and it was as if the sun came out to light up the barn.

Good God. He must have hit his head really hard when he fell.

"I really appreciate it, you know," she said.

"It's no trouble." *Liar.*

"I promise I won't leave you alone again."

That's what he was afraid of. "Like I said, no problem."

She tucked some hair behind her ears. "So . . . did you feed them?"

"Of course."

She nibbled her bottom lip. "Um—"

"Why do you do that?" If he had to watch her tuck her hair back one more time, he might just say the hell with all his good intentions and do what he wanted to do right here and right now.

Moonlight was a powerful thing. Of course, Livvy herself was pretty powerful, too. He could only imagine what could happen if she were actually aware of the power she could wield over him.

"Why do I do what?" she asked, nibbling some more.

"That. The lip thing." *That sexy-as-hell lip thing that turns me on to the point where I'm actually shoveling alpaca shit without complaining so could you cut it out, please,* he wanted to add, but didn't.

There was a reason he didn't add it—and he knew what it was, but when his tongue darted out to lick her lips again, the reason disintegrated.

"I don't know. Habit, I guess." She shifted off her knees, plunking her cute little backside on the floor next to him.

Stay back! his common sense was screaming. His libido, on the other hand, was going full out with, *This way, sweetheart.*

He was losing his mind. "Livvy, there's no need for you to be here. I told you I'd take care of the animals and I am. I did."

"I know. I trust you. It's just that . . . sometimes I need to be around them. There's something very soothing, very natural about being with animals." She ran a hand down Davy's back. "Calming."

Funny, he felt like an animal around her and *calm* was not the word he'd use to describe himself.

"So you said you were going to head out to the maze?"

Another reason not to be calm. She must have overheard him talking to the animals. Dr. Doolittle he was not. "I realized I hadn't been in it yet and I thought it'd be cool to check it out in the moonlight."

Jesus, that was lame.

Livvy bought it, though, nibbling her lip some more. "Seriously? Have you never watched a scary movie? Everyone knows you don't go into abandoned houses or hotels or hedgerow mazes during a full moon. Or a snowstorm. Especially alone."

"I brought my flea and tick and vampire collars for the occasion," he said, hoping some humor would diffuse the utter awareness he had of her bare thigh next to his.

"Funny." She wasn't laughing, and if she nibbled her lip any harder, they'd end up plump and puffy, and the only reason that should happen was if he kissed them.

Which he shouldn't do. Just like he shouldn't do what he was about to do but was going to do anyway. "You're right. No one should go into the maze alone." He sat up and held out his hand. "So come with me." Hell, he'd put the clue back in the sugar bowl so it was only a matter of time before she figured this out anyway.

Livvy looked at it. But she didn't take it.

No, she went with yet *more* lip-nibbling.

"What do you have against the maze, Livvy?"

"Nothing."

Her *nothing* sounded like *something*. "You didn't see *The Shining*, by any chance, did you?"

"Worst movie ever."

"Are you kidding? It's a classic." Since she wasn't taking his hand, he took hers. She didn't pull away. "Come on. It's just a movie and I'll be with you. What do you say?"

She didn't say anything; she just nibbled her lip some more.

God help him. She could get him to shovel alpaca poo forever if she kept that up.

"I got lost in there." She nibbled some more, looking way too sexy in the moonlight that whispered over her curls, catching the highlights in them like shooting stars, her amber eyes twinkling, and for once, Sean didn't mind spouting poetry. Livvy *was* poetry. All beauty and goodness and light, and he was in so much trouble.

"But you won't this time, Livvy. I promise." He, on the other hand, he'd already lost it. "Because I'll be with you."

*T*HAT'S *half the problem.*

Livvy fought those words back as she let Sean lead her to the maze, Sher's words in her head. *Don't be so afraid of the future that you forget to live in the present.*

She *was* afraid. Afraid of losing herself in him. Of putting hopes and dreams and plans into what was between them and losing. Again.

But if she didn't try, she'd definitely lose. And seeing him with her animals tonight, knowing how readily he'd volunteered to help her so she could go to the market, how he was helping her with the treasure hunt, how sweet and gentle and caring and supportive he was being now . . . Sean was here for her and that alone would be appealing enough. Toss in how he made her feel, how he was, how he kissed, how he wanted her, and, well, if she ever wanted a future with anyone, she'd have to take a chance sometime. Sean was worth that chance.

They stopped at the entrance to the maze. Livvy pulled in a ragged breath.

"It'll be okay, Livvy." He cupped her cheek. "I'm here."

He was and that gave her the courage to try one more time—and she didn't mean about the maze.

She slid her hand around the back of his neck, winding her fingers into waves that were a little too long—just the way she liked them—and pulled him into a kiss.

Fireworks exploded behind her eyelids and a symphony struck up the loudest, most downbeat-laded melody, kettle drums thrumming her heartbeat, and she was *all about* living in the present.

Sean made one half-hearted—if that—attempt to pull away, and then he kissed her back. Hell, he didn't just kiss her, he consumed her. He wrapped his strong arms around her, pressing her into him so that there wasn't one inch she didn't feel, one part of him she wasn't aware of, from his lips to his breath hot against her cheek, to the way the stubble rasped along her jaw, the sweet sweep of his tongue against hers, the taste, the scent, the utter *all* of him as he took everything she gave into the kiss and then some.

Only to give back so much more.

She tightened her arms, wanting, *needing*, him to want her like she wanted him. She ran her other hand over his back, feeling the muscles there clench at her touch and she smiled against his lips. Let him stop *now*.

But then he did.

It was slow, but he slid his hand from her head, nipping at her lips instead of the full-on possession of a few seconds ago.

She moaned, snuggling into him. He didn't get to stop. Not now. Not when she didn't want him to.

He captured her face in his hands, drawing out this kiss, tasting her lips so effectively, but so not enough.

"Sean," she whispered, a tiny bit of pleading in the word, but definitely more longing.

"Look where we are, Livvy."

They could be on the moon for all she cared. Matter of fact, she felt as if she was over it.

"Go on. Open your eyes and look."

She didn't want to open her eyes. Opening her eyes would bring the present back. Would bring reality back. For a few moments there, they'd been in the realm of fantasy. The realm of *what if*. She didn't have to think about what her grandmother wanted her to do; she didn't have to remember that no one had ever held her like this, she didn't have to think about how alone she'd been until she'd met Sean, and she didn't have to worry about how long it would last because it'd still been going on.

"Livvy." He kissed the tip of her nose. "Look what you did."

What she did? Her eyes flew open.

They were inside the maze. Just a few feet, but the symbolism was huge.

"See? I told you you could do it."

"So you only let me kiss you so I'd go into the maze?" She was torn between finding it sweet and being disappointed as hell.

"I—" He exhaled and raked a hand through his hair. "No. Of course not. I wanted to kiss you."

"Did you? Really? Because I seem to remember you wanting to stop the last time we were in this position. Something about it not being a good idea."

"It's not, Livvy. It's really not." The look on his face was pained.

Well so was her ego. And maybe just the teensiest bit, her heart. "Why?"

"Because . . . I'm scared of how much I want you."

As far as explanations went, that one was a doozy. How much he wanted her? The man was as strong and honorable as an ox if he was able to put the brakes on if he wanted her even half as much as she wanted him.

"Sher said something to me this weekend that I think I should share."

"What?"

She traced her fingertips over his cheek. "That I shouldn't be so afraid of what the future holds that I don't live in the present." She stepped closer to him. "We're here now, Sean. Right here. Together. I don't want to miss out on what's between us because we're scared of where it could lead or not lead. We'll never find out if we don't take that chance. I'm willing to. Are you?"

Chapter Twenty-five

SHE was going to kill him.

He was trying to do the right thing. The noble thing. The honorable thing, but she was leading him down the path to temptation and, God help him, Sean didn't think he was strong enough to resist, because that same God knew he didn't want to.

"Livvy, I—"

She put her fingertips to his lips. "Do you want me, Sean?"

So much it took his breath away. "You know I do."

"Then let's have tonight. Whatever tomorrow brings or next week or next month . . . we'll always have tonight."

Yep, killing him.

And he went willingly.

He scooped her up in his arms. She was such a tiny thing. A tiny little thing that packed a wallop stronger than any storm, and he kissed her again, willingly going into the maelstrom.

He walked along the path, turning the corner at the end without breaking the kiss, loving the feel of her in his arms.

"I hope you know where we're going," she muttered between kisses.

So did he.

He came to a fork in the path. He'd been in here before and tried to remember which one had taken him to where he wanted to go.

He headed to the right, his memory shorting out as her tongue drove him crazy, and figured instinct was working well for him; he'd let it lead where it may.

He broke off the kiss when he heard the gurgling of the fountain.

Livvy groaned. "No, Sean. You can't stop again."

"I have no intention of stopping." He cupped her cheek so he could look into her eyes. "Look where we are."

She nibbled her lip—puffy from him this time—and looked around. The center of the maze was a large courtyard with a stone fountain and statue in the center, benches and topiaries laid out around it like an English garden, the moonlight blanketing it all in wispy, glistening silence.

"Oh, it's so beautiful."

"Not half as beautiful as you."

Her cheeks flamed then and Sean was lost. The hell with the property, the clues, investors and balance sheets, what was best for her and what was best for him . . . Nothing mattered in this moment but Livvy and the way she was looking at him. The way she wanted him. The way he wanted her. *That* was what was best for both of them.

Sean sank onto one of the benches, wrapped his arms around her, and let the future take care of itself.

KISSING Sean was an experience all of its own. Livvy sat up on his lap, wound her arms around his neck, and dove in. He wasn't stopping this time; she could feel it. Whatever reason had held him back was, if not gone, at least put aside. She hoped it was something that wouldn't make things hard between them later, but given what *was* hard between them right now, she was willing to worry about the future in the, well, *future*.

"Are you sure, Livvy?" Sean growled against her lips, the look in his eyes taking her breath away as much as his kiss was. "Because if we go on any longer, I'm not going to be able to stop." He ran his tongue over her bottom lip and she'd never been surer of anything in her life. "I won't *want* to stop." Then he licked her upper lip. "I *don't* want to stop." He kissed her. Quick and hard and wonderful. "I want you." This kiss was sweet and delicious and skin-shiveringly good. "Here." And another. "Now."

She turned in his arms and slid a leg between them so that she was straddling him on the bench. There would be *no* doubt exactly how much she did want him.

There certainly wasn't any question about what *he* wanted. His erection strained against the silky fabric of his shorts, leaving nothing and everything to her imagination.

She moved against him.

Sean's hands flew to her hips and he wrenched his mouth from where it'd been doing delicious things to her neck. "Hold still. It's too much all at once. I can't take it."

"Ah, you say the sweetest things, Sean."

"If you think that's sweet, you're going to find what I say next downright decadent."

"Oh? What's that?"

He skimmed a hand over her hair, then along her shoulder and down her arm, which wasn't *exactly* where she wanted him to touch her. About two inches to the right would be perfect. Perfectly decadent.

"That you better stop moving like this if you don't want me to toss you onto the grass and have my wicked way with you."

She moved against him.

And moved again.

"Ah, God, Livvy, don't." His lips twitched as his smile morphed into a grimace, but Livvy wasn't buying it. A certain part of him said he was as into the moment as she was, so she was taking his *don't* as *don't stop,* because it'd been far too long for her and Sean was far too potent, and if he had an issue with that, well, he could just make love to her until they both got it out of their systems.

Hmmm, how could she ensure that he *did* have an issue?

Shoving the bench slats with her heels, Livvy backed herself up to the very edge of his knees. He wanted wicked? She could do wicked . . .

He tugged her hips. "Hey, where are you going?"

She crossed her arms and pulled her camisole off, then shook her head to tumble her curls down her back, wanting his hands in it—and on her.

She didn't have long to wait.

"Oh my God." The words came out in a rush as his breath *whooshed* out of him. "You have the most gorgeous hair." He brought a fistful of it to his face and brushed it across his lips before trailing it along her nose and over her own lips. Then lower, along her throat, down to her collarbone, then feathering it down the center of her chest.

Too.

Damn.

Slowly.

She arched her back, her breasts aching for his touch. "Please, Sean."

He sucked in a breath every bit as harsh as the ache she was feeling. "God, Livvy, do you know what you're doing to me?" He dropped her hair and instead ran his palm from the base of her throat down between her breasts, his fingertips spanning the distance, teasing her with how close they came to her tight nipples.

So she teased him right back. "Yes, I think I do." She drew *her* palm down *his* chest, smiling when *his* breath caught as *her* fingertips brushed his erection. "So what do you think? Do I know what I'm doing?"

"Jesus, woman," he said on a long exhale. Then he slid his hands under her butt and pulled her back into him. "Last chance," he whispered against her lips.

"Not taking it," she said, nipping his bottom lip.

He turned the tables on her, sucking *her* bottom lip between his teeth and sliding off the bench onto the soft grass in front of it.

"You are so utterly gorgeous, Livvy." Sean, kneeling over her on all fours, leaned down to kiss her. Their lips were the only point of contact, but the power in that small point was enough to drive her wild.

She lay on the ground below him, shivering with desire, her breasts aching to be pressed against him. To be touched by him. "Stop teasing and kiss me, Sean."

"I just did."

"I mean *really* kiss me." She fisted his shirt and pulled.

He didn't budge. "Impatient, are we?"

"*We*, apparently, are not. *I*, on the other hand, am. So are you going to get down here and get the job done or are we going to spend our night verbally sparring instead?"

"Not the whole night." He kissed her. Short and sweet and wonderful. But not what she wanted. "There. Satisfied?"

"Seriously?" She raised her eyebrows.

"What? You want more?" Sean leaned in, his groin brushing hers, making her forget what they were talking about.

She didn't, however, forget that his shirt was in her hands. She ripped it.

It seemed like the easiest way to get it off him.

Sean looked down at his chest, then into her eyes, and he smiled. "Like that, is it?"

She nibbled her bottom lip. He liked when she did that. "I don't know what you're talking about."

"Uh huh." Sean adjusted his weight and lifted an arm from beside her to work it out of the sleeve.

"Don't tell me you can do one-arm push-ups." Because she found that a complete turn-on. She had no idea why, but seeing a guy able to do that did it for her.

The look Sean sent her did it for her, too. "I can if I'm motivated."

She nibbled her lip. "Is that enough motivation?"

He brushed her nose with his. "Not quite."

"What about this?" She ran both hands down his chest, then around to his backside and squeezed. He had an amazing backside.

"You're getting warmer."

She certainly was.

"How about this?" She raised her head and flicked his nipple with her tongue.

"Holy shit." His elbows wobbled and he caught himself at the last second before he fell onto her. "Damn, woman, that's not fair."

"We're playing fair?" She licked the other one. "How is it fair that you're all the way up there and I'm all the way down here?"

"Oh, is that a problem?" He adjusted his stance so that his

legs were directly over hers in a classic push-up pose, holding himself there effortlessly and making no move whatsoever to come closer.

So she pressed down on his butt.

Sean didn't fight her on this. He lowered himself onto her, still keeping the bulk of his weight off her, but teasing her with the most delicious points of contact ever. He swayed back and forth slightly, his chest sending her nipples on high alert, and she wished to high heaven that'd he'd follow her lead and do some clothes-ripping of his own. She needed to feel him against her.

She pressed on his butt some more.

Then she grabbed it.

That did the trick. He *finally* lay on her and it was utter heaven.

He angled his head to the other side, moving his weight to his elbows, and cradled her head in his palms as he deepened the kiss.

She wrapped her arms around the small of his back. God, he felt so good pressed against her. All hard strength and coiled desire. He *did* desire her; of that there was no doubt.

And now she had none about what they were doing. About how far she wanted it to go. Sher was right; there was no sense living in the future if she never got there. One day the future would be the present and this was as good a time as any to realize it.

She slipped her hands beneath his waistband. "I want you, Sean."

He sucked in a breath—and her tongue—and his arms gave out.

He recovered quickly—too quickly—and lifted himself off her. But, thank God, nowhere near as far from her as he had been before. "Jesus, Livvy. Do you know what you're saying?"

"I do. Absolutely." And for the first time in her life, she was acting on it without thinking it through to the nth degree of ramifications. They were two consenting adults who had no other agenda besides the one fate had lobbed at them, and she was more than willing to knock it out of the park.

"No," she breathed when he rolled off her, breaking the kiss. "Sean, you—"

"Shhh." He smoothed her hair from her cheek. "I'm too heavy for you." He rolled onto his back and in a move that almost defied gravity, he pulled her on top of him.

"This is how it should be. This is where you should be." He bunched her hair into a ponytail with one hand and ran the other down her back.

She shivered.

"Like that?"

She nodded.

"How about this?"

He squeezed her butt.

She licked her lips.

"Ah, hell, Livvy. I have no defense against that." He pulled her down and kissed her again.

And then she kissed him. Being on top gave her a certain freedom she didn't have when he was over her. Now, she could move a bit to the right and press her thigh against his erection.

He groaned.

She smiled.

"You're going to kill me."

"I certainly hope not." She nipped his jaw. "That'd kind of ruin the night."

"You think?" he growled when she nibbled her way down his throat, the just-right amount of chest hair tickling her chin as she kissed her way from his collarbone to his navel. And maybe lower if the spirit so moved her.

Right now, it was moving her to run her tongue over his nipple. She wanted to hear him gasp in that same breathless sense-of-awe whisper she felt.

You are so in over your head.

Her conscience was right, but for once, she wasn't going to listen to it.

He let her tease him, his hands fisting in her hair, his chest—his gorgeous six-pack perfect enough to inspire fantasies—quivered beneath her fingertips.

Somehow, her shorts joined her camisole. She didn't know how and really didn't care. Now if she could just get her darn thong off.

Sean helped with that.

So she helped him and the next thing she knew, they were naked on the grass.

Naked on the grass. She never thought she'd see the day when she was naked in the moonlight, rolling around on the lawn with a god of a guy who looked as if he were the model for the one in the middle of the fountain.

Eros.

No real man could compare to a god, but Sean was pretty darn close. There wasn't an ounce of fat on him, a fact she confirmed with all ten fingers. And a set of lips. Her cheeks. And her breasts. Oh, how her breasts confirmed that, gliding over every cut line of his abs as she kissed her way down his body. She moved slightly to trace that sexy line by his hip that she was sure had been designed by those very same gods to tempt women into losing their minds, and she wanted to be first in line.

"Livvy, come here."

She didn't bother raising her head. The scent of him was calling to her. She wrapped her fingers around him.

"Jesus."

"No, *Livvy*. Let's not forget who we're with here."

Sean slid his fingers under her jaw and tilted her head. "Then why don't you get up here and remind me? Where you are right now? I'm not liable to remember *my* name in another minute or so, so you might want to take it a bit slower or this will all be over before it's even started."

She uncurled her fingers from around him one at a time. Slowly. "Can't have that now, can we?"

Then she scraped her nails gently up his length.

He moaned. "Oh, God."

"No. *Livvy*." She kissed her way back up his body, never taking her hand from him, her fingertips circling over the head ever so gently.

He speared his hand beneath her hair, cupping her face, and pulled her in for a kiss that defied description. Every perfect move, every sexy, sensual feeling, started in that kiss. It was a kiss like no other; it asked her, it cajoled her, it told her, and demanded things of her, and all she wanted to do was lose herself in it. In him.

She dragged her lips from his, gulping in oxygen in the

vain hope that her heart rate would come down out of the stratosphere so she could hear herself think, but she wasn't thinking all that much at the moment. She was feeling.

And she was feeling that they needed to move this along. She looked around for her shorts. There. About four feet to the left. Thank God he hadn't tossed them too far away.

"Where are you going?" Sean grabbed her ankle as she crawled over to her shorts.

"You'll see." She stretched out to reach them, her fingertips crab-walking the last few inches to get them. "Sean, let go. You'll be glad you did. I promise."

"I'll be glad *not* to let go." His fingers flexed against her skin.

His words warmed her heart and she allowed herself to dream for just a second what that could mean. Where it could go. But only for a second. Dreaming was a big step for her. She hadn't dreamed of anything like this for a very long time.

She hooked the belt loop with her middle finger and pulled her shorts over, then she scrambled back by Sean's side. "Here. These are what I was after."

She pulled two condoms from her back pocket.

"*You* brought condoms?" He sort of chuckled, sort of groaned.

Good, just the way she wanted him: off-kilter but enjoying the moment. "A girl has to protect herself."

The left corner of his mouth ticked back. "I'll protect you, but it's good to know we have these. I obviously wasn't expecting this to happen."

"Why not?"

"Huh?"

"Why *not*? It can't be that big of a surprise. The kitchen countertop was unfinished business. Or was I reading it wrong?"

"What? No. Yes." He exhaled and propped himself up on his elbows, the rise-and-fall of his sexy-as-all-get-out chest creating a ripple effect across his abdomen that was mesmerizing. She could watch him all day.

All night, too.

"No, you weren't reading it wrong, Livvy, but it's one thing to fantasize about, well, *that*. You. But to think it could happen and prepare for it . . . That would presume a little too much."

"But *I* presumed. I thought about it, and I presumed it, and now we're here." She held up the condoms. "So *carpe noctem* and pick a color. Red or Green?"

"What am I, a Christmas tree?"

She looked at his groin. "Well, you're at least a Douglas fir, and maybe even a mighty oak."

"I'd go with a giant redwood."

She really wished she'd mastered the art of raising one eyebrow for this. "Thinking a bit highly of ourselves, are we?"

He smiled. "If I don't, who will?"

She tapped her lips, enjoying the way his eyes flared when they focused on her finger. "What? There aren't legions of women lining up to do the honors? A guy like you, I'd think you'd have a harem at your beck and call."

She said it flippantly, but it was actually something she was worried about. Oh, sure, she knew they weren't declaring their undying love for each other and swearing monogamy 'til death did them part, but still . . . A woman did like to know she was special.

He sat up and slid his fingers up her arm until he reached her jaw. He splayed them there, his thumb beneath her chin, each one like a torch, starting a slow burn throughout her entire body.

"There's no harem, Livvy. There's not even one. Only you. You're the only woman I've been fantasizing about."

"You've *fantasized* about me?"

He tilted her chin up a tiny bit more. "Is that wrong?"

Yes.

No.

She didn't know.

He'd fantasized about her. What if she didn't live up to that fantasy? What if she let him down? Couldn't be what he wanted?

What if he never wanted to see her again?

He dropped his hand. "God, I'm sorry. I guess that does sound bad, thinking about your boss that way while living under the same roof. I promise, Livvy, it won't happen again."

"I don't want that promise."

"Huh?"

"I said, I don't want that promise. I want what you said earlier. About wanting me. About the here and the now and fantasies. You don't get to take that back."

He was the only man—the *only* man—to ever tell her he'd fantasized about her, and as a fantasizer herself, she knew just how powerful those fantasies could be and just how good. Now that she had the chance to make one of her own come true, she wasn't going to stop. And neither was he if she had anything to say about it.

She tossed the red condom onto the grass and tore open the green one with her teeth.

Sean looked at it, then at her.

Those ripples increased in tempo across his abs.

She sat back on her heels and very purposely, very determinedly, rolled the condom down. "So what did we do in your fantasy?"

SEAN gave up. He gave up trying to hold back, he gave up trying to stop what she so obviously wanted—what he wanted—and he stopped trying to figure it out. The will and the clues and the property . . . Hell, he'd sell the only property he had left if that'd fix the situation, but he'd deal with it later. Right now, there was only Livvy.

"This." He splayed his hand on the back of her neck and pulled her to him, tasting those lips with an intensity that shocked him.

She tasted amazing. She looked amazing and she *was* amazing, sitting there so proud and sure of herself, with the moonlight cascading over her amazing body, and the whole thing was just, well, amazing.

He groaned into her mouth, wanting this.

He cupped her breast, his thumb finding her nipple and he circled it. Rubbed it. Smiled against her lips when it hardened for him.

Smiled more when she groaned.

"Like that?"

She nodded, her breath catching.

"And this?" He cupped her other one. "Do you like this, Livvy?"

She nodded, nibbling her lip.

He swept her up in his arms and lowered her onto the grass, this time needing no invitation to lie on top of her. No moment of indecision, no questions. This was where they needed to be, and the rest would work itself out.

She wrapped her legs around him. "I want you, Sean."

He buried his face in the sweet curve of her neck, inhaling the scent that was all Livvy. Apples and lavender and something else. Something indefinable that reached out and wrapped around him, inviting him in.

He couldn't say no. "God, I want you, too."

"I keep telling you, it's *Livvy.*" She gasped when he nipped her shoulder, and cried out his name.

"I'll call you whatever you want just to hear you say my name like that again."

He nipped the other side and she said it again, a shot straight to his soul.

He was in a lot more trouble than he'd ever thought possible and right this minute, he couldn't give a damn.

He slid his hand down the curve of her body, over her perfect hips, and slipped it beneath her thigh. He was going to run his tongue up that thigh at some point, but right now, there wasn't any time. "I have to have you."

She lifted her leg. "Then take me."

He did. She opened for him and he slipped inside her and it was as if everything was right with the world. As if it'd been off-kilter and suddenly it was level. Even. Coherent.

Which was more than could be said for him. Especially when she looked up at him, her eyes blinking . . . Oh, no. He'd never been good with a woman's tears. "What is it, Livvy?"

She smiled, a soft smile, tinged with so much emotion that her bottom lip, the one she nibbled on so provocatively, was trembling. "This is so much better than any fantasy."

"*You're* better than any fantasy." He pulled back then, wanting—needing—to move.

"Don't go." Her amber eyes darkened as she tightened her arms—and her inner muscles—around him.

Nothing would make him leave. "I won't." He tilted his hips and sank back into her—in more ways than one.

She relaxed her hold a little and the corners of her mouth tilted up. "Do that again."

"With pleasure." And it was.

She closed her eyes and arched her back, her neck curving so enticingly that he had to taste it again.

He kissed a path from her ear to her jaw, down that sweet soft throat, feeling every beat of her heart with his lips. His own matched it.

He moved inside her, reveling in the feel of her body accepting his, of her taking him inside her and caressing him, clasping, wanting him. He quickened the pace, the night air warm against his back, the grass smooth beneath his legs, and Livvy so soft and silky and perfect beneath him.

She wrapped her legs around him, her heels digging into his ass, her nails scoring his back, and Sean couldn't go slow any longer. He had to have her. Had to drive her as crazy as she was making him. Had to give her the same pleasure he was feeling.

He kissed her again, long, drawn-out, pouring every ounce of want and need and feeling into it as he surged inside her.

"That's it, Sean. Don't stop."

As if he could.

He thrust into her and it felt so damn good he didn't ever want it to end.

He slipped a hand around her waist, then down to cup her perfect backside. He stroked her, smiling when she sucked his tongue into her mouth on a gasp.

She liked that.

He stroked her again and Livvy shifted, and it was as if the entire universe converged on that one spot where their bodies were joined. Heat and need and want and sheer unadulterated pleasure ricocheted through him, and Sean had to grab hold of her butt with both his hands and press her against him as he tried to, well, *absorb* her.

"Oh, God, Sean, yes. Like that." She grasped his back, his ass, his shoulders, her knees clenching him, and Sean couldn't hold back.

He groaned, tearing his lips from hers so he could arch

into her, the moment fraught with anticipation, and he hung there for all of about two nanoseconds before the feelings poured through him, and he surged into her over and over, the climax building inside him. And in her, as she closed her eyes and arched her back and oh, God, yes. There. Once more—no twice—and then . . . and then . . . she cried out his name, taking him over the edge with her.

He was in so much trouble.

Chapter Twenty-six

SOMETIME in the middle of the night, or maybe it was more toward morning since it was no longer dark, Livvy came awake in Sean's arms.

The only place she wanted to be.

She brushed her cheek against his, loving the raspy feel of his stubble, the steady beat of his heart, and the taste of him still on her lips, half afraid that she was loving *him*.

Wait. *Love*? Was she out of her mind? She couldn't be in love with him. She barely knew him. It'd been all of what? A week since they'd met? People didn't fall in love in a week. And they didn't do so after one night of making love. Sure, it was amazing, hot, sexy, intense love, but still *one* night?

Her mother was perfect proof that she was misinterpreting last night's emotions and what they meant. Illogical hormonal reactions weren't love; they were chemistry. Love was *emotion*. It was shared hopes and dreams. Liking each other, being friends. The sex was just an added bonus.

And what a bonus it was with Sean.

"There's a bird staring at us." Sean's arm tightened around her.

"What?"

"A bird. There." He nudged her.

She opened one eye.

A beady black one stared back at her surrounded by jeweled teal and aqua feathers.

"Oh. The peacocks."

"Peacocks?" Sean stiffened beside her.

She glanced down to see if something else had stiffened.

Darn. He'd covered himself with his hands.

"I don't think the peacock cares that we're naked, Sean."

"I don't, either. I just don't need it pecking at me."

She giggled. "Pecking at your pecker? Peacocks eat grain, not meat."

"You didn't just say that."

"Oops, I think I did."

The peacock strutted closer.

"I don't know, Livvy. That thing looks like it might want to go for my eyes."

Its yellow, pointed beak could be dangerous. Peacocks could be aggressive. She couldn't think of a worse ending to their night together than to be running around with a peacock nipping at their private parts.

Livvy sighed and sat up. The bird backed up just a smidge. Cheeky bugger. Though could she expect anything else from Merriweather's affectation?

"Shoo!" she flicked her hands.

The bird just blinked.

"Go on! Get out of here!" This time she ripped some of the grass and flung it at him.

He still didn't move.

Sean got to his feet, dropped his hold on his precious package, spread his arms, hunched his shoulders, and . . .

Squawked.

The bird ran around the base of the fountain screaming its shrill cry as if it were running for its life. Livvy had the hiccups when she finally stopped rolling on the ground in laughter. "*What* was that?"

Sean sat down beside her cross-legged, as if it were the most natural thing in the world to be sitting in the middle of an English-style maze in northeast Pennsylvania bare-ass

naked, squawking at a peacock. "I did what you're supposed
to do with threatening animals. Act bigger and more ferocious
so they fear and respect you and do what you tell them."

"Please tell me you don't apply that to human animals."

He arched an eyebrow. The look was entirely too sexy on
him for her to take offense. "You're saying you weren't an
animal last night?"

"Oh my God. I can't believe you said that." She smacked
him on that very toned, very smooth muscular shoulder.
"That's not very gentlemanly."

"You weren't into me being a gentleman last night."

Damn, she blushed. She hated that she blushed.

"I love when you blush."

Or maybe she didn't. "Why?"

He brushed his hand over her shoulder. "Because you get
this look on your face. It's almost shy, but not. It says so much
with so little. I love that you're not afraid to show your reactions. Most people behave the way they think people expect
them to, to fit in and be valued. But not you. You stand behind
your convictions. You don't go along with the crowd. Do you
know how rare that is? How rare *you* are?" He brushed her
hair off her face. "How special you are?"

Special. She'd never been special before.

She got to her knees and cupped his face. Ran her thumb
over his lips. No way was she going to be able to walk away
from Sean when her sentence was up. Somehow, they were
going to have to work out the logistics.

Or maybe, just maybe, she might consider keeping the
place and living here. He'd keep his job, her animals would
keep their barn, and she could have what she'd always wanted.
A home. And someone to share it with.

The thought, for once, didn't make her wince. For Sean, she
could live here. There was no law saying she had to sell it right
away. She could stay here for a while. Figure things out.

That was sounding more appealing by the moment.

"You make me feel special." She traced his face some
more. His gorgeous, sexy face that was every bit as perfect
as his movie-star brother's, but infinitely more precious
because of the person behind it. The person she'd . . .

She couldn't go there. Not now. Not yet. She was only

willing to cop to wanting him more than she'd wanted anyone before, and for Livvy, that was a big admission.

"Livvy." He groaned her name when her fingers feathered over his lips.

"Yes?"

"I want you."

She looked down. He definitely did.

Livvy smiled. "And you, Sean, shall have me."

All of her. Inside and out.

Because no matter what she tried to tell herself, no matter how she couched it, it all came down to one thing: she was falling in love with Sean Manley.

Chapter Twenty-seven

❧❧❧

"THERE has to be a clue around here somewhere. We have to look harder."

He didn't need to do anything harder; his cock was hard enough. And it'd be so much more helpful if she'd put on some damn clothes. Even her barely-there camisole and those Daisy Duke shorts would be better than her perfectly heart-shaped ass, all toned and curvy and *naked*, sending him into dry-mouth every time she bent over to look under a bench or at the brick path surrounding the fountain. Then there were her breasts. Bigger than a handful—and that old saying was wrong, he liked her large breasts thank you very much—her nipples flat against the pale areolas, each and every freckle surrounding them tempting him to lick them into delicious peaks. He hadn't seen all her freckles in the moonlight, but this morning when she'd been on top of him . . . He'd pulled her down to lick each one and damn if he didn't want to do it again.

"Merriweather *had to* include the maze in her scavenger hunt. This place is too prominent for her not to want to teach me all about it. Who did what to whom and how our illustrious family reaped the rewards. Sheesh, you'd think she'd have a trophy wall or something."

Like an emblem in the barn.

Ah, nothing like guilt to deflate an erection. He ought to try that more often around her. God knew, he had enough to feel guilty about.

Which was why, when she'd come up with the idea to search the fountain area all on her own without any clue, Sean had gone along with it. He still didn't know what he'd do if he found it first. Would he tell her or would he keep it for himself?

How could he after last night?

Last night had been . . . It'd been amazing. She'd been amazing. They'd been amazing. Having sex with Livvy was unlike being with any other woman. There'd been something more than just the physical—and it'd scared the shit out of him. It was one thing to admire her and like her and want her, but to feel connected?

Yeah, the universe was rolling with laughter at him. The one woman he'd ever connected with and he was going to sabotage her.

He couldn't.

There it was. He just couldn't do it. But how the hell was he going to pull this off *and* keep Livvy in his life?

If it weren't for his brothers' trust in him, their help and their money, he'd walk away. He'd take his losses and rebuild. He'd started from scratch in the beginning; he could do it again. But building something with Livvy . . . If she ever learned what he was planning to do, it'd destroy the very foundation of what they were building.

He couldn't let that happen. He had to figure out a solution.

"Here! Sean, it's here!"

There was her perfect butt again, bouncing—of course—as she pointed to a statue on the edge of the fountain. A few other things were bouncing, too.

Yeah, he had to figure this out.

He scooped up their clothes and jogged toward her. Let a few of his parts bounce and see how she liked it.

Her amber eyes darkened when he got close.

"Nice," was all she had to say, but it said a lot.

She took her clothes and if there were clubs for reverse stripping, she'd be the star of the show. He'd never seen anyone put *on* a camisole in a way that begged him to remove it more provocatively than she did. And the way she shimmied into her shorts, foregoing her thong—and it was anyone's guess as to whether that was a good thing or not—had him ready to rip the damn things off her.

"Enjoy the show?"

He gulped. "Yeah."

She laughed when he yanked on his own shorts. His T-shirt, however, got a different reaction. It was in tatters and they both remembered why. How.

She started to tuck her hair behind her ear, but Sean stopped her. "Let me."

She smiled up at him and it took him a few seconds to be able to breathe. He used those seconds to do what he'd wanted to do with that wayward bit of hair since he'd first laid eyes on her. "You said you found a clue?"

She nodded, spilling those curls that had trailed across his abdomen so erotically last night over her shoulders. "The girls at school used to tease me that my family must have buckets of money lying around, so when I heard about the special bucket at this fountain that actually *did* have coins in it, I'd had to come see it. Hence the getting lost in the maze thing."

"You're kidding, right? There's a bucket of money just hanging out on the property?"

"It has pennies for people to make wishes with. They get recycled when the fountain guy cleans it out, but still. The idea *is* a bit much. Right up Merriweather's alley." She rocked back on her heels—her naked ones and not the combat boot ones, thank God—and smiled that smile that could get a rise out of him at first glimpse.

And he meant that literally. "I give up. What?"

"This." She held up a little oval oblong silver tube. Looked like a bullet on steroids with a seam around the middle. "The next clue."

"What's it say?"

She opened it.

Well done, Olivia. Five more to go. Will you finish in time or are you angry enough at an old woman to throw in the towel?

You might not want to do that just yet, though. You'll need that towel—and a swimsuit—for this next clue. But while you're here, study the fountain. The stones come from our lands in England and the statue was commissioned for Phillip Martinson in honor of his wife, Catherine. Legend says this maze was their trysting place, gifted to her by him on their wedding anniversary. A true love match. Sadly, not all Martinsons have been as lucky in love. That is why this land and this home are so important. Never count on anyone but yourself to make your way in life. People can leave; the land is permanent.

Do I sound like Mr. O'Hara? There was a lot of truth to his words, and I do know you enjoy that movie.

"Ah ha!" Sean laughed. "That explains the alpacas."

"Well, duh."

"So why not Mammy and Melanie and Ashley and the rest of the crew instead of the Beatles?"

"The other animals were all rescues. Rhett and Scarlett were the only ones I got to name."

It might be a good thing Livvy didn't want children: Sean could only imagine having a son named Ashley.

Wait. What the hell was he doing imagining children with Livvy? He had to make sure there was a relationship, *and* that he'd have the means to provide for those kids before he could even *think* about having them. Then there was convincing Livvy *to* have them—

"And here's the bad poem."

Sean listened with half an ear as he tried to shove the image of Livvy carrying his child out of his head. It didn't want to go.

"So I guess we're off to the lake next." She rolled the clue up and stuck it back in the tube. "Shall we go get our bathing suits or are we going *au naturel*?"

It might kill him if they did.

TWO hours later, after the animals had been dealt with, they'd put on their suits, pulled together a picnic lunch, and headed out for the lake on the property.

Sean had big plans for the lake. There was an island in the middle of it that would make the perfect setting for small weddings. If he could get utilities to it, he might even think about putting up a honeymoon cottage there, too. That would go before the zoning board the minute he took possession of the estate.

"Oh, look! A bald eagle!" Livvy pointed to the right of the golf cart where the white-headed bird soared in for a landing on top of the island's tallest tree.

This place was a work of art. *The* perfect property for what he had in mind. He *had* to find some way to get it. Absolutely had to.

"Livvy, I was wondering . . ."

"Yes?" She turned toward him with a big, hopeful smile on her face, her eyes dancing, her fingers clenching his, excitement and happiness literally buzzing off her like an electric current.

If only that explained why he was so wired.

"Isn't it gorgeous? I can't believe I never came out here. I wonder if there's fish in the lake? What a great place to just hang out and relax."

Or hold a wedding reception.

For guests. Not for himself or Livvy. No. He was thinking strictly along the lines of business. That'd been his first thought when he saw the lake. The edges were perfectly manicured, every stone and patch of moss and foliage all strictly planned out and maintained. Merriweather had been meticulous like that.

Sean jerked the golf cart to a stop two feet from the water's edge. "So, um, where's the next clue here?"

"Good question." Livvy got out and grabbed the picnic basket from the back seat. "I've never been here so I have no idea." She pulled out the previous clue. "She mentions something about needing our towels, so I guess we'll be going in the water."

"The island. The clue's on the island."

Merriweather had been very interested in his ideas for weddings on that island, though concerned about the impact on wildlife. Sean had earmarked a hefty sum in his budget for an environmental impact report, that, luckily, he hadn't ordered yet. He could postpone that project and use the money for Livvy's asking price.

It wasn't enough, but it was a start.

They set the picnic basket and blanket beside one of the springs that fed the lake, the cool water trickling over smooth stones in a soft serenade.

The lake water was pristine. And cold. Merriweather had said a snow runoff reservoir filled the lake, and it was just the thing Sean needed when Livvy took off her skirt—she was back to skirts—to reveal a bikini.

His hands itched to take it off and memorize her curves all over again.

It only got worse when she went in the water and her nipples went on high alert.

Sean dunked himself, praying it'd do the trick.

It did. Until he saw her again.

So back under he went, holding his breath for as long as possible before he had to come up for air. Luckily, the island wasn't too far now and he walked out. He'd never been so thrilled for shrinkage in his life.

LIVVY took her time getting to the island. Sean was standing there, looking every bit as perfect as Eros—except for the shorts, that was—and she wanted to enjoy the scenery. She still couldn't believe he was as into her as she was in him.

Maybe he's seeing dollar signs.

Well there was a thought to suck the pleasure out of everything.

But, hey, there were no guarantees she was going to end up with the place anyway, so Sean, if he *was* hedging his bets, could be doing it all for nothing. But he wasn't, because he wasn't that kind of person. She knew that about him. She didn't know how she knew; she just knew. Instinct had served her well all these years, kept her going all on her own, so she wasn't going to disregard it.

"Aren't you cold?" he called from the water's edge, his hands on his hips, shaping his abs into a nice V with those broad shoulders. Shoulders that she'd run her lips over last night. And this morning.

Too bad she hadn't brought more than two condoms out with her. Speaking of which, she needed to go to the drug store at some point.

"Nothing like cold water to wake a person up." And calm their nerve endings down.

She joined him on the beach and it was the most natural thing in the world to take his hand. So she did. Or he took hers. Either way, it didn't matter because they were touching each other as they started searching the island.

H E shouldn't hold her hand. He forgot things when he held her hand. Important things. Things like Bryan and Liam and a whole bunch of money. Things like the future and his plans and what he wanted to do with his life and what he had to prove to not just everyone else, but to himself.

The thing was, he hadn't counted on Livvy. On wanting her. And not just in the carnal sense—though there was that—but in *every* sense. He wanted to see her away from this place. Away from the barn and her animals. Just to take a walk somewhere new for both of them. Something they could call their own. He wanted to see her little farmhouse and the life she'd carved out for herself. He wanted to hear about her childhood and soothe her fears. He wanted to make all the loneliness go away and promise her that she'd never be alone again.

Sean stumbled on a rock. At least, he thought it was a rock. Maybe it'd been a metaphorical one because what he was thinking . . . was heavy. Way heavier than he wanted at this point in his life, but if he thought for even a second about letting go of her hand and taking a step back—and another and another—he just couldn't do it.

Because this—her, him—it felt right.

Get your head back into the real game, Manley.

Funny, he'd swear his conscience sounded just like his accountant.

Millions of dollars.

Yeah, it did sound like Don.

But Don would be looking out only for his financial interests, so Sean tried to focus on something else.

The shrubbery was interesting. He wasn't familiar with that particular plant. It lined the beach like a fence with walkways cut through it, but they were starting to grow over. "She pensioned off the gardener, too, didn't she?" Yes, that was it. Focus on the grass. Guaranteed to destroy any moment.

Livvy nodded. "Somebody's going to be doing a lot of hiring."

He already had the specs in to a staffing agency.

They walked through an orchard of fruit trees.

"Oh, wow!" Livvy clapped her hands. "Pears and apples and peaches and cherries. And, look. Blueberry bushes as well. This is awesome." She touched the budding fruit almost reverently. "Do you know how many pies I can make with these?"

"Let's not forget the scones."

She smiled at him, her amber eyes twinkling like sunshine. "Would you be willing to help?"

"I didn't do so badly last time, right?"

"No. You were great. *It* was great."

And just like that, all his good intentions shifted. The flora and fauna were no longer interesting. He couldn't care less about the island and the pristine water surrounding it, or that it'd be the perfect place for a private getaway.

He'd like to get away with her. Just the two of them, with nothing between them: no secrets, no clues, no history or future, and definitely no clothes.

He reached out to tuck that errant curl back again, but she cleared her throat and turned away.

It bothered him that she did. It bothered him that it bothered him. He ought to be glad she could walk away. If she could, so could he, and then the whole issue of the inheritance wouldn't be an issue. They could enjoy each other, then go their separate ways, doing what they needed to do.

Except he wasn't wired that way. Gran had instilled a strong sense of right and wrong. A sense of self-pride. Fairness.

"I don't think the clue is going to be here," she said, leaving the orchard. "The last clue mentioned something about fishing."

Sean nodded and followed her, not trusting himself to speak—not sure what he'd say. He wanted to come clean. Tell her what was going on and ask her help in resolving it. But what would be the point? She wanted out of this place and she needed the money. Only a fool would give it up for a guy she'd in all likelihood hate when she heard the full story, so why bother?

"Ah ha!" She pointed to yet another statue, this one on the beach.

From the watermark on the guy's leg, Sean would guess that at some point the statue had been in the water.

"Merriweather did love her statues, didn't she?" Livvy checked out the life-sized stone carving and real tackle box slung over his shoulder. "Aha again!" She held something up. "Bingo. Another clue."

Sean walked over as she unfolded it.

Your great-great-grandfather, William, my beloved Henry's father, loved to fish. Your father asked for this statue for his tenth birthday, the year his grandfather died. They would go fishing together every Sunday in the summer, and I've never known your father to be happier. He was never the same once his grandfather died. To cheer him up, we had this statue commissioned and Lawrence would keep it filled with lures. Behind the stand of white pines is a small shed with other fishing items for anyone to use. He lost that part of himself as he grew older, and I'm sad to say his father and I didn't think to fix this. I did upon his death, and I hope you will continue this tribute to both men if you inherit.

If she inherited. Merriweather *still* didn't think she was capable of figuring everything out.

Livvy stuffed the rest of the letter into the back pocket of her shorts.

"Who's he? What's the next clue?"

Sean had stood by silently while she'd read it. Thankfully, she hadn't read it out loud. She didn't need him to hear about her grandmother's utter lack of faith in her.

"He's my great-grandfather. He loved to fish. Used to hang out here on Sundays with my dad." She shielded her eyes from the sun and looked out across the lake. "You know what? Let's forget about the clues for a while, okay? It seems like that's all I've been thinking about since I got here and I could use some time off."

"First of all, it's not the *only* thing you've been thinking of." There he went with that eyebrow-raising thing again. "And second, you just went to the market, so you've had some time off, and third, isn't your deadline looming? I'd think you'd want to find these clues as quickly as possible."

"You'd think." She shrugged, putting as much nonchalance into it as she could muster. Either that or break out in tears over her grandmother's brutal honesty. "But I don't. I could use a nice, relaxing afternoon. Let's go eat lunch and then maybe we'll figure it out."

Sean looked a little impatient and she couldn't blame him. His future was tied up with these clues, too. Would he have a job or wouldn't he?

"You know," she said as they headed back into the water. "If you're worried about your job, don't be. I told you I'm going to put some money aside to help you get over the hump if the new owners don't want to renew your contract."

"I don't want your money, Livvy."

She liked that he was proud. Liked that he had scruples. But she'd been in the position of having nothing and it sucked. She was about to have more than she could ever use, so she could afford to help him out. But with the way his tone had changed about the clue, she should probably get some food into him before continuing with the subject. "I just didn't want you to worry, is all."

"I'm not worried."

Uh huh. That's why those gorgeous lips of his had tightened

into a straight line and his shoulder muscles were standing at attention.

About fifteen feet from shore, she decided to do something about it.

"Sean!"

He turned around and got a face full of water. "What was that for?" he asked, shaking his hair out of his eyes and spitting out lake water.

"I thought you needed some fun."

"You call drowning me fun?"

"You were never in any danger of drowning and you know it."

He raised an eyebrow again. "You're playing a dangerous game, woman."

"Who's playing?"

She loved the look in his eyes now. Narrowed and focused on her, their blue color so vivid it made her catch her breath.

And then he started swimming toward her.

Uh oh.

Livvy looked back at the shore. They were halfway across. She'd never outswim him and even if she could, he'd outreach her.

"Should have thought about that before you splashed me," he said, his voice low as he glided through the water like a deadly crocodile.

Darn. She was in for it.

Then he slipped below the surface.

Jaws was up there with *The Shining* on her Worst Movie Ever list.

She turned to the right and kicked as hard as she could.

Once.

Then his hands clamped around her ankle and he yanked her under.

She gulped some air and went with it. Too much fighting would deplete her energy, and while she might not be able to outswim or outreach him, she was going to try to outsmart him.

She didn't fight him when he grabbed her around the waist, and she tried not to smile when he glared at her, the crystal-clear water making his blue eyes shimmer.

Then she kissed him.

It surprised him all right. He let go of her waist and his hands were drifting up toward her head, but Livvy kicked hard and got away.

She poured on the speed, zigzagging across the lake, and managed to drag herself onto the shore before he got to her.

"I call foul!" He stomped onto the beach.

"All's fair in lunch and war!" Livvy was on her feet and running toward their blanket.

She didn't make it.

Sean came running up and scooped her into his arms, barely breaking stride. "I've got you now, my pretty!"

He sure did. And she was going to let him have her.

He plunked onto his knees on the blanket before setting her down. "I win."

"If that's what you want to believe, go ahead."

"What are you talking about? The only reason you're on this blanket with me is because I didn't run past you. If it weren't for me, you'd still be running."

She let her fingers dance up his forearm. He had really nice forearms. Strong and muscular with just the right amount of hair that tickled her skin in so many delicious ways. "Yup. That's right. You're the winner."

He looked at her hand. Then he looked at her, the cutest bit of confusion on his face. He'd figure it out sooner or later.

"We both won, didn't we?"

Sooner. Definitely sooner.

She nodded. And nibbled her lip just because.

"Ah, Livvy." He bent down to kiss her.

She wrapped her arms around his neck and hung on for dear life, because, seriously, that's what this felt like.

Her senses went on high alert. Everywhere Sean touched her—from his hand stroking down her back to where her thighs rested across his to the catch in his breath and the stroke of her breast that was much too light—made Livvy utterly and completely aware of him. How his arms tightened as he lifted her to him, how his thighs bunched beneath hers as she shifted to kneel up straighter, how his tongue thrust between her lips like he'd thrusted into her last night—Livvy couldn't stop the groan at the memory.

Sean answered it with one of his own, tearing his lips from

hers to bury them against her throat. "I want you. Here. Now."
He untied the back of her bikini one-handed.

Talented guy. As she knew firsthand.

"We don't have any condoms." She'd realized that when
she'd packed the basket, but short of going off-property to
the closest drug store, which was about twenty minutes away,
she hadn't had a choice. The two she'd had last night had been
in her luggage. She knew for certain there weren't any more
in there.

"We don't need condoms for what I have in mind."

She could only imagine what was in his mind . . .

"If you want to find out, that is."

"I want." That was a no-brainer.

His eyes flared and he sucked in a breath. "You can't possibly want as much as I do."

"Wanna bet?"

"No betting. Just you and me and . . ." He flicked his
thumb over her nipple. "This."

She shivered down to her toes.

And that's where he started kissing her. All ten of them.
One at a sweet, too-long time.

Then he moved to her instep. Then her ankles.

It took him forever to get to her calves, and by the time he
reached her knees, Livvy wasn't sure what a knee was, let
alone how much more of this she could take.

Quite a lot as it turned out.

Sean kissed every inch of her. *Every* inch. Some longer
than others. Some not long enough. But when he returned to
the one place that she really needed him, he took his time.
Made it worth her while. And if his growl of satisfaction was
anything to go by when she cried out his name on a wave of
pleasure that was so amazing she was sure the sky had opened
right up and given her a glimpse of heaven, it'd been worth
his, too.

"See?" he said when she could finally open her eyes to see
him kneeling between her legs, his smile of satisfaction probably as large as her own. "No condom necessary and all the
pleasure you could want."

Smug bastard. She bit back a smile. "Oh, I don't know. I
want a lot more."

He flopped onto the blanket beside her. "Jesus, woman. You're going to kill me."

"I'm going to kill you if you don't get my name right. It's Livvy, not Jesus. And while I'm more than happy for you to think of me as a divine being, I do so enjoy *my* name being the one you call out when you come."

"And when I do, I'll be sure to do that."

"When you . . . Is that a challenge?"

He lifted that one eyebrow. "If you want it to be."

Oh she wanted.

Livvy sat up and kicked her bikini bottom off her left foot where Sean, for whatever reason, had left it. She wanted complete freedom of movement because when he'd challenged her, he'd had no idea what he was going to get.

Neither, as it turned out, did she.

Livvy took her time exploring every inch of his body. Well, not quite *every* inch; she wasn't as much into toes as he'd been, but there were certain inches she was *very* into.

"Jesus—God, Goddess—Livvy," he called out, his fingers tightening in her hair as that final moment approached, giving her scant warning so she could pull back to watch the pleasure overtake him.

"At least you got my name in there somewhere," she said, settling her head in the crook of his arm, her fingers still wrapped around him, enjoying the shudders that wracked him afterward. The heck with outswimming him; she might have just out-*sexed* him.

"Sweetheart, I knew exactly who was doing what to whom." He threaded his fingers through her hair, the tugs zinging through her.

She played with his chest hair, wanting to return the favor. "So you want to tell me why this isn't a good idea?"

He stiffened then. Darn. She shouldn't have brought it up.

But then he relaxed. "Never mind. I was wrong."

"Wow. A man who can say those three little words and not shrivel up in the sun. You *are* amazing."

He turned his head and tilted her chin. "Bad experience?"

She shook her head. "Long ago. I shouldn't have said anything. You're nothing like him."

He tapped the tip of her nose. "And don't you forget it."

He was teasing, but she wasn't. She rolled onto her stomach and worked her hand beneath her chin as she lay on his chest. "It's true, Sean. You aren't like any guy I've ever been with. I like you much more."

He stiffened again momentarily, but then he smiled. Okay, so maybe she shouldn't have been so candid.

"You're just saying that because I do windows."

Okay, she could go with levity. "And toilets. Don't forget that you scrub toilets."

"As if I could."

"And shovel alpaca poo."

"Ah, but that's going to cost you."

She licked her lips. "Name your price."

He groaned and dropped his head back onto the blanket. "Damn, Livvy, you're not supposed to say that. Not when we're out of condoms."

"Well then we'll just have to get *in* condoms now, won't we?"

He chuckled. "I'd like to see you get in a condom. Where would you put it?"

She reached down. "Right here of course, silly." She ran her fingers up the length of him.

"Holy hell." His breath whooshed out. "Damn, woman, I can't—"

"Oh yes you can."

And she showed just how much he could.

T was late when they got back to the house. Later still after they fed the dogs, ate dinner, and took care of the barn chores, both of them grinning when it came time to muck out the alpacas' stall.

"Who would have thought this would become our little joke?" Sean said as he shoveled the last bit into the wheelbarrow. "Don't most women want romance? You can't tell me this is romantic."

She took the pitchfork from him. "I'm not most women, and having had to do this for years by myself, you can't believe how romantic it is to have someone help me."

"Someone? Or me?"

She kissed him. "You of course, silly. I don't see anyone else here."

She turned to leave, but he grabbed her around the waist and pulled her into him. "Good thing."

Then he proceeded to show her how a proper kiss was done. Or rather, how an *improper* kiss was done.

"You don't, by any chance, happen to have any condoms on you, do you?" she asked.

Sean shook his head, then rested his forehead against hers with a sigh. "Sadly, no. I wasn't expecting this to happen when I'd be living here by myself."

"What about dates? I would've thought that living alone in a big ol' mansion would lend itself to some extracurricular bachelor activities."

"If one were so inclined to extracurricular bachelor activities, then you might be right. I, however, have other things on my mind."

"Like what?"

Shit. Yeah. Like what? Like how he was going to bilk her out of millions?

He'd let his guard down. Now he had to scramble to shore it back up. "I, uh, am only working for Mac until a couple of business ventures I'm working on pan out."

"What sort of business ventures?"

Yeah, genius, what sort? The take-over kind you don't want to talk about?

"Flipping houses." Because, really, he did flip them. Into B&Bs.

And now vacation resorts.

"Oh, I had a friend who did that," she said, settling herself against him in a way that made it hard to concentrate. Then again, just thinking about Livvy made it hard to concentrate. "He made a killing until the housing market went bust."

Which was why Sean turned them into B&Bs. People were always looking to get away, especially when the economy went south. He'd never had an issue with vacancies. It was one of the reasons this project had been so attractive to investors and why he'd decided to go with Bryan and Liam, hoping to share the winnings with them. An idea that was now coming back to bite him in the ass.

"Yoo-hoo, Sean." She waved a hand in front of his face. "You still with me?"

He worked a chuckle out of the back of his throat. "I am. I'm just thinking that, for the first time in my professional life, I wish I'd been more focused on something other than business. If I had been, I'd be better prepared and we could end this night in my bed."

She kissed his neck. "We still can. If you remember, there are lots of things we can do without condoms."

"I remember."

And they discovered a few more.

Chapter Twenty-eight

A GONG was going off inside his skull.

    Sean dragged a hand to his head to get it to stop.

His hand, however, wouldn't move.

That's because there was a person in the way.

Livvy.

Last night.

The lake.

Ahhhh.

Sean smiled and closed his eyes again, wanting to revisit the memories. But the damn gong wouldn't let him. What the hell?

"Livvy."

"Hmmm?" she murmured, shifting so that her breast brushed his stomach.

Holy hell.

There went the damn gong again. Talk about the opposite ends of the spectrum for ways he wanted to wake up.

"Livvy. The doorbell." If that's what one called it. Only Merriweather would want her house to have the bells of Notre Dame peeling through it, trying to impress visitors. Or intimidate them. Or both.

"Livvy, come on. I think we overslept and your grandmother's friends are here now." Which meant Gran was, too. Great. He needed to be somewhat on the ball after spending the night doing condom-optional things with Livvy 'til the early hours.

"Mmmm," Livvy murmured again, this time her lips pursing so sweetly he wanted to kiss them. Then have them do that around a certain part of his anatomy.

"Come on, sweetheart." He nudged her instead. If he kissed her, Gran and her friends would be waiting for hours. "We've got company."

"Don't wanna. Need sleep."

"You can sleep later. Right now, we've got three old ladies to entertain."

"Seniors."

"Huh?"

She opened one eye. "Call them seniors. *Old ladies* will get you a handbag to the head."

"Oh. Right. Well, come on. Being late will, too, no matter what I call them."

He slid his arm out from under her, every cell in his body protesting. And not because of lack of sleep. Funny how his body could run on no sleep when it was engaged in such pleasurable activities. Which, sadly, was not going to be the case today.

He yawned. "Come on, Livvy. You invited them."

"A gentleman wouldn't remind me of that." She dragged herself to a semi-upright position and flipped her hair back over her head with her forearm like a lion's mane. She'd had *him* growling all night long, that was for sure.

And if she didn't cover her gorgeous breasts, he would again.

He tossed a pillow at her. Then pulled another one off the floor where it'd fallen and stuck it in front of his groin. "You jump in the shower. I'll stall them."

"Like that?" She looked him up and down.

He felt that look the entire way. "Well no, obviously. I'll put on some clothes."

"Pity." She sighed and climbed out of bed. Without the pillow. "I'll just be a few."

Sleepy and disgruntled, and she could still have him standing at attention. That'd be a problem when he saw his grandmother.

Luckily, the thought of his grandmother was enough to put the guy to bed, and five minutes later, after Sean had pulled on a pair of khaki shorts, a golf shirt, brushed his teeth, scrubbed his face, raked his fingers through his hair, and answered the door, he was in much better shape.

"Hey, Gran." He kissed her on the cheek.

"You kept us waiting, Sean. I didn't raise you like that."

"Sorry. I was in another part of the house and, well, it's big."

She pursed her lips. He'd never been able to put one past Gran. "These are Merriweather's friends. Dafna Fine and Hetta Rothenberger. Olivia invited them."

"Yes, I know. She'll be here in just a bit. She, uh, had a late night last night."

He could feel the blush blaze over his skin. This was ridiculous. He was a grown man, for Christ's sake, and if he wanted to make love to a gorgeous woman all night long, he had nothing to feel guilty about.

Well, okay, perhaps with this particular gorgeous woman he had a *lot* to feel guilty about, but making love to her wasn't why and it was none of Gran's business anyway.

"Hi!"

Speak of the devil, Livvy traipsed down the staircase with her hair up in a messy ponytail, her skin still damp from her shower, and for the first time since he'd met her, she wasn't wearing a camisole. Well, one he could see. But her shirt was one of those blousy, lightweight Indian-print things, so she probably had one on under it.

Yeah, he didn't need to be thinking about what was under Livvy's clothes with his grandmother standing across from him.

There. Mention Gran and his dick went back into hibernation. Should make for an interesting day with Livvy beside him and Gran across from him.

"I'm Livvy. Dafna, it's so good to see you again." Livvy shook Dafna's hand, then reached for Hetta's. "And you must be Hetta, because this lovely woman is obviously Sean's grandmother." She shook Gran's hand with both of hers. "He looks just like you."

She thought he looked like his grandmother? Well, shit. His shrinkage might just be permanent.

"Our Merri talked about you," said Hetta, shuffling into the foyer, her slow, pained gait making him feel guilty for even those five minutes he'd kept them waiting.

"Why don't we go into the, uh . . ." He was going to suggest the salon, but he didn't want Merrriweather's friends to see the animals' destruction. "The study? You can all have a seat and I'll bring some snacks in."

"Snacks? Sean, it's almost eleven o'clock. We don't want to ruin our lunch."

Eleven? Where had the morning gone?

Livvy's face blazed when he looked at her. Oh, yeah. Sleeping off a night of great sex, that's where.

"Then I'll see what I can do about lunch."

"Hang on." Livvy held up her hand. "I'll do it. And let's all go into the kitchen. I'm sure you want a tour, and that's the best place to start."

"That's true," said Gran, helping Hetta along. "The kitchen *is* the heart of a home."

Sean followed along behind them, worried that Hetta wasn't going to make it. She surprised him when she not only did, but also climbed onto one of the barstools. Amazing what a determined woman could do.

"How do you like the kitchen?" asked Hetta, adjusting her skirt around her. "Merriweather had the designer research the best appliances for baking when she was redoing it. That's why there are different brands. She wanted to make sure that you had something you'd like when you moved in."

"Oh, but—"

Sean squeezed her hand. No need to destroy the women's delusions. Well, two of them. Gran didn't have any. Though holding Livvy's hand might give her other ones. She'd been after all four of them to settle down and give her great-grandchildren.

The thought started a slow burn in the middle of his chest. He'd love to do that for Gran, but he hadn't found the right person yet. And with Livvy's moratorium on children, he still hadn't, no matter how much he was attracted to her.

IVVY felt a little guilty when she saw Sean's grandmother narrow in on their joined hands, but she'd been glad of it after Hetta's little bomb. Her grandmother had made over the kitchen with her in mind?

Livvy glanced out the window expecting to see a raging snowstorm as Hell froze over, but, nope. A sunny, cloudless sky, the vibrant blue looking just like a postcard.

"That's right." Dafna slid onto the barstool next to Hetta. "She was adamant about getting you a convection oven *and* a traditional one. *And* she called the nurse from your school to get your height so she could have the baking counter at just the right level."

Livvy was *not* going to look at Sean. She was certain Merriweather hadn't had *that* in mind when she'd been doing her measuring.

But what had she been doing with the measuring? And the stove situation? Did Merriweather think she was capable of inheriting this house or not?

And why was the answer so important?

"And the cooktop. Remember, Dafna?" Hetta tapped Dafna's arm. "She talked about having a ten-burner stove custom designed for you, with a griddle and a grill and a couple other gadgets, but the decorator convinced her that a six burner with a warming tray was more manageable. What do you think, Olivia? Was the decorator right? Would that have been overboard?"

This whole revelation was overboard. She'd had no idea that Merriweather had gone to so much trouble. And she had no idea why. But it didn't change things. She couldn't stay here. She was one woman and this was a mansion. A tribute to ideals she didn't agree with. She couldn't be bought for a set of high-end appliances.

She did, however, use those high-end appliances for making lunch—and enjoyed them way too much. Hetta and Dafna kept up a running commentary of the different renovation stories "Merri" had shared with them, as well as snippets of her grandmother's life. Things she'd never have known if she hadn't invited them over.

There was the fire engine Merriweather donated to the local fire station with the extended ladder. Probably to ensure they could save the highest turret on the Martinson estate, but, still, she *had* donated it. Then there was the circus she'd arranged for the local church's fund-raising event. Livvy would have thought her grandmother would have just written a check, but instead she'd done something everyone could enjoy. Livvy was surprised to hear her grandmother had turned down the honor of opening the event, saying that it was all about the community, not the family.

"And then there was that elderly couple who lost their house," said Hetta. "Remember, Dafna? It was so out of character for Merri to do something so personal. What was that couple's name again? I can't remember it."

Dafna got a weird look on her face. "It's not important now, Hetta."

"Sure it is. I'm sure Olivia would love to know who her grandmother helped." Hetta put a hand on her throat. "My memory's not as good as it once was, I'm afraid." She poked Dafna in the arm. "Come now, Dafna. If you remember, tell the girl."

Dafna fiddled with a button on her blouse. "It was the Carollas." She looked at Livvy. "Merriweather rebuilt your grandparents' home. She was saving it for you."

Livvy didn't know what to say. She didn't know what to *think*. Merriweather had done *that*? For *her*? Why? Her maternal grandparents had disowned both her and her mother. If anything, Livvy would've expected Merriweather to be the one to burn the house in the first place in retaliation for sending her mother out on the streets with an illegitimate Martinson. Bad enough she was illegitimate, but homeless, too? It was a wonder Merriweather had waited until Livvy was five to push for the adoption.

But to rebuild the house for her . . . It just didn't make sense.

"I don't know what to say."

"Well, there. See? It *is* important." Hetta smiled and

squeezed her arm. "Your grandmother did care a great deal for you, even if she didn't show it."

"*Show* it? She never even contacted me."

"She had her reasons, I'm sure."

"There is no reason to not contact your granddaughter." Mrs. Manley crossed her arms. "Why, I couldn't imagine one day without speaking to my grandchildren, let alone weeks."

"Years." Livvy winced. She hadn't meant to let her bitterness seep out.

"Years?" Hetta and Dafna asked, their eyes wide.

Livvy squinted. "Um . . . yeah. It was years. But that's not important anymore. As you said, she was doing what she was capable of doing." The fact that Livvy had wanted so much more wasn't necessary to discuss.

Matter of fact, she was darn near done discussing any of this. She'd had quite enough of this trip down Memory Lane so she jumped up to clear the table.

Sean's grandmother helped. "Lunch was delicious, but then, I didn't expect any different. I love that pepper loaf you make. I made the boys try it when they came for dinner Thursday night. Sean really enjoyed it, didn't you, dear?"

Livvy looked up at him. Thursday night? That would have been the night he'd had *plans*. Plans that included his grandmother. Was there anything *not* to love about this guy?

"You should taste her scones." Sean replied, but the look he sent to her said he wasn't talking about scones.

She felt the blush wash over her again.

Saw him notice it, too.

Remembered what he'd said about it, and she got warm in a totally different way.

"If your offer is still open, Olivia, Hetta and I would love a keepsake to remember Merri by," said Dafna when she handed Livvy her lunch plate.

"Of course."

"No," said Sean at the same time.

They all looked at him.

"No?" His grandmother arched an eyebrow. No surprise that it was only the one. "I believe Livvy is the one who has the right to say how the contents of this house are disposed of."

Equally as puzzling as Sean's reaction was his grand-mother's. Livvy appreciated the support, but she didn't need it. She *was* going to give them something and there was noth-ing Sean could do to stop her.

"Uh, you're right, Gran." He smiled at the ladies, but it didn't reach his eyes. "Sorry. It's just that, well, the estate should be preserved as is." He looked at her and there was something in his eyes all right, but it wasn't a smile. "Every piece of it has a story to tell. A clue to the past. You know how particular Mrs. Martinson was about this place. I doubt she'd want it dismantled."

"They're not talking about dismantling it, dear." His grandmother patted his arm. "They merely want a remem-brance of her. Olivia did offer."

Livvy would love to take a picture of the moment. This big, tall, hunky guy who looked like he could walk into any room and own it—including one that his movie star brother was in—was backing down from a little old, gray-haired lady's glare. It was almost comical.

Almost because Livvy read between the lines of his little speech. He was worried she'd give away a clue, and while it was sweet of him to look out for her, it didn't change her mind.

"I did offer, and I meant it. Was there something particular you have in mind?" she asked them.

They looked at each other, then smiled. "There were some lovely Lladró figurines from our birthday trip to Spain," said Dafna.

"I think that's a lovely idea. I don't see how a statue you bought recently could be a clue to the past."

Sean was trying to speak to her with his eyes as she led them out of the kitchen. Or rather, he was trying to yell at her with his eyes, but Livvy just smiled as if she didn't have a clue what he was trying to say. Telling her guests *no* . . . As if he had the right to do that.

Ah, but what if he did? What if it was just the two of you here and you made it permanent? You, him, the house, the whole she-bang. Isn't that what you've always wanted, Livs?

She led the ladies toward the salon, hating that her con-science sounded like Sher because she *had* told Sher that was what she wanted. The ultimate dream: a normal relationship, a life together, maybe even children.

Her tummy tingled at the thought of having babies with Sean. *Had* she found that guy? The one who could make her believe in happily-ever-after?

She glanced back over her shoulder. He certainly looked like Prince Charming. Tall, dark, and gorgeous, funny, sweet, thoughtful, loved little old ladies and animals, with a great personality. Not to mention being an incredible lover.

"It must be a big job keeping this place clean," said Hetta. "Quite the enterprising young man you are, Sean, to hear your grandmother talk about you. In our day, no man would be caught dead with a feather duster."

"I don't use a feather duster."

And he cleaned, too.

Yup, having Sean Manley in her life just might make it perfect.

But then Sean opened the French doors.

Chapter Twenty-nine

❧❧❧

"SONOFA—!" Sean stared into the room. Not again.

"*Sonofabitch!*" Orwell was perched atop the *open* door to the patio.

"Oh, no," said Gran.

"Oh, my," said Dafna.

"Oh, *dear,*" said Hetta.

"Actually, that's a goat." Sean wanted to groan. Why was Dodger in the salon? And how did he even know that *was* Dodger? And how had Orwell opened the damn door? That bird was looking a little too pleased with himself.

"What have they done now?" Livvy slid past him, and for once, he was more aware of something other than her soft breasts brushing against his back and the scent of the lavender that would forever remind him of her—

Okay, maybe he wasn't *more* aware of the nightmare in the salon, but he definitely couldn't ignore it.

Dodger leapt onto the sideboard with a clatter of hooves. Thank God the top was marble so he wouldn't damage it, but the crystal pieces on display . . .

"Livvy, get your goat!"

Livvy snorted as she ran past him. "You do know what that saying means, right?"

"I don't care what it means. You have to get the damn goat before he breaks something." He looked at his grandmother. "Sorry for the language, Gran."

Gran waved his comment away. "I appreciate the apology, Sean, but save the crystal."

Sean smiled at her before he frowned at Dodger. And now Digger. Randy, too, and the other one. What was its name? How the hell had Orwell gotten them out of the barn and in here? And why?

Livvy was trying to catch them, but the animals were using the furniture as their own personal mountain range and—hell. One of them jumped onto the fireplace mantle— the mantle that held Merriweather's collection of crystal balls. Very fitting for a woman who wanted to control the future to collect instruments to see it, but he didn't need one to know about the chunk they'd take out of the marble hearth below if one of them rolled off.

Sean vaulted over an ottoman and righted the chair he almost knocked over, and would have done a sliding save onto the hearth if the ball the goat had knocked from its pedestal hadn't snagged on something and stopped rolling toward the edge.

Then Digger nudged it with his hoof.

"Nooooooo!" Sean dove, bracing himself for the impact of hard, unforgiving marble.

Instead, he landed on something soft. Bouncy.

Feminine.

"*Oof*!"

Who, thank God, was still able to talk.

"Would you *please* get off me?"

"Are you okay?" He rolled off her and brushed the curls off her face. "Livvy? Did I hurt you?"

"No, but—oh my God—*move*!"

Sean looked up as he rolled away to see the crystal ball careening toward him. He shoved out a hand and caught it at the last second, the force stinging his palm.

"Good catch." Gran waved at him.

He smiled at her, a sick feeling in his stomach. If he hadn't rolled out of the way, if he hadn't landed on Livvy, *she'd* have gotten a bad crack on the head.

Damn goat.

He sat up and rubbed a hand through his hair. "You okay?"

Livvy sat up, adjusting her blouse—yep, there was the camisole. "I'm going to have a nice bruise on my knee tomorrow, but other than that, I'm good."

Sean hopped to his feet and held out a hand, refusing to think about how *good* she was. Gran was here. That ought to be enough to put the freeze on his hormones.

Then Livvy looked up from beneath her eyelashes, and Sean had to fight hard to remember that *anyone* but the two of them were here in this room.

"Thanks."

"My pleasure." He held her hand a little longer than was necessary because, yeah, it was his pleasure.

And then the goat bleated, killing that moment.

"How'd they get in here?"

She pointed to the damn bird. "I told you that Orwell knows how to unlatch the doors. He must have gotten out of his cage. He likes to be around everyone. I shouldn't have left him alone in my room so long."

Digger walked up beside Livvy on the mantle and leaned over to nibble her hair.

Damn goat.

Sean picked it up, ignoring its bleat of protest. And its butting head. "One down. Let's round the rest of them up and get them back to the barn."

"Or, better yet." Livvy poked her head out the door and whistled. "Davy? Come on, boy!"

"What are you doing?" They didn't need any more chaos in the room.

"Trust me. Wait 'til you see what Davy can do. Put Digger down."

Sean was skeptical, but that changed when the poodle roared into the room and began rounding everyone up as if he were a border collie and they his sheep, er, goats.

Digger and Randy and Bo came willingly enough, but

Dodger was another story. He wasn't having any of it, jumping from piece to piece to avoid the snippy little poodle.

So Davy went after him, leaping onto the sofa, and then onto the back of it.

Which he slipped off of.

Sean once more found himself diving to catch something, but this time, he didn't make it in time.

Poor Davy paid the price.

That leg didn't look good.

WHAT if he dies?" Livvy asked for the fourth time since they'd left the vet's office hours later.

Sean pulled his truck into the small lot at the back of the estate by the kitchen. "He's not going to die. Dr. Carston knows what she's doing. She said it was a simple fracture. Davy will be good as new in no time."

"But what if he doesn't wake up from the anesthesia?"

He turned off the ignition and faced her. "Livvy, don't go borrowing trouble. This is a routine procedure."

"No, it's not." She shoved her hair behind her ears. "It's not routine for a dog to break his leg chasing after a goat in the drawing room of a mansion. Don't you see how *not* natural all of this is? How could I have even thought for a minute that I could stay here? They're not used to this place and with all the upheaval in their lives . . . I promised them—and myself—some stability. Yet here I am, jumping to Merriweather's demands and risking the safety and security I promised them when I adopted them."

Sean grasped her hands that were clenched in her lap. "Livvy, they're animals. They'll adapt. Don't keep beating yourself up over it. Davy will be fine."

She yanked her hands away and raked them through her curls. "They're *not* just animals, Sean. They're *my* animals. I'm responsible for them and I don't take my responsibilities lightly."

She didn't say it, but he heard the *unlike my parents* and suddenly, he understood. This went far beyond a broken leg. This spoke to who she was, what shaped her, what her hopes

and dreams were. Livvy needed stability. She needed someone there for her who would give her the security she needed.
She needed someone looking out for her, caring about her,
who'd be there for the long haul. He had no business starting
an affair he couldn't finish. And as for stealing her
inheritance . . .

It was his turn to rake his hands through his hair. A no-win
situation.

He pulled out his cell phone and called the vet's office.
"Hi. I was just in with Livvy Carolla and the poodle with the
broken leg. Please have Dr. Carston give Livvy a call when
Davy's awake." He thanked the receptionist, then ended the
call. "Okay? Nothing more we can do tonight. Let's go in and
I'll make you something to eat. You look pretty wiped out."

"Thanks, but I'm going to head out to the barn. I need to
make sure they're all right."

He didn't argue with her. She wasn't going out to see if
the animals were all right; she was going to out to make sure
she was all right.

"Want me to come with you?"

For a second there was a flash of something in her eyes,
but then she shook her head. "No. I need some time alone
with them."

He brushed her hair off her shoulder. "Okay. But if you
need me, just call."

She promised she would and headed to the barn, stumbling
over the brick in the path that he hadn't yet fixed. Sean
reached out to catch her for a brief moment before she was
on her way—a metaphor, he was afraid, for their entire
relationship.

That was it. Things had to change. Which meant that he
had some calls to make.

Chapter Thirty

❧

LIVVY didn't come to bed last night.

It was Sean's first thought on waking up alone and it felt wrong.

He bypassed a shower and pulled on shorts and a T-shirt before heading downstairs and out to the barn.

He never made it that far.

She was asleep in the salon, her menagerie around her. Well, the dogs and Reggie were, and they didn't look all that comfortable smashed up against her.

Livvy, however, looked sexy as hell. Her hair tumbled over her shoulders as if he'd spent the night running his fingers through it. There was one curl across her lips that puffed every time she exhaled. Her lips were pursed, and her long lashes rested against her cheeks as if pointing to each and every adorable freckle. One leg was curled up over Ringo—lucky dog—and she'd draped an arm over Petra, her fingers brushing Reggie's back as the pig slept on the floor, his bells tinkling softly with each breath.

"*Sonofabitch.*"

And Orwell was on the back of the sofa, his head stuffed under his wing, muttering in his sleep.

Livvy stirred and opened her beautiful eyes. It took a few seconds for her to wake up, but when she did . . . whoa. That smile. He could wake up to that smile for the rest of his life.

"Good morning." Her voice was husky with sleep and it took Sean a few moments to be able to respond because he was still stuck on the *rest of his life* comment.

"Hi."

"I, uh, fell asleep here."

"I can see that."

"I got in late."

"I know." Because he'd listened for her.

"It was . . . peaceful in the barn."

He walked over to the sofa and nudged Ringo so he could sit down. "You don't have to explain yourself to me, Livvy. It's your house."

She disentangled herself from the dogs, her bare leg brushing his, and every cell in his body went on high alert. More so when she swept her mane of hair back over her head in a sexy cascade of curls.

"What would you think if I stayed here?"

That got his attention off her. "Stayed here? In this house? As in, don't sell?"

She nodded. "I know it's really big and needs a lot of upkeep, but I've been thinking about what the ladies said yesterday. How Merriweather went to all that trouble with the kitchen and what she's trying to do with this treasure hunt, and, well, I'm wondering if I'm being too quick to want to cash out. It might be kind of nice living here. I don't have to worry about the roof leaking and the barn . . . It's perfect for everyone. And the lake . . . the geese would love it. I could build a shelter for them on the island and they'd have the whole place to themselves. It's at least three times as big as the pond back home that they share with all the other birds. I could build Rhett and Scarlett a big outdoor pen, and the dogs already love the yard."

"And this room. Don't forget how much they all love this room."

"True." She laughed and her smile socked him in the gut.

So did the idea of her actually staying in the house. He hadn't expected that. She'd been so adamant about leaving that he'd never considered for a minute that she'd want to stay.

So much for all the calls he'd made last night to sell his last B&B. A couple of people expressed interest and hadn't balked at his asking price. If he got it, he could actually pull this deal off if Livvy inherited and wanted to sell. He'd been hopeful. Now, however . . . If he sold his place and she decided not to sell hers, he'd be back to square one, with nothing. "So you're really thinking of staying?"

"It's still in the weighing-the pros-and-cons stage. I'm not counting anything out yet. I'll miss everyone on the co-op, but, really, there's no reason for me to live there anymore when there's a waiting list of people who want to move in. It's only fair since I'll have so much. Hey, maybe I could make *this* place a co-op. We've certainly got the acreage for it."

Now Sean's stomach took another hit, but it wasn't because of her smile. This place was worth a fortune and she was going to turn it into a co-op? The property value would take a nosedive and as for the surrounding properties he'd bought and would need to sell to pay back his brothers . . . A co-op would cut their value in half.

"You might want to check with the zoning board before you go that route, Livvy." That would be his next call. "So, I'm assuming Dr. Carston called?"

"Yep. Davy's doing fine. We'll be able to bring him home today. Thank you for taking us yesterday. I know you probably wanted to spend more time with your grandmother."

"No problem. And Gran understood." Gran had understood too much; he hadn't minded leaving.

"I should call her and the other ladies to apologize for running out. They never got what they came for."

Gran certainly had. She'd had her say *and* saw him holding Livvy's hand. When he'd called her last night after they'd gotten back from the vet, she'd said only one thing. "I approve of her, Sean, but I don't approve of what you're planning. I know you'll do the right thing."

As if he needed any more guilt over this situation.

"If you're staying, you'll have all the time you need for them to visit again. But to do that, we have to find the next clue. Any idea where to start?"

She tucked her hair behind her ears. "My grandmother said it had to do with my grandfather Henry. Something about his pet project. Any ideas what that means?"

He did, but as a housekeeper, he shouldn't know about the amusement park her grandfather had built. As an interested party in Merriweather's will, however, he did.

"I'm sure it's not that hard to find out with a couple internet searches."

"Which means it's back to the library for me again. Want to come?"

"Actually . . ." He pulled out his phone. "Smartphone. I picked it up when you went to the Market. Search away."

It took her less than five minutes to discover what he already knew.

"You're never going to guess what it is." She handed him the phone.

"Okay." He didn't let go of her hand.

She rolled her eyes but smiled anyway. "Aren't you even going to try?"

"You said I wouldn't, so why bother?"

"Seriously, Sean, you're no fun."

He arched an eyebrow.

"Okay, you are, but you could at least humor me."

"All right. Let me see. Did he build a road?"

"No."

"An office building?"

"Nope."

"Shopping mall?"

"Not even close."

"Gee, this game is so much fun."

Livvy rolled her eyes again. "All right, Mr. Sore Loser. It's an amusement park."

"I am *not* a sore loser, and you're right. Never would have guessed an amusement park. You're planning to go there, aren't you?"

"Unless you have other plans for the day."

"There's just one problem."

"Oh?"

He tugged her closer. "Yeah. You see, I have this thing

called a job. For which I get paid. And my boss is kind of a stickler for keeping the clients happy."

She flattened her palms against his chest and suddenly Sean wasn't finding anything amusing in their situation. Hot and heavy, a turn-on, sexy, yes. Funny . . . Not at all. He wanted her with an intensity that was almost frightening.

"Well *this* client would be much happier if you accompanied her to an amusement park instead of vacuuming the stairs, so unless you have some weird aversion to amusement parks, I guess that means you're going with me." She pushed back on his chest and he reluctantly—very reluctantly—let her go. "Give me fifteen minutes to get ready, and then we can go."

"Sounds good, but why don't we get something to eat first?"

"Good idea. Let's check out that diner on our way to the interstate. My treat."

"Sounds like a plan, but it's *my* treat. I've never let a woman pay for a meal in my life and I'm not about to start now."

She shrugged and the way her breasts moved was payment enough if she wanted to be a stickler about it.

"Okay, fine by me. But just so you know, I'm in the mood for a really big breakfast."

S HE hadn't been kidding.

Livvy was the first woman he'd ever taken to a restaurant who actually *ate* her food. All the others had taken little nibbles and pushed it around on their plate, but not Livvy. She was right; she wasn't like any other woman.

Not that he'd needed her to point that out.

She polished off her third fried egg and washed it and the fourth piece of toast down with her second glass of grapefruit juice.

"Where do you put it?" Sean asked, trying to look at her objectively. Yeah, that wasn't happening.

"Too much? Sorry, but I was hungry."

"Don't apologize to me. I'm glad to see you have a healthy

appetite. Even if you were a little nutso with the multi-grain bread."

"Hey, I had to know if it was organic or not. I don't expect a teenage waitress to know that. Easiest way to find out is by looking at the packaging."

"I'm surprised you didn't ask if the butter was hand churned."

She balled up her napkin and tossed it at him. "Now you're just making fun of me."

"No, I'm enjoying you. All your little quirks and issues."

"You don't mind?"

He reached for her hand. "How could I? They're what make you you."

She swallowed, then licked her lips. It wasn't a nibble, but it was just as potent. "Thank you for saying that. It was really sweet."

"So are you, Livvy." He lowered his voice and leaned in. "And I wouldn't mind tasting you right now."

He got the blush he'd been aiming for. He also got a raging hard-on, but then, he'd been at half-mast ever since she'd walked down the stairs in a pair of shorts and sandals that made him want to run his hands up her legs, and her requisite cami with the open blouse over it that was more of a peek-a-boo turn-on than anything that hid her curves.

"You can't say things like that," she whispered.

"Sure I can. It's the truth."

If it was possible, her blush got deeper. And it spread down her neck and beneath that blouse and that cami and, hell, he'd love to trace its path with his tongue.

"I think we should go," she said, pulling her hand from his and sitting back.

"So do I, but unfortunately, if I get out of this booth, I'm going to embarrass you, myself, and everyone here."

It took her a few seconds to get it, but when she did, she blushed all over again.

Sean groaned. "Livvy, please stop blushing."

"Then stop saying things like that."

"Can I still think them?"

She rolled her eyes. "You're incorrigible."

"No, I'm in pain. Take pity on me and let's talk about something . . . oh, I don't know. *Cold*."

"Like a glacier?"

"That's a good one."

"Or how about a frozen lake."

"Even better."

"Polar bear?"

"That works."

"Me naked in front of a roaring fire with snow falling outside the window behind me?"

"No fair."

She flicked a lock of hair that'd fallen onto his forehead.

"All's fair in lunch and war, remember?"

"I remember very well, thank you, but this is breakfast." He remembered seeing her stretched out, naked in the sun with the gurgle of flowing water surrounding them, the blue sky overhead and not a soul around for miles, and they'd made love as if they were the only two people on earth, in their own private Eden. "You're blushing again."

"That's *not* a blush."

The look she gave him told him everything he needed to know. "Keep looking at me like that, woman, and I'm not going to be liable for the consequences."

"I'd love to explore those consequences with you, but there are rides waiting for us."

He'd give her a ride . . .

He didn't have to say it—she started blushing all over again.

Today promised to be a lot of fun.

Chapter Thirty-one

❧❧

ET'S go again!" Livvy was bouncing all over the place, God help him. Down the steps from the ride, across the macadam, circling around him like her dancing poodle. Though a hell of a lot cuter.

"You want to do that *again*? Aren't you about to toss up your three eggs, four pieces of organic multi-grain toast, and two glasses of grapefruit juice?"

"Technically, it was only one and a half."

"Oh, right. Big difference there. So if it'd been two full glasses *then* you'd be tossing it?"

"No, silly. I love that ride. When the bottom falls out, it's like that feeling you get in your tummy when you . . . You know." She nibbled on her bottom lip and Sean had a feeling he knew exactly what she was going to say.

He tugged her against him and linked his hands against the small of her back. "You mean like the feeling you get when I do this?"

He kissed her. Right there in the park in front of everyone, he kissed her as if it were just the two of them like at the lake. As if he couldn't wait to take her home.

He couldn't. "I want you, Livvy." He had to murmur it against her skin.

"Sean, we're in public."

"Trust me, I know." He tugged on her earlobe with his teeth. "Just wanted to make sure *you* did."

She arched her back slightly, thrusting her belly against his erection. "Oh I know."

He exhaled on a laugh and kissed the tip of her nose. "How long do you think we can stay like this before someone notices?"

"Probably a lot longer than if you let go and turned around right now."

"Good point."

"I say we try the log flume next. That water will be sure to cool you down."

"Until you end up soaking wet."

"Oh, right. Good point. How about the fun house instead?"

"Sounds like a plan."

It was a good plan. Those moving stairs sent her careening back into him. And that rope climb . . . Good thing Gran had taught him to be a gentleman; he'd let her go first.

"Cotton candy?" she asked once they'd worked their way through the hamster wheel and onto the platform at the end.

"Cotton candy? You?" Sean put a hand on his chest and pretended to stagger back against the cordon ropes. "Isn't that full of chemicals and dyes and nitrates or something?"

"Sugar and air. Maybe some food coloring. Not too bad."

"Go figure. The stuff mothers warn kids about passes muster with you."

She poked him in the chest. "Mothers also warn girls about guys like you, yet I'm not listening to that, either."

Sean wouldn't let her pull her hand away. He plastered it against him, more than willing to use any excuse to get her hands on him. Hell, he had it bad for her. "Hey, I'm a good guy. Mothers love me."

"I bet they do." She waggled her eyebrows and tugged her hand free as she headed on to the next ride.

Sean followed her, quickly catching up. Bryan was the one every woman loved. And that was okay with Sean. He didn't need to be the object of every woman's fantasy. Just one certain one.

One special one.

Livvy.

"Sean? You okay?"

Livvy turned around when he stopped moving. Hell, he thought he'd stopped *breathing*.

"Sean?"

"Huh? Uh, yeah. I'm fine." In a my-world-just-tilted sort of way.

"Can we do the swings? I love spinning around like that."

She ought to try spinning the way he was right now. Holy hell, he was falling for her. And not because the sex had been great. Though it had been. But he wanted her smiles in the morning and her moans at night. Her kisses all day long. He wanted her laughter and her insecurities and her jokes and her sighs when she was sleeping. He'd even take the dogs if it meant he got Livvy. And her blushes. Oh, how he wanted her blushes.

"Or do you want to do that pirate ship ride?

He looked to where she was pointing. A giant ship swinging from side to side until it was almost perpendicular to the ground. Nah, he didn't need to go on that one; his insides were doing that all on their own.

"Or how about the Double Shot? It's a rush."

He didn't need any more of a rush. But he couldn't exactly tell her that. "Sure. Sounds fun."

He was *falling for* Livvy.

LIVVY couldn't remember a better day. Well, maybe the one by the lake, but this was a close second. Sean was so much fun and such a good sport and the perfect guy to hang out with at an amusement park. He, of course, hit the bell on the strong man game. He popped all six balloons with his darts, winning her a stuffed hippo "for her menagerie," and didn't mind powdered sugar all over his face from the funnel cake.

Of course, that might have had something to do with the fact that she kissed it off of him, but still . . .

They went on every ride, some twice, bought all of the overpriced pictures the rides took of them, watched a clown juggle, a sword swallower swallow swords (obviously), and the trained dog act got her seriously thinking about her own animals. Hers were smart; they could learn to do tricks like these. Maybe she could put on shows at senior centers or children's hospitals now that she'd have time to do such things—*if* she found the rest of the clues.

She gave in to eating a hot dog—it was pretty good, though she wasn't going to admit it to him—when Sean brought their drinks back to the table.

"Here. I got you an iced tea. Figured the cotton candy and funnel cake were enough sugar for you today, so I bagged the soda. Didn't want to overdo it." He plucked the hot dog from her hand. "Including this. All those nitrates you know." He downed it in one bite.

"Hey! That's my dinner!"

He raised an eyebrow. "Really? You were enjoying that? I thought you were eating it to appease me, since there's no corn-fed beef around here."

She crossed her arms and exhaled. "I was appeasing *me*. My appetite."

He pulled out some more cash. "Oh. In that case, I'll get you another one."

"Never mind. It's not like I need any more. Besides, I have this." She held up her tea. What an utterly sweet gesture. "Thank you."

"No problem." He took a good chug of his soda, then wiped his mouth with the back of his hand. She hid a smile. "What's so funny?"

"Nothing."

"Uh huh. Not buying it. Your nothings always sound like something to me, so spill. I want to know why you're laughing at me."

"I'm not laughing at you; I'm *smiling* at you."

"Same thing. Tell me."

She shook her head. "You wouldn't understand."

"Try me."

She arched her eyebrows and lowered her voice. "I already did."

She loved teasing him. Loved the way his blue eyes darkened. Loved the way his shoulders got straighter as he sat up. Loved that tic in his jaw that said he got her innuendo and was remembering exactly what she was remembering.

"You're going to pay for making that comment in public, Carolla." His look let her know exactly what he was talking about.

"I'm counting on it." She picked up a few hot dog bun crumbs from her napkin. "So, we should probably find the next clue before it gets dark. You haven't seen a plaque or anything proclaiming the great Martinson name around here, have you?"

Sean looked at her a few seconds longer with *the look*. "Actually, I did. What will you give me if I tell you where it is?"

"What do you want?"

"You know the answer to that question."

"Yeah, I do."

"And?"

"And I'm in complete agreement." She stood up and held out her hand. Whatever Merriweather's plans for the treasure hunt were, Livvy was just glad they included Sean. "Let's go find that clue so we can spend the rest of the evening together."

Chapter Thirty-two

❧

IT was late morning when Livvy woke up in some budget motel that probably rented rooms by the hour.

She smiled. For her and Sean, it was cheaper to rent it by the night.

She looked at him asleep beside her. She loved his face. Oh, not because he was good-looking, though he was, but because it was so expressive. Sean held nothing back. He looked at her with such care in his eyes, so clear and direct and honest . . . It felt as if she could see into his soul when she looked into them. His face was so strong, so masculine, so perfectly chiseled, as if Mother Nature had been intent on making not only the most perfect *inside* of a man, but *outside* as well. She'd gotten it right on both counts with Sean.

Livvy reached up to trace his nose. She'd done that a lot last night. There was something about Sean's nose . . . and his lips . . . and his chin . . .and—

"See something you like?" He caught her hand and brought it to his mouth to kiss her fingers.

And to steal her breath.

"Yeah." She more than liked it.

He rolled onto his side facing her, still holding her hand,

then tucked it against his chest. Against his heart. "Me, too."
He kissed her.

It was a soft kiss. Sweet. Undemanding and simple. But
filled with a world of goodness that brought tears to her eyes.
She didn't know how she'd gotten so lucky with Sean, but she
wasn't going to question it. For the first time in her life, she
didn't have to work hard for something good to come her way.
It was as if the universe was acknowledging all her efforts
and giving her a big reward for never giving up.

"Mmmm, you taste good," he whispered against her lips.

"You said that yesterday."

"You proved me right last night."

Yep, she blushed again.

"Ah, Livvy, come here." He wrapped her in a big, tight
hug, and pulled her against him. Her arms went around his
waist, her face into the crook of his shoulder, and there was
no place on earth she'd rather be.

"Housekeeping." The door opened.

Okay, maybe she'd rather be at home so no one would
interrupt this moment.

"Hey!" Sean scrambled the sheets over her, then sat up.
"We're in here!"

"Oh, I'm so sorry!" The maid backed out of the room,
probably redder than Livvy was.

"That is *not* the way I wanted to wake up." He ran his hand
over her back and Livvy shivered. Yes, Mother Nature had
done wonders with Sean.

She tossed her hair back and raised herself onto her
elbows. "At least we know the rooms are clean."

Sean laughed, then tossed the covers off and swatted her
behind. "Come on, you. I could stay here all day and do
nothing, but we've got a dog to pick up and a clue to find. You
do have the one from the park, right?"

She searched for her bra, giggling when she found it hanging from the lamp on the nightstand.

"What's so funny?"

"This." She held it up.

"Lingerie is comical? Not to men."

"Not the bra, but where I found it. No one's ever tossed
my bra onto a lampshade before."

"Their loss. It was fun. Especially what came after."

He was too gorgeous to pull off a cheesy leer. It just made her want a repeat of last night. But he was right; they didn't have time. The clock was ticking on her inheritance. She still wasn't sure if she wanted to live there or not, but she wanted the ability to make that choice.

"So where's the clue?" he asked, pulling on his shorts. Commando.

Livvy tried to swallow but with her suddenly dry mouth, it didn't happen.

She coughed and pulled the clue they'd gotten from the manager of The Merri Jeweler shop in the park from her bra. Sean had figured it out from the line, "something more precious than jewels" in the previous clue. "Uh, here."

"That wasn't there last night," he said. "I checked."

"It was between the fabric and the lining. You weren't looking in the right place."

"Trust me, I was in the right place."

She felt the blush start all over again.

"Ah, Livvy, it's too easy with you. Don't ever lose that blush, okay? I'd miss it."

"I'll try not to." And if he kept saying things like that, she wouldn't need to try.

They grabbed a quick shower—separately so that they actually *left* the motel—tossed the travel toiletries they'd picked up at a convenience store last night into the trash, then Livvy read the clue to him again when they were on their way.

"A locket? That ought to be easy to find."

"It would except it's in the safe. And she didn't give me the combination."

"I'm sure Scanlon has it."

"But I can't ask him for it. See where she says, 'On your own'? I have to figure out the combination by myself."

"That could take years."

"Tell me about it."

Sean exhaled and tightened his grip on the steering wheel. "It's almost as if she wants you to fail."

"Or the combination is so obvious that I should be able to figure it out."

"If it were that easy, anyone could do it. Merriweather

wasn't stupid. The number has to be significant to you." His cell phone rang. "Hang on. I have to take this call."

He tapped his screen. "Manley." His lips tightened as he listened to the person on the other end. "Yeah, that'll work. One's good. Where do you want to meet? Okay. Right. Got it. See you then."

"So where are we going?" she asked when he ended the call.

"*We* aren't going anywhere. *I*, however, have a business meeting, so you're going to be on your own for clue hunting. You up for it?"

"Puhleaze. I'm a born clue hunter. I only let you tag along because I feel sorry for you all cooped up with chemicals and mops and vacuums and alpaca poo. I'll be fine." She tucked the clue back in her bra, totally enjoying the heat flaring in his eyes when she did so. "So does this business meeting have to do with your house-flipping business?"

"Yes. A potential buyer."

"And that's good, right?"

He blew out a breath. "Yeah, it's good."

"You don't sound very excited."

"It's a double-edged sword. On one hand, I'm glad to sell the place, but on the other, I hate parting with it. The place has sentimental value to me and it's in an area that's about to become the *in* place to live in the next few years, probably quadrupling my investment if I could hang on to it that long."

"So why don't you?"

He exhaled again, this time scratching his jaw. The rasp of his morning stubble reminded Livvy exactly how it'd felt against her stomach. Her thighs . . .

"Sometimes a deal comes along you just can't pass up. This could be one of those."

"Oh. Okay."

He *did* have to make money after all, especially now that they weren't sure if he'd have a job, so that was yet another reason for her to keep the house. She could give Sean the job permanently. Or, better yet, tell him to forego the cleaning altogether, and just hang out and keep her company. Except, Sean was proud. He wouldn't want a handout from her and that, alone, made her fall a little more for him.

So did his tenderness when they stopped by the vet's office

to pick up Davy on their way home. He carried the poodle out to the car and gently set him on her lap, making sure the newly casted front leg was lying comfortably. He petted Davy a few times on the way home and didn't pull his hand away when Davy licked him. Sean was definitely coming around to her animals.

Just like she was coming around to the idea of calling this place home.

Chapter Thirty-three

SEAN walked out of the restaurant his broker had wanted to meet at and headed back to the estate with a sick feeling in his gut and a sense of relief in his head. It was done. The cottage was sold. With this and putting off the island electrification, he had a shot at matching the offers he'd heard. His brothers' ROI was still in question, but he'd cross that hurdle when he got there. *If* he got there. There was no guarantee she was going to sell. Or that she would sell to him. Not once she found out he'd wanted this place the whole time.

Sean exhaled. One more thing to worry about.

At least his conscience was clear, though. The sense of relief he felt as the burden of his lies left his shoulders was huge. Now he and Livvy could deal on a level playing field with no secret sabotages between them.

He parked the truck and was heading toward the kitchen when he noticed the door to the salon was open. Now what?

He changed direction and—oh hell. They'd destroyed the room. Again.

Muddy paw prints of all sizes were everywhere. The furniture, the floor, on the floor-length curtains, on the walls, the paintings—

The *paintings*? How the hell did that happen? *Why* the hell did it happen?

"Livvy?"

Nothing. Not even Orwell's *"Sonofabitch."*

He walked farther into the room. "Livvy? Orwell? Davy?" Thank God the Lladró were still standing in the curio cabinet, but they were about the only thing that was. Lampshades were cockeyed, pillows mashed onto the floor—paw-printed, of course—and one of the coffee table legs had given way so the thing listed drunkenly against the sofa. The table corner had torn a hole in the sofa's upholstery. Great. There went more money.

He pulled the doors to the hallway closed behind him. They, thank God, stayed shut. "Livvy? You here?"

"Upstairs!" came her disembodied voice.

He found her in her bathroom, a slew of candles tumbling lilac and rose and some sort of berry scent through the room, the perfect set-up for a seduction.

"Sonofabitch."

Or, with Orwell in there, maybe not.

He turned the corner and was greeted with a smile that would have lured him into the tub with her *if* she weren't fully dressed and knee-deep in soap suds and wet dogs. There were four in with her, one trying to get in, and two others rolling around on towels on the floor. Davy was sitting on a towel on the toilet lid, his casted leg crossed daintily over the non-broken one.

"What happened?"

She puffed a swath of hair out of her face.

It didn't stay.

She brushed it away with her shoulder.

It still didn't stay.

Sean leaned over and tucked it behind her ear.

"Thanks." She took a deep breath. "It was the damn peacock. He was on the other side of the hedge, taunting the dogs, who, I guess, finally had it. Near as I can figure, Ringo went first and the others somehow managed to wiggle out of the fence. I don't know. All I do know is we've got one practically tail-less peacock running around that could use some therapy or medication, a walkway that's been dug up and destroyed, hedges that need to be reshaped, and I've been picking prickers and thorns out of their noses, fur, ears, tails, and the pads of their feet for the past four hours. And trying to bathe them because whatever they chased that peacock through does not smell good."

That explained the candles.

Sean grabbed a towel, rolled it up, and stuck it next to the tub for him to kneel on. "What do you need me to do?"

She looked like she was ready to cry. "Nothing. This isn't part of your job description."

"Haven't we established that I don't *have* a job description? Besides, I want to do this for *you*, not because I'm on the clock." He grabbed a brush from her. "Who's next?"

"I could kiss you for this."

"Good. I'll hold you to that when we're finished here. So who needs a bath?"

"Paula. No, Petra. No, I think I did her already." Livvy sat back on the far edge of the tub, her shorts getting soaked. "I'm not sure."

Sean grabbed the shampoo bottle from the edge of the tub. "Okay, then we'll just start over. The two on the towels; are they done?"

"Yes. John and Mike were the worst so I did them first."

"Okay, two down, one out of commission, five left to go."

He was soaked by the time all the dogs had been bathed. So was Livvy.

That was a plus.

Her cami was clinging again, her nipples had tightened, and she'd lost the blousy thing along the way. With his first-hand knowledge of her body, it was a good thing he had *eau de wet dog* to keep his senses engaged, otherwise he'd be as hard as the porcelain they were bathing the animals in.

He gave Georgia a good rubbing down. She was an older dog; he didn't want her to catch cold, but the others were twisting the towels into corkscrews. He helped Livvy out of the tub so she wouldn't slip on the water the dogs flung all over the place when they shook themselves dry.

"Now what do we do with them? We don't need a repeat of the salon in every room in the place."

She sighed. "They destroyed it, I know. I'll take care of it."

"It's no big deal. I've cleaned it before; I'll clean it again."

Some fire came back to her eyes. She straightened and scraped her hair back and twisted it into a weird, messy bun. That was sexy as hell.

"Oh no you *won't* clean up after them. They're my animals; I'll do it."

"You don't have time. It'll take you the better part of a day to clean that mess up and we need to find that clue, remember?" Sean did a mental double take. If he wanted her to fail, why was he pushing her to go searching? "We'll put them on the patio, but this time, we'll use leashes."

"They'll hate it."

He grabbed a pair of soaking wet towels off the floor and tossed them into the tub. Another thing he was going to clean. He was definitely hiring Mac once he bought the place.

Bought the place sounded so much better than *tricked her out of her inheritance*. Now he could be with Livvy and not have to lie to her anymore. It felt so good to have the knot in his stomach gone—only to be replaced with something else when she tugged on her soaking wet cami.

"And I'll hate bathing them again even more. So which do you want? Angry, tired, frustrated dogs, or angry, tired, frustrated, *cranky* Sean?"

Livvy handed him another soaked towel. "Can't I have Um-Sean the Pool Boy instead? He was a lot more fun."

"Are you saying I'm not fun?"

"Well, Um-Sean would suggest playing catch with them in the yard to tire them out before tying them up on the patio."

"Um-Sean doesn't have to clean up after them," he muttered, scooping yet more towels off the floor. The washing machine was going to blow a circuit by the time this mess was through with it.

"They're going to be miserable."

He flicked some soapsuds off her nose. "Better them than us." He rubbed the small of his back and tried to stretch it out. "Look at the bright side: the peacock will thank you."

"I'd rather tie the *peacock* up. Damned nuisance. First thing I'm going to do when I officially own this place is donate that thing to a local zoo."

"Speaking of which, any thoughts for the combination to the safe?"

She shook her head. "I didn't get a chance to try. The Great Peacock Fiasco happened pretty much as soon as I got in."

"Then there's no time like the present to give it a shot."

Livvy picked up Davy. "Can't we shoot the peacock instead?"

FIVE hours later, Livvy was ready to forget the peacock and shoot whoever had designed this stupid safe. She and Sean had tried every number combination they could think of: birthdays, anniversaries, death dates, important dates in history, the summer and winter solstices, holidays . . . but the darn thing hadn't budged. To add to the fun, they weren't even sure how many numbers were in the darn combination, so the whole thing was one giant crap shoot. She was *so* over Merriweather's little game.

"What about one-two-three-four-five?" She flopped onto the Chesterfield sofa beneath the windows in the study.

"Didn't we try that?"

"I don't know. I'm seeing strings of numbers behind my eyelids every time I close them." She tossed an arm over her forehead. "We're never going to figure this out."

"And I don't have much longer to try."

"Hot date?" She tried to put a whole bunch of nonchalance into the question, but really, it practically choked her.

Sean turned around. "Are you actually expecting me to date someone else after sleeping with you?"

"There wasn't a whole lot of sleeping going on." She was trying to be blasé about it, so cool and hip and with-it, but sex was a pretty big deal to her.

"Exactly my point. Why would you think I'd have a date?"

"I didn't." Well, not for more than a second.

"I don't buy it, Livvy. That shot out of your mouth so fast you didn't have time to come up with something to be cute. You meant it. Now why? What have I done to give you the impression that you were so unimportant I'd see other people? I don't jump into bed with every beautiful woman I meet, you know. I didn't think you did, either."

She was blushing again, but this time it was in anger. At

herself. She'd jumped to conclusions and hurt his feelings when he'd given her absolutely no reason to think what she'd thought. "I don't jump into bed with every beautiful woman I meet, either."

"Not funny."

Okay, so humor was out.

Livvy sat up and tucked her feet beneath the sofa and her hands beneath her thighs. "I'm sorry. I guess . . . I guess I'm just a little scared. What I'm feeling for you . . ." She blew out a big breath. "It's new. And it's exciting, but it's also a little scary. I don't exactly have the best track record with people caring about me."

Sean stared at her for so long she wanted to shrivel up and die of humiliation. Great, now she'd put the pressure on. Caring about her—God. When would she learn not to get her hopes up? When would she learn to just accept what someone was willing to give and not want more? It wasn't as if sex with Sean wasn't amazing enough. She should have just kept her big mouth shut and enjoyed this for what it was and not let herself get all caught up in the moment.

But, dammit, she was *tired* of having to settle. Of going along with another person's program. And she wasn't just talking about guys. Merriweather, her mother, her father . . . All the people who were supposed to love her unconditionally hadn't. They'd all dumped her on someone else. Why would she expect a guy to waltz in on his vacuum cleaner and be the answer to her prayers?

She needed to stop believing in fairy tales. She was no Cinderella and he was no Prince Charming and maybe that hadn't worked out so well for ol' Cindy in the long run anyhow. Those Grimm brothers never did put out a sequel. Maybe because there hadn't been one.

"Livvy?"

She didn't want to look at him. "It's okay, Sean, I—"

"Livvy, look at me."

She did. She couldn't *not*.

"I have to go. My brothers will be waiting and I have a lot of things I need to discuss with them. But when I get back, we'll talk, okay?"

She licked her dry lips. "Okay."

And this is why you get your heart broken every time. You believe in people, and they always let you down.

Sean wouldn't.

Uh huh.

He wouldn't. He wasn't that kind of a guy. He wouldn't leave someone he cared about. He wouldn't betray their trust, dash their dreams, mess with their life. Sean was a good guy.

And maybe, after their talk tonight, he'd be *her* guy.

MANY more hours later than he'd planned, Sean let himself in the kitchen door—*after* he'd checked the ones to the salon. Thankfully, they were still jimmied shut from the inside so the barnyard animals were where they were supposed to be. Good. He wasn't up for dealing with them tonight.

He looked at his cell. Actually, it was this morning. He hadn't planned to stay out so late, but his brothers had drilled him on what he was planning to do all the while taking his money in the poker game, and while it hadn't been fun, at least they were now all on the same page. Though Bry did think he was nuts for giving up his dream for a woman.

"And you're not even married to her," he'd said.

Funny he should say that . . .

Sean glanced at *the* counter. The thought of Livvy there, like she'd been before Sher and Kerry had interrupted . . .

They would think he was completely out of his mind if they knew what he was thinking. But why not? Why couldn't Livvy be The One? He wasn't talking immediate proposal, but down the line? She made him smile, she made him laugh; she certainly made him horny. Livvy was a go-getter who didn't let the world beat her down. He admired that about her. He liked her sunny spirit, her strong work ethic, and her fierce loyalty to those she cared about, be they two-legged or four. She had a soft, caring heart, a willingness to give, and the way she blushed . . .

Yeah, he could definitely see *forever after* with Livvy.

He walked into the foyer and checked the salon. No Livvy, thankfully.

Sadly, there were also no dogs—because they were in his bed. Livvy was there, too, along with one of the goats—looked like Digger—leaving very little room for him.

Sean had to chuckle. He'd stopped at a drugstore on his way home, never imagining he'd be put out of his bed by *dogs*.

And he wouldn't tonight.

He pulled off his shirt and shorts, then nudged Paula and Georgia over. They grumbled, but moved. A few inches.

He slid between the sheets and faced Livvy. The moonlight filtered through the blinds onto her face, and he wanted to trace her profile. To touch her. Show her that what he felt for her was not fleeting and shallow. He didn't, though; no sense waking her up with a menagerie between them.

He did, however, capture a few of her curls, loving the silky feel of them between his fingertips. And on his abdomen. His thighs . . .

Sean sighed and tried to settle into a more comfortable position, but Mike growled at him from the foot of the bed.

Oh, well. He'd just have to make the best of it and prayed he got a few hours' sleep.

Then "*Sonofabitch*" wafted from the bureau in the far corner.

Great. Damn bird talked in his sleep. Between that, the dogs, and the box of condoms mocking him from the bedside table, it was going to be a long night.

Chapter Thirty-four

❦

"WHO'S been sleeping in my bed? Come on, Sleeping Beauty. Time to get up."

Livvy peeled one eye open.

Sean was propped up on an elbow, his chest bare, and he was running some of her curls through his fingers.

"You've got your fairy tales mixed up," she grumbled. She hadn't slept well, trying to stay awake for when he'd arrived home so they could have their discussion, but entertaining her troops so they wouldn't do a number on another room in the place had worn her out. Looked like that ten-minute "nap" she'd decided to take had turned into a ten-*hour* one.

"I was never big on the whole dragon-fighting scenario anyway." He reached out to pet not her, unfortunately, but Digger. "Hey, little guy. What sort of chaos got you to bed down in here?"

"He kept crying when Davy and I were leaving the barn last night. I figured he'd fall asleep and I could put him back. But the dogs were climbing all over us on the sofa, so I came up here. You can see how well that worked. I'm sorry."

"No need to apologize. My brothers and I had a lot to discuss."

"Did you get everything done that you needed to?"

"Not quite, but enough." He sat up—practically naked. Man, if the animals weren't in here with her . . . "So are we back to safe-cracking or did you come up with the combo last night?"

"Sadly, it's back to safe-cracking."

"You don't need me for that, right? I've been neglecting my duties around here."

"I was planning to get to the salon."

"Don't worry about it. You take care of the safe and I'll do the room."

T was a decision he questioned over the next four and a half hours as he hauled the damaged furniture out to his truck. Some of it was probably beyond repair, but he had to at least try. Now that he was going to buy this place at a higher price, he wouldn't have the capital to invest in some of the improvements he'd planned on, so what was here had to work.

"*Sonofabitch!*" Orwell had squawked his catchphrase throughout the house until Sean had brought him into the salon in the hopes of getting him to shut up.

He should have known it wouldn't work.

"*Sonofabitch!*"

"Hi, Orwell." Sean tapped the cage for the twelfth time, and for the twelfth time, Orwell broke into song. So far, they'd been through Journey, The Police, some Tom Petty, Red Jumpsuit Apparatus, and Michael Bublé. He'd have to ask Livvy where *that* came from. The bird had quite the repertoire.

"You want some lunch?" Livvy stuck her gorgeous face in the room.

"No luck with the safe?"

Her curls bounced when she shook her head. "I'm now trying birth dates of every English monarch. So far, no luck. I'll start on the Plantagenets after I eat something."

T was close to dinner before Sean heard another peep out of Livvy. Though it was more of a shriek.

He tossed the last thirty-foot length of really heavy fabric that passed for a curtain that he'd had to remove from the rod thanks to the pig snout impression on the lower panels, and went running into the study. "What happened? Are you hurt?"

She looked up from the sofa and twirled a locket around her finger. "I got the safe open. Here's the next clue!"

"You figured it out?" What were the odds?

"I actually called Dafna and asked if there were any numbers or dates special to my grandmother." Livvy took a deep breath—which was very nice when she was wearing a camisole. "The combination is October 7."

"Three digits? That's it?"

"No, eight. She chose the date that I . . ." Livvy cleared her throat. "The day she bought me from my mother."

"You mean when she adopted you."

"Same difference."

Sean didn't know how to respond to that, other than to ask if she was okay.

"I'm fine."

Uh huh. That's why her voice went up an octave and she answered him before he'd barely finished the question. "Livvy."

"All right; I *will* be fine." She shoved her hair behind her ears. "It's just a date after all. She probably chose it so I wouldn't ever forget that she deigned to own up to her son's responsibility and bring me into the fold. For all the good it's done me."

He wanted to hug her, to reach beneath that so-tough exterior to the woman inside who'd been dismissed by her grandmother and her entire family her whole life. "But, Livvy, she's giving you the family legacy. She's entrusting you to carry on the name, something she prized beyond everything else."

"Even her own flesh and blood."

"Exactly. She's giving you the keys to the castle. Literally and figuratively. From what we know about Merriweather and how she felt about the family name, this is huge. She's giving you everything."

"That's only because she has no choice. If she hadn't gotten sick, I wouldn't be here now. With all her options of what to do with this place, I was probably the lesser of all the evils. But I guarantee you, she's got a plan B in case I fail. Perhaps it's a little less attractive to her than keeping the estate in the family, but she's got another plan."

Yes, Merriweather did. *He* was Plan B.

HEY, you did a great job in here." Livvy flopped into one of the few remaining chairs in the straightened-and-cleaned salon in front of the fireplace Sean had started a fire in.

"Thanks. How'd you make out?"

She opened the locket for the umpteenth time, staring at the pictures of her parents as she never remembered seeing them. Side by side. Together. That'd never happened when they'd been alive.

Illusion, all of it.

"Look how young and happy they were. So different from what I remember." Mom had been bitter and angry and scared. Dad—Larry—well, he'd been a good-time Charlie for all of his short-lived life, and Livvy's one recollection was of him smiling and laughing a little too loudly when he'd been around that one week she'd come here. He hadn't done any "dad-like" things with her and he definitely hadn't picked her up to hold her. That, she did remember.

"They were kids, Livvy."

"I guess." She closed the locket and slipped it into her pocket.

"Did you figure out what the clue meant?"

"No and my brain is fried. You want to give it a shot?" She handed him the paper that'd been inside the locket like a fortune cookie.

He took her hand instead. "I'm fried, too. Let's sleep on it. We have some time, and as your alpaca's namesake said, tomorrow *is* another day."

Except tomorrow ended up being a long and frustrating day.

Chapter Thirty-five

❧❀❧

*T*OMORROW was also a lost day. The rep from Livvy's biggest client had called and needed an order of specialty desserts for the next day, and Livvy couldn't afford to tell him no. Especially with the last clue escaping them. If she failed, she was going to need that client more than ever.

Another round of baking ensued—though this time without a repeat counter incident. Pies were more involved than scones and when she started in with the soufflés, Sean was afraid to breathe for fear of deflating them, let alone anything else.

They loaded up his flatbed and Sean drove like a little old lady on a summer Sunday to deliver the order.

He drove like a bat out of hell on the way back, though. "We've still got a few hours left to search for that clue."

"It doesn't make any more sense to me now than it did last night." She climbed out of the cab before he could get around to her. She leaned against the closed door, and stared at the house.

Sean joined her. "It'll be okay, Livvy. We'll figure it out."

"I hope so."

"We will. Come on, let's go in."

She followed him down the path, avoiding the bricks the dogs had dug up on their little jailbreak/peacock episode.

"I'll fix that tomorrow," he said as he held the kitchen door open for her.

"Don't bother. If I can't figure out the clue, it's pointless. The new owners can do it."

She stared at the kitchen with a bleak look on her face.

What he wouldn't give for one of her blushes. "Come on. It's not over yet. You can't give up. Read the clue to me again."

Never mind that if she *did* give up, he'd win. He didn't want his glory to be in her defeat. Not if there was some way to prevent it, which meant he wasn't about to let her give up without trying.

She exhaled and recited the poem from memory, a testament to how often she'd read it today.

> *You've walked with the generations of*
> *Martinsons who've come before you,*
> *Building everything you see,*
> *But there is one clue left to test your sincerity.*
> *Your way is clear, the reward is great*
> *If you watch what steps you take.*

"I've been to every statue on the property," she said, hiking herself up onto the barstool and plopping her chin in her palm. "Forty-seven commemorative hunks of granite, not including the lawn ornaments, testifying to the greatness of my ancestors, and not a clue on any of them. I have no idea what she means."

Sean didn't either, but if the clue wasn't outside, then it must be *in*.

"We need fresh eyes."

Livvy peeked out from beneath the hand that was rubbing her forehead. "And how, exactly do you propose getting those? You saw how gaga Sher was with this place; if we bring him here, he's just going to get distracted by all the antiques."

"You leave everything to me. I'll take care of it." Sean slapped the countertop. *The* countertop. "In the meantime, let's go take care of the animals."

"They're my animals; I'll do it." She slid off the barstool, fatigue etched in every droopy fall of her shoulders.

"Hey, none of that." Sean wrapped an arm around her and steered her toward the back door. "We'll do it together. All of it."

TOGETHER had a nice ring to it . . . Until about midnight. Then *nothing* had a nice ring to it because Livvy was beyond tired and their inability to find the last clue was driving her nuts.

"I quit. I can't do this anymore." She walked away from the stack of books in the family library. They'd decided to start there after bedding down the animals in the barn for the night, but so far, she'd only found two torn pieces of paper with numbers on them, three old pictures, and one ripped page in the family bible. "I give up. Merriweather won."

Sean replaced the heavy old book on the shelf above her head. "No, she hasn't. We still have two more days."

"Less than forty-eight hours."

"We'll do it, Livvy."

"How can you be so sure? What if we don't? What if I fail? I'll be exactly what she's always said. Unworthy. Useless. An embarrassment."

"She said those words to you?"

"Well, no, but they were implied. I mean, I was her granddaughter for Pete's sake and she couldn't even bother to visit. Not even once. I never got a birthday card, and forget a graduation present. I reached out to her over the years and got nothing—*nothing*—in return. Now all of a sudden, out of the blue, she wants to hand over the reins of a dynasty to me? I'm not buying it. She's doing this just to rub salt in the wound."

Damn it, her voice hitched. She was *over* this. Had been for years. But two weeks in this place and the bandage she'd put over the hurt had been peeled back so slowly that she hadn't noticed it until now. And the wound was just as raw as it'd been the first time. And the second. And the third. That's why there'd been no fourth; she'd stopped letting Merriweather get to her. She'd stopped writing, she'd stopped phoning, and she'd stopped asking for even a shred

of simple human decency and kindness, more than willing
to let Merriweather rot out the rest of her life in some out-of-
the-way monstrosity, clinging to ideals of the past and dead
people.

Livvy had made the conscious decision to move forward
with her life, yet this treasure hunt was pulling her back into
the swirling morass of her past. She wanted out. And if it
meant walking away from the inheritance, well, so be it. She
was done with the Martinsons. Well and truly done with the
family. She didn't need them.

"Livvy? What are you thinking?" Sean brushed her cheek
with the backs of his fingers.

She nibbled her lip.

Yup, his eyes narrowed right in on them.

"I'm thinking I don't want to search anymore. The one
thing I have control over in this situation is how *I* react to it.
Merriweather is dead and she needs to stay that way. She
never wanted me around here in my childhood, there's no
reason for me to hang around now. This was her home; it was
never mine."

"You don't mean that. We're too close."

"I do, Sean. I'm done. Merriweather might think she's
won, but I have. I took back my life. *I* make my decisions.
And I'm deciding that I don't want to do this anymore."

SEAN should be glad about this. He *should* feel elated.
He could get the house without sabotaging her and she
would be fine with it. Or, if not fine, she couldn't be mad at
him if she made the decision to walk away.

But she didn't *want* to. That was the thing. She wouldn't
have fought this hard to not get the house. He couldn't let her
give up now.

"Livvy, you're tired. That's why you're saying this. But
you can't give up. You can't let her win."

*What are you doing, Manley? You're throwing it all away.
It's right there for you!*

He, too, was taking his life back. He wanted the estate,
but not this way. She'd regret giving Merriweather this power
over her someday and he couldn't let her do that.

He scooped her up in his arms. She shrieked and wrapped her arms around his neck. "What are you doing?"

"I'm taking you to bed. Things will look better in the morning when you're rested."

He made it to the second floor before she said anything. And when she did, Sean was glad she'd waited.

"I don't want to sleep, Sean. I want you."

He was also glad his room wasn't too far down the hall. And that he had a king-sized bed. And that he'd bought condoms.

"Livvy, you're tired."

"Don't tell me what I am, Sean Manley. I'm pretty darn *tired* of people telling me what I am and am not. *I* know what I am. *I* know what I want. And I want you. Are there any reciprocal feelings inside of you that you might want to act on? Because, if so, here's your chance."

God, she was amazing. She fluttered her legs so he'd set her down, then she shook her mane down her back and lifted her chin, her gaze drilling into him with the force of her desire. Then she pivoted on her heel and walked into her room, a curvy, sexy package of willing and assertive woman, dropping her clothes every step of the way.

Sean ran into his room, grabbed the box of condoms, and ran after her.

Gotta love a woman who knows what she wants.

And, yeah, he did.

Chapter Thirty-six

❧

SEAN called in the troops the next morning, and the Manley crew descended on Casa Martinson ready and willing to help out. He could always count on his family.

"Hey, Livvy," said Liam when he arrived. "Still on for a repeat trouncing, er, racquetball game? Cassidy and I will give you a chance to win back your dignity, but I wouldn't hold your breath if I were you."

"When this is all over, you're on. Be prepared to lose and lose big. Right, Sean?"

"Uh, yeah. Sure." If they were still talking at that point, that was.

Mac walked in then. "Come on, Jared. Either you're going to help or not, but you don't get to claim invalid status when it suits you." Mac walked around Jared's crutches with a lack of patience that wasn't like her.

Bryan's, on the other hand, was perfectly normal for him. Hell, with the three kids he'd brought along, it was downright heroic.

"What's with the kids, Bry?" Sean asked, taking a fist-thump from the twins. The youngest, a little girl, just stared

up at him with big brown eyes and a baby doll in her arms
that was almost as big as she was.

"Don't ask," Bry grumbled. "Tommy! No lightsaber bat-
tles in this house. You'll break something. Shit." He took off
running after the twins.

Maggie, their little sister, shook her head and sighed a sigh
that was bigger than she was. "He'll never learn. The boys
will never give up the lightsabers."

Sean coughed to cover his laugh. Bry definitely had the
worst assignment out of all of them.

IVVY was used to working with a group of people, but
ones who knew each other as well as these guys did made
for an, um, interesting day. Lots of laughs, lots of insults,
but also lots of work. They made quick time in the downstairs rooms, covering every inch she and Sean had and then
some.

They moved upstairs after lunch, converging on the hall
of portraits by mutual decision.

"It's got to be here," said Liam. "*Generations of Martinsons* has to mean this. They're all here."

His brothers and sister and their friends took down every
picture and searched the frames for clues while the kids ran
up and down the hall, playing hide-and-seek and running the
poor dogs ragged.

Maggie hit maximum overload an hour after lunch, plunking herself, her doll, and Davy down in the middle of the hall,
stuck her thumb in her mouth, and let the Stormtrooper battle
wage on around her.

Livvy sat down next to her. "I never had any brothers.
What's it like?"

Maggie blinked up at her, sucking furiously on her
thumb, her little face all scrunched up, adorable as anything.
"Noisy."

Livvy laughed. "I get that."

Actually she could *hear* it. The crash and yelp that accompanied an "*en garde*" from the bedroom on the right didn't
bode well.

She got up and held out her hand to Maggie. "You want to come with me while I see what your brothers are up to?"

"Are you gonna punish them?"

"No, honey. I wouldn't do that."

"You should. That's what Kelsey says."

"Who's Kelsey?"

"My sister. She says the boys are fences."

"Fences?"

"Menaces," said Bryan as he hung Martinson Relative Number Fifty-Six back on the wall.

Lady Heather Martinson Capshaw of the Baltimore Capshaws. An advantageous marriage since Livvy remembered hearing that name. Big in exporting.

"And she's right; they *are* menaces. Their mom needed a break, so I took them for the day. How the woman does this day in and day out, I'll never know."

"Because she loves them." *Real* mothers did what it took to keep their families together. *Real* mothers didn't abandon their kids.

But real mothers also wanted what was best for their kids and maybe Sean was right; maybe her mother *had* thought the best thing for her would be to have the Martinson millions at her back.

Livvy shrugged. She'd never know now. It was too late to ask any of the players. It was what it was and there wasn't anything she could do to change it.

Not the past, but what about the future?

"Yo, bro." Bryan balanced another frame in his hands. "Wanna check out the top of this frame? Looks a little—"

"Loose?" Sean leapt over Petra and caught the frame before it landed, the two of them handling it as if they'd done it a thousand times before.

Maybe they had. They'd grown up together, knew each other in ways no one else could.

She looked at Mac and Liam. Mac was handing Liam a piece of wire to restring the painting he'd checked, no words necessary between them.

They'd come when Sean had asked, no bones about it, and pitched in as if this was as big a deal to them as it was to her.

They were a family.

She took Maggie's hand. "Come on, sweetie. Let's go see what your brothers are up to."

SEAN watched Livvy and the little girl walk down the hall together, *want* rooting him to the spot. She'd make a great mother. For all her lack of a role model in that department, Livvy knew what was important in a parent. As a child who'd been practically abandoned by hers, she'd make sure nothing like that would ever happen to *her* children.

Sean knew first-hand how important security and stability were to kids.

He wanted kids with Livvy. Wanted to see her face in theirs, see her mannerisms as they grew, watch her caring and loving them in a way parents should. He'd been lucky to have Gran; Livvy had had no one. Not really. Merriweather leaving her the estate was too little too late because when it came down to it, money was only a means to providing a house for kids; parents provided the home.

"You've got a funny look on your face," said Liam.

"That's his normal look," said Bryan. "It's always funny."

"Ha. Ha." Sean rolled his eyes. "Come on. Let's get back to work. We're almost halfway done."

Mac groaned. "Halfway? You mean there are more portraits? How many generations are we talking?"

Sean pointed down the next hallway. "The Martinsons loved to show off every member of their families."

Jared tapped her on the arm. "Buck up, buttercup. We've got a long way to go."

MAC'S boyfriend, or whatever he was, hadn't been kidding. They'd decided to *re*tackle the library when the portraits didn't yield anything on the chance that she and Sean had missed something. There were enough things to search in that room that Livvy didn't try to talk them out of it.

She still couldn't believe they'd come to help her.

Sean played gopher as the rest of them searched the books,

bringing them dinner and drinks, and keeping the kids occupied. He'd brought a few animals down from the barn into the salon. Livvy had raised her eyebrows (still both of them!) when he'd suggested it.

"The kids are more important than any room," he'd said. "At least in that one, we know the potential problems. I've cleaned it before; I'll clean it again."

He'd even cooked dinner. If everything else hadn't sealed the deal on her feelings for him, that, and his family, did.

She wanted one. Just like them. With kids running all over the place, significant others around, and the security of knowing someone would always have her back.

The thought choked her up. For so long she'd thought she'd never have a normal life, with kids and a house full of in-laws, but now, seeing this, she wanted it. Wanted to be part of a big, boisterous, chaotic family.

Maybe even this one.

There was so much love between them, she could have felt left out if they'd let her. But they hadn't. They'd included her in every conversation, explaining references she didn't understand. They'd included the kids in their discussion. Even Bryan was overly attentive to the kids, cutting their chicken for them ("Knives are weapons," he'd said) and helping Maggie "feed" her baby doll.

The domesticity was worth more than any mansion, and when they hadn't found the clue by the kids' bedtime, Livvy was okay with it. What they'd shown her today, what they'd given her, was worth more than money.

"We'll find it tomorrow," Sean said as they waved good-bye to everyone from the front steps.

She allowed herself to lean back against him when he rested his hands on her shoulders. "We'll *try* to anyway."

"We'll find it, Livvy. We will."

She turned in his arms. "It's okay if we don't. The inheritance would make my life easier, but it'd never been part of my plan. This isn't the be-all for me; it was a nice *what if*. But if it doesn't happen, it doesn't happen. I still have a life to go back to."

One that she hoped would include him. She didn't say it, though. There were still too many variables and they didn't need to examine their future right this minute when the next twenty-four hours were so crucial.

It was the next eight of them, however, that she wanted to focus on.

She led him upstairs.

Chapter Thirty-seven

❧

D DAY had arrived.

Sean came awake to the scent of Livvy's lavender shampoo and her breath fluttering across his chest. Not a bad way to wake up. And not a bad way to go to sleep. They'd made love well past midnight and he still couldn't get enough of her. If today weren't the deadline . . .

"Come on, Livvy. Time to get up."

"Mmmm. Don't wanna."

She was utterly adorable in the morning. All day, she was on the go with a fire and passion he loved, but he loved this time, too. The soft, cuddly, softer side of Livvy.

Face it, Manley. You love her.

Now *that* was a way to wake up.

"Come on, sweetheart. We don't have a lot of time left."

"I know, I know." She shifted off him and Sean wanted to pull her back.

Tomorrow he'd do that. After this was all over.

"I'm going to go to the historical society," she said, dragging the sheet with her as she stood. "Maybe they know something. Want to come?"

Sean grabbed a pillow and stuck it across his groin. Yes,

actually he did, but not to the historical society. "No sense both of us doing something one can. I've got a few things to do around here and see if I can come up with anything else. You go and we'll meet back here."

"Before going to Mr. Scanlon's office to concede defeat, you mean?"

"Hey, it's not over 'til someone starts singing. And lucky for you, I can't carry a tune."

He walked her out to her car, catching her when she stumbled on that stupid brick, then waved good-bye as she left.

First order of business: he was fixing that brick and the rest of the path that'd been damaged in the peacock hunting frenzy.

It turned out to be the best peacock hunting frenzy in the history of Martinson peacock hunting.

He'd found the clue.

Chapter Thirty-eight

SEAN stared at the clue. Here, buried beneath that cock-eyed brick, was the ticket to the rest of his life.

And the end to Livvy's plan for hers.

Sonofabitch.

He crumpled the paper, wishing it were that easy to get rid of it. *Do I or don't I?*

Should he tell her? Should he make *her* dream come true or *his*?

Sean raked a hand through his hair and looked around him. There was no guarantee that he had enough money to buy the place. Yes, he hoped he did—as far as the last offer he'd taken on the phone, he had enough to match it, but there was still the variable of Scanlon. What offers was the lawyer fielding?

But this clue . . . This was the guarantee. Keep it from her and the place was his at the original amount. He'd be able to buy back the cottage and build that honeymoon suite on the lake's island. This was it. His dream. His way to make a name for himself. To have the chance to achieve the same level of success as his brothers. To be a leader in his field.

Or give it all up so Livvy could bake her pies in her family's ancestral home and her sheep could eat his golf course.

He'd never forgive himself.

He leaned on the shovel, his chin on his chest. There was his answer. Because, in the end, it came down to what he thought of himself, not what others thought of him. He had to live with himself. Face himself in the mirror every day.

He couldn't if he hurt Livvy.

He ran back to his room, booted up his laptop and his smart phone, and went through the necessary hoops to have the clue read to him.

This is the last one, Olivia. You needn't figure anything out or find anything more. Simply present it to Mr. Scanlon by the specified time and date, and he will have the answers to all your questions. I congratulate you. You have now, truly, become one of the Martinsons, a fine, illustrious family.

~Merriweather Knightsbridge Martinson

There it was. Livvy had won. The house would be hers.

Sean smiled. He probably ought to be crying, but he liked that Livvy would get it. Liked that Merriweather hadn't defeated her in this. Liked that she'd won.

He smoothed out the clue. All Livvy had to do was present this to the lawyer by—he looked at the clock on his laptop. Shit. Twenty-two minutes. And Livvy wasn't back yet.

He was going to have to take it in.

Luckily, the dogs were still tied up on the patio, so he could leave them there. He grabbed his keys and his phone and ran out to his truck, then peeled out of the driveway. He'd call her once he delivered the clue because he needed to focus on driving the thirty miles to the attorney's office or it wouldn't matter what he'd decided because if this clue didn't get there on time, Livvy would be SOL.

LIVVY pulled into the driveway with fifteen minutes left on her deadline. Even if she *had* found the clue, she'd never make it to the lawyer's office in time. It was over. She'd lost. Merriweather had been proven right.

Self-pity was threatening as she climbed out of her ratty old Baja until she heard Davy howl. She ran down the path to the house, bypassing the area Sean was fixing, then onto the patio. Why were the dogs out here alone and where was Sean? And why was Davy hanging from the fence by his cast?

She looked over the hedge. The stupid, tail-less peacock hadn't learned its lesson, standing there preening as if it still had all its glory.

She really didn't like peacocks.

She took Davy off the fence and sat on the warm slate with him. The others gathered around, their wet noses and warm, breathy snuffles soothing her disappointment over losing out on her inheritance.

Stupid really. It was just a house. If the day with Sean's family had shown her anything, it was that *people* mattered. Relationships mattered, not houses or money. You couldn't put a price on relationships.

And the one with Sean was priceless. If nothing else came from this treasure hunt, he had. He was the greatest treasure of all, and she wasn't going to let another minute pass without telling him so. Merriweather wasn't going to suck the joy out of her life any longer. Livvy had given her too much power already. That, too, was over.

She shortened Davy's leash so he couldn't reach the fence and set him next to Micki with a stern, "Stay" to both of them, then went off in search of Sean.

What she found, instead, was worse than losing the inheritance.

Chapter Thirty-nine

❧

SEAN screeched into the law firm's parking lot. Two minutes to go.

He bypassed the elevator—couldn't wait for it to show up—and took the emergency stairs three at a time. Thank God the firm was only on the third floor.

He rushed through the door, startling the receptionist. "Scanlon? Which one is his office?"

"I'm sorry, sir—"

"I have the last clue! Where's his office?"

Thank God the woman understood what he was talking about. "Third door on the right."

Sean didn't even thank her. He'd do that on his way out.

He dashed into Scanlon's office. "Here! Time!" He slammed the clue onto the desk, his palm flat on top of it. "Livvy's clue," he said, trying to catch his breath. "Made it."

Scanlon lifted an eyebrow behind his wire-rimmed glasses and checked his watch. Then he slid the clue out from under Sean's hand.

Sean stepped back while Scanlon took his too-sweet time reading the damn thing.

"Yes, this is the last one." The lawyer set it down on his desk. "But I'm afraid Olivia must be the one to present it. Mrs. Martinson was very clear about that."

"No. No way. You don't get to gyp Livvy out of her inheritance that way. She couldn't make it. Her car broke down."

"Then why didn't she come with you?"

"It broke down on her way home to *get* the clue to bring it to you. She was panicked. You should have heard her on the phone." He was improvising here, but that was a talent that had served him well in negotiations and this was for the biggest deal of his life. Livvy's life. Perhaps theirs together.

"Yes, I should have." Scanlon pulled a file from his top desk drawer and adjusted his glasses as he read the paper inside. "Hmmm, it does appear that Mrs. Martinson *didn't* spell it out to that degree in her instructions, though that was her intent."

"If it's not in writing, Livvy can fight you for it. Do you really want that kind of battle on your hands? She found the clue and if it weren't for her broken down *old* car that she can't afford to fix until she gets her inheritance, she'd be here in my place." Sean crossed his fingers behind his back, praying his nose wasn't growing. He'd been doing a hell of a lot of lying recently and it bothered him how naturally it was coming to him. But *this* was for a good cause. The *right* cause. Livvy deserved her inheritance and he wasn't leaving here until she got it.

"If she'll just confirm it—"

"She'll be in. I'll bring her in, but we wanted the clue to get here first."

Mr. Scanlon peered over his glasses. "I'm surprised *you* brought this in. Quite surprised."

"Livvy deserves her inheritance." Shit, the guy *did* know who he was. What he'd been after. "Why didn't you tell her?"

"It wasn't my place. Unless and until she inherits, I work for the estate. I have my instructions." He tapped the file, then closed it on his desk blotter. "I'll need to speak to Ms. Carolla as soon as possible."

"Will you tell her?" Sean didn't want to have given up the estate only to lose her. Not that that was why he'd done it, because turning in the clue was the right thing to do, but if Scanlon told her, she'd question everything that'd happened between them.

Sean didn't want her to do that because what was between them was real. Regardless of the estate situation, he'd meant everything he'd said to her and more. And he needed to say more to her. Needed to tell her how he was feeling. What he wanted.

"I see no reason to tell her, since there will be no challenge to the will, is that correct?"

The man could convey a lot with a glance over the top of his glasses. Sean felt as if he were in the principal's office. "Correct."

"Very good." Scanlon slid the file into his top drawer. "I look forward to speaking with Ms. Carolla."

Summarily dismissed, Sean headed back to his truck. It was out of his hands now. He'd done what he'd had to do; now it was time to deal with the consequences.

LIVVY stared at the computer screen in Sean's room.

He had a computer.

More importantly, he had the clue.

He also had plans for the estate. *Her* estate.

She swiped the touchpad to scroll down. Blueprints. Estimates. Numbers. Dollar signs. Projections.

A letter from her grandmother.

If the computer and ledger sheets hadn't pulled the rug out from under her, this letter could do it all by itself. As it was, Livvy had to sit down.

She sank onto his mattress in his room, trying *not* to remember the last time she'd been in here. What they'd done in here. Together. On this bed.

Where his betrayal now mocked her.

She scrolled through the numbers. New carpeting, staffing, linens, housekeeping, a chef, golf pro, maintenance crew, concierge . . .

There were plans for a golf course. An infinity swimming pool with a pool house-slash-outdoor dining area.

He was planning to turn this place into a hotel.

She looked at the expenditures column. Architectural, engineering, permitting, land . . . The amount in that column was staggering. Amounts already spent.

What the hell was this? Where did Sean come up with these numbers? *Why* did he come up with these numbers? How did he go from flipping houses to . . . to this?

She opened a search window and typed in his name and *hotels.*

What came up was as staggering as the numbers.

Sean owned bed and breakfasts. Quite a few of them.

He was planning to add this house to his list of properties. And Merriweather, according to her letter, was practically *giving* it to him at a price well below market value. It even *stated* that it was below market in the letter. What the hell?

Livvy clicked back to the projections sheet and did some quick math. He needed that price. Based on projected revenue, his ROI would be significantly lower if he paid more for the estate than what Merriweather had promised him.

Had he been working here all along—sleeping with her all along—expecting her to go along with this? And when was he planning to tell her, before or after she inherited—

Oh, God, she was going to be sick.

Livvy felt the room spin and she gripped the footboard to steady herself. Had everything been a sham? Had he been lying to her all along and she, poor, pathetic, lonely fool that she was, had fallen right in with his plans?

And the clue . . . If he had the clue, that meant . . . that meant that he'd kept it from her. Was that why she hadn't been able to find it? Had *he* been the one to send her on a wild goose chase instead of Merriweather? Had she been blaming the wrong person this whole time?

Livvy clicked back to the clue.

I congratulate you. You have now become one of the Martinsons—a fine, illustrious family.

~Merriweather Knightsbridge Martinson

Congratulate her? Seriously? The woman thought *this* was such a prize? How about the money it would bring? *That* was the prize, not some antiquated, outdated feudal knight-hood that meant nothing in the twenty-first century.

Especially when her knight-in-shining-mint-green had betrayed her.

He wanted the estate.

She ought to feel some sort of satisfaction that Merri-weather had betrayed him, too, but right now all she could feel was hurt.

He'd used her. That was worse than being ignored and unclaimed by her family. He'd taken her feelings, her gener-osity, her *trust,* and used them for his own gain.

He had the clue.

She couldn't get that out of her head. He'd kept it from her. He'd made sure she wouldn't win. Wouldn't be able to claim her inheritance.

If she weren't already sitting, that realization would have pulled her legs out from under her. Who *was* he? He wasn't the guy she'd thought she'd known. The one who wanted her and cared for her and liked being with her. He'd used her for his own purposes.

Seems she was like her mom after all.

Livvy shook off that depressing thought. No. She wasn't like her mother. She wasn't going to beg and plead with the guy to want her. She wasn't going to wait around for him to "come to his senses." And she also wasn't going to sit here and wait for him to throw her out.

Oh, God, here she'd been thinking of how to keep him around forever, and he'd been wanting her gone all along.

No wonder he'd pitched such a fit over the rug and furni-ture. No wonder he'd been tagging along on every clue hunt. She'd thought he'd been so helpful, so generous with his time. That he cared about her enough to want her to suc-ceed, when, all the while, she'd been doing his dirty work for him. She'd led him right to the way to ensure her failure.

For once she was grateful for the without-a-purpose chairs lining the hallway; she didn't get far before her legs got shaky. She sat down and dropped her chin into her palm.

Was he there right now? In Mr. Scanlon's office, crowing about how he'd beaten her? Was he writing the check at this very moment to buy the place out from under her as she sat here powerless to change the outcome? Was she going to be out on the street before dark?

What was she going to do about the animals? The dogs she could probably get in her car. They weren't going to be thrilled about it, but she could get all of them in there if she had to. But the ones in the barn . . . She'd need at least a day to rent a truck. Surely Sean wouldn't toss them out? He'd bonded with them; he couldn't fake that. Animals would know. They'd all accepted him, coming when he called, greeting him when he entered the barn. Even Rhett had let him near Scarlett. Animals could spot a phony a mile away. Why hadn't they this time?

Why hadn't *she*? Was she so hard up for affection that she'd jumped at the first chance that came along? *Was* she as needy as her mother?

That got her to her feet. No. She was *not* her mother. Or her father *or* her grandmother. She was Livvy Carolla. Her own person. And she was in charge of her future. Not fate, not Merriweather, and definitely *not* Sean.

"Sonofabitch!" Orwell said when she stormed into her room. For once, she didn't mind his potty mouth. Yes, Sean was a sonofabitch and it was only fitting that he'd been the one to teach Orwell that word.

She tossed Orwell's cage cover over him. While she agreed Sean was a sonofabitch, she didn't need Orwell reminding her like a broken record.

She threw her clothes into a duffel bag, scooped her toiletries into another, and dashed off a note to the son of a bitch telling him *exactly* what she thought of him and that she'd be back for the rest of her animals tomorrow. Ten minutes and she'd erased her existence from this room.

It was too sad to contemplate. Besides, she didn't have time for contemplation. She needed to get out of here pronto so she wouldn't have to face him when he came back. Gloating.

Chapter Forty

LIVVY'S phone rang for the sixth time in as many minutes. She didn't need to look at it to know it was Sean. He could keep calling for all she cared; she wasn't going to answer it.

It rang again. Georgia started to whine.

Oh, God no. Livvy grabbed the phone. She'd rather talk to Sean than have Georgia set off the rest of the dogs.

"Look, Sean, I don't want to—"

"This is Mr. Scanlon, Ms. Carolla."

"Oh. I'm sorry. I—"

"I was wondering when you would be coming in. There are matters we need to discuss."

"Look, Mr. Scanlon, I know all about what Sean did. What more is there to talk about?"

"The disposition of the estate."

She almost laughed at the estate's "disposition," but *her* disposition wasn't in the mood to find any of this funny. "Do I really need to do this now?"

"I'm afraid so. There are certain guidelines to be met and this is one of them."

Her grandmother must *really* be gloating from beyond the

grave: She'd been proven right *and* she still had Livvy jumping to her tune.

"I'll be here for another half hour but then I'm meeting my wife—er, another client and will be unavailable."

Crud. He was giving up time with his wife for her and there wasn't enough of it to go back to the house and get the dogs situated there—not to mention running the risk of seeing Sean.

Call her a sucker for true love, but she wasn't going to make Mr. Scanlon or his wife wait on her or the son of a bitch. The dogs would just have to stay in the car. "I'll be there in a few minutes."

SEAN kept hitting *"redial"* on his phone, trying to catch Livvy, but her calls were going straight to voicemail. After leaving a third message, he gave up. She must not have her phone on her.

He hoped to hell she wasn't flopped on her bed crying because she'd lost it all. He had to tell her she hadn't. Had to tell her she'd won.

Now to tell his brothers that they'd lost.

Well, they'd been prepped for it. They'd both tried to talk him out of it, warning him against giving up his life for a woman. Liam had been burned like that and Bry had taken the lesson to heart. Sean was the only romantic left in the bunch, but it hadn't clouded his vision. Livvy was a great person. A good human being. An amazing woman. And she'd make an incredible wife and mother. His wife and mother of *his* children. He wanted her for forever and he was going to do his damnedest to get her. Her and her crazy menagerie and her eight dogs and profanity-spouting, song-lyric-mangling parrot.

Her car wasn't in the driveway when he pulled up. Maybe she'd gone to the lawyer's office?

He called there, but the call went to after-hours voicemail. So where was she?

He headed to the kitchen door. Where were the dogs?

He tried her phone again, but *again* got voicemail.

"Livvy?" he called when he went in.

Nothing.

"Ringo?" He figured the big dog would come bounding through the doorway when he heard his voice, and Sean didn't have to worry about what the husky's claws would do to the floor. It was Livvy's headache now.

"John?"

Nothing.

"Davy?"

Double nothing.

"Anybody home?" Where could Livvy have gone with the dogs? And in what? Her POS car wasn't big enough to handle even Ringo, let alone seven others.

He didn't find them in any of the downstairs rooms, so he headed upstairs. She wouldn't have put them in the bathroom again, would she? She'd been so annoyed when he had.

Sean smiled at the memory. She'd been so indignant, with her hands on her hips and her hair wild around her shoulders. He'd had to concentrate to contribute to the conversation because all he'd wanted to do was haul her up against him and kiss her senseless.

Which, he thought as he headed toward her room, was what he was going to do just as soon as he found her.

The first thing he noticed was that Orwell was gone. *Good riddance* crossed his mind, but then he realized her closet was empty. And that there was a note on the bed.

It wasn't a clue.

Sean picked it up. It was one big mess of swirls. Of course Livvy would have swirly handwriting; it went with the pink toes.

Too bad he didn't understand a word of it, and his computer program didn't do well with swirly writing. Still, he had to give it a try.

He headed across the hall to his room to scan it into his laptop and—

His laptop was out.

It was open.

It was on.

He toggled the touchpad and the screen came to life.

Holy hell. Merriweather's letter.

He sank onto the mattress. Livvy couldn't have seen this.

He looked across the hall at her empty room, praying it didn't mean what he was coming to suspect it did.

He clicked on another open document.

The clue.

A spreadsheet was open, too, and Sean didn't really need to click on it to know what it was, but he did anyway in the vain hope that his world wasn't crashing down around him.

The projections. *And* there was a search window open.

He clicked on it.

She knew. Or at least, she thought she knew.

Sonofabitch. Here, he'd gone and done the right thing and it'd blown up in his face. He shouldn't have done it. He should have just kept the clue quiet and stayed here and—

No. No, he shouldn't have. He'd done what was right and could look himself in the mirror knowing that he had. Whether Livvy would ever look at him again or not, he'd done the right thing.

He picked up his phone and dialed her one more time. Voicemail again. This time he did leave a message.

"Livvy, it's not what you think. Let me explain. Please."

He stopped because what more could he say? Either she wanted him or she didn't.

But then he said the one thing he had to tell her. The one thing he'd regret for the rest of his life if he didn't.

"Livvy . . . I love you. It has nothing to do with the house. Nothing to do with what I thought I'd wanted when I started working here, but everything to do with you. You've made me realize what's really important in this world and I hope you'll give me the chance to tell you in person. I love you, Livvy. Whether you're living on the farm or in the estate, or in a tiny little apartment with the animals sleeping on the furniture, it doesn't matter to me. Anywhere you are is home and that's where I want to be. Please give me a chance. Give *us* a chance."

He ended the call before he started pleading, though if that's what it took to get her to listen, he'd do it. He couldn't lose her, too. Because, ultimately, she was the only thing that mattered.

Chapter Forty-one

M AY I be the first to offer you my best wishes." Mr. Scanlon extended his hand, completely unfazed by the eight
dogs she'd had to bring in with her. Georgia had started whining when Livvy had parked the car and the others had started
in. She hadn't wanted the interior shredded when she returned,
so she'd brought them with her. Thankfully, they were on
their best behavior.

Unlike a certain son of a bitch she knew.

"Don't you mean condolences?" She jostled the leashes to
shake his hand. She didn't know why she bothered, but it
wasn't his fault that she'd failed. What was the poor guy
supposed to say when he told her she just lost out on more
than a few million dollars?

"Well, I suppose you might look at it that way, but it was
your grandmother's sincere wish that you would come to love
the place. Or, at the very least, feel enough for the family
history to keep it in the family. But if not, I can tell you that
I have been fielding several offers should you wish to sell."
He handed her a piece of paper. "Here are the larger amounts,
and I dare say you could go higher. You, young lady, are set
for life should you wish to sell."

He was speaking English, but it wasn't computing. Sell what?

She took the paper and sat in a chair facing his desk. The dogs settled at her feet.

Whoa. Those were some big numbers. Lots of zeroes.

"I'm sorry, but I don't understand."

"The Martinson estate is a highly prized piece of real estate. As I said, those are preliminary numbers. Once it's actually up for sale, I expect them to increase."

She shook her head. "I'm sorry, Mr. Scanlon, but what does this have to do with me?" Was he under orders to rub salt in her wound?

Mr. Scanlon smiled. It didn't look like a sadistic, in-your-face sort of smile, but then, she'd thought Sean was on the up-and-up so what did she know about human nature anymore?

"I gather that this is a lot to take in, but my firm and I personally are ready to handle the sale of the estate on your behalf."

"My behalf? But I don't own it."

"A mere formality." He removed a blue-bound stack of papers from a file on top of his desk. "You may wish to have your own counsel review these documents, but you will find them in order. Your grandmother made sure of it."

Livvy took the documents, scanning them to make sense of—

Deed jumped out at her.

And there was her name.

And the estate's address.

She *really* didn't understand what was going on.

"Mr. Scanlon, I don't have the clue."

"Yes, I understand."

She wished she did. "But you're telling me I don't need it? That the estate was mine all along? Did my grandmother send me on a wild goose chase for nothing?"

The dogs shifted as her voice level rose. John stared at the attorney with a rumbling growl.

"Oh, no, my dear. The treasure hunt was very real. If you hadn't delivered the clue in time, I had my instructions for disposing of the estate."

"To Sean."

"Well, er . . ." Now Mr. Scanlon looked *fazed*. "Uh, yes. Mr. Manley would be the purchaser of record."

"So why isn't he? I didn't deliver the clue."

"But he did in your place." He held up another piece of paper. "Surprised me, given how keen he's been to take ownership, but deliver it he did. Told me all about your car breaking down, too. The estate is yours."

She didn't know which to process first. The bald-faced lie about her car, or the fact that Sean had handed her the estate, lock, stock, and barrel, losing out on all that money.

And she'd written him that letter . . .

Oh, God.

"Ms. Carolla, are you all right? Would you like a glass of water?"

Wine would be better. A big jug of it. Ohmygod, what had she done?

"I have to go." She jumped to her feet—and got tangled in the leashes when she tried to leave. The dogs didn't share her sense of urgency.

"But, Ms. Carolla—Olivia. May I call you that? You can certainly take your time having your attorneys review the deed, but I do need to give you this." He produced yet another letter. This guy was like Santa Claus handing out gifts on Christmas morning.

"It's from your grandmother."

Or maybe that was coal.

Livvy sat back down. It was all too much. Sean's betrayal-that-wasn't, her letter-that-shouldn't-have-been, and now Merriweather's gloating.

"I can't really read this right now."

"I understand you're overwhelmed. But your grandmother felt that this might help. I do, too." He held out the envelope. "Please. Read it."

Livvy took the envelope and the letter opener Mr. Scanlon offered and slid it beneath the flap. She pulled out a piece of parchment.

Of *course* it was parchment. Nothing as mundane as copy paper or scented stationary for Merriweather Martinson.

"I'll leave you to read it." Mr. Scanlon stood and took a step, then paused. "If I may, Olivia?"

Livvy looked at him through a haze of . . . something. Confusion? Surreality? "Yes?"

"I see a lot of your grandmother in you. I think she did as well. And that's a good thing." He tapped the leather blotter once softly, cleared his throat, then walked out the door, the latch clicking shut.

Chalk another one up on the Surreality Board. She was like her grandmother? Not in this lifetime.

She sat back in the chair and unfolded the parchment, the spidery scrawl she'd expected being replaced by a strong, bold hand.

Olivia,

I was wrong. These are not words I've said before in my life, but here, at the end of it, I find I must. Yes, I was wrong.

I should have embraced you for being my granddaughter, illegitimate or not. You were not to blame for the circumstances of your birth; that I leave to my son and his predilections. But you, you were innocent, and in my anger and disappointment, I forgot this.

As one's life draws to a close, one has the opportunity to reflect upon many things. I will never regret the vigilance I placed upon protecting the Martinson name. It is a name that has survived the centuries with both admiration and condemnation. I was determined that, under my tenure, the admiration would continue. But in doing so, I failed you.

I will not and cannot make excuses. A child, as I well know, is always a blessing. Having been able to bear only one, this tenet is foremost in my mind. I wanted Lawrence, your faithless father, to become the man his father would have been had Time given him the chance. But it seems Lawrence was one of the Martinsons who would bring condemnation to our name. And so I hid you. I ignored you. I didn't want the blight on the family.

Now I see that the blight was put there by me. Had I only embraced you, welcomed you into the family, made your father own up to his responsibility, this self-induced stain on the family name—and my conscience—would never have been. And you would have had the family you deserve.

I did try with that one visit, but . . . well, there are no excuses. I am a stubborn woman and always have been.

Truly, Olivia, you are a strong, determined individual, not unlike myself. While I had privileges all my life, you did not. And, for that, I have only myself to blame.

I wish to make amends and I hope you won't allow your pride—and I know it is a fierce one, for I share it—to stand in the way. You are a Martinson. You are every bit as strong and determined and fierce and loyal as your grandfather, my beloved Henry. If only I had allowed myself to see this in you before fostering the chasm in our relationship, things would have been different.

Obviously I cannot make up for what has gone before, but it is my wish that you will come to embrace this family, with all our faults, and take up the heritage you so richly and rightly deserve.

The clues probably frustrated and angered you; I know they would have were it me. But I wanted you to see where you came from, who you are, before you threw it away. I had hoped your fierce sense of justice and fighting for the underdog would keep you going to the end. That you would want the opportunity to embrace your heritage and use it for those things you believe in, not sell out to some corporate giant out to make a buck on those more privileged than most. That is the reason I accepted Mr. Manley's offer: I liked what he'd planned to do with the estate. But I had hoped that you would want to claim it.

That you are reading this is proof that I was right about you.

I have followed your progress over the years, Olivia. Right or wrong, I needed to see what you would make of yourself. Your commune lifestyle seemed to justify my distance, at least to myself. That you were exactly like your parents. I had had such high hopes Lawrence would take it upon himself to marry a woman of good character

*and breeding, with a son to carry on our family name. I
was deluding myself.*

*You are not like your father. Whether or not you have
some of your mother in you, regrettably, we shall never
know. But I think not, Olivia, for neither of your parents
had the inner fortitude you have shown in building your
life on your terms.*

*I have tasted your cakes and breads. Your baking
skills are superior to mine, which would be why I've
always had a chef. But even with your talent, it is your
belief in yourself, your utter determination when the odds
are stacked against you that show your true mettle. You
are a survivor, Olivia, because you keep fighting for what
you want. I wonder what would have become of you if I
had fostered that fighting spirit instead of thwarting it.*

*It was my intention to contact you before this, but
knowing of your pride, I knew it would be only upon my
death that you would return to this house. And so I prepared this game for you. It gave me great pleasure to
focus on giving back what I've taken from you. It's also
given me great remorse for what we could have had.*

*I have come to realize I am not perfect, which is quite
an admission from the old battle-axe. Yes, I knew of your
nickname for me and secretly relished it, for that was the
image I wanted presented to the world. The proud, strong
woman at the helm of the Martinson ship.*

*I am honored to be able to turn that title over to you.
I am proud of who you are, Olivia, and I hope that someday it will mean something to you. I am proud of you for
putting the past and your pride aside to take control of
your legacy despite your hatred of me. I am proud that
you stood so strongly in your beliefs to continue trying
new ventures. I am proud to turn over to you centuries'
worth of Martinson heritage and entrust to you the con-
tinuation of that name.*

*I am proud to call you my granddaughter and wish I
had found this truth decades ago.*

*But, in the end, I have found the one thing I wish I had
said to you all those years ago is stronger than my*

protectiveness of this family. What I wish I had said to
you in person, and will go to my death not doing so—my
biggest regret—is,
 I love you, Olivia.

Your grandmother,
Merriweather Knightsbridge Martinson

Livvy stared at the last sentence until the words ran
together from the blotches of her tears. Her grandmother
respected her. Apparently even loved her.

Livvy clutched the letter to her chest and bent over, as the
tears she'd fought so hard for so long wracked her body. All
those wasted years. All the loneliness. All the lonely holidays
and empty seats in the auditorium for the school plays. All
the summers shuttled from one friend's home to another
friend's home, never having a place to call her own. All the
resentment and hurt and questions . . .

It would take a while for the anger to go away. For the
hurt. Her grandmother had misjudged her and in doing so,
had caused her grief she'd never deserved.

Ohmygod—she'd done that same thing to Sean.

She stood up, wiping her eyes and untangling the leashes.
She had to go to him. Had to tell him . . . What? That she
forgave him? Of course. That she understood? Yes. She did.

That she couldn't live without him?

Yes. That, too.

That she loved him?

That, more than the rest, was what she had to tell him.

Mr. Scanlon and even Merriweather herself might think
there was a lot of her grandmother in her, but the one big
difference between them was that Livvy knew when to admit
she was wrong and ask forgiveness for it.

"Come on, guys." She tugged on the leashes. "Let's go
home."

Chapter Forty-two

S EAN cursed as he tried to type the second line of Livvy's letter into his laptop. Damn, he missed his tablet with its read-aloud capability. This was going to take forever.

Was that an *E* or an *A*? He couldn't tell and it was driving him bat-shit crazy. He was going to have to call Mac for help and that was going to blow. And so would she when she found out he was leaving, but Livvy's absence and the note did not bode well. She wasn't going to want to see him when she claimed the estate, and he didn't blame her.

Mac would, though. Blame him, that was. And there wasn't a damn thing he could do about it because he was guilty as charged.

He struggled with the rest of the word, but then gave up. Printing was hard enough to read, curlicue cursive was next to impossible for him. He'd be better off with hieroglyphics. At least those were pictures.

He closed his laptop. He should probably leave, give her time to process the inheritance, what he'd done, and what he'd said in his message, but he wanted to see her. Wanted the chance to say it all in person. To fight for her. If anything in this world was worth fighting for, it was Livvy.

He looked out his window. The barn. The animals were probably wondering where dinner was. And why their stalls were filthy. He could do that to kill some time. God knew, he deserved to shovel more shit.

Surprisingly, the animals were subdued when he went in. Probably sensed what he was feeling. Or, it could be because he didn't have Davy, the troublemaker, with him. He missed that little guy.

Come to think of it, he missed all of them. He'd miss all of these guys, too, if Livvy called it quits.

"You know, Rhett, I never thought I'd say this, but I'm jealous of you, man. Your lady is right there with you, day after day, by your side, loving you."

Rhett must have understood because he walked up behind Scarlett and nudged her.

Sean shook his head. The alpaca was just showing off now.

But Scarlett turned on him this time. She swung around and spit at Rhett. Hit him square in the face. The big guy looked so surprised it'd be comical if Sean didn't know just how he felt.

And they both deserved it.

"Next time, try some tenderness, buddy. Show her you care. Offer her first dibs on the alfalfa."

"Or hand in the clue that gives her the estate and bankrupts your company."

Sean spun around. "Livvy." In yet another one of her skirts, wearing another one of her drab green camisoles and those clunky boots, and she never looked more beautiful. "I can explain—"

"Yes, you'd better." She walked toward him, the setting sun streaking fire through her hair. "Mr. Scanlon told me what you did. I want to know why."

She stood in front of him, her chin tilted up. "Why did you help me, Sean?"

He fought the urge to tuck that one piece of hair behind her ear. He didn't have the right to do that anymore. "Did you listen to your voicemail?"

"My what?"

"I left you a message."

She shook her head. "Sorry, but with the whirlwind of the

last two hours, I didn't even think about it. Why? What'd you say?"

She didn't know how he felt. "Why are you here, Livvy?"

She raised her eyebrows. "You of all people should know it's because I own the place."

"I mean, why are you *here*? In the barn. Now. Looking for me."

Her tongue slicked over her lips. "I want an explanation."

"You don't want to throw me off the property?"

"Depends on your explanation."

She hadn't said *no*. There was still hope.

Sean took a deep breath. Time to play his cards and show his hand. He hoped to hell he didn't get the same kind of surprise he'd gotten when he'd played with Mac. He'd thought he'd had a winning hand then.

He needed one now more than ever.

He took her hands in his. It was promising that she didn't pull back.

He took a step closer.

She didn't move back. Another promising sign.

"I know you saw my laptop, so you know about your grandmother's acceptance of my offer. You know that I'd planned to turn the estate into a resort."

She nodded.

Sean swallowed. "I planned this long before I knew about you. I put the wheels in motion once I met with your grandmother. She liked the idea of the estate remaining in this condition. Of not being used for a group home or turned into office buildings and the land sold off for residential properties. That's what most of the offers Scanlon's firm has received are about. This is a prime location. A big piece of property that won't take as much investment as others in the area to build on. What I was proposing to do with the property was in keeping with Merriweather's view on the importance of the estate. So I moved forward with my plans. After all, her only heir was a granddaughter she'd never had anything to do with. I never saw the change in her will coming."

He got a smile then. Small, but it was there.

"You weren't the only one."

He nodded. "So when Mac needed someone to take over

here, I figured it was perfect. The estate would be mine in a few weeks; I had the chance to get a jump on the renovations. It was a good plan. Until you showed up."

She nibbled her lip.

God help him.

"I was torn, Livvy. You deserve this place. But I had too much invested. Too much to lose. It's not just my money; my brothers are in on the deal and I've spent a lot on the preliminaries."

"I know. I saw the projections. Architect, engineers . . . You really put everything into this."

"It was to be my coming-out in the luxury resort business. The property itself would be a draw, plus the amenities we'd offer. The location is perfect, within driving distance of some of the largest cities in the country and the perfect blend of rural and urban to cater to tastes across the board. It was a home run."

"Until I showed up."

"Yes."

"So why did you give him the last clue?"

He dropped her hands then and raked his through his hair. "Because I couldn't do that to you. I couldn't steal your dream, your future from you. If we hadn't found the clue, that'd be one thing, but I did and, well, it wasn't up to me. She'd left it to you. It's yours."

"I've never had anyone give up a shot at millions of dollars for me before."

"You're worth so much more than mere millions, Livvy, and never let anyone tell you differently. Your grandmother was a fool not to have realized that from the moment she first laid eyes on you." He swallowed, committing himself. "Because I definitely did."

Her amber eyes flashed. "You . . . did?"

He nodded. "Yeah." His voice was hoarse, choked with emotion he was both terrified of and yearning to show her. Never had anything meant more to him than this moment.

"I love you, Livvy. I know you have no reason to believe that, but I do. And I want you. In my life. Forever. And if you want me to sign something refusing any rights to the estate,

I will. I never want you to think I want to be with you to get my hands on this place." He smiled then. "The only thing I want to get my hands on is you."

She licked her lips, not returning his smile.

But then she reached for his hands and put them on her waist. She looked up at him from beneath her lashes. "Now that you have your hands on me, what are you going to do about it?"

Sean stood there for a heartbeat—or five—to absorb the moment. To understand that it was really happening. That she, well, if she hadn't forgiven him, was willing to try to.

"Sean? I'm waiting." Those amber eyes had twinkles in them.

He dropped to one knee. Totally unplanned and completely unprepared. No ring, no idea what he was going to say, but this just felt right. "I'm going to ask you to marry me. To be in my life forever. To wake up with me in a huge king-sized bed every morning surrounded by dogs, to help me muck out alpaca poo, catch wayward parrots and dancing poodles, and make babies so we can make this mausoleum a home."

She was crying by the time he finished, but these tears he could deal with.

"I'm sorry, Livvy. For not telling you the truth. But you have to know, you have to *believe* that I didn't use you. Every time we were together, every touch, every look, every kiss . . . They were all real. All about us. The estate didn't come into play."

"I know."

"I've been trying to figure out how the hell I could make it work out for both of us this whole time, but, in the end, I couldn't. Because I couldn't take what was yours from you."

"I know."

"No matter what happened between us, I couldn't deny you your birthright."

"I know."

"I—you know? You believe me?"

She finally smiled and oh what it did to the inside of the barn. It was is if the sun rose and the animals sang and the heavens rained down happiness—

He was spouting poetry again.

"I love you, Livvy. In your co-op, leaky-roofed farmhouse or here, it doesn't matter. I love *you*. And your Noah's ark."

She tugged on his hair. "Good because they love you, too. And . . ." She licked her lips. "So do I."

"Thank you, Jesus." He swept her up in a kiss that gave him the chance to pour only a tiny bit of his feelings into it. The rest would take years. At least fifty or sixty.

When they finally broke apart, she yanked his hair, this time a little harder than a tug. "You know, I keep trying to get you to remember that the name is Livvy. L-i-v-v-y C-a-r-o-l-l-a."

He tugged hers right back—right into him for another kiss. "No, it's not," he said when they came up for air a second time. "It's L-i-v-v-y M-a-n-l-e-y."

"Well, it *will* be."

"Damn straight. Just as soon as I can find a justice of the peace. I hope you don't want a big wedding."

"Who would I invite? You're all the family I have."

He kissed her nose. "No, I'm not. You have all of them." He nodded his head to the menagerie behind him.

"They can't come to the wedding, silly."

"So let's bring the wedding to them. What do you say about getting married right here. With your family looking on?"

She threw her arms around him. "I say that you're the craziest sonofabitch I've ever met."

He pulled back. "*Sonofabitch*?"

"Consider it a term of endearment. After all, with Orwell around, you're going to be hearing it for a very long time."

"Then you better get used to hearing *Jesus*."

"I won't mind. Because every time you kiss me, it's divine."

Guys' Night . . . Plus *Three*

❧❧

EIGHTEEN months later

"Call."

"Read 'em and weep, guys." Cooper Wexford fanned out his three aces on the poker table in what used to be the French provincial main salon of the Martinson estate, but was now the game room at the Hideaway Hills Bed & Breakfast. "Better luck next time." He scraped the chips toward him.

"Hang on." Kerry set down his margarita and picked up his cards. He tossed them onto the table. "Full house."

"Son of a bitch!"

"*Sonofabitch!*"

"Orwell, hush." Livvy tapped the bars of his cage as she passed by it with her signature organic salsa and homemade chips. "Sorry, guys," she said, placing the snacks on the edge of the table. "Play on."

"Thanks, Livvy," said Cooper, scooping a generous portion. "Eat up, boys. It's on me."

Livvy rolled her eyes. The salsa was a house staple and didn't cost the guests anything extra. And Cooper, their landscape contractor, knew it.

"You having some, babe?" Sean slipped his arm around the small of her back.

"Can't. It doesn't agree with them." She rubbed her belly.

"Couple more weeks, then you can."

"A couple more weeks and I'll be breastfeeding and I *really* won't want spicy food then."

"Come on!" said Bryan. "No talking about my sister-in-law's . . . Well, *that*. It's game night. Sheesh."

"I'm out," said Drake Fletcher, tossing his two pair onto the table. The author was a regular every six months, when he'd hole himself up for the week of his book's deadline to pull a marathon writing session and finish it.

Livvy had never seen him in the game room, so she could only imagine he'd finished early. Pity he'd come out only to lose.

She recognized that look on her husband's face. Sean might have a good poker face to the rest of them, but she knew him. Knew that face intimately and all his moods. Most of his thoughts, too, since they worked together every day and slept together every night.

She rubbed her belly, testament to the success of *that* venture. Three more weeks and the twins would arrive.

"Whatcha got, Bry?" Sean tapped the edges of his cards on the felt.

Bryan rolled his eyes. "More than enough to beat you bozos." He tossed out four twos.

"You do realize tonight's the third Saturday of the month."

"Aw, shit." Cooper sat back and swiped a hand across his mouth.

Kerry choked on his margarita. "Sher is going to kill me."

Bryan just turned green. A certain *mint* shade of green.

"What? What's going on?" Drake looked around the table.

Sean couldn't stop smiling. "The third Saturday of every third month is Maid Night."

"*Made* night?"

"As in m-a-i-d," said Cooper before he gunned his beer.

"Loser has to do maid service here for a week," said Kerry.

Sean just grinned as he laid down his straight. "Looks like you're it, Drake. I'll have my sister fit you for a uniform. Welcome to Manley Maids."

TURN THE PAGE FOR A SNEAK PEEK AT
THE NEXT MANLEY MAIDS NOVEL

·

What a Woman Needs

*COMING IN JUNE 2014 FROM
BERKLEY SENSATION*

Guys' Night . . . Plus One

❧

HE'D lost.

Bryan Manley stared at the cards on the table in front of him.

Straight flush. Jack high.

It beat his full house. It beat Liam's four queens and Sean's nine-high straight flush.

He'd lost.

To his *sister*.

The one who'd never played poker.

And she'd not only beaten him, but all *three* of them. Mary-Alice Catherine Manley had beaten the Manley men at their own game.

And now they were going to have to play hers.

Bryan cleared his throat, disgust burning the back of it. He, leading man, paparazzi fodder, starlet heartbreaker, and *People* magazine's Next Biggest Thing, was going to be someone's maid.

"I believe, dear brothers, you all need to be fitted for Manley Maids uniforms," Mac said as if it weren't the death knell for Bryan's image.

"I'm not wearing an apron." The words were out of his

mouth before he'd even thought that far, but it just proved his
instincts were right on. Every director he'd ever worked with
had said so, and Bryan was damned glad for it right now.

An apron. Christ. The tabloids were going to have a field
day with this.

Interestingly, none of the brothers tried to talk Mac out of
this ridiculous pay-up. They'd made their bets and lost fair
and square.

But, Jesus. A maid.

"When do you want us to start, Mac?" Liam was the first
to recover—if that's what it could be called. Bryan just felt
sick.

"Whenever you can. I've got the business."

If Bryan didn't know Mac better, he'd swear she was trying
not to laugh. But that wouldn't be like Mac; she'd always
idolized the three of them. Called them her knights in shining
armor. Or football pads on occasion. But never this. Never
an . . . an *apron*.

He'd swear it was a joke, but Mac had bet the only thing
that could come anywhere close to what he and his brothers
had bet: four weeks of cleaning service if she lost, four weeks
of indentured servitude if she won. She wouldn't risk her
business for a joke.

"I've got the time now. I'll get started first thing Monday."
Sean stacked the poker chips. Meticulously, which was the
only indication of Sean's emotions. He was pissed. At himself,
probably. They'd gone against their instincts, all of them, and
had let her play when she couldn't afford the stakes.

The fact that they were the ones paying was immaterial.
They'd been protecting Mac, their baby sister, for pretty much
all of her life, since their parents had died and Gran had taken
them in. They should have stuck to their "no girls" rule for
this game, but she'd wanted in so bad and they'd all always
been pushovers for her.

And now she was going to be their boss.

A maid. God.

The one plus was it looked like Gran's cleaning lessons
were going to pay off. Their grandmother had had her hands
full with four young kids, and he and his brothers, especially,
had been pretty rowdy and messy.

He never would've thought he'd be grateful for those lessons. Hell, he even had Monica, his own maid from Mac's company, to keep his condo in shape just so he *wouldn't* have to dust off those cleaning lessons.

"Hey, can I do my place?" Kill two birds with one stone, so to speak, though the PETA people would probably take issue with that saying.

Mac frowned at him. "You'd put Monica out of a job to weasel out of the bet? Really?"

When she put it like that . . .

"I'm not weaseling out of anything." That's all he'd need the tabloids to pick up on. "You can count me in for Monday, too. I've got some time between projects and was looking for something to do anyhow." He'd hoped it would've had something to do with a certain actress, a beach, and a couple of Heinekens, but that wasn't going to happen. At least he was out of the public eye for a while; maybe he could pull this off without anyone getting wind of it.

Yeah, and Gran was going to up and leave her new place for the mansion he'd been wanting to buy her, too.

Chapter One

❧❀❧

BETH Hamilton tripped over a big, yellow, hard-as-all-get-out toy truck, banged her shin on the coffee table, slipped on a page of shiny stickers, and landed butt-first in a basket of dirty laundry.

Again.

It'd be hysterical if it weren't so common.

She was constantly tripping over things. Constantly swerving to avoid an incoming wet dog or the twins chasing each other with lightsabers, only to end up on her butt anyway.

The sad part was, she had enough padding there that the falls didn't do a lot of damage to her body—not like the extra padding did to her self-esteem.

But then, what widowed mother of five could afford self-esteem? Especially when one of the five had attained teenager status, another was fast approaching, and the twins came up with daily nicknames for her from their favorite sci-fi movies—Princess Leia not being among them. No, she got stuck with names like Frodo, Chewy, and the ever-popular Voldemort. At least they hadn't gone for Barney. Yet.

Thank God for Maggie. The five-year-old still thought Mom could do anything.

If only she could.

The clock on the mantel chimed ten. Great. The cleaning service was going to be here any second and her house looked like a tornado had hit it. Tornado Hamilton. It came through on a daily basis. Sometimes twice just for kicks.

"Jason, did you finish straightening up your room?" She picked the toy off the hardwood floor, wincing at the nick the rotor blades made. They'd probably done the same thing to her shin.

"Uh-huh." Jason muttered from somewhere beneath the mop of hair he called *cool*, but which she called a bowl cut. If she'd given him that hairstyle as a toddler, she'd never hear the end of it whenever she pulled out baby pictures, yet he'd actually *wanted* her to pay someone to do that to him. *Teenagers.*

"Your laundry is put away and the bed made?" Yes, she knew it was silly to clean up before the cleaning service arrived, but if the woman got a look at her house now, she'd either take off or double her fee. Maybe even triple it.

"Uh-huh."

Odds were Jason's *uh-huh* should be *nuh-uh*, but Beth had too much to do down here to run up the stairs to check out his story.

And Jason knew it, too.

Beth sighed. It'd been two years since Mike's death, and while the kids had seemed to sprout right before her eyes, every day of those two years seemed to last longer than their allotted twenty-four hours.

What she wouldn't give for Prince Charming to ring her doorbell.

BRYAN ran his finger under the collar of the golf shirt and adjusted his hold on the bucket of cleaning products while he seriously contemplated not ringing the doorbell of Mrs. Beth Hamilton's home.

He was a freaking maid. A *maid*!

He checked over his shoulder. No one had seen him yet, unless the tabloids had sent out a slew of covert reporters— and the likelihood of that was on par with those alien abduction stories they wrote about. No, those people were like dogs with a bone and they traveled in packs. He'd never miss them.

Still, he tapped the rim of the baseball cap down another half inch. Not technically part of the Manley Maids mint green polyester nightmare of a uniform, but he didn't care. His face and build were recognizable enough; he needed some protection from prying eyes—

Like the ones staring at him from behind the sheer curtain on the sidelight beside the door.

Snagged.

Taking a deep breath and straightening his shoulders, Bryan bit the bullet and rang the bell.

Instantly a chorus of barks, shrieks, and a couple of "*Expelliarmus!*"es erupted, followed by a nasty crash and some muttered cursing.

Then *she* opened the door.

For a moment, Bryan just stared.

Then his PR training kicked in and he ramped up the Charmer smile that was not only his signature look, but one that came naturally around beautiful women.

And *she* was stunning. From her artfully messy, wavy brown hair, to the curves just hinted at beneath the open neckline of the mis-buttoned blouse, to the yoga pants that hugged shapely legs that went on forever, the woman was almost as tall as he was and built like a woman should be, rounded in all the right places with just enough to hold on to for the ride of a lifetime.

Maybe this wasn't going to be such a bad gig after all.

Then the kids hit the scene, heads popping out behind her like some dance number in a musical.

And they didn't *stop* popping. Three. Four. Five. She had her own basketball team.

Bryan reined in the smile. He didn't hit on married women, and he didn't hit on moms.

He especially didn't hit on married moms.

Of five.

"Who are you?" Kid number two, or maybe three, said.

"Honestly, Kelsey, that's no way to greet someone." The woman rolled her gorgeous coffee-colored eyes as she flicked her finger under the girl's chin, then she wiped away her annoyed look and smiled at him.

This time his Charmer smile appeared of its own volition. Bryan couldn't help it. When she smiled, she was beyond stunning, and it made him glad he was a man—but annoyed that she was married.

And a mom.

Of five.

"Can I help you?"

Let me count the ways. Bryan caught himself before he started spouting sonnets. "I'm here to clean your toilet."

Way to go, idiot. Brilliant opening line.

"I beg your pardon?"

She could beg for whatever she wanted, and he'd give her every single thing.

Bryan cleared his throat. "I'm a Manley Maid."

The shaggy teenager snorted before he walked away, the picture of utter teenage disinterest.

Bryan rephrased his intro. "I mean, I'm Bryan. I work for Manley Maids. You hired us to clean for you?"

"*You're* the maid?" The little girl tugging on her mom's shirttails had no idea she was in danger of popping Mom's button and giving Bry a glimpse of something that, in any other circumstance, he'd be thrilled to see. And Bryan wasn't about to educate the kid.

But *she* was married.

And a mom.

Of five.

The other teenager lost interest and the younger two—twins from the look of them—took their crooked wands back into the den, leaving him and Mrs. Beth Hamilton alone with a preschooler.

Where was *Mr.* Beth Hamilton?

Bryan put his game face on. He'd dated dozens of beautiful women. Had slept with a lot of them. Beautiful women were a dime a dozen in his world.

But he wasn't in his world anymore. He was in Mac's and Mrs. Beth Hamilton's, and he'd better play the part before she cited him for either sexual harassment or failure to deliver.

Either one would do more damage to his public image than being caught in a maid's outfit would.

He'd like to see her in a maid's outfit—

"Yes, I am the maid." He tapped the little girl's nose. "Do you need something cleaned?"

Big brown eyes blinked up at him. Solemn and serious. "Uh-huh. My castle. Mrs. Beecham made a mess."

Bryan looked toward Mrs. Beth Hamilton for translation.

"Our cat likes to take naps in Maggie's dollhouse and tends to leave enough fur to weave a rug, but we haven't read *Rapunzel* yet, so that's not happening."

Rapunzel. Wasn't she the one with the hair and the tower? It was an image Bryan did not need as he looked at Mrs. Beth Hamilton's shoulder-length, windblown hair.

He liked it like that, not fake photo-shoot windblown hair. Mrs. Hamilton had come by her messy hair naturally and there was something about that kind of unselfconsciousness and abandon that just screamed *sexy* to Bryan.

To Mr. Beth Hamilton, too, if the guy had an ounce of red blood in his veins, and considering there were five little Hamiltons running around, apparently he did. And unfortunately for Bryan, that guy had every right to fantasize about everything Bryan did not.

It was going to be a long four weeks.

From *New York Times* Bestselling Author
JACI BURTON

*M*elting *the* *I*ce

Everything's coming together for budding fashion designer Carolina Preston. Only months away from having her own line, she could use some publicity. That's when her brother suggests his best friend as a model—hockey player Drew Hogan.

Carolina and Drew already have a history—a hot one, back in college. Unforgettable for Carolina, but for Drew, just another slap shot. This time, though, she could use him.

Drew is all for it. Plus, it would give him a chance to prove to Carolina that he's changed. If only he could thaw her emotions enough to convince her to let down her guard—and let him in just one more time...

"Hot enough to melt the ice off the hockey rink."
—*Romance Novel News*

jaciburton.com
facebook.com/AuthorJaciBurton
facebook.com/LoveAlwaysBooks
penguin.com

M1387T1013

Erin...the good girl
Cole...the bad boy
The attraction...off the charts!

From *New York Times* Bestselling Author
CARLY PHILLIPS

A SERENDIPITY'S FINEST NOVEL

Assistant District Attorney Erin Marsden, is Serendipity's quintessential good girl. The only daughter of the ex-police chief, she has never made a misstep, content with her quiet, predictable life...or so she thinks.

After years of deep undercover work in New York City, Cole Sanders returns to Serendipity to help his aging father and to find his moral compass once more. Not to get involved with wholesome Erin. Even as a rebellious teen, he knew a girl like Erin was off-limits and that hasn't changed. But neither one of them can resist their off-the-charts chemistry, and a one-night stand brings complications neither Erin nor Cole expected.

"Carly Phillips has me addicted!"
—*Joyfully Reviewed*

carlyphillips.com
facebook.com/CarlyPhillipsFanPage
facebook.com/LoveAlwaysBooks
penguin.com

M1262T0213